'A scathing exam
justice system .
this one fo

SARAH V
ANATOM

'A diamond-class legal thriller . . .
I loved every moment . . . Five stars'

JANICE HALLETT, AUTHOR OF
THE TWYFORD CODE

'If you want to know how the law takes its course with people's lives, you won't get a more accurate picture than this. It's truly fascinating to see it turned into a page-turning story'

WENDY JOSEPH, AUTHOR OF
UNLAWFUL KILLINGS

'Like a front row seat at a hotly contested murder trial. Fast, furious, fascinating and impeccably plotted . . . Legal thrillers don't get better than this!'

NEIL LANCASTER, AUTHOR OF
DEAD MAN'S GRAVE

'Weaves a really compelling plot-driven story with great characterisation. Pacy. Intriguing. Thrilling'

IMRAN MAHMOOD, AUTHOR OF
FINDING SOPHIE AND *YOU DON'T KNOW ME*

THE EXPLOSIVE THRILLER FROM THE NO.1 BESTSELLER

'Gripping and often poignant, *The Cut Throat Trial* carefully paints a stark picture of what a murder trial is like and how dramatic, and unexpected, its conclusions can be'

DAILY MAIL

'Edgy and sinuous . . . a memorable legal thriller and a must-read for the many fans of the genre'

CRIME TIME

'Draws the reader in and keeps you reading'

BELFAST TELEGRAPH

'Compelling and authentic – this had me hooked'

PRIMA

'This book is phenomenal!'

NICOLA STURGEON

THE CUT THROAT TRIAL

The Secret Barrister is a junior barrister specializing in criminal law. They write for many publications and are the author of the award-winning blog of the same name. Their first book, *The Secret Barrister: Stories of the Law and How It's Broken*, was a *Sunday Times* number-one bestseller and spent more than a year in the top-ten bestseller list. It won the Books Are My Bag Non-Fiction Award and was shortlisted for the Waterstones Book of the Year and the Specsavers Non-Fiction Book of the Year. *Fake Law: The Truth About Justice in an Age of Lies* and *Nothing But the Truth: The Memoir of an Unlikely Lawyer* were instant *Sunday Times* top-ten bestsellers on publication. *The Cut Throat Trial* is their first novel.

Also by The Secret Barrister

The Secret Barrister: Stories of the Law and How It's Broken

Fake Law: The Truth About Justice in an Age of Lies

Nothing But the Truth: The Memoir of an Unlikely Lawyer

THE SECRET BARRISTER

THE CUT THROAT TRIAL

PICADOR

First published 2025 by Picador

This edition first published 2026 by Picador
an imprint of Pan Macmillan
The Smithson, 6 Briset Street, London EC1M 5NR
EU representative: Macmillan Publishers Ireland Ltd, 1st Floor,
The Liffey Trust Centre, 117–126 Sheriff Street Upper,
Dublin 1 D01 YC43
Associated companies throughout the world

ISBN 978-1-0350-4670-6

1 3 5 7 9 8 6 4 2

A CIP catalogue record for this book is available from the British Library.

Typeset in Minion Pro by Palimpsest Book Production Ltd, Falkirk, Stirlingshire
Printed and bound in the UK using 100% Renewable Electricity by CPI Group (UK) Ltd

MIX
Paper | Supporting responsible forestry
FSC® C116313
FSC www.fsc.org

For Oma

I didn't become a magician, but I did write you a gruesome book. I hope this will do.

x

Exhibit LJD/1/140224 – Extract from download of iPhone JP/22/010124

28 December 2023

- *YouTube link SENT*
- *Wat dat?*
- Bro, u wanna play a game?
- *Wat game G*
- Need 3 2 play
- *K*
- Basically we all bang sum1 out . . .
- *Ye?*
- But only 1 at a time
- *Wat u mean?*
- So like u hit him then I hit him and we go round circle til sum1 wins
- *How u win?*
- Lol when he's dead u daft fuk
- *Sick bro*
- Srsly, u up for that?
- *Haha yeman maybe*
- NYE?

[END OF MESSAGES]

WITNESS STATEMENT

(Criminal Procedure Rules, r. 16.2; Criminal Justice Act 1967, s. 9)

Statement of: Rita Hooper

Age (if under 18): Over 18 Occupation: Retired

This statement (consisting of 4 page(s) each signed by me) is true to the best of my knowledge and belief and I make it knowing that, if it is tendered in evidence, I shall be liable to prosecution if I have wilfully stated in it anything which I know to be false, or do not believe to be true.

Signature: *Rita Hooper* Date: 03/01/2024

I am the above named person and I reside at the address overleaf.

I am the wife of Bernard Hooper. We met in 1979 through the Methodist Church Music Society. I vividly remember that first day. I walked into the community hall on a Sunday morning in early April, to be greeted by the sound of Chopin's Piano Sonata No. 3. It was so note-perfect that at first I assumed a record was playing. It was only as I went to hang up my coat that I noticed there was somebody sitting behind the rehearsal piano. As I crossed the polished floorboards towards him, he lifted his head and smiled. I smiled back, transfixed by the kindness in his deep brown eyes. 'If I am being a chore, please do say and I'll stop,' he said to me, still playing, still holding my gaze. I shook my head. I could have listened to him for ever.

We swiftly became inseparable. Bernard's infectious enthusiasm for everything that life had to offer, which he paired with a quiet, private, romantic side, swept me away. We married in 1981 and had a son, Christopher, who lives in Australia. Christopher and his wife have recently celebrated the arrival of a baby girl, after many years of trying. Bernard's Christmas present to me was aeroplane tickets for us to fly out and visit our first grandchild.

Although our roots have always been in Ableford, Bernard's teaching and my work with the church have taken us on adventures around the world. The places we have seen, the people we have met and the wild stories that we became practised at regaling in tandem to our friends, are all a testament to Bernard. His joy and curiosity took me out of myself. He made my world bigger and more colourful than I ever thought it could be.

Little could I have imagined on that very first day, standing in the community hall with my soggy coat in my hand and staring in rapt fascination at this gifted stranger summoning those most beautiful sounds, how exciting and complete a life we would build together.

On New Year's Eve 2023, Bernard and I had arranged to spend the night with friends in Broxton. At around teatime, Bernard came into the living room and told me that he couldn't get our Vauxhall Astra off the drive. Our house is at the bottom of a steep gravelly lane and when it is snowy or icy, it is not uncommon for the car to get stuck.

Because of this, Bernard suggested that we stay in and make a night of it. We snuggled on the sofa and watched a James Bond film, *Die Another Day*, which ended at around 10.45. When it finished, Bernard realised that we didn't have any champagne in the house. Tradition was very important to Bernard, and he said that it wouldn't be a proper New

Year's Eve if we didn't have some bubbles at midnight. Bernard decided to walk twenty minutes into Ableford town centre to see if he could find a shop that was open and selling champagne. He kissed me goodbye and said that he would be back by 11.30.

I next heard from Bernard around half an hour later. He sent a text message telling me that he had struggled to find any champagne, and so would be back a little later than planned, but definitely by midnight.

When Bernard was not home by midnight, I tried calling his mobile phone. It rang through to voicemail. By this time, I was becoming worried. I kept trying his phone, but it kept ringing out. When the clock struck 1 a.m., I contacted the police.

Around ten minutes after I dialled 999, there was a knock at the door. I opened it to be greeted by two police officers. They told me that my husband was dead.

Bernard was the centre of my world. We were married for forty-two years. We have grown together. We have defined each other. I do not know who I am, or what my life is, without him. When the police officer uttered those terrible words, I assumed that he had made a mistake. I am still not able to make sense of any of it. All I keep thinking is how Bernard will never get to meet his grandchild. How that little girl will never know the wonderful, incomparable man who was her granddad.

The police keep using the word 'random'. I do not know if that is supposed to be a comfort. That Bernard could be taken from us for no reason, not by God but by the wickedness of people he had not met and did not even know, affords me little solace. I have been told that, due to the manner of his passing, I am not even able to see Bernard one last time to say goodbye.

Bernard was a husband, a father, a grandfather, a musician and a teacher. He was a man guided by his faith but defined by his kindness. It is what made people gravitate towards him. It is what he was known for.

I simply do not understand how anybody could take him away.

Signature: *Rita Hooper*
Signature witnessed by: *PC Percival*

PROLOGUE

Ableford Crown Court is a shithole.

That assertion, whether or not rooted in truth, can at least be said to endure, scribed as it has been in four-foot-high faded fuchsia on the building's concrete cladding for ten years and two months. Whether it followed or inspired the Tripadvisor review posted in identical terms around the same time is a subject of occasional speculation among regulars, but the efforts at deletion by the court administration have been equally ineffective.

If evidence were being sought for the proposition, however, the court's exterior might be a fertile starting point. In a spasm of 1960s permissiveness, Ableford Metropolitan Borough Council granted consent for the town's four-roomed red-brick magistrates' courthouse to be extended into a state-of-the-art 'combined court centre', a sprawling complex intended to accommodate twelve new Crown courtrooms. The battle between brutalism and Victorian was ultimately resolved in favour of the former, and giant panels of raw concrete were erected in what the developer described as 'bold geometric forms', but which a passing tourist might mistake for an approximation of a child experimenting for the first time with Duplo. The completed extension most closely resembled a half-finished multistorey car park with added, inexplicable, glass; in this case, wall-to-ceiling windows running the perimeter of the first floor, exposing the administrative offices boxed within to the glare of the onlooking public, should any of those members of the public harbour any curiosity as to what court administrators do at their cubicles.

What the outside walls lack in charm, they more than atone for in rust-streaked water staining, which has the unintended advantage of disguising much of the older, more conservatively coloured graffiti. Whatever epithets those might contain are at least not immediately visible to the naked eye.

The building's extension was expected to generate a heavy daily footfall, and ease of entry and egress at peak times might have been aided by – to quote one regular patron of the criminal courts – the installation of more than 'one single fucking revolving door'. Even more so if that door was not prone to sticking with such regularity that the glass has already had to be replaced three times this year, fractured on each occasion by an angrily thrust palm. Patience is not always abundant with those patrons. But that is barristers for you.

Airport-style security has been a relatively recent addition to the process of entry. As a result, attendees can expect to queue around the building for twenty minutes to pass through an archway detector and be interrogated, frisked and relieved of their contraband by a security team led by self-appointed 'head bouncer' Annette, a five-foot engine whose time served in this building corralling society's least desirable has given rise to her own lore and law.

Locals still revel in the fate of one visitor several years back, who, anticipating an unhappy outcome before a famously difficult judge, arrived at the back of the lunchtime queue brimming with a morning's worth of Dutch courage and a tenner's worth of Colombia's finest. Seeing the size of the line before him, he staggered up to the fire exit door and manoeuvred himself through, announcing to the onrushing security that they could go fuck themselves, actually, because he was, in fact, a fucking King Daddy who could not be late for his sentence in front of 'that fat bell-end in Court 5'. Annette dropped him to the ground and – depending on who is narrating the story – either knocked the man out cold (Annette) or sat awkwardly on his legs for eight seconds until the court police officer arrived (every other witness). Whichever version is preferred, the man does not emerge well. But that is barristers for you.

Inside the court building, the imposing green-carpeted marble staircase that greets you as you pass through security is best not climbed; it leads to a first-floor door marked 'RESTRICTED ACCESS', and then up to a second-floor door marked 'RESTRICTED ACCESS'. Only when you reach the third floor is it a different story. There is no marking on the door, but a firm push will confirm that access to what lies behind is, indeed, restricted.

No, to go anywhere that court users might wish or need to go to, one must travel down an undesignated corridor to the left, through four sets of double doors and past the darkened, long disused canteen, from within which a redundant hum can still be heard. A hum of a different kind also pervades the corridors: an ever-present whiff of hospital ammonia, notable not only for the thwack it reliably delivers to the back of the throat, but for the absence of evidence of any cleaning that might explain it.

Through the final pair of doors, a less splendid flight of concrete steps heaves into view, adjoining an unburdened lift. This – 'the Grand Staircase', as it has been named – spirals up to four floors of corridors, each corridor boasting three courtrooms, each courtroom's interior an identikit hybrid of faux-Victorian features and lacquered pine, as if a nineteenth-century architect had run out of inspiration halfway through and made a frantic trolley dash through Ikea.

Whether by design or accident, no natural light is permitted entry to the courtrooms. This prohibition extends to the entrance doors having been fashioned out of heavy slabs of timber with no window slots, so a passer-by wishing to discreetly see what is happening within has to haul open the doors and reveal themself, the whine of the hinges liable to rudely interrupt whatever is proceeding.

Were such a passer-by in residence today, and had they scaled to the heights of the fourth floor, and had they walked along the chipped tiled corridor towards Courtroom 11, and had they taken the risk of heaving open the door, what they could expect to rudely interrupt right now, as the morning's business draws towards its end, is the reading of an indictment. Now this exercise might not, immediately, strike the passer-by as significant or interesting. But it bears a moment's attention.

The reading of an indictment by a court clerk to a defendant – or, on this particular day in this particular case, more than one defendant – may sound like a fusty formality, but it heralds something important: a jury is being put in charge of a defendant's destiny. A defendant – or, on this particular day and in this particular case, three defendants – is each having their liberty placed in the hands of twelve strangers, who right now know nothing about the accused, and nothing about what they are said to have done, other than the snapshot that is teased by the formal reading of the charges that the indictment discloses.

It is the start of a process in which the lives of those twelve strangers, and the persons they are judging, will become inextricably bound and irreversibly entangled. It is a voyage on which the jurors and defendants travel together, but which will end with those at the wheel deciding the fate of those riding pillion. They will not speak, these two groups; indeed, a threat of imprisonment hangs over any juror who solicits any conversation with, or poses any question to, the persons now in their charge. Instead, the information that the strangers are deemed to require, and the rules that they must follow, will be filtered, moderated and debated by costumed lawyers with no personal interest in the outcome.

But in charge those twelve strangers are. They each carry personal responsibility for taking decisions which will never be reasoned nor justified to those affected, but which will irreversibly fix the course of three human lives. More than three, of course, because the stakes in the verdicts that those twelve will be required to reach are incalculably high, not only for the blank faces in the dock and those whom they are said to have wronged, but for all of us who tell ourselves that we walk our streets safe under the protection of the criminal law.

This is the start of a murder trial.

Let the game begin.

URN 08AF0468325

INDICTMENT

IN THE CROWN COURT AT ABLEFORD

THE KING v. CRAIG MERVYN-SCOTT, ARRON FREEMAN AND JAMAL LOWTON

CRAIG MERVYN-SCOTT, ARRON FREEMAN and JAMAL LOWTON are charged as follows:

Count 1

STATEMENT OF OFFENCE

MURDER.

PARTICULARS OF OFFENCE

CRAIG MERVYN-SCOTT, ARRON FREEMAN and JAMAL LOWTON on the 1st day of January 2024 murdered Bernard Hooper.

Officer of the Court

PART I

THE PROSECUTION CASE

DAY 1 OF TRIAL – WEDNESDAY

CHAPTER 1

Aliyah (the prosecutor)

The air feels tight as I survey the benches to my right. The sensation never dulls, not for me at least. Ever since my first opening speech in my first magistrates' court trial – prosecuting a woman caught leaving Asda with forty pounds of sirloin steak in her knickers – I've never lost that buzz, that sting of nervous energy surging from my stomach and dispersing out to every toe and every fingertip.

The prosecution opening is the prosecutor's opportunity to set the scene. It is the prosecution's advantage, as I like to remind juries when I am defending. The prosecution tells the jury what will happen, and then produces evidence which fits with what the jury has been told will happen, and a convincing but wholly illusory confirmation is subtly engineered. The jurors feel immediate sympathy towards the prosecution witnesses because what they are saying fits the story the jury has been told.

You need to build trust, right from the outset. From the moment the panel of prospective jurors file into court, staring around them at the be-wigged and be-gowned figures on counsel's row and taking in the underwhelming faux-majesty of the court furniture, it is imperative to maintain composure. Suppress that energy, maintain poker rigidity. It's why I wear flats in court. It's not as if I need the height, and they allow me to plant my soles flush to the floor, both hands on the bench in front of me, palms pushing down. It earths me, channelling the adrenaline down to the ground as I sit and wait for my moment. When I eventually rise to speak, I will find a side panel or a chair leg with the outside of my foot – whichever is available – and push outwards, as hard as I can. An old trick taught by my pupil-master twenty-five years ago. *It stops you from jiggling*, he had whispered to me, his fingers curling around my thigh as he demonstrated his technique.

Forty pounds in value, I should clarify. Sterling, not weight. Four steaks each costing a tenner, which you might just have a hope of smuggling past a distracted supermarket security guard. Four packs of supermarket luxury brand sirloins, inevitably to sell down the pub. Always *down* the pub. Never *up* the pub. Purloined sirloin. For the bargainous combined cost of a single wrap. A precious ten-pound note, to be immediately, desperately converted into the instantaneous warmth that a shot of muddy, street-purity diamorphine intravenously delivers. Detached relief for a few hours, until the effects wear off and the cycle begins anew. The point is, it is important to be accurate. It is important to be precise. It is the smallest detail on which a criminal trial can hinge. A loose word from a witness, an ambiguity in a formal admission, an ill-chosen expression from an advocate – the slightest vagary in the weather can turn the climate for good. This is why my opening speech is always written verbatim. Every word is road tested. Any ambiguity neutralised. The craft is hidden, but it is essential. I want the jury to accept unquestioningly what I am telling them. They may come to doubt parts of it as the evidence unravels and witnesses buckle under cross-examination, but the stronger the narrative I can construct now, the greater chance of the foundations holding when the defence bulldozers move in.

I lift my head slightly and observe the jurors. One or two are displaying the first signs of restlessness, a bit too eager to get into the action. Most are staring obediently at the judge. Not long now, ladies and gentlemen. His Honour Judge Letts is approaching the end of his introductory homily, and the minutes until my opening are receding into seconds.

There is a side that Jeremy Letts saves especially for us, the professionals. But with a jury, he is sweetness and temperance incarnate. The very image of a people's judge. Fair, open-minded and accommodating, but also willing to give the bad guys a damn hard kicking if the press gallery is occupied. *We try this case together*, he tells the assembled fourteen. *You are the judges of the facts, I am the judge of the law.* The obligatory warnings against jurors conducting personal research on the internet or social media are denuded by practised chuckles and affected affability, right down to the knowing reference to 'social media sites such as Myspace – or, as I am given to understand is now more popular, the TikTok', a minor defiance of expectations guaranteed to raise a smile among the younger jurors.

I am your captain for this flight, is the tenor of his pitch to the jury. Well, fuck off, Jeremy. This is my plane. And I have been studiously watching the passengers, planning how best to get them on board.

Identifying the foreperson-in-waiting is key. Since the panel entered the courtroom, I have been making calculated assumptions based on their age, sex, race and, in particular, the way in which they swore their oath or affirmation when reading the card handed to them by the usher. Anybody stumbling over the words or having to be asked by the judge to repeat themselves after omitting or mangling the construction – they are out of the picture as far as who gets to play foreperson. *I will faithfully try the defendant* is a reliable litmus; insert a superfluous *to* after *try* and they will always falter, a failure of their not having understood the meaning of the solemn vow they are making. I will still try to engage those stragglers, of course. I cannot afford to lose any of the twelve votes. I will look into their eyes and smile gently when I am addressing them, ensuring to keep my language precise yet accessible, but they will not be the centre of my world. That will instead be the foreperson;

the woman or man who has not yet been elected by their peers, but whose confidence, demeanour, dress and accent persuade me of that inescapable destiny. My initial impression may change as the trial progresses, and the jurors' levels of attentiveness or distraction are given away by the furious taking of notes or the drooping of eyelids, but my instinct is usually correct.

I am in the zone. Laser focus. That is what a case of this gravity demands. Nothing less.

Prosecuting, you see, is about fairness. It is about measure. It is a calling. And I take it seriously. Empathy is my prosecutorial style. Remembering, at every turn, the enormous privilege that I have. Prosecuting, by definition, is a privilege that confers immense power. I am conducting the might of the state, flexing the coercive muscle of thousands of police officers and thousands of prosecuting lawyers, all gathering under the banner of the Crown. As prosecuting counsel, I am the Crown's representative. And I must always act in a way consistent with the weight of that responsibility.

I am not Robo Prosecutor, pitilessly gunning down any strays in my path. My speeches and cross-examination are intended to be quietly devastating; no shouting or badgering, much less crowing or insulting. I prosecute in sorrow, not in anger. This is how I gain the jury's trust.

Take these three boys in the dock, right now. Boys. Seventeen, each of them. They are accused of something truly wicked, but they are, at the same time, still children, in the eyes of the law at least. There can be no doubt that they are scared. Nor can there be any doubt of the disparity between our lots in life. Their advantages are few, mine are many. I have read the Social Services material, the psychological reports, the intermediary assessments. I can recite the litany of educational and social misfortunes that have defined their existences. I know, from my own experience of defending children just like these, the absence of opportunity to escape their circumstances. I know that if they have been broken, they have been broken on the axis of the society into which they were born.

And so I will treat them fairly. With consideration and respect and compassion. Even when I am doubting them with my questions, and disbelieving them in my speeches, I will do so with civility and moderation and even-handedness. The defence barristers enjoy greater latitude; they may ramp up the pathos and let passion run free. But not me. My voice will ooze patience, my deportment will radiate calm. For this is what the Crown, and the jury, expect.

I will be the grown-up in the room. I will be the jury's Sherpa, and they my confidantes. I will hold their hands throughout the trial, modulating my every word and reminding them with modesty and humbleness that *it's entirely a matter for you whether you agree with my arguments.*

And, at every stage, I will be doing everything in my power to convict these feral little fuckers of murder.

CHAPTER 2

Aliyah (the prosecutor)

The passengers sense the imminent descent. One juror, a tall woman in her early forties, rotates her neck, shaking loose the stiffness built over the last eighteen minutes. Juror number twelve, separated from the others by an empty seat strapped in yellow and black tape, clasps his hands together and stretches them in front of him, his throat bulging as he strangles a yawn. A contagious shuffling of papers suddenly breaks out across the front row. I glance one final time at my laptop screen, triple-checking that the text of my opening speech is the correct size (22-point, Calibri, 1.5 spacing).

Letts winds down his homily by thanking the two extra jurors who will stay with us today for the opening speech, in case one of the other twelve discovers overnight that they are unable to stay for the full four weeks. He volunteers an anecdote about a juror in a multi-handed Section 18 wounding who, upon returning home to tell her boyfriend that she had agreed to sit on a six-week trial, forced the poor sod to reveal the surprise engagement trip to New York that he had spent six months arranging. The slip into legalese does not distract from the point that Letts probably was not intending to make: you don't even have to set foot in a court for the Criminal Justice System to fuck up your life.

Fucked-up lives are, of course, the lifeblood of the criminal courts. None of us would be in this room without them. Many of these jurors will have internalised a bright dividing line between what goes on in court and their lives outside. They are still in cinema mode, excited for the drama that is about to unfold. They are not yet dealing with real lives; their fingertips are not yet tracing real blood.

My speech is going to change that.

'I will now invite Miss Arshad KC to open the case for the prosecution.'

HHJ Letts gestures towards me, and I rise, straightening my black silk robe and placing my laptop onto my lectern.

'Members of the jury,' I say, 'I prosecute, on behalf of the Crown. My learned friend Mr Wyatt of King's Counsel represents the first defendant, Craig Mervyn-Scott. Mr Evans of King's Counsel represents the interests of the second defendant, Arron Freeman, and Miss Rennie represents the interests of the third defendant, Jamal Lowton. His Honour, the learned judge, presides over the trial to ensure that it is conducted fairly. And the three defendants, by convention, sit in the dock.'

I speak slowly, allowing the jurors time to turn their heads to each character as I introduce them: from the barristers, sitting in benched rows running the width of the courtroom, me as prosecutor furthest from the jury box, the defence barristers closest; to the judge's bench, front and centre and raised high above the well of the court; and finally to the floor-to-ceiling Perspex screen at the back of the room, and the three small figures sitting mutely behind, heads bowed and flanked by thickset security staff.

I explain that what I am about to say to the jurors is not evidence in the case, but rather a summary of what the prosecution say the evidence will prove.

And then, turning, almost imperceptibly, meeting the eyes of juror number seven – white male, late forties, tortoiseshell glasses, open-necked long-sleeved blue shirt – I begin the tale of New Year's Eve 2023.

'The thirty-first of December 2023 was a bitterly cold evening, one which you may well remember. The city had been carpeted in a thick blanket of snow, causing havoc for many people's celebrations.

'Rita Hooper certainly remembers it. It was the night that she and her husband, Bernard, a retired teacher, had to revise their plans to go and see friends because they couldn't get their old Vauxhall Astra out in the snow. It was the night that she gave Bernard a quick kiss goodbye as he popped out to the supermarket to grab a bottle of champagne for them to share as they saw in the New Year. That was to be the last time Rita would see him alive. They would never get to see in the New Year.'

I stop, allowing the staccato sentences to fall through the air like snowflakes, and waiting for them to settle, break and dissolve. Every back in the jury box is upright, and every face pursed.

Excellent.

'On his way back from the shop, Bernard Hooper had the terrible misfortune to encounter these three defendants.' I raise my left arm, palm open, not moving my head but inviting the jury to turn their collective gaze towards the dock. Most of the jurors oblige. Number seven is still returning my stare. I think I have found my foreperson.

'These three defendants had one thing, and one thing only, on their minds that night: to experience the thrill of violence in its most gratuitous, extreme and lethal form.' I start to increase my pace. 'High on cocaine, they armed themselves with weapons and headed into town. And when they happened across seventy-four-year-old Mr Hooper, they saw the opportunity to act out their twisted, vicious fantasies.

'They pursued the lone Bernard Hooper down Rowe Street, steering him away from the safety of the revellers gathering as the clock struck midnight. They led him away from the Christmas lights strung throughout the town centre, and lured him towards the darkness of a secluded alleyway, known as Garth Yard.

'And then they armed themselves with *this*.'

An eagle-eyed observer – or perhaps one with any bird's eye view – might have already spotted a package on the seat to my left. Bending slightly, I retrieve the prop – a large transparent plastic cylinder – and hold it aloft with both hands, bending my elbows to lend emphasis to its weight. The dark item visible within still bears the discoloration of fingerprint powder, but the ornate shape and size are what deliver the impact.

'This,' I explain slowly, 'is an illegal weapon known as a "zombie knife" – because it is specifically designed and intended to cause fatal injuries.'

I allow the jury a first look at the sixteen-inch cutting edge curving upwards to a sharp point, and then at the twenty serrations on the other side, and then at the five-inch hilt emblazoned with the word 'SLAUGHTER'.

'This was the weapon used by the three defendants as they inflicted over sixty wounds to Bernard Hooper's head, face, torso and legs; a frenzied attack that lasted several minutes. The post-mortem would later establish that he died of blood loss from those wounds, which severed major arteries in his neck. A pathologist said that one such wound was consistent with an attempt to sever Mr Hooper's head from his body.

'In other words . . .' I pause, inviting the jurors to silently fill the blank, 'to decapitate him.'

An audible murmur from the jury box hints that I have hit my mark. As I summarise the other blunt force injuries inflicted on poor Bernard Hooper – the breaks and fractures and bruises consistent with either the use of other weapons or heavy and sustained punches and kicks – the greenish pallor of my new pal, juror seven, confirms that I have.

There will be evidence in abundance, I promise the jury, from CCTV cameras and horrified eyewitnesses; and compelling forensic scientific evidence proving that each of the three defendants played his part in the murder.

But it is not only the evidence of third parties that they will receive. 'A particularly callous feature of this case –' I lower my voice – 'is that while Bernard Hooper lay dying on the ground, the defendants prodded his body with the knife, taunting him with the words: "How does it feel to die?"

'We know this because we live – do we not, members of the jury? – in a social media age. And, after the defendants had done what they came to do, after they had exhausted themselves with the violence, they made a video recording of Mr Hooper's final moments; a digital trophy, to be shared across their social media channels. A preview of what the police would find when they arrived at Rowe Street: the three defendants coated in Bernard Hooper's blood, and the sixteen-inch blade embedded in his chest.

'This, the prosecution say, was killing for the sake of killing. A brutal and sadistic murder, committed by three young men who wanted to experience the thrill of taking a life, and of doing so in the most violent, bloody and merciless way they could imagine. They lured Bernard Hooper to his death, and they took their time – three long minutes – in inflicting the numerous, agonising, fatal injuries.'

I take a moment for a sip of water, and hear one or two jurors gently exhale. If they think the worst is over, it is a false hope. This is merely the summary of the summary. The deeply unamusing *amuse bouche*. We have a long way to go yet.

I notice that the judge's attention is diverted behind me, and I turn to see Jamal Lowton's intermediary, sitting next to him in the dock to help him follow the proceedings, motioning for a break. HHJ Letts looks at me pointedly, and I nod to reassure him that I am about to reach a natural pause. I turn back to the jury.

'All three defendants deny that this was a joint attack. Each denies being a party to murder. And each has their own, very different account of how the defenceless, blameless Bernard Hooper met his fate.'

CHAPTER 3

Craig (the first defendant)

The judge says we're having a break. Every forty minutes or something, my brief said. It's what the intermediary reckons Jamal needs, coz he's supposedly too fucked in the head to pay attention. It's the skunk. That's what's fucked his brain. Dickhead.

It's hard to listen to, I'm not gonna lie. I'm glad for the break. That prosecutor woman hasn't even begun, Arron whispers to me. There's hours left. Apparently this is just the introduction, like. Where she says basically 'this is what went down', so the jury think bad of us right from the start. But she's then going to tell the jury about all of the evidences, in detail. So like 'this witness says this, and that witness says that'. And that's before the witnesses even come in and say it themselves. So the jury are hearing this shit like three or four times.

How is that fair? Three or four times for the jury to be told, 'They're all guilty, they all killed the old man,' when it didn't even go down like that. I get to say that once. If I'm allowed. My brief says we have to wait to decide if I even give evidence or not. Because apparently it's not always a good idea. I don't get that. If I don't say something, surely the jury's gonna think it's because I'm guilty? But my brief says it's more complicated than that.

Probably they're worried that the prosecutor is going to make me look even more guilty. That's what she's paid for. Making bare money to make people look guilty, even if they're not. Asking sly questions and tripping them up. Getting them to say shit they don't mean. Fuck that. My brief says the prosecutor's a fucking bitch once she gets going. She doesn't look that scary though. All skinny and lanky with a big nose and a wobbly neck like a turkey, like fucking Big Bird. I was watching her fidgeting while the judge was talking. Reckon she has a habit. Drink maybe. Or a smoker. She's got that twitch.

My mum was the same. Not my birth mum, obviously. But Paula. She was a forty-a-day woman, and the minute she started aching she was scratching and flicking her fingers like that, almost clicking them, without even noticing she was doing it. Like her hand was trying to distract her brain from wanting a smoke. Once she'd started, she couldn't stop even when she'd got her smokes. She'd still be clicking in between drags. It used to make my stepdads proper vexed. I didn't mind it myself. It was just her way. The sound was like a hoover or the fridge. Just a noise in the background letting you know it was there. I liked that. But not my stepdads. It put them on edge, like it meant they couldn't relax and watch the telly or have a blaze because she was just sitting there on the kitchen stool, *click click click*. Course, it was MJ who put an end to it. He put an end to a lot of things.

Maybe Big Bird is nervous. Maybe she's never prosecuted a murder before. My brief says she's only been a KC for like a year. If she's not done a murder before, maybe I've got a chance if I do give evidence. Maybe she won't be as good at tripping me up. Making me look like I'm lying. I want the jury to hear things from my mouth, not just hers. Not just those witnesses who are lying through their fucking teeth. And I don't want them to just hear from Arron or Jamal, because they're both doing me dirty. If I'm facing life, I want that jury to look me in the eye while I tell them what I need to tell them.

It's like what I tried to tell my brief when I was in the police station. Coz I told him what had happened. Most of it, at least. The bits he needed to know. And I said I want to tell this to the police. But he said nah, go no comment. He said don't start telling the police things, because they can then use those things to make other things look bad.

So he wrote like a piece of paper which I signed saying basically I haven't done nothing wrong, and he read it to the police when the interview started, and then when they kept asking me questions I just had to go no comment, over and over and over. I don't even know what questions they were. I was just like no comment, no comment, no comment, until the words meant nothing. I was falling asleep by the end of it. I'd been awake for two days straight.

We was all taken to different cop shops, far as I could tell. Arron and Jamal definitely didn't come with me, anyway. I was by myself in that van, listening to the siren blaring in my ears. The fed in the back with me made my handcuffs a bit looser when I said they were hurting. He was pretty safe. But then when I got to the cop shop, there was some other fed at the desk who was a dick. I had to take off all my clothes, even my boxers, and they gave me these police prison clothes that were absolutely rank. Stank of pure shit. And then they got this woman doctor who took my blood and my piss and stuck things under my nails and pulled out my hair. And then I had to show her all of my injuries, and there were a lot, obviously. Because of everything that went down.

Now the jury has gone out with that little guy with the glasses – I think he's called Usher – and one of the barristers is standing up. The fat one, Arron's barrister. He's pissed off about something that the prosecutor said in her speech. But he can't just say that. Nah, it's all lawyer. *I wouldn't ordinarily seek to correct a comment made in opening, but I'm slightly concerned about the Crown's use of the word 'blameless' to describe Mr Hooper, in light of the nature of my client's defence and the application that Your Honour has yet to determine.*

All fucking code. Now my barrister is getting up. He's not pissed, but the judge is asking, *What do you say, Mr Wyatt?* And I think he's saying he agrees. *Certainly it is not my lay client's case that Mr*

Hooper's conduct was blameless, although, as Your Honour knows, for very different reasons. Big Bird looks fucked off. She's up on her feet.

Your Honour, it's the Crown's opening. It is how the Crown puts its case. I am a little baffled by my learned friends' objections. The jury will hear how the defence cases are put and can in due course decide for themselves whether my chosen adjective is apt.

How the fuck I'm supposed to follow this, I don't know. But at least it's better than listening to how that poor fucker died. Coz nobody deserves that. Not even him.

CHAPTER 4

Jennifer (counsel for the third defendant)

I catch the courtroom door as it swings back towards me, my outstretched palm flashing in front of my face and taking the weight of the wood with a thud. Baxter Wyatt doesn't look back as he strides down the corridor ahead of me.

'Twat,' mutters a voice to my left, in what wouldn't even qualify as a stage whisper. I heave the door once, twice, three times until there is sufficient momentum for it to swing ajar long enough for my solicitor, Caz, to bob under my outstretched arm and out on to the concourse. I nip through after her and hold the door still for the crowd behind us as the courtroom empties.

'What would it have cost *him* to hold it?' Caz growls. 'Knowing that we're all right behind him? Is there something in the silks' handbook that says once you're in your tights you can't act like a member of civilised fucking society?'

'Serenity now,' I smile winningly at her. The thunder on her face immediately melts and she grins conspiratorially. 'Insanity later,' she completes. There are many, many things I love about my diminutive instructing solicitor. Her zero-fucks-given candour is obviously up there. The steady stream of grisly criminal cases that pay my mortgage, naturally. But her encyclopaedic ability to spot, decode and return an obscure 1990s sitcom reference is by some distance top of that list. It is, as I have told her many times, a remarkable, if utterly useless, sort of talent.

Bob Evans emerges at the threshold and hesitates, before stepping back to allow two women – press? Public gallery? I've not noticed them in court – to pass through before him. He then retreads his steps and thanks me humbly for my services to door-holding, nodding at Caz with a smile.

'I might pop across the road for a coffee-cino,' he says. 'Can I bring either of you anything?'

Caz doesn't even need to look at me before firmly declining on behalf of us both. Our plans for the next twenty minutes are set in stone.

'Wonderful!' Bob beams with unrestrained delight, as if instead of a fairly brusque refusal he'd just received an offer of a hand job in the canteen. 'I'll see if I can tempt Baxter into sin instead.'

'See?' I nod at Caz as Bob rolls away, the tails on his jacket flapping in his self-generated breeze. 'Some silks – very nice indeed.'

'Too nice,' she wrinkles her nose into an affected scowl. 'Can't see him really laying into a witness, can you? No grit. No . . .' She inelegantly shoves her laptop under her arm so that both hands are liberated for an entirely unnecessary and exaggerated mime as she loses her modulation and near enough shouts the word 'balls'.

Concerned for the fate of her MacBook, I gently tug the computer free and place it on top of my own, and pointedly start walking down the hall. Hint taken, Caz follows.

Usually when there is a break in play, we would take the opportunity to speak to the client, but with Jamal buried under layers of Category A security in the cells, that is a futile endeavour in anything less than half an hour. Jamal has instead been told that Caz and I will come to see him at the start and end of each court day, and these precious twenty-minute segments are to be dedicated to a much more important pursuit.

'You got them on you?' Caz demands.

'I'm stopping by the robing room,' I reply, and she nods, satisfied. I can always be depended upon to keep my side of the bargain; a pact now ten years old, terms non-negotiable and set by Caz on the day we first met, as we stood outside Ableford Crown Court in the pissing rain, waiting for a gap in the torrent.

It was only a week since I'd moved up to Ableford, almost a year to the day since we lost Oliver, and the sentence I had just been prosecuting had been unexpectedly triggering. The next day I introduced my new rule with my clerks. So it was that I found myself blinking back tears while rooting for an umbrella, oblivious to the tiny woman creeping up behind me, and powerless when she spied the Marlboro Gold in my bag and stuck her hand straight in.

'I'll keep you in briefs,' she stated, without any introduction, 'and you'll keep me in fags.' I nodded, instinctively withdrawing my Zippo and obediently holding it up, still trying to calibrate myself onto the same social plane as this five-foot, purple-haired pickpocket whose East End rasp put me in mind of Alan Sugar. Whether she was a solicitor or a prospective client was not immediately clear. 'I don't like your chambers,' she exhaled hoarsely through silver plumes, pointing at my branded tote bag. 'But you're a Marlboro girl, so we can be friends.'

Since that chance encounter, Caz's boys have made up most of my defence practice. Her knowledge of the families on the local estates, their histories, their loyalties and their rivalries, their squabbles and the indecorous means and particular weapons by which those are resolved, is omniscient. The families adore Caz for her blunt speaking and respect her for her hard work, and her boutique firm – *Don't ever say 'small', it's fucking boutique, like me* – turns over a heavy churn of very serious crime. Caz herself handles the bulk of the Youth Court work that Caroline Carter & Co. bring in, her control-freakery one of many attributes that bond us. Pride in her client care, although important, only tells part of the tale. There is an equally pressing commercial imperative, about which Caz is entirely open. *Dangerous boys turn into dangerous men.*

The Lowton family has had its share of dangerous boys dutifully so maturing. Prior to his arrest for murder, however, Jamal was not one of them. His older twin brothers, Frankie and Lawrence – both the spitting image of Jamal – were selling crack from the age of fourteen and by sixteen were enforcing the debts with the aid of squeezy water bottles filled with hydrochloric acid. Two years of youth detention presented the opportunity to forge new acquaintances and revamp their business model and, when they were next arrested, three months after their release on licence, they were in possession of the proceeds of their expansion: two bored-out Russian Baikal pistols and twelve 9mm rounds. The mandatory minimum five-year custodial term was enhanced by the sentencing judge to eight, and the family's dissatisfaction with this result was what led to Jamal's mother declining to contact the family's usual firm when Jamal was arrested, and how Caz, covering the duty slot at the police station that night, had happily stepped in.

Jamal's learning difficulties were immediately apparent. Building a rapport and taking instructions has been a slow, delicate and at times near-impossible procedure, like extracting a tooth from a sleeping tiger without waking it. The omnipresence of Mama Lowton, at the police station, at Caz's offices and at court, has been both welcome and complicating. She has been a vital resource in filling in the blanks in Jamal's backstory, yet Caz and I have been mindful of the power that she wields over her boy's decisions. Any dissatisfaction on her part – however trivial and however ill-grounded – could manifest itself in even greater reticence in Jamal's dealings with us; worse, an application to transfer to a new firm.

After two sets of double doors, Caz and I break company at the stairs. She heads down towards the exit, I launch myself towards the robing room. I punch the door code and enter. Suitcases are sprawled on tables that stretch out as far as the eye can see. I locate mine and unzip the front pocket, fumbling through assorted biros for the orange Sainsbury's carrier bag wrapped around my cigarettes and my lighter. I remove two from the box and place them on the table, before re-wrapping and restoring the bag to its hiding place. This is my effort at self-restraint; if I keep cigarettes in my handbag, I know that they will be smoked on autopilot on my walk to and from the station. Zipping them away affords the best chance at successful rationing.

I whisk off my gown, then my wig, and ball the two roughly next to my suitcase, before, slightly more tamely, unfastening my collarette and folding it neatly on top. Some colleagues gather outside to smoke still fully robed. I've never been convinced it's a particularly desirable look if a juror should catch sight of you puffing away in your regalia.

As I make for the door, I hear a familiar braying from behind the partition situated on the far left of the room, to mark out the silks' area. Three freestanding aluminium-framed screens were erected five years ago as a temporary fix when the silks' separate robing room was closed due to a leaking pipe, and quickly became permanent when His Majesty's Courts and Tribunals Service realised that locking the door was cheaper than contracting a plumber. A separate dressing area for King's Counsel makes perfect sense, of course. Heaven forfend that such luminaries should have to put on their wig and robe in front of the likes of me.

The voice is unmistakeably that of Baxter Wyatt. I don't linger to pick up the full contents, but his jeering appears to be directed towards Aliyah's opening. His audience – presumably Bob Evans – is evidently not responding in kind, as Baxter ups the ante from 'pedestrian' to 'snooze-fest' in an attempt to elicit a laugh. When this fails, he mounts a fresh horse. 'And what about that fucking intermediary, eh? What a waste of public funds . . .'

I head downstairs, through the atrium and out the revolving door into what has, since this morning's promise of sunshine, spoiled into a shivery drizzle. Caz is standing alone under the canopy a few metres away, lost in thought, staring blankly towards a pigeon attending to the important business of attacking another pigeon.

She immediately boots into life as I approach and extend my hand towards her. She grabs one of the cigs and I light for us both. No words are exchanged. We both know the value of silence, enhanced by scarcity in the course of a trial like this. Multi-handed murders are chaotic at the best of times. A three-way cut-throat defence involving shifty opponents and a youth client apparently oblivious to the reality of the evidence, and you have a headache that starts pulsing the minute you arrive at court, and stalks you all the way home.

Because one thing is abundantly clear to both me and Caz. Whether it is fear, or functioning, or teenage defiance, or whether it is simply that he knows he is guilty and lacks the wit to invent a tale to extricate himself, extracting meaningful instructions from Jamal has been a long slog, and there are still parts of the prosecution evidence that he is unable, or unwilling, to talk about.

Clients being less than forthcoming is nothing new, of course. I have defended plenty of cases on limited instructions. There is no observable correlation between a client's verbosity and their innocence. Often the innocent – not merely 'not guilty', but provably, horribly innocent – say the least; stunned by a system which, however loudly it swears fidelity to the presumption of innocence, doesn't really believe it. That there is no space for innocence; that every jaundiced official in the state's pay is just waiting for you to admit your guilt – the realisation can break you. And when it does, part of my job – mine and Caz's – is to glue together enough of your fragments so that you can help us to help you.

Whether that is the exercise we have been attempting with Jamal, I still don't know. I haven't yet figured out whether his reticence is a product of his innocence, or his guilt, or of his unmet needs, or of something else entirely. But it is a problem. Those parts of the evidence to which we still have no answer – we are going to need one. Because the snippet that the jurors have already heard is damning enough. Just wait until they hear the full details of the eyewitnesses. And the forensics. And the phones. Oh God, the phones.

Caz is evidently reading my mind. With smoke curling out of her nostrils, she offers her lawyerly assessment. 'He's fucked, isn't he?'

My silence betrays my agreement as I flick my butt on the ground and gesture towards the door.

CHAPTER 5

Arron (the second defendant)

My hands are still stiff from the cuffs. The screws took them off when they brought us back into court, but I keep finding myself shaking them, trying to get the blood pumping again. I look across at Craig, to see if he's doing the same. He's just sitting there with a face like he's got a proper mard on.

When we came back in and one of the screws told us to sit, Craig just stared at him, like *Why, what's the point?* Like we didn't all know that any minute the judge was coming back into the room and that little guy with the glasses was going to shout *All stand!* And, yeah, he's right. But there's no point in arguing. That's just Craig though. You try telling Craig what to do – worse, you try telling him to wind his neck in – and it just makes him go zero to a hundred.

I'm not arsed, me. Sit, stand, whatever. It's a minor.

One thing I don't get, though. I know we're Cat A. And obviously I know what they think we've all done. But the *cuffs*, every time we go out this dock and down the stairs to our pads, and every time we come back up again. What do they think we're going to do? Like, where are we gonna run? We've had near enough a year to sort shit, and we've waited until we're in court to just . . . what? For Craig to give Jamal a slap in front of all the barristers? For me to give Craig a shove on them steps when we're going down?

Nah. I've got no problem with them two. As far as I'm concerned, we're sound. And I reckon they feel the same. I know they're both pointing the finger. But that's just the way it goes. I'm doing it to them. Nobody wants to grass up, but what's done is done. They're saying what they've got to say. I'm saying what I've got to say. There's no point in causing grief.

That's the thing. I'm not actually a violent person. I know what it looks like. But the person the prosecution is describing – that's not me. When she's telling the jury all them terrible things, saying those words – *savage, brutal, senseless slaughter* – I can't even get my head around it. It's like she's telling a story that just didn't happen. Like when you get proper wasted, and the morning after everyone is saying what you did, and you can't remember a thing but you're like *No way did I do that!* – and you don't know who's telling the truth and who's chatting shit. And then throughout the rest of the day, bits of your memory come back but other bits don't, and you're still trying to get the picture straight in your head.

Only this time I *know* what everyone is saying isn't true.

The judge walks in and we all stand up. Then the jury comes back. There's two rows of them, sitting to my right, and I'm looking at them but trying not to look at them. On the one hand, I want them to look me in the eye. I want them to see that I am not that person. But I also don't want them to see me staring.

The prosecutor is talking again. She's going into all the details of why she says we've done what she says we've done. All this evidence that we attacked the guy for basically no reason.

'You will see closed circuit television camera footage, seized from various locations around Ableford town centre which, when taken together with GPRS data extracted from the defendants' mobile phones, enables us to track the defendants' movements on the night, up to and beyond their chance encounter with Bernard Hooper.

'Shortly before eleven p.m.,' she says, 'Jamal Lowton arrived outside the "Reggie's" off-licence on Horcross Road. The footage shows him on his phone, and, indeed, moments later, a WhatsApp message was sent to Mr Lowton's good friend, Arron Freeman, which said, "*MT O* REGG" – or, deciphering the text-speak, "Meet outside Reggie's". Within a few minutes, Jamal Lowton was duly joined by Arron Freeman and Craig Mervyn-Scott.

'All three then entered the store, where the interior security cameras captured Arron Freeman, the shortest of the three, engaging in conversation with the cashier and purchasing two bottles of Jägermeister.'

She says 'Jägermeister' like you'd say 'jelly', and this lad on the jury with this ThunderCats T-shirt pulls this face, and I have to look down so I don't react. Bet she's never had a Jäger in her life, her. Tragic, that.

'The quality of the recording is not the highest, but it is sufficient to clearly show the faces of all three defendants inside the shop – indeed, it is good enough for you to see Jamal Lowton casually smoking a rolled "spliff" of cannabis.

'The exterior camera at Reggie's then records the defendants exiting the store and making their way slowly down Horcross Road and towards the town centre. Although you will hear toxicology evidence confirming that the defendants had all consumed substantial quantities of alcohol and drugs, you can see from their gait and demeanour as they walk through the town that they are still very much in control of their senses. They are not falling over or staggering in disorientation. They are walking with purpose.

'That purpose? You can see that Craig Mervyn-Scott is carrying a navy-blue rucksack. That, the prosecution say, is what was used to transport the zombie knife, the weapon that they intended to deploy when the opportunity arose. And what else you will see from the footage is how intent the defendants were on finding such an opportunity. How hard they searched for their prey.'

Jamal, man! I told him to put out his spliff. I didn't know at the time that he was just standing there, blazing in front of the camera like he's not even arsed with his hands down his pants. It's probably because, whatever the prosecutor thinks, Jamal was mashed out his head. He didn't have a clue what was going on.

I realise that I'm shaking my head, and maybe even smiling a bit at the thought of that dopey scruff, and I stop myself. I straighten my face and try to look serious again, but when I look up at the jury there's this posh-looking woman who is staring right at me. *Shit.*

The one thing my solicitor said to me over and over again was how important it is that I don't piss off the jury. 'Make a good impression,' he said. Something about the way he said it, and the way he fiddled with his tie when he did – like he didn't realise he was doing it – reminded me of Graham. At the home, when they was preparing us for job interviews and that. And Graham would grab the knot on my tie and squeeze it and push it up till it was tight up against my neck – he wasn't rough with it, but it was firm – and he'd say, in his daft posh voice, 'You only get one chance to make a first impression.'

Well, my first impression with that posh lady is not gonna be a good one. To be fair, it wasn't a good one I made for that first job interview either. I remember there was two people interviewing, upstairs in the drive-through on the Ricky Estate, a man and a woman, both wearing grey shirts and baseball caps, and the man had one of them badges with all the stars on it. And there was about ten of us, sitting on chairs in a circle, and the woman said that what they were gonna do was ask a question and we'd then all have to answer it. Their first question was, 'Why do you think you'll be a good fit for Maccy D's?' or something, and as the woman was speaking I realised that my chair was closest to hers, and I could see what was about to happen but couldn't do nothing to stop it. And sure enough, she pointed at me and said, 'Would you like to start us off?' and I just stared at them for what felt like an hour. My mouth was completely dry and in the end I just said the only thing that came into my head, even though it wasn't an answer to their question. I thought that if I said it out loud, maybe my brain would free up space to think up a proper answer. So I just went, 'Your gherkins are proper rank,' and they didn't say anything back. And I started laughing, coz I had no idea why I said it. And to them, I probably looked off my head. And that thought made me laugh even more. When I stopped laughing I said to the guy, I said, 'Mate, I know I haven't got the job, no worries,' and I got up and shook his hand and went downstairs and got me a Double Quarter Cheese, and that was it. My first impression.

I didn't do the best impression in my second interview. Or my third. Or for a fair few after that. But I got there eventually. And Graham was proper smug when I did. Like I was his own personal project, and my wins were his wins too. 'I told you,' he said. 'We'll make a man of you yet, Arron. You keep making the right decisions, and you're going be the best thing to come out of Wythenshawe since Marcus Rashford.' That were one of his favourite sayings, that.

I keep looking over at the public gallery. Like he's going to be sitting there, in his suit and his proper tied tie, watching over me. But he's not. Obviously. Even if he were still here, a court is the last place he's gonna find himself.

It's mad though that they're obsessing about Craig's backpack. The way the prosecutor is talking, it's like she's solved the case. But she doesn't know shit. Like, she says 'Jamal Lowton's *good friend* Arron Freeman', which is a joke. I know Jamal to let on to, but we're not friends. He's Craig's mate, not mine. We'll chill together and that, but I don't feel anything for the kid. I don't know anything about him, other than he's a proper psycho when he's on the haze. Big joke in all this is that he didn't even need to be there that night. Life is about decisions, like Graham said. Jamal made a bad one.

She's getting towards the worst bit now. I'm trying not to look at the jury's faces, but it's hard not to.

'The footage is not continuous: not every building in Ableford is kitted out with security cameras. But it establishes landmarks, around which other evidence can be fitted. The initial encounter between the defendants and Bernard Hooper, for instance, is not captured on camera, but we have a recording from CCTV on Rowe Street at 23:59, showing the three defendants walking in company with Bernard Hooper. Surrounding their quarry. Guiding him towards Garth Yard.

'Garth Yard is a narrow side street – an alleyway, as some witnesses refer to it – that runs off Rowe Street. There are no cameras – there are derelict commercial premises and a run of large bins, and the alley is fenced off at the end.

'This,' she says loudly, 'is significant. Garth Yard was chosen by the defendants as the place to which to lure Bernard Hooper precisely because they knew that what they planned to do would not be caught on CCTV. And because they knew that, once trapped in Garth Yard, there was nowhere for Mr Hooper to run.

'As for what took place in Garth Yard, you will hear from two eyewitnesses: Paul Bell and Farid Suhail. Paul Bell was at that time living in a second-storey flat opposite the junction of Rowe Street and Garth Yard. Farid Suhail lived two doors down from Mr Bell.

'Paul Bell and Farid Suhail will tell you of the sights and sounds that violently rang in their respective New Years, as the three defendants launched a savage and sustained attack that left Bernard Hooper dead, and the three defendants covered in his blood. You will hear scientific evidence which proves that the three defendants were each present and involved when the fatal blows were inflicted; when Bernard Hooper was murdered for the grotesque entertainment of these three boys.'

I'm listening to all this, about meeting the old man and going to Garth Yard, and why we were there, and it's bullshit, of course, but at the same time it all sort of makes sense when she says it like she does.

And on she goes. On about the knife, on about the injuries. And them words she is using again – *savage* and *brutal* and *senseless* – I can't help myself now, I have to look at the jury. And of course they're all looking back at us, sitting in the dock. Their faces show what they're thinking.

And yeah, of course I was there. But that doesn't mean the prosecution witnesses are telling the truth. It doesn't mean that Craig and Jamal are telling the truth.

And it doesn't mean that the old man didn't deserve to die.

DAY 2 OF TRIAL – THURSDAY

CHAPTER 6

Aliyah (the prosecutor)

These three boys.

I replayed these words in my head as I lay in bed last night, scrabbling for sleep. I tossed for hours, well beyond the point at which dawn sluiced through my bedroom shutters and cast the Skimming Stone walls into a grimier shade of Tallow.

Boys.

But they are not boys. Not when I am describing them to the jury. They may not, as a matter of law, be men, but it is vital – especially given the defences that they are running – that I not be seen to accord them the status of children. They can be youths, or young men, or – if I am being faithful to dispassion – defendants. But not boys. Never boys.

I know well the weight of words. I am normally so careful, so focused. I proofread that opening a dozen times, if not more. And yet that careless fragment remained. Infantilising these killers, implicitly accepting the premise that will be advanced, by at least one of them, that they were merely a child dragged into the adult world by the deeds of others. Scared and confused and appalled by those deeds, and in no way a party to them. Just a child. An innocent child.

Because that is the couplet, is it not? We speak of children as we do of bystanders – both are perennially innocent. Our vocabulary struggles to compute *guilty children*. The phrase sticks in the mouth if we try to say it, our brains slamming on the emergency brake to ask, *Is that really what you mean? A guilty child?*

Maybe the jury didn't notice. In fact, I am sure they won't have, consciously. But that is not the point. Trials such as this are lost and won on the margins. Each word that I use in court has to assist my case, or, at the very least, not harm it. If it fails that test, it comes out. Certain words and associations have a tendency to stick in a jury's mind, and, once implanted, can prove impossible to dislodge. I did my best to litter the favourables throughout my opening. *Brutal and sadistic. Bloody and merciless. Killing for the sake of killing.* A Tarantino scenescape; dark and vivid and beautifully, graphically adult. And then, in that single, stupid error, I contaminated it all with a splash of CBeebies.

Possibly the lapse was a sign of rustiness. I had hoped that my time away from prosecuting would not be noticeable, but I suppose it is inevitable that there will be an adjustment period. Not that my whirring nocturnal brain treats that as any sort of mitigation.

The overnight loop of intrusive thoughts is not unusual when I am trialling. Although impeccable in my professional detachment, dissociating myself from my work at home has rarely proved easy. The carefully calibrated equilibrium of the household routine also tilts as I bury myself in paperwork, leaving the management of the evening and weekend activity rota to my husband, Sasha.

The burden of being required to do some actual parenting is seldom discharged with grace. He does not need to say aloud the words *I get enough of this at work* to make plain that he considers corralling two teenage girls an oppressive incumbrance on his free time. Likewise, I do not need to spell out the rejoinder he knows is loaded in my chamber if he articulates his woes: *You chose this 'more fulfilling' change of career when you left the City, dearest. Mentoring 'underprivileged young people' for minimum wage does not relieve you of your responsibilities as a father.* So a steamy brew of passive aggression and mutual resentment hangs in the air, choking the atmosphere, each of us equally irritated at the other's life choices. It is an equilibrium of sorts, I suppose.

My need for time and space has been even more acute given how important this trial is to my career, the success of which – due to Sasha's midlife voyage of discovery – our financial future now depends on. And in fairness to my beloved, he has given me both. He has shown even less interest in discussing this trial with me than he usually would, not even going through the motions of asking how my days have gone, or how I am finding my first murder in silk, or how I am managing the pressure of winning (not that winning matters).

The tried-and-tested morning-after elixir for nights like last night is at least now surging through my synapses as I slam shut the boot of my Discovery and tear yesterday's parking fine from the windscreen wiper. There will be another in its place when I return at 4.35 p.m., but the daily penalty of £70, halved to £35 for prompt payment, is a fair price for the convenience of only having to pull my case twenty metres to the court entrance.

Once inside the building and robed, I make my way in the direction of our courtroom and flash a sympathetic smile and a cheery – but not indecently so – 'good morning' to the Hooper family sitting forbearingly outside. The police family liaison officer is also there – a relief, as it means I can avoid stopping to talk to them. I introduced myself to the family yesterday before the trial began, explaining my role and the likely course of the coming weeks, so there is little I can usefully add at these intervals. While my sympathy for Bernard Hooper's widow knows no bounds, her emotional needs throughout the trial do not fall within my remit, and my precious time out of court is best spent working to secure the verdict that might offer her something approaching closure.

My mind turns to today's agenda. Paul Bell and Farid Suhail are the jewels in the Crown's crown. Both witnessed the attack on Bernard Hooper, with Suhail even having the presence of mind to dial

999, as opposed to Mr Bell, who was somewhat more preoccupied with his takeaway. Nothing like watching a pensioner spill his intestines to work up an appetite. But nevertheless, Bell's and Suhail's accounts of what they could see from their respective vantage points help to fill the gaps in the CCTV footage, thoroughly refuting the ridiculous defences on offer.

Bell is first up this morning. Once I have tracked down Lydia, the CPS caseworker, we can trek across to the other side of the building to the witness suite and make introductions. Check that Mr Bell has refreshed his memory from his witness statement. That he's vaguely coherent. Vaguely sober.

My iPhone squawks, and pulling it free from my Birkin I see an email notification blinking.

> Morning Aliyah! Just to let you know, the van isn't here yet for my lad, so we're looking like a late start. Bob.

He has added a smiley face emoji for good measure.

Processing the implications for this morning's timetable, and trying not to dwell on the indignity of a man in his fifties using emojis, I slip my phone back into my bag, and glide to a small box room at the end of the corridor.

The officer in the case, DS Chris Rose, has demonstrated the initiative to book a conference room for the duration of the trial, on the same floor as the court we are in. I am pleased. There is novelty in the court administration actually permitting somebody to use one of the conference rooms. And even more novelty in this particular officer acquainting himself with his own initiative.

Since I was instructed on this case, it feels as if I have been required to teach DS Rose the basics of a criminal investigation from scratch. His elevation to the rank of Detective Sergeant, and his presence in the Major Investigation Team, is truly a mystery. At our first conference in chambers, while Rose was fumbling an answer to a straightforward question about disclosure, I caught the eye of his DCI. Afterwards, as everyone was leaving, the DCI shrugged at me semi-apologetically.

'Look, Chris is a bit of the old school, but a straightforward job like this is well within his capabilities. I wouldn't worry.'

Well, that's all right then. I mean, it's not a straightforward job, by any definition. A murder involving three kids and cut-throat defences. But I don't need to worry my pretty little head about that, or about any investigative deficiencies that may be obvious from the papers, because Chris is Old School. Old School being shorthand, of course, for *doesn't read the evidence, doesn't care about the law, doesn't know his own case.*

You expect this kind of attitude on Division. The MIT is supposed to be a cut above.

'The original disclosure officer did a solid job,' the DCI had added. 'Since she went sick, Chris has taken on her role as well as OIC, but disclosure is all in good shape anyway.' I bit my tongue.

If I sound touchy about disclosure, it is because I, more than anybody, recognise its importance. Ensuring that the defence are provided with all material capable reasonably of assisting the defence case or undermining the prosecution is not, as officers of Rose's vintage perceive it to be, an administrative inconvenience. It is an essential function of a fairly prosecuted trial. All the more so when the stakes are this high.

All the more so when the defendants are so obviously, provably guilty.

CHAPTER 7

HHJ Jeremy Letts (the judge)

The Frodsham carriage clock on my desk shows that the time has now crept past twenty to eleven. We are late starting. I expect better from silks.

My habit when in my chambers is to keep the lights low and the curtains closed. For one, it aids concentration. For two, the construction work on the residential development that backs onto the court has rendered this room overlooked by fluorescent men for eighteen months, and, while it would take a particularly malevolent twist of fate for the developer to employ somebody who had appeared before me, such coincidences are not unheard of.

I turn the dial on the radio, increasing the low whisper to a moderate hum. The Tudor Consort's recording of *Caligaverunt oculi meis* by Tomás Luis de Victoria fills the space, and I close my eyes as I lean back in my chair.

It doesn't work. I still can't shake the irritation. It was Andrew Warner who, following the latest 'quiet word' from the circuit leader, prescribed mood lighting and BBC Radio 3 as the balm to salve the abrasions of the office. '*Essential Classics* to ease you into the morning, with the *Lunchtime Concert* to see you through the short adjournment. Might just help to, er, reduce the temperature,' he had said. 'And it means that I can say that I have "put measures in place to address counsel's concerns". Might help to keep the wolf from the JCIO's door.'

The view at which I am swiftly settling is that, whatever purposes *Essential Classics* might serve, putting me in better humour is not among them. If it comes down to a straight choice, I think I would rather suffer the full colonic irrigation of the Judicial Conduct Investigations Office than another morning of this dirge. I twist until the tuner locates talkSPORT, and am treated to a witless former Scotch international gravely opining that some useless football manager might have 'lost the dressing room'. Well, whoop de fucking doo.

Sandra, my clerk, knocks on the door to my chambers. 'Enter,' I say, adjusting the dial back to Radio 3.

'Judge,' she says. 'Just to let you know the vans have now arrived, but Mr Evans says that they're going to need a little time in the cells with the defendants. I've asked that the jury be kept upstairs for now so they can enjoy a cuppa.'

Sandra's a good girl. I have had her now for several years, and she is well versed in my ways. She knows not to enter unless I expressly give the command. She knows that I abhor inefficiency and delay, even more so where it leads to juries being kept waiting without explanation. More often than not, like all the best help, she is able to read my intentions and show initiative accordingly. So if, for instance, we are productive enough to finish a list by two-thirty, she knows not to indulge the inadequacies of my brother judges by volunteering to 'help out' in taking other courts' work.

Today, however, she has misjudged. I am in no mood for further forbearance. We are already losing time because of that bloody intermediary for D3 – an application that I certainly wouldn't have granted had it come before me for case management instead of one of the girls from the family court – and there are three youths in custody and a jury with better things to do than to sit upstairs drinking tea at the taxpayer's expense.

'No,' I tell Sandra as I stand up. 'Put out a call over the speaker system. I want them all in court.' I walk to the Corby press and carefully lift out my trousers, silently embracing the residual warmth and admiring the sharp creases. Now this was a recommendation that Andrew got spot on. Possibly the best money that I have ever spent. Nobody in court ever sees my lower half behind the bench and beneath my robes – indeed, rumour abounds that a judge in Southwark once got away with sitting for a full day's list with nothing under his robes but his underpants. But that is not the point. It is the feeling of completeness, of being fully and impeccably attired, that only a £169.00 spend at John Lewis can provide.

As Sandra bustles out, I tie my bands, reading one of the press clippings pinned on my noticeboard as my fingers search behind my neck for the loop, before slipping on my purple robe and adjusting my red tippet. My bench wig sits on a dresser, displayed atop a polished mahogany stand next to my full-bottomed ceremonial. I carry it to the mirror and check that the wig and bands are straight. Within a few minutes, the door creaks again. It is the usher; a fey willowy boy from an agency, which the bean counters calculate is somehow a more prudent use of funds than recruiting permanent staff. Suffice to say he would not be my first choice. He is ostensibly polite, but there is something in his manner, in his levity, that is deeply grating. His buoyancy, like his thick-framed red spectacles, exudes insincerity and a lack of respect for the gravitas of the court's business.

I follow him in silence back through the judicial corridors as he witters inanely, his rising inflection misleadingly cueing questions that never arrive, and which, even if they did, I would likely have no interest in answering. When we arrive at Court 11, the boy knocks three times, and I enter as Sandra addresses the court.

'Court rise! All persons having any business before His Majesty's Crown Court, draw near and give your attendance.'

I bow to the assembled court, and they bow to me. Or technically, they bow to His Majesty's coat of arms, affixed to the wall behind me but, to casual observers, counsel's bowing doubtless has the appearance of deference. Which is no bad thing.

Two of the straggly adolescents in the dock stare impassively. The third is whispering with his intermediary. Cold and dead behind the eyes, all of them. Remnants of a society that long stopped caring about the lot of the underclass, content to leave the dregs to their own devices unless and until their conduct became unignorable. I have read the defence statements and applications in this case and the histories thereby revealed are all too predictable. The real tragedy is that those who spawned these creatures are not in the dock with them. They remain at liberty to repopulate the estates with replica murderous offspring.

But what is in my power, is the disposal in respect of these three. And I cannot wait to pass sentence in this case. I started preparing my remarks when this case was allocated to me a fortnight ago, and I already know the minimum term that each will receive when convicted. There will be furious applications to the Court of Appeal, of course. They may even get leave. But that will not deter me from doing right by the people.

I realise that my fingers are stretching and uncurling, and I slam my palms flat. Baxter Wyatt, counsel for D1, is getting to his feet and asking for time on behalf of all defence counsel. He's a decent sort – he prosecuted me in a rape when I was at the Bar, and he's not a half-bad advocate. You know you're in for a firework or two if he's in your trial. Bob Evans, for D2, is not to my taste – a little chummy and cloying – but I am told by others that he is considered to be effective. I am not familiar with the oeuvre of Rennie, the junior girl for D3, but I obviously have the inside track on the personal history, even if there has been an assiduous expunging of the online search results.

As for the prosecutor, I've had the dubious pleasure of Arshad in my court as a junior for some time. She is competent on the law, but her voice – the nasal shrillness and that *accent* – is nails on a chalkboard. The reaction in the judicial dining room when her name appeared on the silks' list last year was one of surprise, to put it lightly. The widespread assumption had been that any chance she might have had of elevation had been eliminated following all that unpleasantness a few years back. Time was that even being subject to that sort of investigation would have left an indelible mark when the Lord Chancellor's office was sifting applications. A diversity hire, I remember saying to Andrew Warner over lunch. He didn't say anything in response, but there can be no doubt that he agreed.

That she is now also entrusted to prosecute again – even as a late return due the unavailability of first-choice counsel – is yet another indicator of the Crown Prosecution Service's slow march into the abyss.

'I am not delaying the jury any further,' I tell the assembled rabble. 'The Crown have a witness waiting. We have lost enough time this morning. This witness . . . what is his name, Miss Arshad?'

'Paul Bell, Your Honour. I've—'

I cut across the extraneous wittering. 'Mr Bell can give his evidence in chief, and further defence instructions can be taken if needed when we take a break for the defendant who is . . .' I stop momentarily, and, in deference to the wokery of the *Equal Treatment Bench Book*, alight upon 'apparently in need of special assistance' as an alternative to 'allegedly retarded'.

Jennifer Rennie is on her feet now. For Christ's sake. 'Your Honour, my concern is that the breaks to which Your Honour refers are breaks for my lay client to rest, as recommended in the intermediary report, rather than breaks to give me and my solicitor instructions. So might I instead invite Your Honour to—'

'I've given my ruling,' I say, demonstrating venerable restraint by not adding out loud that she and that preposterously dressed solicitor will just have to forego their little fag breaks and do some actual work.

'Now Madam Clerk, jury in, please.'

CHAPTER 8

Jennifer (counsel for the third defendant)

'With Your Honour's leave, the Crown calls Paul Bell.'

Aliyah adjusts the position of her lectern, angling it away from the jury on her right and towards the witness box on her left, as the usher hurries out to fetch the first prosecution witness. She returns moments later, shepherding a spindly, heroiny little man engulfed by a light grey T-shirt and heavy black cargo shorts. I watch the jurors' reactions as Paul Bell emerges into the aggressive strip lighting, and try to gauge how many of them have clocked the track marks on his arms. Not that that is a novel aesthetic in Ableford.

Aliyah exudes this slightly frantic energy which I find deeply relatable, if a little disconcerting in a prosecution silk. I've not been against her before. I've heard the stories, obviously. But the closest our paths have come to crossing was about six years ago, when I was at the back of court while Jeremy Letts took delight in berating her for a trivial error by the CPS. *I don't care if the reviewing lawyer is on 'maternity leave', Miss Arshad. You are going to get her to this courtroom today to provide me with a full explanation for not complying with my direction, and you are not leaving the building until she arrives. 'Childcare' commitments or not.* With his little gnome-sized hands making air quotes around 'maternity leave' and 'childcare'. I found her restraint in not chinning him admirable.

Once Paul Bell has been escorted to the box and has grunted his way through the oath, Aliyah throws some introductory soft balls to warm him up, before directing him and the jurors to an A3 map folded inside the jury bundle, the slightly dog-eared lever arch file doled out to each juror containing the key documents they will need.

Jurors summonsed to Ableford Crown Court can now live as far as forty miles away – the legacy of a court closure programme that auctioned the other two Crown Courts in the county to the private developer with the deepest ministerial ties – so there is no guarantee that any of these twelve will be familiar with the charms of Ableford. Aliyah therefore uses Bell – the world's least appealing tour guide – to help the jury with the geography.

Rowe Street, as the map shows, is a long road linking the concentrated town centre with Ableford's sprawling residential estates, not quite arterial but channelling a steady stream of traffic in daytime, which condenses to a trickle of returning commuters and a twice-hourly night bus after dusk. The lower reaches of its terraces cloister takeaways, off-licences, vape shops and second-hand electronics stores, some of which shoulder residential flats on their second and third floors. One such flat – 133A Rowe Street, perched above Mickey's, a perennially customerless milkshake parlour – was in December 2023 the home of Paul Bell.

From his living room window, Bell was able to see partway into an alley on the opposite side of the road, offset about forty metres to his right. He confirms that a blue sticker on the map accurately marks the location of his flat, and reads out the street name of the alley: Garth Yard.

Before Aliyah can get out her next question, Bell blurts out, 'That's where it happened. The New Year's Eve Massacre.'

I remember the first time I heard that phrase. On the evening of 3 January, as I sat at my kitchen island staring at my frozen laptop and eating cold, well-past-their-prime leftovers from my New Year's Eve soiree-for-one (Starter: Domino's, Main Course: Chinese, Dessert: Prosecco), my phone blared from the worktop where I'd left it charging. I stood and dragged my MSG-sodden body across the room, wiping my greasy hands on a tea towel before answering.

'What took you so fucking long?' Caz had barked.

'Mmm?' I replied, trying to liberate a stringy piece of mozzarella from my front teeth.

'I'm at the station,' she continued without pausing. 'I've picked up one of the Lowtons. The youngest one, Jamal. It's the New Year's Eve Massacre.'

The killing of Bernard Hooper had been reported in sober and factual terms by a local news outlet the previous day, only to be picked up and repackaged within hours by a tabloid website, which in its eagerness to coin a headline, missed the point that the murder had actually occurred in the very first minutes of New Year's Day. In any case, I had managed to avoid the whole story in a New Year's hangover fug. Picking up on my confusion, Caz texted me a link, and waited silently as I clicked on it and read.

The silence grew longer as Caz, uncustomarily, struggled to select her words.

'I know,' she eventually said, 'it's knives. I do. And under normal circumstances, I wouldn't ask. Obviously.'

'Mmm hmm.' Non-verbal was as much as I could muster. Ordinarily any such requests would be filtered out by my clerks, who would give the standard polite rebuff and direct the solicitor in question to alternative counsel. Confronting this . . . *this*, head on, was something I was not used to. And Caz knew that, the fucker.

'You fucker,' I murmured down the line.

'I know,' she repeated. 'I do, Jen, I do. But this kid is in a world of shit – ASD up to the eyeballs – and you are the only person I would trust with him. And I don't expect you to say yes, but I wouldn't be doing right by him if I didn't at least ask.'

I wandered over to the island, phone cradled between my ear and shoulder, picked up the sodden pizza box and swept the remaining slices into the bin. I wouldn't eat again that night, I knew.

'Please, Jen. I wouldn't ask, you know I wouldn't. But . . . there's something about this kid. I don't feel like I'm getting him, you know? There's something there. And I don't know anyone else who . . .'

As she faded again, a million reasons to decline were flooding my mind, including those I have practised for a decade. But bobbing amid those, one why I should agree:

It's My Job. Caz was asking me to do my fucking job, and help her. To be defined not by the worst thing that has happened to me, but by what I choose to do. And I did know she wouldn't ask unless . . . unless.

Standing up straight and sucking as much air as I could into my lungs, I expelled it slowly and evenly, recalling my exercises. On the count of ten, I broke the silence.

'OK. I'll do it.'

'I love you, you know that? Thank you. Really.'

I mumbled something indistinct, and Caz's tone returned to its natural freneticism.

'We've had two interviews so far. We've got another in the morning, then I expect they'll be charging. He'll be in the mags' on Thursday – any chance you can come to hold his hand? Bit of a PR exercise?'

The tradition of solicitors instructing counsel by contacting their clerks was abandoned by Caz a couple of years into our relationship. 'I don't wanna have to deal with the monkey – I'd rather speak to the organ grinder and get it straight from the horse's mouth,' she had declared in a baffling trifle of zoological metaphor. Putting her on speakerphone, I pressed my calendar app and scrolled through my diary. I had a Crown Court sentence listed on Thursday afternoon, but could squeeze in a trip to the magistrates' court beforehand. 'As it's you,' I replied.

'You're a star,' she said. 'I'll call you after tomorrow's interview and give you a proper rundown. And thank you, again. I do know, you know?'

I know she knows. But it doesn't make this case any easier.

Aliyah allows the word 'massacre' to hang in the air for just long enough before affecting a stern expression and telling Bell that 'it is important that we please keep to the plain facts and take your evidence in stages'.

She steers Bell back to the beginning with a series of clipped questions, and I type his answers, cross-referencing them with his witness statement for any inconsistencies.

It was just after midnight, Bell tells the jury, that he was at home waiting for his takeaway. He was looking out of his living room window onto Rowe Street, hoping for signs of a Deliveroo driver, when he saw three kids with an older man, all walking together and towards Bell's flat, albeit on the far side of the street. 'There was like one of the younger ones either side of the older man, and one of them a bit behind.'

Aliyah asks him to describe the four characters he could see. 'Perhaps, to help the jury, we can refer to the first person you are about to describe as "Male 1"', Aliyah suggests, hoping that adopting the language used by the police when drafting Bell's witness statement might jog his memory.

Bell thinks for a moment. 'All right. Male 1 was the one with a black hoodie and dark bottoms. He was white, late teens – they were all late teens – and he had blond streaky hair. Oh, and he was carrying a rucksack.

'Male 2 was a white lad with short dark hair. He had a blueish top and bottoms, I think. He was the one hanging back at the start. And Male 3 was dark – what d'you call it? – mixed race? He was also to the side of the old man.'

'Miss Arshad.' A yap from the bench breaks the flow. 'Miss Arshad, the identification procedures will be dealt with in agreed evidence, I presume?'

'They will, Your Honour.'

'Yes. Well, is there any reason that the jury cannot be told now that Mr Bell positively identified "Male 1" as Craig Mervyn-Scott and "Male 2" as Arron Freeman? Just to save a little time?'

It's a dick move, interrupting just for its own sake. I would be tempted to tell him to shut his baldy little face and let me present my case how I fucking well please. But Aliyah is a professional, and probably twitchier than most about offending the Bar Standards Board, so she just forces a smile. 'Not at all, thank you, Your Honour.'

She steers Bell back to his living room window. He watched the group walk down the street towards him, he says, until they stopped at the entrance to Garth Yard.

'Then my Chinese arrived,' Bell says – although, to the winces of several jurors, he doesn't say 'Chinese' – 'and I walked away from the window.'

'And was that,' Aliyah asks, in a tone suggesting she is genuinely unaware of the answer, 'the last you saw of that group of people?'

'No.'

'What else did you see, and when?'

'It was no more than a couple of minutes, and then I heard the old man shouting.'

'Could you hear what he was shouting?'

'No, I couldn't make it out. So I went back to the window to see what was going on.'

Aliyah raises her palm off her lectern, no more than six inches, but sufficient to cue to the witness to pause. She wants this part of his evidence to land.

'And what,' she asks, 'could you see?'

Bell shakes his head. 'It was mayhem. One of them was waving this giant knife around and they was in the alleyway, well, he was at the end of the alley, so like he'd just stepped into the alley off Rowe Street, and—'

'Just taking that in stages, please. You say *one* of them had a knife. Can you first describe the knife, please.' It is a command, not a question. And while Bell fumbles with his hands to indicate size and shape, and stammers a jumble of 'spiky sharp edges', it doesn't actually matter, because Aliyah is reaching to the seat on her left, and hoisting aloft the tube containing the intimidating, bloodied weapon.

'This is the knife you are describing?'

Bell nods. 'Yeah. That's it.'

Aliyah nods back.

'And which one of the three males,' she asks, 'did you see waving this weapon before – how was it you described it . . .?'

She pauses for effect.

'. . . before the massacre.'

CHAPTER 9

Craig (the first defendant)

I remember what my brief has said about not reacting to what the witnesses are saying. It's hard, though. When you hear things that you know are wrong. You just want to shout out and make it right. That's what Mr Wyatt is for, I know. But it's still hard, even just hearing this prick's bullshit descriptions of what we was supposedly wearing. It was a black Berghaus jacket, not a fucking hoodie. Twat. But I don't say anything. I try not to look at the skinny little prick when he's talking. Easier that way. I stare at the barristers instead.

Big Bird looks well fucked off whenever the judge gets involved, telling her what to do. He's all polite with his voice and what he says, but it's obvious that she thinks he's having a dig. Like he's trying to do her job for her, or something. Like he sounds all nice to the outside world, but it's painful for her deep inside coz she knows what he really means.

That was MJ's thing. What he was good at, with my mum. To everybody else he was this proper safe guy, and he'd never shout at her when other people were around. When we were out in the park or when his mates were there, he would talk to her in this special voice. Really calm and really . . . not aggressive. He didn't say insults – but the words he used, I could tell that they cut deep. It was like they had this power. So, like, I remember when we had a birthday party for Kayla when she was eight, I think. I would have been ten. And my mum had made this proper effort, she'd arranged for a load of Kayla's friends to come with us to Nando's, and if you'd seen how my mum was back then, you'd know that that was big for her. And she got these fresh garms from the market, this frilly yellow dress thing with white spots and one of those little hats on like a headband, and she knew it was dumb because it was only Nando's, but she wanted to make the effort, and you know what? She looked decent. And you could tell that she was really happy with herself, like she was being a proper mum for once.

And so we got to Nando's, and loads of Kayla's friends were already there, but then this one girl, Lola, arrived, and her mum was wearing this bright pink dress that was so tight and short, you could basically see what God had given her, you know what I mean? Like, really not the sort of dress you wear to a kids' party.

And when she came in, MJ was sitting with me and my mum and Kayla, and he just got up and walked straight over to this woman – I don't know whether he'd seen her before, or what – but he was talking to her and touching her waist, and she was laughing at everything he was saying and kept putting her hand on his arm. And he spent basically the rest of the party just chirpsing this woman until she left. He didn't even come back over when Kayla was blowing out the candles. And when this woman went, he walked back to where we were sitting, and he leaned over to my mum and smiled and said to her, in front of everyone, 'Maybe with a bit of hard work, you'd be able to fit into something nice like that.' It was like the words were encouraging, but you could see in her eyes that she was hurting. Like he knew the one thing to say that would get to her the most. And my mum, she said nothing on the bus all the way home, and when we got in she just went to the bathroom, and we could hear her crying from the living room until MJ went in to make it stop.

He had a special voice for Kayla, too. He would never shout at her. Even when she was kicking off, or she'd been fighting in school, even when my mum lost her shit with Kayla, MJ was always calm.

Always quiet. He'd just look at her, and then when he spoke it was low and quiet – a different quiet voice to the one he spoke with to my mum. Softer. But it always worked. It was like he had her trained, or something.

Fair play to MJ though, he was right about the bleach. When I first did my hair when I was ten, he was pure raging, said I looked like a gay and he smashed my mum's nose for raising 'a queerboy'. He said I would get myself into trouble, attract the wrong attention. And that's one of the things that's done for me, says my barrister. 'We are in real difficulty challenging what the witnesses say about identification because of how distinctive your hair is,' he said at one of our first meetings.

And yeah, he's right. Coz right now, everyone in the room is staring at me, and the witness is saying 'the blond kid', and Big Bird is saying, 'The blond kid – Male 1 – was the one you saw with the knife when the shouting began?' – just to make it stick in the jury's heads – and he's going, 'Yeah, the blond kid, he must have took the knife out of his backpack.' And I can feel my fists clenching, and it's taking everything I have not to shout out *YOU FUCKING LIAR*. But I remember what my brief and my barrister told me and I just stare at the floor, digging my fingernails into my palms.

The guy is asked where the others were, and he says they were deep at the end of the alley, and that he couldn't properly see all the way down coz of the dark, but could see people moving. What about the old man? the prosecutor asks, and he says that the old man was further into the alley than the kid with the knife, but not as far back as the other two. And then he talks about how he saw the glint of the blade, and how the old man was screaming and they all disappeared into the alley, and all the man could hear was the noise – 'the whooping and hollering, like they were egging each other on'. And then I remember.

I remember the noise. I can hear those sounds now. They're rushing in my ears, like waves smashing onto rocks. Drowning out what the man is saying. I squeeze my eyes shut to see if it helps me to concentrate. I feel like I'm swaying, like I'm about to fall off my chair, and I'm gonna crash onto the floor. But when I open my eyes it's all in my head, and I'm not actually moving at all. But the waves are still crashing and smashing. On my mum's life, I can hear Arron and Jamal. I can hear Jamal bragging, like he always did about his brothers, and the things they did. I can hear his voice getting louder and louder, I can hear him laughing and saying how it's nothing to cut a man. I can hear myself too, my own voice, telling Jamal that nah, I'm not like that. That I'm all about a fair fight.

I shake myself, like physically shake myself to break out of it. And I'm back in the courtroom, and Big Bird is asking the man if he saw any of us three again, and he says that he seen us when we all ran out of the alley and got arrested. Which is bullshit, but anyways. And she says nah, could he see anything during the whooping and hollering – and she stresses those words, taking her time to say them. Whoooooping. And hollllllllering. And he says yeah, that not long after the slashing started, he could see the old man's feet like he was lying on the floor, and the three kids were like moving around his body, coming in and out of the light.

The prosecutor wants to know if he could hear any of the words that anyone was saying. And even though the answer he gives is a bad one, bad enough to make me stare at the ground again – 'I opened my window and I could hear the old man was begging. Just saying, "Please, please stop," over and over and over' – that's not why I'm looking away from the jury. It's because I can see where the questions are going. And I've read his statement and I know what's ahead.

And then she asks it: 'Did you see Male 1 – Craig Mervyn-Scott – again after that?'

I don't even need to hear it said. I close my eyes again, and I can see the veins of my eyeballs inside my eyelids, and it's like they are filling up, about to burst. The whole world is going red, and my throat is burning dry. I can feel the weight in my hands. The coldness. The adrenaline.

'I next saw Male 1 when he ran out of the alleyway.'

'Was there anything about him that caught your attention?'

'Yeah. He was waving the knife. And he was head to toe dripping with blood.'

CHAPTER 10

Aliyah (the prosecutor)

I pause and straighten my back, leaving Bell's reply to percolate. In my peripheral vision, I can see twelve heads slowly turning towards the dock, each trying to catch the reaction of Craig Mervyn-Scott. Each suddenly picturing him not as the silent teen lounging unthreateningly in his grey sweater and joggers, but as I want them to picture him: Savage. Bestial. Painted with the blood of his prey.

Their imaginations are now giving vibrant form to Paul Bell's testimony – scrabbling for fragments from horror films and nightmares, scenes folding into one another, yanking the jurors out of the courtroom and dropping them into the darkness of Garth Yard. They can hear the curdling war cries of the monsters and feel the ripples as the air is cut by the swinging blade. They can see the fresh crimson pooling around their feet.

The remainder of Paul Bell's testimony is of little consequence, so I wrap up my questioning, hoping that the impression we have created is strong enough to last. When I sit back down, several jurors are still staring at the dock. A woman on the front row looks as if she has lost a bit of colour. Excellent.

I whizz my fingers over the trackpad of my laptop and open a new document, which I save as 'Cross-examination of Paul Bell (Baxter Wyatt) v1.1'. Now comes the part where we learn how robust Mr Bell can be when challenged. And, given what I know of

Baxter Wyatt, whether Mr Bell can keep his composure in the face of relentless provocation.

With his first response, I fear the worst.

'Mr Bell, you have described what you saw in two parts. There was the part before your takeaway arrived, and the part afterwards.'

'If you say so.'

'Well, no,' Wyatt spits. 'Not "if I say so". Do you accept that your account of what you saw is in two separate parts?'

'Fine, whatever.'

Wyatt then leads Bell through what will now be termed 'Part One'. *No*, Bell agrees, *I wasn't paying much attention to the group when I first saw them. Yes, my mind was on the arrival of my takeaway*. But, more importantly, Wyatt wants to reframe the image that I have so artfully constructed.

'There was no aggression being displayed by any of the young males in "Part One", was there?'

'Not that I could see.'

'No animosity?'

Bell stares. 'You what?'

'No animosity, Mr Bell. No hostility. No enmity. You are looking blank. Do you understand the words I am using?'

Letts intervenes.

'Mr Bell has accepted that there was no aggression, Mr Wyatt. Perhaps you should just move on.'

Wyatt smiles fawningly. 'Very well. I'll try to formulate my questions into a more . . . digestible form.'

Bell is not a bright man, but he knows when he is being made to look a fool. He is flinching, struggling to contain those surges of aggression which, I know from his lengthy list of previous convictions, he is not good at containing. To his credit, he manages to keep the volume of his response respectable. Just not the substance.

'Yeah, maybe you should speak in plain fucking English, mate, yeah? And not ask me the same shit questions over and over again.'

Baxter Wyatt widens his eyes and blinks affectedly at the jury, as if his delicate ears have never been exposed to such vulgarity. He glances up at the bench, waiting for the inevitable judicial admonishment with the glee of a child who knows that her sibling is about to be punished. The judge disappoints.

'Please just answer counsel's questions, Mr Bell.'

But the tone is set.

'Mr Bell, would you agree with this? Had it not been for "Part Two", you would never have given what you saw in "Part One" a second thought.'

'I dunno.'

'You certainly would not have involved the police, would you?'

I can anticipate – because I have seen Craig Mervyn-Scott's defence statement – the question that Wyatt wants to build to. But it's a question which Paul Bell is unlikely to agree with. So before we get to that, Wyatt wants to take the jury on a credibility-bashing detour, teasing out inconsistencies and exploiting Bell's volatility, in the hope that, by the time Wyatt asks that final, killer question, Bell is so damaged in the eyes of the jury that it doesn't really matter what he says. And this line of questioning – Bell's dealings with the police – is the first stop on that journey.

'The police?' Bell repeats. 'Nah.'

'No,' Wyatt shakes his head. 'And in fact, even when you did see something of significance in "Part Two", even then you did not call the police, did you?'

'I can't remember.'

Wyatt mugs again towards the jury box.

'You can't remember whether or not you called the police?'

'I'm not sure.'

'Well, in fairness to you, Mr Bell,' Wyatt says, picking up and brandishing a document, 'you were candid enough in your witness statement to indicate that you had been drinking throughout the evening. Ten or eleven cans of lager, you estimated. Is that why you can't remember whether or not you called the police?'

'It's not a crime to have a drink, is it?'

'Good heavens, no,' Wyatt agrees. 'I would not for one moment seek to come between a gentleman and his . . .' Wyatt peers at the witness statement, 'his *Carlsberg*. No, the question is, was your alcohol consumption the reason that you now can't remember whether or not you called the police?'

Paul Bell grits his teeth. 'I *do* remember. I didn't call them, no.'

'Right. So now you agree you *didn't* call—'

Bell doesn't let him finish. 'I don't trust the police.'

Oh no. No no no. I stare at my laptop screen.

'I beg your pardon, Mr Bell, what was that? You don't trust the police? Dearie me.'

'Yeah, well,' Bell shouts, 'if your missus had fucking lied about you battering her and they had fucking taken her side . . .'

He trails off. Wyatt allows just long enough for the words to sink into the jurors' minds.

'Is that why, when the police arrived on the scene, you didn't bother to leave your flat to tell them that you had witnessed, in your words, "a massacre"?'

Bell thinks. After an agonising silence, he settles on a defiant, 'It was none of my business, mate.'

And just like that, my star independent witness – the concerned, plain-speaking neighbour minding his own business when he happened to see a terrible crime – is transformed. I expected questions about Bell's omission to call the police. I just rather anticipated that he might offer *I was in shock*, rather than *I'm a drunken wifebeater who doesn't think murder is a big deal.*

The damage is as much as Wyatt could have hoped to inflict, as he now limbers up for the trickier part of his cross-examination:

putting before Bell – and this jury – the ludicrous defence that Craig Mervyn-Scott is asking them to accept.

'Moving to Part Two of your account,' Wyatt says, somehow rendering 'account' sarcastic. 'This began, you say, when you were away from the window and were alerted by shouting.'

'The old man shouting,' Bell interrupts. He has no idea where Baxter Wyatt is going, but a whiff of defiance is detectable in his tone.

'Indeed,' says Wyatt. 'The *older* man shouting. Your evidence was that there were "a couple of minutes" between your leaving the window to answer the door to receive your takeaway, and your returning to the living room to hear the older man shouting.'

The lack of a question nevertheless draws a nod from Bell, who proceeds to agree that, when he answered the door to the delivery driver, he was paying no attention to the group on the other side of the street.

'It follows, doesn't it,' Wyatt says, slowing just a fraction, 'that you are not able to assist the jury with what took place among the members of that group in those "couple of minutes" immediately before the shouting?'

'No.'

Wyatt turns the page on the blue notebook lying flat on the lectern in front of him. His fingers trace the top line, silently emphasising for the benefit of the jury the significance of what he is about to say next.

'So if I were to suggest to you that the older man was acting in such a way as to provoke the coming together of this group of people, you would not be able to say whether that was right or not?'

Bell appears to know that he is boxed in. 'I couldn't say.'

'No,' says Wyatt softly, shaking his head. 'Well, have a think about this: you used the word "shouting". Not "screaming" or "crying", but "shouting". Does it follow that the older man sounded angry, or maybe aggressive?'

Bell stares at Wyatt, searching for the least helpful answer. 'I couldn't hear what he was saying.'

'So again, it follows, doesn't it, that if I were to suggest certain words to you, if I were to suggest that the older man was shouting threats, you would not be able to say whether or not that was correct?'

'No, I don't know what he was saying at that point,' Bell says after a lengthy pause.

'Thank you,' says Baxter Wyatt. 'Now can we please turn to what you say you could see in the alley.'

One or two of the jurors are leaning forward in their seats, as if bracing for impact.

'You have already indicated to my learned friend who prosecutes,' Wyatt says slowly, 'that you could not see down to the end of the alleyway. You could see only the first few feet, and beyond that it was too dark for you to make anything out, yes?'

Bell replies that he could see 'shapes but not faces', repeating his earlier description of the scene as 'mayhem'.

'Lots of movement,' Wyatt suggests, helpfully. 'Lots of noise, and people – and shapes – moving quickly in and out of sight?'

'Yeah.'

'Not easy to follow precisely what was going on?'

'No,' Bell agrees, but then grins, exposing his sparsely populated gums. 'But I know that your lad – the blond kid – was slashing the old guy with a machete.'

I clatter my laptop keys, a noisy hint to the jury that this is a good point for the prosecution; that Bell is sticking fast to the part of his evidence which condemns Craig Mervyn-Scott.

'Well, let us look at this again, please,' Wyatt says. 'When you first saw the person holding the "machete", as you call it, how long was he in your sight before he disappeared into the alley?' Paul Bell is unwilling to volunteer an estimate, so Wyatt gladly fills the gap. 'A couple of seconds maybe? A fleeting glance?'

'Probably.'

'And the knifeman was not looking in your direction, presumably? He was looking down the alley, yes?'

'Yeah.'

'And walking away from you?'

'Yeah.'

Baxter Wyatt's demeanour suddenly shifts. It is as if he is stepping out of character, vacating the pomposity conferred by his wig and gown, and speaking to Bell – to everyone in the room – as equals. As collaborators trying to figure out a problem. The sharp edges of his accent soften, and he even appears to lose a little height, as he drops his volume down low and confides.

'Because the thing is, Mr Bell, what I'm getting at is this. Now I agree that the person you saw *after* the older man had been struck – the person you say was "covered in blood" – that *was* the blond boy. But I am going to suggest that the person you saw with the knife *beforehand* – the boy making the first slash – was in fact one of the other two boys.'

Paul Bell's face collapses, trying to compute this judder into first gear. He stammers, 'I don't think so.'

It's all Wyatt needs. He wrenches straight back into fifth; wig, gown and attitude immediately restored.

'You don't think so – so you don't actually know?'

'What do you mean?'

'Well, let me put it this way: might it be possible that, when you were playing this back in your mind when you gave your statement, you recalled seeing the blond boy with the knife immediately afterwards, and you *assumed* that it was the blond boy who'd had the knife at the start. That you put two and two together. Do you understand the question?'

He does not wait for confirmation. 'I am suggesting that you were not, in fact, able to see "Male 1" – the blond boy – waving the knife *before* the group were all in the alley, rather that the person with the knife at the beginning – the person slashing at the old man – was "Male 2". Is that possible?'

'I don't think so. I don't know. Maybe. I don't know.' Bell looks pleadingly towards me for respite. There is nothing I can do.

'That's a veritable smorgasbord of answers, Mr Bell. I'm going to ask you to choose one. Do you agree that it is *possible* that the person with the knife when the violence began was Male 2?'

Something in Bell breaks. 'It's possible.'

'Right. And as for who was doing what in the alleyway, you cannot say with any certainty?'

'Are you going to keep asking me the same fucking thing? No, mate. For the last time.'

'So . . .' Baxter Wyatt turns forty-five degrees away from the witness and half-faces the jury for the last furlong. 'All you can say is that a male, who you *assumed* was Male 1, but who you now accept might have been Male 2, was slashing with a knife, and then went into the alleyway. There was a commotion, a lot of movement, and you then saw Male 1 leave the alleyway carrying the knife?'

It takes a moment for Bell to process, and then to agree.

'And when you saw him carrying the knife out of the alleyway,' Wyatt says, again dropping the tempo, 'you could not see how he came into possession of it?'

Bell pulls a face, and Wyatt tries another tack.

'As you can't say who was doing what in the alley, you cannot say whether, for instance, Male 1 had the knife because he had just disarmed one of the others in the alleyway?'

'For the last time,' Bell raises his voice to a dangerous decibel, 'I don't know what happened in the alley.'

'And,' Wyatt continues, now turned to face the jury directly, 'when Male 1 came out onto the street, covered in blood, you cannot say whether he was in fact trying to remove the weapon from the scene to prevent it being used again?'

This question, Wyatt knows, is a liberty, and I stand to object.

Letts waves at me to sit down, and begins to request that Wyatt return to a more permissible line of interrogation, but His Honour's words are drowned out, then cut short, by a bellow from the witness box.

'I. DON'T. KNOW. WHAT. FUCKING. HAPPENED. IN. THE. FUCKING. ALLEY!'

It provokes a momentary fuzzing on the microphone in front of Paul Bell, which gives way to pained silence. Wyatt inhales it, then allows himself a slow, smug sip of water. All that can be heard is the heavy wheezing of the witness. I try not to look at him lest the jury spot how wretchedly fucking disappointed I am with his bin fire of a performance. Wyatt now has his centrepiece for his closing speech. It doesn't matter, he will say to the jury, what Mr Bell *thinks* he remembers about that night. What is important is what he admitted in his own words: *I don't know what fucking happened in the fucking alley*. It's a cheap point, cheaply extracted, but I expect it will be effective.

This, now, at the moment of ultimate weakness for the Crown's witness, is when Wyatt is going to put the Question. Before we had begun, I was at least confident that, whatever concessions he might be forced to make, Bell would be solid when the utterly absurd defence advanced by Craig Mervyn-Scott was put to him. But at this rate . . .

As one or two jurors shuffle in their seats, Jeremy Letts interrupts the silence.

'Mr Wyatt, I think the jury may have the point that Mr Bell did not see what happened in the alley. And it is not for this witness to speculate about what may or may not have been in the mind of your client or anybody else.'

'Of course, Your Honour. One final question, please, Mr Bell.'

And so we reach it. Even now though, Wyatt will not be rushed. He looks down at his notebook, and then up again at Paul Bell, like a high jumper measuring the bar, plotting the curve of his run-up.

The crucial part of his client's case, the proposition that the prosecution do not accept, that I am still praying Bell – useless, collapsing, shit-for-brains Bell – will not accept. He *can't* accept it. He can't. Because if he *had* seen what Wyatt is about to ask him, he damn sure would have led with it in his witness statement. Wouldn't he?

'I'd like to take you back to the beginning of "Part Two", when you heard the older man shouting aggressively.'

Bell says nothing, waiting. I stop typing and stare at the jury. I cannot help myself. I have to see how this lands.

'Mr Bell,' Wyatt says, lowering his voice, forcing the jurors to lean in to hear. 'Were you able to see a knife in the older man's hand?'

CHAPTER 11

Jennifer (counsel for the third defendant)

Baxter Wyatt sits down with what I imagine he thinks is a dramatic flourish. To my eye, it looks more like enthusiastically bouncing on a whoopee cushion, but I appreciate that I am not his intended audience. And, to his credit, the knife was a sharp point (shit pun absolutely intended) on which to finish. The jury, of course, have heard no evidence to substantiate the question, and Bell was emphatic in his rejection of it, but the seed has been planted.

Wyatt turns to his solicitor sitting behind him and crooks his eyebrow in a shameless fish for praise. He is duly rewarded, as his chalk-striped suitor leans forward and whispers something that causes the corners of Wyatt's mouth to momentarily twist upwards, before he recovers and shakes his head in faux modesty. An email notification bursts onto my laptop screen. It is Caz.

If you ever get that needy, I'll fucking shoot you.

I swivel around, nod solemnly and mouth *Thank you* at her.

This is the first time I have seen the Wyatt legend made flesh. He didn't attend any of the pre-trial hearings, on each occasion sending some poor pupil or junior in his stead. His reputation is circuit-wide and varies according to the beholder, traversing the gamut from fearless to abrasive to obnoxious to a bit of a prick to quite a lot of a prick actually. Our initial encounter in the robing room yesterday – 'Could your solicitor not be bothered to apply for a certificate for a silk?' he had oh-so-jokingly whinnied upon seeing that I was co-defending – has me pegging him well towards the less favourable end of that scale.

I've been assured that his courtroom abilities atone for, or at least mitigate, his personality. I scoured the jurors' faces for reactions during his cross-examination of Paul Bell. If there was any sympathy for Bell, or any hint of discomfort at the obvious inequality of intellectual arms, it was well masked. If anything, they seemed to be enjoying rubbernecking as Wyatt superciliously kicked Bell around the wreckage of his evidence.

This, doubtless, is the reaction that Wyatt is used to. His schtick is far from unique; the trope is so overplayed as to almost be back in fashion. Leaning into the stereotype, giving the jury *what they've come here to see*, the affected poshness, the booming voice, the pantomime swivel towards the jury box when a witness says something of significance – it's all perfectly valid courtroom artifice. It just rankles to see that it still, apparently, plays well.

Bob Evans is standing and waiting for HHJ Letts to give him the nod, and as he obliges with the words, 'Mr Evans', Paul Bell visibly deflates. The poor fucker hadn't realised that the past half-hour was only Round One. Nor that no number of knockouts can prevent this match going the full three rounds.

I expect that Bob intends to drag the witness back towards the prosecution case, which, although far from favourable to his client, is closer to Arron Freeman's version of events than the narrative teasingly hinted at by Baxter Wyatt's questioning. Neither version helps Jamal, of course, but my opportunity to put Jamal's case – if his instructions can be said to amount to a case – will come.

As Bob Evans smiles warmly at the jury, and then radiates towards a momentarily startled Bell, it is immediately clear that, however Bob intends to move Paul Bell away from the damaging concessions he has just made, dragging will not be the mechanism. Coaxing, enticing, seducing – those are the tools of Bob Evans's trade. He is the cheese to Wyatt's chalk. Pure fucking brie.

Kindly Uncle Bob is so mild and soft and inoffensive that Paul Bell has no idea that he is being trussed up for carving.

'Mr Bell,' Bob beams, as if greeting a long-standing professional acquaintance, rather than an intemperate stranger who has just inconveniently placed a murder weapon in the hand of Bob's client. 'I represent the interests of Arron Freeman, who has been referred to as "Male 2".'

The lack of response does not dent Bob's bonhomie.

'I hope I shan't be too long, Mr Bell. If there is anything I ask that isn't clear, then that is my fault, not yours. I apologise in advance if that does happen, but please do say if I need to repeat or rephrase anything.'

Paul Bell studies Bob warily, waiting for the sting. He glances in the direction of Baxter Wyatt, apparently fearing some sort of tag-team distraction strike, but Wyatt is busy doing something with an iPad. When satisfied that there is no imminent threat, Bell replies, exhaling an 'O . . . K' for a good five seconds, like releasing air from a balloon.

'Now there is absolutely no criticism intended of you *at all*, Mr Bell,' Bob lies, 'and I am not for *one moment* suggesting that you are doing anything other than your very best in giving your evidence to the ladies and gentlemen of the jury.'

Even Bell can sense the *but*.

'However, I wonder if I might ask if we could please look together at what you told the police back in January? That was at a time when events were fresher in your memory than they are today, would that be fair?' Bob Evans is still smiling, and Paul Bell is moved to agree that, yes, that would indeed be fair. He also agrees that he spoke to some police officers at his home twice – first on New Year's Day when they came knocking door-to-door, and again six days later when they returned to take a formal witness statement – and on both occasions signed something to confirm that what the police had written down was accurate.

From this, Bob adroitly restores Bell's evidence to where it was prior to Wyatt's hatchet job, putting the zombie knife back into the hands of Craig Mervyn-Scott when the violence began.

Yeah yeah, Bell agrees. *I did tell PC Monroe on 1 January, when events were fresh in my memory, that it was only the blond boy, Male 1, who I saw with the knife. Yeah yeah, I did put that same thing in my witness statement six days later.* And *yeah yeah, at no time did I mention ever seeing Male 2 holding a knife. Yeah yeah, had I seen that, I would definitely have included it in my witness statement.* And *yeah yeah, perhaps I have got a bit confused today about what I did or didn't see.*

No shit, dipshit.

'Now, Mr Bell, I promise I don't have too many more questions for you. But you must please say if you would like a break at any point.'

'Nah, you're all right, mate,' Paul Bell says, still nestled comfortably in Bob's palm.

'Well, what I'd like to ask now, please, is about what you could *hear* taking place in the alleyway. You told my learned friend Ms Arshad that you could hear somebody saying the words "Please stop", is that right?'

'The old man was saying that, yeah.'

Bob Evans nods thoughtfully. 'Well, this was what I wanted to ask you about, Mr Bell. Because as I understand it, you couldn't see anybody's face at this point, could you?'

'No. They was in the alley.'

'So – and again, no criticism at all – but would it be fair to say that you *assumed* it was the older man saying, "Please stop"?'

'It sounded like him, to be fair. I'd heard him shout earlier.'

'Ah yes, well, that is fair,' Bob agrees. And Paul Bell nods again, agreeing with Bob Evans's agreement, and evidently relieved that this exchange remains, despite this emerging difference, so agreeable.

'But may I just clarify,' Bob adds innocently, 'you hadn't previously heard Male 2 speak, had you?'

Bell considers this. 'Not that I can remember, no.'

'So would it be fair to say that, as you didn't know what Male 2's voice sounded like, you can't be sure that it wasn't Male 2 who was, in fact, the person saying, "Please stop"? Would you agree that that might be *possible*?'

Bell pauses. He thinks. And then he delivers. 'Yeah, I'd say that's *possible*, but . . .'

'And does it follow – and I really am sorry if it feels like I am whiffling on – that the "whooping" you say you heard, again you can't be sure whether this was Male 2 or whether, instead, it might have been one of the others?'

An even longer pause. 'Yeah.'

Bob beams. 'Thank you, Mr Bell.'

Bafflement reigns. Who of Craig Mervyn-Scott and Aaron Freeman had the knife at which point in Bell's addled chronology, nobody – least of all Bell himself – is now sure. Who was shouting 'Please stop', who was whooping and hollering – there are no certainties to which anybody, let alone the prosecution, can cling. Aliyah's irritation radiates as she hunches over her laptop. She would be a sitting duck at poker. I have some sympathy. Them's the breaks when prosecuting. You can make your case look so pretty on paper. But you can't stop your star witness stepping into the box and shoving a grenade down his own trousers.

As it happens, however, Paul Bell isn't the Crown's star witness. Aliyah doesn't even need him. The real jewel is Suhail, the 999 caller. He's the one who, if he comes up to proof and gives the jury the detail in his witness statement, will electrify the Crown's case against all three. He's the one whose evidence Jamal still can't, or won't, explain.

Bob retakes his seat next to me. A female juror on the front row is frowning at Bell, who blows out his cheeks and nods to himself, apparently pretty pleased with his own performance. Not missing a flicker, Caz fires another email into my inbox, a meme pasted into the body of the message: A cartoon dog perched happily on a chair as a fire rages around him, emitting a speech bubble containing the words, 'This is fine.' Caz's professional email signature is emblazoned incongruously beneath.

'Miss Rennie?'

The judge is indicating for me to begin. Standing slowly, I yank my robe straight and then knit my fingers behind my back. People assume that advocates are paid to speak. Sometimes, however, we are paid to know when not to speak. If a question does not need to be asked, it needs to *not* be asked. A gratuitous, unfocused question can undo an entire case; it can throw a lifebelt to a witness who was thought sunk. On behalf of Jamal, there is very little I need to ask Paul Bell. His general credibility is already through the floor; all I need to do is extract two extra nuggets.

'Mr Bell, first I want to ask you about "Part Two" – the incident in the alleyway. Have I understood your evidence to be that you were watching what was happening continuously, from when you saw one of the males on Rowe Street with a knife, right up to the point at which the police arrived?'

'Yes.' Bell stiffens.

'You didn't look away at any point?'

'No.'

'You're quite sure of that?'

'Yes.' His tone is sharpening with each answer. He does not follow the purpose of my questions, but Bell correctly recognises that, unlike the delightful Mr Evans, I do not come to praise him.

'And you are also sure that there were three males in the alleyway with the older man?'

His irritation is rising, not to the altitudes scaled during Baxter Wyatt's sparring, but definitely pitching a tent at the same base camp. 'I've said yes, haven't I?'

'Might you only have seen two males in the alleyway, with the older man?'

'No, I've told you. There were three. Definitely three.'

I take a sip of water from the plastic cup to my left. I am not thirsty. I want to give this answer the space to breathe.

'Mr Bell, I want to ask you about something you told the jury earlier, when giving your evidence in chief. You said this: "They all ran out of the alley a few minutes later and got arrested." So that we understand each other, do you mean that you saw each of the three young males run out of the alleyway and straight into the waiting arms of the police?'

He sighs. 'Yes.'

'Now, I want to be fair to you, Mr Bell,' I say. 'You have already admitted that you have been wrong about quite a few parts of your evidence. Might you be mistaken about this – about seeing all three young males run out of the alleyway and be arrested?'

Bell knows I am needling him. But, unable to understand why, and mistaking it for sport, he is incapable of rising above it.

'No,' he bristles. 'I'm not wrong. I am definitely right.' He pronounces it as 'def-i-nightly'. I can hear Caz behind me thumping this answer onto her keyboard.

'Are you as sure about that,' I ask slowly, turning to the jury as the words drop, 'as you are about the number of people you saw in the alley?'

'Yes. I am def-i-nightly one hundred per cent sure.'

I nod, taking another sip of water as I prepare for my final move.

'And lastly, Mr Bell. You were asked earlier about two identification procedures that you attended at the police station. And you confirmed that you positively identified "Male 1" –' I turn to face the jury – 'who the jury have heard was Craig Mervyn-Scott. And you also made a positive identification of "Male 2", who the jury have heard was Arron Freeman. But it is right, isn't it, that you in fact attended a third identification procedure?'

'Yeah.'

'And it was the same format – you were shown a video displaying a sequence of nine videos of males all matching the description that you gave of "Male 3". And you were asked whether you were able to recognise any of them. And, again, you made a positive identification, didn't you?'

'I did.'

'And, again, is it right that you were one hundred per cent, definitely sure about that identification? Or might you have been mistaken?'

The question hangs as Bell slowly chews it, running his tongue over the gap between his front teeth. 'No. I'm sure.'

'So, pulling that all together, you are sure that there were three people in Garth Yard, sure that you saw all three being arrested by the police when they ran out, and sure that "Male 3" was the person you identified?'

'Yes.'

I sit down hurriedly before Bell can say any more. My pulse is thumping. I allow a small smile to unfurl; nothing too overt, but obvious enough to be caught by any watching jurors. I want them to know that *this is fine*. Genuinely. That *I am not the dog meme. I am not on fire.* Right now, all twelve are probably struggling to see how any of those questions benefit Jamal; in their eyes, all I have done is invite the prosecution witness to hammer home the fact that he saw three people involved in the killing and positively identified all three.

But the jury don't yet know what is coming. They do not know the evidence that will be put before them once Paul Bell is safely out of the witness box.

They don't yet know that Paul Bell, in insisting that he saw all three defendants being arrested when they ran out of the alley, has committed himself – def-i-nightly, one-hundred-per-cent – to something which is completely, provably wrong.

They don't yet know that one of the best points Jamal has – the one thing about which he has been entirely consistent, and which will be confirmed by the police witnesses – is that he wasn't even at the scene when the police arrived.

And they don't yet know that the person who Paul Bell picked out on the identification procedure as positively, def-i-nightly being Male 3 – it wasn't Jamal.

DAY 3 OF TRIAL – FRIDAY

CHAPTER 12

Aliyah (the prosecutor)

I push open the door of the boxy conference room and knock redundantly as I enter. All nineteen stone of DS Chris Rose are implausibly squeezed behind a small pine table pushed up against the back wall as he jabs at his iPhone. My entrance does not disturb whatever critical police business is occupying him – initially I assume social media, but then notice a row of coloured gemstones reflected in his spectacles – and even placing my macchiato on top of his closed laptop does not elicit eye contact.

'Ah! Aliyah!' he says to his phone screen. 'Just the ladywoman. Bit of a problem, you may have heard, with the, umm, witness, Farid . . .'

He squints and trails off. I deign to finish for him, doing my best to disguise the panic in my voice.

'Suhail? No, I haven't heard.'

'Hmm?'

'The witness Farid Suhail?'

'Yeah. Yeah. That's, umm . . .' He falls silent again, prodding furiously at his phone, and I wonder whether he is actively inviting me to drain my macchiato over his perfectly square head.

'Oh!' he suddenly cries. 'You bastard!'

I do a double-take of my immediate surroundings for reassurance that I have not acted out my fantasy, and am relieved to see my KeepCup still perched on his laptop. Instinctively I pick it up, just as Rose sends his phone skidding across the desk. Finally he looks up at me, all smiles. 'Sorry. You were saying?'

'What is the problem, Chris?'

'It's nothing really. I've just been stuck on that level for what feels like—'

'What. Is. The. Problem. With. The. Witness. Farid. Suhail.'

'Oh, right. Yes. Farid. Now, he's the one who . . . remind me, is he the—?'

'He's the fucking 999-caller, Chris. The one whose statement says, quite crucially, that—'

'Yeah, yeah. Yeah, he's been a bit, shall we say, problematic.'

I wince. After the shitshow of Paul Bell's evidence yesterday, Farid Suhail's significance has magnified overnight. Presentationally, it would be nice if the prosecution could produce at least one civilian witness who did not repel the jury. More important still, however, is what he will tell them. His view of Garth Yard was superior to that of Paul Bell, two doors down. His witness statement, made to the police in the early hours of New Year's Day, contains the detail around which, once he repeats it in evidence, I intend to construct my closing speech; the detail that will nail all three defendants to the wall.

'Suhail is problematic *how*, exactly?'

'Well, we've got him here, that's the important thing. He is in the building. But he's – well, let's just say he's enjoying the company of a new friend from patrol, and he probably wishes his hands were, umm, available, to, er, rub his eyes.'

I sigh deeply. 'Right. Do I want to know?'

'Want to know what?' He reaches towards his phone and I clamp my hand onto his wrist.

'Do I want to know why the key prosecution witness in our murder trial has been PAVA sprayed and handcuffed to one of your colleagues minutes before he is due to give evidence? And before you answer incorrectly, take it that, yes, I *do* want to know.'

'Your laddo didn't react well to this morning's early knock-on. Took a swing at one of the PCs who'd turned up to escort him. And became a bit bitey with a PCSO. He thought they were there to arrest him.'

Behind me, the CPS caseworker Lydia opens the door and steps half into the room. I wave her in fully and motion for her to shut the door.

'But Chris, why did he think he was being arrested? You told us yesterday that you had spoken to Farid Suhail over the weekend, that he was fully on board and that you'd discussed giving him a lift to court.'

'Yeah, honest to God, Aliyah, I thought I had. But the funny thing is that I've got another job with an Asian witness with a similar name . . .'

I don't need him to finish. I do not need the mental clutter of a random man from an entirely different case, who is right this minute sitting at home expecting a police escort to a trial in which he is not a witness, while our actual witness is downstairs in handcuffs having bitten chunks out of the officers who gave him an unsolicited wake-up call. This can all very much be filed under Shit I Absolutely Do Not Need.

I raise my palm for silence. 'This . . . incident will all need scheduling for disclosure, Chris. In the meantime, Lydia and I will go and speak to Mr Suhail and see if we can pacify the tiger before we release him into the playground.'

As I move towards the door, I suddenly remember.

'On the subject of disclosure, Chris, where are we up to with the counselling records?'

Rose stares at me. 'As in . . .?'

'As in, do we have them yet, and have you, as disclosure officer, reviewed them yet?'

'I shall triple-cooked-chip check and get back to you.'

Further words would be wasted on him. In particular, words

pointing out that his answer sounds awfully like a no, and that the question of obtaining and reviewing the counselling records should have been answered in the affirmative when it was first posed several months ago, and, failing that, on each of the dozen subsequent occasions it has been repeated.

As I walk out of the room and along the corridor, Lydia at my elbow, I offer myself – not for the first time – the reassurance that DS Rose's rewards will come in heaven. And by 'heaven', I mean 'cross-examination by the defence', when Rose's decisions and non-decisions as investigating and disclosure officer will be forensically dismantled.

The glow of anticipatory schadenfreude quickly fades. Because, much as I would have it otherwise, our respective functions and fates, as OIC and prosecuting counsel, are intertwined.

Where gaps or errors arise, it ultimately counts for little whether the fault lies with the police or the lawyers. All of our names attach to the consequences. All of us bear the weight of a potential miscarriage of justice.

And it matters.

I am not oblivious to the robing room rumours. I hear the whispers, born of ignorance and spread in malevolence. The affectation of surprise with which certain counsel say, 'You're *prosecuting* again?' as if there was any genuine substance behind what happened five years ago. As if it was actually my fault.

I care about fairness. I care about doing right by the defendants. And I care about the safety of the convictions which – irrespective of the incompetence around me – I am damn well going to deliver.

CHAPTER 13

Arron (the second defendant)

The banging only really stops in court.

It's there in the night when I'm in my pad – usually the scruff across the landing screaming for his meds, or just trying to get a rise out of the screws. They ignore him – it's not them he's stopping getting any kip – but he just thinks they haven't heard, and so he carries on thumping his door.

It's worst in the sweatbox on the way to court. On the way back it's not as bad. Everyone's a bit quieter. Less excited. Like the energy has all drained away. Maybe it's because if you're on the van back to prison, your day in court hasn't gone as you'd hoped. But on the way there, even though we've all been up since five and we're all locked up in our little boxes stinking of vom, people are buzzing and the banging is mad. Sometimes it's coz someone is gagging for some water. Or it's some lad who's had too much water and needs the screw to push him a piss bag under his door. Sometimes the banging's not coming from someone's fists, but someone's head whacking against the plastic seats as the driver takes corners like he's on speedway.

Right now, the other seven lads in the van are banging coz while we're stopped for the electric court gates to open, there's three teenage girls in trackies on the pavement. They can't see us, but if we twist our necks we can see them out our tiny tinted windows, though everything outside is coloured pink, like we're watching a film from the olden days.

As the girls walk past the side of the van, close enough almost to touch them, everyone bangs harder, and two of the girls jump and squeal. One of them turns and I see her face, and summat about the way she has her hair makes me look twice. Just in case. But it's not her. Or if it is, she's not letting on to me.

I'm still thinking about her as we pull into the loading bay and my box is unlocked. Still thinking about her as I'm cuffed to a screw and walked through the metal doors and down into the court cells. Still thinking about her twenty minutes later as we're pulled up the stairs and into the courtroom. Could it have been her?

I'm seeing things everywhere at the moment. The way the van goes to court, it takes us past the Rosewoods estate, and from this angle it looks exactly like Mossfields. If I didn't know this was two hundred miles away, I'd swear down I was back in Wythenshawe.

If I squint I can almost see myself up on the thirteenth floor, seven years old in my United top and fake Adidas pants, running across the landing from our flat to the kid on the corner, ten-pound note in my hand. And then running back again, and racing indoors and seeing the look of relief on my mam's face as the door slams behind me and I walk into the kitchen and hold out my hand. I loved that look. Truth be told, I don't think my mam ever really did happy. But that look, when she knew it was coming, was close to it.

The only other time I saw it was when there was a knock on the front door and she answered thinking it was the social but it turned out to be somebody else. Pure relief. She had her problems, but her family mattered to her. I mattered. I do know that. And every time the knock on the door was the social, and every time it looked like I was being taken away again, I do think it cut her. Like, she felt bad that I had different schools all the time coz of all the different foster families, and when I was twelve and she got clean and the social said I could go back with her properly, she swore down that it would be different, and that I would have one home and one school. And I really think she meant it.

Fuck cancer, man.

After the court said I could go live with my nana, I did only have one school to be fair, so even if it wasn't what my mam meant, I did sort of get what she wanted for me. Don't get me wrong, it wasn't always easy. But I had one home, with my own bed in my own room, not just a pull-out in the living room, and there was always scran in the cupboards. And I had one school, and new mates I knew I'd see every day. And my nana went to work every day, even with her health, and then came home and sat me down at the kitchen table every night before tea and made me do my homework. We didn't have to deal with the social and we never ran out of leccy. And even though I was miles out of Manchester and away from everything I knew, it was the best year of my life.

Seriously, fuck cancer.

When she passed, that's when I got moved to Ableford, coz even though it's like an hour and a half from my nana's, it's the same council or summat, and that's where they had space in the home. And when I first got to Rosewoods Family Centre, I didn't really think I'd find what I had with my nana again. Even when I first met Graham, I wasn't sure. I've never been sure about anybody new who says they are looking out for me, coz usually what they mean is they are looking out for themselves. But Graham was decent to us. Like my nana, he was all about keeping out of trouble and making more of myself and all that. A lot of kids at Rosewoods ignored him, and even I took the piss out of him at first. But I did see what he meant. He was sound when you got to know him.

There's no way that Nana or Graham would have expected me to end up here. I'm just thinking about how mad it is, how different it all could have been. It's like I'm gonna have to tell the jury, we wouldn't even be here if Craig hadn't learned what he did about the old man.

Now though, there is no banging. Just the silence of the courtroom as the judge comes in. I take a deep breath. I enjoy it.

The next witness who's coming – someone Suhail – he's the one who Mr Evans says causes real problems for us. Mr Evans says he will do his best, but I need to prepare myself to hear some things I don't want to hear. Just sit and watch, he says. And don't react.

So I sit. And, as the police bring this guy into court, I watch him. And I don't react. I don't react when I see his purple swollen eyes and squashed nose. I don't react when I see – I swear down – that he's wearing fucking pyjama bottoms.

The jury do though, of course they do. When they all come in and they see this skinny little guy sitting there, with his red eyes poking above the witness box like one of them lemurs at the zoo, I see they are thinking like, *What the actual fuck?* When the guy is told to read out the oath, he wipes his nose with the back of his hand and when he pulls it away he's like broken his scabs and he starts bleeding, and the usher is rushing around looking for a box of tissues. But I'm doing what I'm told, me. I'm saying nowt, even as Craig next to me is creasing.

The mad thing is though, when Miss Arshad starts asking this guy like what's his name and where was he living, it's like they're all pretending this is just dead normal. She's telling him to look at the map in the jury folder and asking if his flat was opposite the ginnel, and literally a drop of blood falls out of his nose and onto the page, and I'm like, *Am I the only one that's seen that?* Because, again, nobody lets on.

The guy, Mr Suhail, he is not happy though. He's not looking at her when he's giving his answers, and he's saying only like one or two words, and you can tell it's getting under her skin. She's like, *How would you describe the view of Garth Yard as you look out of your bedroom window?* And he's like, *Fine*, and he's basically giving her nothing. When she tries to get him to talk about New Year's Eve, it takes her for ever. Like twenty minutes or something just to get him to say that he was watching telly with his girlfriend, and that he heard shouting just after midnight when he went to his bedroom to get his skins for a rollie. He starts going on about how that's just the way it goes round his, how Garth Yard is where all the smackheads hang out, but she stops him and gets him to say that he could see a group of us in the ginnel. He says he could see us all near the bottom of the fire escape, just where the light from the street lamps was starting to fade. And then he tells the jury that he could see one of us waving 'an enormous fuck-off knife'.

This is the bit where he's gonna hurt us. We'll obviously say to the jury that he's got it all wrong, Mr Evans has told me, but if Suhail says to this jury what he's put in his statement, I don't need a barrister to tell me how bad it is for us all.

'How many people could you see?' she asks.

'Three or four.'

'Can you help us with *precisely* how many?'

'Like I said, three or four.'

'You have described one of the people as waving a knife. Who or what – if anything – was he waving the knife towards?'

'He was waving it towards an old bloke.'

'Right. So that's two people – the person with the knife and the old bloke. How many others, besides those two, could you see, and what were they doing?'

I close my eyes.

'One, maybe two. I dunno. Can't really remember. I was only there for a few seconds and then I went to call the police.'

I open them again. That's not what . . . is it? Maybe I'm misremembering. Miss Arshad leans towards the woman with the laptop in front of her and gets this piece of paper which she holds up.

'Would it perhaps assist, Mr Suhail, if you were permitted to refresh your memory from the statement that you gave to the police on 1 January? That statement was made at a time, was it not, when these events were fresher in your memory than they are today?'

OK, I get it. He's forgot what he put in his statement, so she's gonna let him jog his memory. For a minute there I thought maybe he wasn't gonna say it. But Suhail is shown the piece of paper and says that yeah, this is his statement and this is his signature, and I close my eyes again because now I know what's coming.

'Now, taking a moment to refresh your memory from page two of your statement, can you tell us how many people you could see, and . . .' Miss Arshad pauses and then stresses every word, 'what you could see them doing.'

I can see Suhail's lips moving as he's reading his statement to himself, tracing his finger over the words. Then he looks up.

'Does that assist you with recalling how many people you could see in Garth Yard, and what those people were doing?'

Here it comes.

'Not really, no.'

What the fuck?

Miss Arshad has this mad smile on her face as she says to him, 'Not even, say, paragraphs six to eight?'

And without looking at the page, Suhail says to her, 'No. I know that one of them younger ones hit the old bloke with the sword, or the knife or whatever, but I was in and out of the room. Looking back, I can't even be sure that what I put in that statement is right, to be honest. I think the police got some of it wrong.'

I glance at Jamal on my left, but he's in his own little world. I look at Craig on my right, and our eyes meet, and I can tell he's thinking the same as me. I don't want to say anything to him in case the jury see, but then Miss Arshad is saying something to the judge, and the jury are getting up and walking out, stretching their arms and rolling their necks. And when the door has closed behind them, Mr Evans turns to me and gives me like a 'just chill' sign with his hand – not that he'd ever use them words, but you know what I mean.

And I'm trying to chill, I am. I'm trying to work out what is going to happen next. Because I'm no lawyer, but I don't need to be to know that Farid Suhail – the prosecution's star witness, the one who was gonna screw us all – is not saying what the prosecution was expecting.

CHAPTER 14

HHJ Jeremy Letts (the judge)

I maintain my poker face as the jurors exit and the witness is escorted out, but let there be no misunderstanding: this is fucking hilarious. Arshad's first murder in silk, and her witness has gone bandit. She is on her feet, trying to maintain composure in her voice, but fooling nobody. The panic all but drips off her.

'Your Honour,' she squawks. 'In light of the answers given by the witness on oath, as contrasted to the contents of his witness statement, I am bound to apply for leave to treat him as hostile.'

I nod. 'So the Crown submits that Denman's Act is engaged?'

'We do, Your Honour.'

It is an unsurprising application. I made enough of them during my time at the Bar. When a witness goes rogue, sometimes your only option is to ask for permission to treat them as hostile. If the judge agrees, you can then cross-examine them in the same way you would a witness for the other side, and put to them, in front of the jury, the details in their witness statement that they are declining to give in their evidence.

I bring up Farid Suhail's witness statement on my computer and remind myself of what he was expected to say. Most of it overlaps with or repeats what the jury have already heard – the sound of raised voices on Rowe Street just after midnight; the word 'money' distinguishable above the din; the witness idly drawing back the curtain and seeing four males in Garth Yard. Three young wearing dark hooded clothing. One older, in a light-coloured coat.

But those, of course, are not the parts of Suhail's testimony that the prosecution are so desperate to adduce. It is the three paragraphs that follow, which have disappeared from the evidence he has given today.

One of the hooded males was holding a long implement, which may have been a plank of wood or a pole. Two of the hooded males were holding knives. One of the knives had a curved blade approximately sixteen inches in length. The other knife was smaller and looked like a kitchen knife. The male with the large curved knife then swung it towards the older male, hitting his left arm. The older male screamed.

I immediately ran to my living room to get my mobile phone to call the police. While I was on the phone to the police, I returned to my position in the bedroom. The group had moved further back into Garth Yard, but were still visible from my vantage point. It looked like the three hooded males were taking it in turns to hit the older male, who was now on the floor and trying to get up. The larger curved knife was passed between the hooded males, who each struck the older male. He fell to the ground and rolled out of sight. The group then moved further back into Garth Yard and behind the fire escape, obscuring my view.

I left my bedroom and returned to the living room with my girlfriend as I did not want her to see any more of the violence. I could still hear the screams. The sound was like a fox being torn to pieces. The whole incident lasted a few minutes. The hooded males are not known to me and I do not believe that I would recognise them again. I can only say that there were three of them and they were all using weapons to attack the older male. And they continued to attack him even after he fell silent and stopped moving.

'Well, gentlemen?' I address the defence counsel, remembering slightly too late the chubby presence of Jennifer Rennie. 'And of course, ladies. If,' I jest, 'we are still permitted to use those terms.'

Baxter Wyatt is up first. 'Well, Your Honour, if I might start by offering the reassurance that I, certainly, will not be making any urgent referrals to the Woke Police.'

We share a smile.

'In response to the Crown's application, the Court of Appeal authorities make plain that "adverse", for the purpose of Denman's Act, means "hostile", and not merely unfavourable. The question for Your Honour is not, "Has Farid Suhail failed to give the evidence that the Crown had hoped for?" but "Does Farid Suhail appear *not desirous of telling the truth*?" It is a very different test, and one which in this case is not met.

'Mr Suhail has explained the position clearly. Having had the opportunity to reconsider his statement, he does not believe that the police constable who deposed him has accurately reflected his recollection. It is disappointing for my learned friend, of course. But that does not make the witness hostile.'

'Your Honour,' Arshad interjects. 'This morning, in the cells, Mr Suhail was provided with a copy of his statement and expressed no concerns about its contents. This volte face has taken place without warning in front of the jury. That is why the Crown submits—'

I cut across her. 'In the cells? Not the witness suite?'

She stops in her tracks.

'This isn't something which ought to have been disclosed to the defence and has *not* been, is it, Ms Arshad? That would be . . . unfortunate.'

She flushes red. She thinks I am going to bring up the history. But I am not a vindictive man. On the bench, I am the epitome of fairness, as faithful to my judicial oath as I am to my mistress.

'Miss Arshad, is this reference to the cells linked to the – how shall I put it – *presentation* of Mr Suhail today?'

'Does Your Honour mean the, erm . . .'

'I mean the fact that somebody relatively handy has apparently knocked seven bells out of him at some point in the last twenty-four hours. Are those blemishes, and his attendance today in the cells, merely sequalae of his general lifestyle, or do they have any relation to his role in this trial?'

Bob Evans interrupts. 'Your Honour, can I make plain, the Crown certainly did disclose the unfortunate circumstances surrounding Mr Suhail's attendance today. I wouldn't wish for there to be any criticism of my learned friend in that regard. She has acted entirely properly.'

I have had enough of this circumspection. 'And what are those unfortunate circumstances? Is anybody going to tell me, or is there a new judicial bench book on divination that I've failed to read?'

Before Arshad can reply, Wyatt is up again. 'Your Honour, as the defence understand it, the police went round to Farid Suhail's home mob-handed this morning, having forgotten to warn him as a witness, and in the ensuing brouhaha he sustained the numerous injuries that Your Honour has observed.'

I raise an eyebrow at Arshad. 'And you wonder why he is not a paradigm of good humour and cooperation?'

'Your Honour, the point is—'

'The point, Miss Arshad, is that my discretion as to whether to allow the Crown to treat Mr Suhail as hostile is absolute, is it not?'

'It is, Your Honour, but—'

'And is your submission that, in exercising that discretion, I should condone the Crown beating up its own witness and then complaining when his evidence does not emerge as they would like?'

'My submission,' she prattles, 'is that both the content of his evidence and his demeanour demonstrate that, for whatever reason, he is now hostile to the prosecution. The materiality of his evidence does not need to be emphasised.'

'Oh, worry not, Miss Arshad. I fully appreciate *why* you want to get the line-by-line contents of his statement in front of this jury. Its value to the prosecution is not lost on me, a mere judge of the Crown Court though I may be. But the question is whether, in all the circumstances and applying the law as I must, I should allow you to do so.'

Another matter that is not lost on me is the inevitable outcome of this trial. These three yobbos are going to be rightly and justly convicted, come what may. The Crown's case theory may well, based on what I have read, be an exercise in backing the wrong horse, but irrespective of the competence of the prosecution, the defendants are going to sink each other with their defences. The very last thing we need is frivolous defence complaints about this ruling prompting the Court of Appeal to stick its oar in. I have not had a conviction in my court overturned yet. And I do not propose to allow this trial to blacken that copybook.

'Sit,' I direct as Rennie moves to rise. 'I don't need to hear from you.'

I address all counsel. 'The Crown may not cross-examine Farid Suhail, and may not put the contents of his statement before this jury. I am not satisfied that the witness is hostile, as opposed to merely unfavourable and, even were I so satisfied, I would still not exercise my discretion to allow the prosecution to put his statement to him, in light of what I have been told about his treatment at the hands of the Crown.'

Arshad looks shell-shocked.

'The police have made their bed, Miss Arshad,' I beam at her. She nods obediently. Defeated.

'Your Honour, yes.'

I click my fingers towards Sandra to bring the jury back in.

CHAPTER 15

Jennifer (counsel for the third defendant)

In every trial, you will get a lucky break. Usually it is something minor, and ultimately inconsequential to the verdict, like winning a trivial legal argument you expected to lose, or your opponent missing an opportunity to trip up a witness in cross-examination.

Every once in a while, however, a lucky break can do just that. It can break a case.

Farid Suhail failing to come up to proof, and the judge refusing to allow the prosecution to tell the jury what is in his witness statement, ranks in the God Tier of lucky breaks. It does not solve all of Jamal's problems – far from it – but it tosses the cards up in the air, forcing the prosecution to scrabble on the ground and frantically reorder the pack.

Without Suhail putting weapons in the hands of the three defendants – without him even being sure that there *were* three defendants – the case against Jamal takes on a different complexion. I mentally run through my checklist: *Not at the scene when the police arrive; Paul Bell a demonstrably unreliable witness; no positive ID of Jamal by either witness; Farid Suhail accepting the possibility that there were two, rather than three, hooded males present when the violence began.* Tick, tick, tick, tick.

Everything else – even the DNA and the phone material – is explicable, can be made to fall into place, if we can just cast doubt on Jamal's presence when the first blow landed. And Farid

Suhail – beautiful, bloodied shithouser-in-chief Farid Suhail – looks to have done just that. I don't need to discredit him, because his evidence is no threat: if there were potentially only two defendants in Garth Yard when Suhail started watching, there is a gap for Jamal to have left the scene before it all kicked off.

On that aspect of his instructions, Jamal has been clear since we first met, deep in the bowels of Ableford Magistrates' Court. Two days after Caz's call, I had arrived outside the magistrates' court at 8.50 a.m. and stood on the curtilage, dodging the rain streaking through the cracked grey awning. As I lit up, with an unusual heaviness in my stomach, Caz appeared on cue, and we stood enveloped in awkward smoky silence until the chimes signalled 9 a.m. and security permitted us to enter.

We made our way downstairs and towards the heavy beige door marked 'CELLS', and once through security were ushered into a yellowing, peeling room smelling bountifully of BO and piss, and squeezed ourselves behind one side of the screwed-down table next to the wall. A few minutes later Jamal Lowton appeared, hands cuffed and flanked by two skinny male cells officers. He towered over both of them, but there was no menace. His eyes were dull and he exuded a gentle grogginess, like a captive wild animal under sedation. Three nights spent in a police cell will do that to you.

Once Jamal was safely bundled inside the conference room, one of the officers took out a small key and gently removed the handcuffs, before backing out and locking the door behind him. Caz spoke first.

'Jamal, this is Miss Rennie. She will be your barrister when the case goes to the Crown Court.'

I smiled and introduced myself. Conscious not to overwhelm him with information, I kept the briefing short. 'This,' I told him, 'will be the first of many meetings we will have. Today is only the first court hearing, and all that will happen is that the magistrates will send the case to the Crown Court, where there will be another hearing in a few days. Don't worry about speaking – all you need to say is your name. Leave the rest of the talking to me. That's my job.'

I paused, hoping for some outward sign of understanding. Jamal remained rigidly blank, his face giving away nothing, his eyes avoiding mine.

'We have plenty that we need to talk about,' I continued, speaking slowly and carefully. 'There will be lots of evidence and lots of questions that we will need to go through. But there is no rush. You don't need to tell me everything now.'

There is always a risk, when meeting a client for the first time – especially somebody young and inexperienced – that they will blurt out something that they later wish they could take back; something I cannot unhear.

It transpired that there was no such risk with Jamal. The monosyllabic instructions he had given Caz at the police station did not fit with the evidence that the police had initially disclosed, and so Caz had advised Jamal to give no comment throughout his interviews. She had reasoned that, with his limitations, he would be better off waiting to see the full evidence before telling us chapter and verse. But we never got chapter and verse. Or even an abridged edition of the events of New Year's Eve. Just a tagline on the dust jacket: *I wasn't there, miss.*

Jamal's disinclination to explain other, slightly damning, parts of the prosecution evidence has not helped us. But his having left the scene has been a consistent refrain. Just entirely inconsistent with the rest of the evidence.

Until today. Today, Farid Suhail has given Jamal a lifeline.

The key now is navigating three defence cross-examinations without any of us stepping on a landmine. The very last thing needed is for a loose question to give this mad volatile fish the opportunity to blurt out something damaging from his statement. Given the current state of his evidence, none of us should be asking any questions at all. We should be banking what we currently have.

Baxter Wyatt, drawing himself to his full towering height, has probably never cashed in his chips in his life. He is the type who always fancies that he is just one more spin away from not just beating the house, but repossessing it entirely and evicting the occupants. And so it is little surprise that he thinks there is more to be won from Farid Suhail.

'Mr Suhail,' he booms. 'Just the one question, please.'

As predicted. Just one more spin.

'You have already accepted that you had only an intermittent view of what took place in the alleyway, and that you only looked out *after* the shouting had started. You have also accepted that you are not able to offer any meaningful descriptions of the two or three persons involved, other than to say that one of them was armed with a large knife. So I shan't ask any questions about any of that.'

I stare at my laptop screen, willing Wyatt to shut up grandstanding and just ask his question. Why the fuck is he doing this? Save it for your speech – don't give the witness an opportunity to backpedal. Or, worse, give the prosecution a chance to revisit this turf in re-examination.

Mercifully, Suhail remains as useless to the prosecution as he was in chief, and does not quibble with Wyatt's dicey characterisation of his evidence.

'So what I want to ask you,' Wyatt peers over his tortoiseshell glasses, 'is simply this: it is right, isn't it, that when you heard somebody shouting, there was a reference to "money"?'

Suhail ponders this, and, seeing little advantage to be gained by the prosecution in his cooperating, nods. 'Yeah, I think so.'

'But,' Wyatt continues, 'you of course cannot say who of those in the alleyway was doing the shouting?'

'No.'

Without thanking the witness, Wyatt sits down. He has as much as he needs to make the points for his client.

Bob Evans is clearly thinking along the same lines as me, as he barely raises himself out of his seat to nod at the judge: 'No questions on behalf of Arron Freeman, thank you.'

'No worries, mate.' While not exactly demob happy, Suhail is visibly relaxing as he senses the end.

Letts turns his stare to me. 'Miss Rennie?'

That's all from me too, folks, I ready myself to say. No questions from me, now please get Farid Suhail the fuck away from this jury. But as I rise, so does a noise from my right. Baxter Wyatt is leaning back towards his solicitor, and misjudging the register in which he whispers a mocking 'No worries, mate.' It catches in the silence and bounces around the courtroom.

Suhail suddenly fixes his head towards Wyatt, eyes firing, as if somebody has just rebooted him. 'You got something to say, mate?'

I pause on my ascent, body curved in an awkward half-crouch. Wyatt stares at his cufflinks.

'You taking the piss, yeah? When I'm doing youse all a fucking favour?'

No no no no no. What the fuck have you done, Wyatt?

'Well, I'm taking it back then. You wanna know what I actually saw?'

I don't know where to look. I don't know how to stop it. Instinctively, I straighten my back and bark, 'Mr Suhail!' But I don't know where I'm going next.

Nowhere, as it turns out, because the judge is already on it, a smirk behind the eyes as he extends his hand to stop me. 'Miss Rennie, please let the witness finish. Now, Mr Suhail, was there something you wanted to say?'

I can feel the bile catching at the back of my throat as Suhail's words begin to spool.

'Yeah, there was. Turns out I do now remember what I saw, yeah?'

I swallow. And I brace.

'I saw three youngers in that alley. And I saw all three of them laying into the old man.'

The stillness is broken by Jeremy Letts. 'Just to make sure my note is accurate,' he purrs, slowing down to ensure the jury cannot miss just how important he considers this piece of evidence to be. 'You said that you saw all three of the young males laying into the old man – do I have that right?'

As Suhail agrees, I feel all eyes in the courtroom on me, still crouching, trying to work out how to reverse out of this cul-de-sac in a fucking upside-down wheelbarrow. Fucking, fucking, fucking Baxter Wyatt. All I wanted to do was ask no questions and bank what we had. And now this entirely avoidable shitstorm means I have to say something.

But what?

I can't suggest that Suhail has made this up on the spot, because we know that this piece of evidence – and much worse besides – was in his witness statement, and Christ knows we do not want to give the prosecution a second chance at getting that in front of the jury. But I obviously can't leave what he has said unchallenged. Because to do so would be to accept it.

'Mr Suhail,' I say as a I straighten my back, straining for composure, trying to make my challenge as non-confrontational as possible. If he starts talking about us all holding weapons, it is game over. 'You are mistaken about what you saw, aren't you?'

'Sorry, love,' he gurns, exposing a row of bloodied gums. 'I'd like to help you out. But you don't fucking forget something like that.'

DAY 4 OF TRIAL – MONDAY

CHAPTER 16

Craig (the first defendant)

Friday was a head fuck. Before that man walked into court, my brief was all like, 'He is going to fuck you all, bruv,' and then he goes and says barely any of the shit he was going to. He fucked us all a little bit right at the end, but the main thing is that the shit he was supposed to say about us all being strapped and taking it in turns with the old man – he didn't say it! All those little details about who was doing what, he couldn't remember them. Or he pretended like he couldn't remember them, whatever. It doesn't matter. Mr Wyatt says that their case is still strong, but that now we've got a chance.

The door to my pad shakes, and voices are shouting that it's time to get on the van. Second day in a row there's no time to shower or clean my teeth. On Friday I told the screw, the fat one with the eye that doesn't look at you straight, that I needed to shower before court. I told him that the washers are broken downstairs and I've been in the same filthy garms for a full week now, but he just said if I didn't go straight to the van, they'd tell court that I refused to come, and what would the jury think about that?

It's the same screw today. When I walk onto the landing and say to him that today I *need* to shower, that the hot water has been broken all weekend, he smiles at me. Then he says, 'You were offered the opportunity to shower on Friday, and you refused, Mervyn. Now get on the fucking van.'

So I smell rank, but to be fair that makes me no different to everyone else. And at least I don't have to actually do anything at court. It's just watching CCTV today, Mr Wyatt says. Showing the jury who was going where and when.

The big problem, he reckons, is Arron. He doesn't give a fuck about Jamal, he said – he actually said that, in his deep posh voice. 'I don't give a fuck about what Jamal Lowton says. The chap's a fucking imbecile.' But he is vexed about Arron. I'm vexed about Arron, too. I'm vexed about the jury listening when he starts chatting bare shit. And I'm worried that the CCTV sort of backs up what Arron's going to be saying.

I had a visit off Kayla on Saturday. First I've seen her in time. She says she's had loads on with school and with her new foster family, but I know it's just excuses. Truth is she can't stand seeing me in here. When this all started, she was gassed for our visits. But on Saturday, the minute she walked into the hall and saw me she just cried and cried and cried. It was the same when she had to go. She tried to give me a hug, and the screws ran over and it got bare ugly, and she was just howling and scrapping. It was like all of a sudden she wasn't fifteen, she was a little girl again, sobbing her little heart out at being pulled apart from her big brother.

It made me think of that day when she'd not been long going to primary school. I think she was five and I was eight, and I walked from home to pick her up. I wasn't going to school myself at that time for my own reasons, and when I got to the school gates she saw me from the playground and came running over to me in her blue and white checked dress, as fast as she could. She was so excited that she didn't look where she was running and she went crashing over a tree root and onto the concrete, and she scraped all the skin off her knees. It was messy. But even though she was just five, on my mum's life she just got straight back up and carried on running, with the biggest smile on her face, and literally jumped into my arms.

And then when I put her down and wiped the blood from her knees with my sleeve, and told her we had to go the hospital, her little face crumpled and she just lost it. Like she did at visits. She was just sobbing and sobbing. She didn't understand, and kept saying that her knees were OK, and we could just get the little orange plasters with the farm animals on and that they would make her better. And as we walked away from school and crossed the main road and went into the churchyard, I tried to explain. I told her that she didn't need to worry. I said that we weren't going to hospital because she'd banged her knee. But I didn't know how to tell her why we *were* going.

She guessed though. She asked, after we'd been walking for about half an hour, if we were going to see Mummy. I couldn't lie to her – I could never lie to her – but I also couldn't tell her the complete truth. So I said that yeah, Mummy had fallen over and hurt herself, but that the doctors were going to make everything better. I told her that Mummy was having a rest, and that the doctors had put lots of tubes around her to help her feel well again, so that Kayla wouldn't be shook when she saw her.

And when we got there, and Kayla saw MJ standing outside Mum's room, talking to one of the nurses with this look on his face like he was really worried for her, Kayla knew. I didn't need to tell her. She knew. Even before MJ came over and winked and whispered to us:, 'She's a careless woman, your mum. She needs to make better decisions.'

And when the feds turned up, because the hospital had called them probably, and MJ was taken away, I made Kayla a promise. I couldn't swear that MJ wasn't coming back – coz of course, he did. He always came back. I couldn't swear there would be no more visits to the hospital. Because there were. Lots. But I did swear that I would never, ever let anybody get away with hurting her. And I meant it. I kept that promise.

I just didn't think that this is where it would end up.

CHAPTER 17

Aliyah (the prosecutor)

Rage is not a constructive emotion. That I of course knew prior to therapy, and, given the detachment I have perfected between my cases and my feelings, it is a cliché that rarely intrudes into my professional life. I remain, eternally, the swan, irrespective of the turbulence of the waters.

Still, if ever there were a cocktail that might cause me to quietly remind myself of the futility of fury, it would blend a witness like Farid Suhail and an OIC like Chris Rose. At times on Friday I did wonder if, as my daughter would have it, I was being 'punked'. It was only the predictable, petty malevolence with which Jeremy Letts refused my application that convinced me of the day's aching realism. That, and the pained silence from my senior clerk Rick when I rang to ask about the gap in my diary looming after next month. 'Better make sure you win this one then, miss!' he eventually said. 'Get some more nice juicy prosecution briefs! We can't have our top silk on the breadline, scrimping and saving on the finer things, miss!' *Or, here's an idea*, I should have said, *stop being so fucking familiar and do the job I pay you to do*.

Still, we press on. The Crown suffers no defeats nor glories in victory. All I can hope to achieve as prosecuting counsel is my best efforts, and the remainder falls on other shoulders: the legal decisions on the judge, the verdicts on the jury. I merely present the prosecution evidence. I have no stake in the outcome. And in any event, there remains a compelling case against all three. I still expect to win.

The scope for surprise in today's evidence is, at least, minimal. It is an SOE and CCTV day – hours of taking the jury, line by line, through the colour-coded A3 'Sequence of Events' chart. This impressively laminated and spiral-bound document is the prosecution timeline, chronicling the movements of the defendants and the deceased over the final hours of New Year's Eve. There are no civilian witnesses to wrangle, just – and even as I think this, I can feel any sense of reassurance dissipating – DS Chris Rose to stand in the witness box and, with my assistance, tell the jury what the timeline shows.

Now, I sit at the desk in our court conference room, keeping an eye on my phone as the digits creep towards 10.00, examining the pages of the SOE for a final time. I was up until 2 a.m. last night checking its accuracy – also enjoying a screaming match with Esme after discovering inappropriate messages to some older boy on her phone, but mostly checking the accuracy of my exhibit. I do not dare to hope, much less expect, that Chris Rose has spent his weekend doing the same.

Eight minutes before we are due to begin, Rose heaves open the door and barrels in, shaking loose the collected rainwater from his puffa jacket and spattering the desk. The page I have open carries a still image from the CCTV footage, which shows Bernard Hooper standing inside the Co-op at quarter past eleven, paying at the self-service checkout for a bottle of champagne. It is a high-quality image, capturing the moment at which Mr Hooper turns to alert a member of staff to remove the security tag on the bottle. He is staring down the camera lens, his soft pink features reddened slightly by the elements, a kind smile forming at his mouth's edges. A fat droplet of water lands right in the middle of the page, causing the ink to bleed and the topography of Hooper's face to disintegrate.

'Sorry I'm a smidge late,' Rose says with an impressive absence of sincerity, as he hangs his sopping coat on top of my Burberry. 'Just the SOE today, right?'

'And the CCTV compilation, yes,' I say, lifting my Birkin off the empty chair as he throws his bulk down.

Rose nods, smoothing the crumples on his jacket sleeves. 'Impressive work, I thought, from the digi boys.'

For once we are in agreement. The digital forensics team has enhanced and condensed hundreds of hours of CCTV footage, taken from dozens of security cameras across Ableford, into a twenty-four-minute compilation, which has been spliced with maps and moving graphics to create a compelling re-enactment of the night. Nobody watching could be left in the slightest doubt as to the defendants' intentions and motivations.

'Yes,' I say. 'There is, however – and I appreciate that my shopping list for you never seems to end, Chris – the matter of the outstanding statements and viewing logs from the camera operators and the officers who reviewed the raw footage.'

'Oh, right,' Rose says. 'Well, those will exist somewhere.'

I smile patiently. 'I'm sure they will, but the point is that they need to be obtained and either served, if they underpin footage that we rely upon, or scheduled as "unused" if they don't.'

'Gotcha.'

'It's continuity evidence, nothing more. It's not going to affect anybody's case – the footage shows what it shows. We just need to know that it's all been reviewed and dealt with.'

'I'll get on it today.'

'Thank you. And on the subject of my shopping list, I hesitate to ask but do we have any update on the counselling records?'

His pause tells me all I need to know.

'Aliyah, I . . .'

'Today, please, Chris. They need to be bottomed out. The case against Arron Freeman might depend on it.'

CHAPTER 18

Arron (the second defendant)

He's a big lad, the main cop. He weren't the one who did my interviews – they got in some retired ones, apparently. My solicitor said they're like special police, who they get in to do the proper serious murders. And you can tell. Obviously I'd never been interviewed before so I don't know, but the questions they were asking, and the way they were asking them, it was like they were trying to tell a story with the questions. The wrong story, obviously. But I still found myself listening and thinking maybe they're right. It's mad how they can twist it.

And that's what they're doing now, of course. Telling their story. Miss Arshad is talking and the cop is basically just saying yeah and agreeing with everything she says as she reads bits out, turning through all them pages with pictures on. They are too big for all of us to have our own in the dock, so I'm sharing with Craig, and the screw between us has got the folder open on his lap and we're both leaning in. The kid reeks, I swear down.

The first page just has our names and the photos they took at the police station. Craig's sucking his teeth like he's got a proper cob on, a proper attitude. Jamal just looks wasted. Me, I'm wearing the blue jumper and pants they gave me when they took all my clothes for forensics, and my eyes are wide open. I look a bit scared. I don't think I look like a killer. If that's worth anything.

The next pages are just full of lines. Miss Arshad keeps playing bits of video and then stopping to read out what is in those lines. So she's like, 'At 22:35 Jamal Lowton arrives outside Reggie's off-licence on Horcross Road holding a mobile phone.' And after each line, the prosecutor and the police talk about what they think it means.

And some of the stuff, although the words and the pictures are obviously right, they are twisting. The little things she says, like, oh, and this means this, and some of the comments the police are saying – it's just snide. Just pure making shit up.

Some of it I would have to agree with, obviously. So like right now, the police officer is telling the jury that Jamal had two mobile phones, and he used his second phone, the Nokia one they're calling 'J2', to message me at 22:37 and say, meet outside Reggie's. It would be stupid for me to get up and say, nah, that didn't happen.

And then, obviously, the video shows at the same time the old man is arriving on the other side of town and walking to the Co-op, and then buying champagne and putting it in that bag for life, and then walking out checking his phone. And again, no point arguing that.

The jury are then watching us leaving Reggie's, Jamal with his zoot hanging out his mouth, and Miss Arshad pauses the big screen and asks the cop about what we are wearing. She uses this laser to put a red dot on Craig and asks, 'What can we see here?'

And the police says, of course he does, 'We can see a blue rucksack being worn by Craig Mervyn-Scott.' And then it's like he's practised or something, because he says, 'The zombie knife recovered from Bernard Hooper's body had a sixteen-inch blade and a five-inch hilt, and would have fit comfortably inside that blue rucksack.' When he says this, I can see some of the jury writing something down on their pads. They obviously think it's important.

When I get to tell my side, I'll have no choice but to say that yeah, the knife was in Craig's rucksack. That he's my mate but at the same time, he's the one who got us all into this mess. That he is why I am locked in here when I haven't even done nothing wrong.

Mr Evans says for the jury to properly understand, I need to tell them how it was at Rosewoods. How hard it was when I first got there after my nana passed. All the stuff that I don't want to think about; the beatings and the pissing in my drinks and the shitting in my bed. It's all written down by the staff, my solicitor told me, and the police got the notes and gave them to us. Mr Evans says that the things that the social workers put down about me, words like 'polite' and 'naive' and 'meek' – that's all important. 'Risk of exploitation by criminally sophisticated peers' – that's one he kept saying. Some of the other lads in the home trying to get me to do robbing and that. I didn't, of course. Graham did all he could to try to keep me straight. But the point is that even with all that going on, I never got into trouble. And Mr Evans says that's one of the best things I've got going for me. He says the jury needs to see that I'm not like Craig and Jamal. That we've got different stories. He says we need to make the jury understand how I could get dragged into something that has nothing to do with me.

Miss Arshad's now playing some videos which show us all leaving Reggie's, and walking behind this guy whose name they don't even know. And the video shows us walking behind him down all these streets for basically ten minutes, until he walks into this block of flats and we then turn round.

And this right here is what I mean by their sly little games. Miss Arshad asks if the police know who the old guy on camera is, and the police officer says that was 'the initial random target'. He reckons that we were 'stalking' this random for like ten minutes because we wanted to attack him, and that the only reason we didn't is because he went indoors and we missed our chance. He says that's why we then went into town looking for someone else.

Miss Arshad then plays another bit of the video again. It's the bit just after this guy goes inside his building, and you can see Craig shaking his head and saying something to me and Jamal. And now the judge is getting involved and asking the police, 'Do we know what they are saying?' And the police says, 'There is no audio, but our belief is that Craig Mervyn-Scott is expressing irritation that the defendants have lost their initial random target.'

I try not to laugh, me. He'd kick himself if he knew the truth.

I find that I'm scratching my face during the next bit, and have to sit on my hand to stop. There's videos showing Hooper leaving the Co-op and walking on Dalston Street towards Rowe Street, and then ten minutes later it shows us running the same way. So the prosecution are saying that we've basically seen Mr Hooper alone on Dalston Street and have chased him all the way onto Rowe Street.

Then the jury are told to look at one of the other maps they've got in their folders, and to see the green square which points out where Hooper's house was. 'This,' says the police officer, 'is significant.'

'Why?' Miss Arshad asks, although, again, she knows why he says that.

'Look at the direction the group are walking,' the police officer says. 'It is the opposite way that Bernard Hooper would need to travel to get home. He has no need to go down Rowe Street.'

'So what conclusion do you say can be drawn from that?'

Our barristers all stand up but the judge waves them down again. Let the cop answer, he says.

'The conclusion,' he says, 'is that Bernard Hooper was either being lured, or coerced, towards Garth Yard.'

At least half of the jury are now staring at us. And I get it. It sounds like a good story. Bits of it are right. But the bits that they've got wrong, they've got proper wrong. Like when Craig got annoyed after we followed that random old man? That wasn't because we had 'lost our initial random target'. That was Craig realising. That was Craig telling us, 'That's not him.'

And there's the bits they are missing too. Like the gap in the CCTV when we first met Hooper, coz apparently there's no cameras on that part of Dalston Street. If we could show the jury how that all started, what actually happened, they would see.

They would see that the person who went up and talked to the old man – the one who started all of this – was Jamal.

CHAPTER 19

Jennifer (counsel for the third defendant)

The aggressive glare from the strip lighting obscures my view of the jury's fifty-five-inch flat screen. I have watched the CCTV compilation a dozen times, if not more, and could follow along now on my laptop. But that's not the point. I know how it appears viewed through the strained eyes of a lawyer. I want to encounter it afresh; to see what the jurors see, in its magnified, piercing technicolour.

What do they see, I want to know, when Jamal Lowton first slinks into camera shot outside Reggie's, casts a quick look at his surroundings and pulls out his phone? A bored teenager texting his mates? Or a collected killer setting a plan in motion?

MT O REGG.

That Jamal chose to send this message to Arron Freeman from his burner phone – presumably a dirty phone, for sundry dirty deeds – is a small feature of the evidence, but I don't like it. If you're just casually meeting your mates, you'd use your normal phone, wouldn't you? Yet one of a hundred questions we have asked Jamal without getting an answer.

As he stands outside the shop for thirty-five minutes and thirty-one seconds waiting for his co-accused to arrive, is he – as Jamal has instructed us – mindlessly passing the time listening to music? There are no headphones visible, but that doesn't necessarily mean much. Or is he planning? Is he weighing options? Processing permutations? Running through his knowledge of the town centre, marking in his own mind the very best route to entrap and slaughter? The psychometric tests scored Jamal in the bottom percentile for working memory and processing speed. A detailed planner he is not, if the psychologist is right. The brains of this operation, it seems clear to me, lie elsewhere. But what do the jury make of him?

The still image from inside the store, of a hooded Jamal staring straight to camera, the green of his eyes heightened by the ambient lighting and a roll-up hanging over his bottom lip, could in another context be almost iconic. The inscrutable face of a moody advert, rather than an adolescent who knows that, within an hour, he will have taken a life.

And what of his demeanour in motion? When the three defendants begin to pursue that stranger – and it *is* a pursuit, there can be no sensible suggestion otherwise – Jamal is not leading the chase. He is, if anything, dawdling. He occasionally opens his mouth as if speaking, but there is little in the reactions of either of his co-defendants that would indicate conversation. Doing my best at objectivity, I do not think he looks aggressive. In fact, I muse to myself, Jamal looks barely interested; along for the ride, wherever that may take him.

I stop myself at that second clause. That is absolutely not a sentence to repeat aloud in front of the jury.

As DS Rose drones on, I shuffle and tilt awkwardly to my right, hoping that the slight shift might bring me closer to the jury's perspective, but the monitor is still half-bathed in glare. I concede defeat. I would need to be sitting in the jury box to replicate their view. *Or in the public gallery*, a small voice reminds me. I silence it. I know where that voice leads. Now is not the time.

I return to my wish list of helpful adjectives, of the Jamal Lowton that I hope the jurors are seeing. I idly start typing into a blank Word document:

Being led, not leading.

Uninterested.

Not aggressive.

Does not look like a killer.

I pause. I immediately regret that final sentence and my finger springs onto the backspace key, holding it down until the page is empty. I know where my subconscious wants to take me, and I cannot allow it to. But the door has been opened. *Does not look like a killer*, the voice returns. *But as you know better than anyone – the most dangerous often don't.*

At the same time, my brain summons a picture; not a memory, but a photograph once pinned to my fridge, of Ollie – my beautiful, purest Ollie – in his green Cubs uniform, arm around his new best friend, Finlay. Finlay with the sharp dark eyes, who 'goes to the school you said wasn't very good, Mum'. Finlay who was loud and brash and rebellious and everything that we had successfully scared Ollie into not being. And who, having barged his way into Ollie's affections at the age of eight, would remain a fixture in our lives and on our fridge, until . . . Until.

I try to clear my mind of everything, emptying every thought and re-focusing solely on what DS Rose is saying as the CCTV rolls on.

While there was no CCTV from inside Garth Yard, Rose tells the jury, there was footage showing part of the entrance. As you turn right out of Garth Yard, he explains, there is a newsagent on the junction with Rowe Street – marked on the map – which had a fixed exterior camera. This was pointing up Rowe Street, and captured the group moving towards the camera, disappearing out of view at 00:02 as they turned into Garth Yard. The video rolls, and the jury watch the three defendants, by this point clustered together, roles indistinguishable, shepherd Bernard Hooper off camera.

The screen fades to black. The compilation picks up again at 00:05, when two figures reappear and can be seen briefly turning to look behind them, before sprinting back up Rowe Street. Zoomed in, the pair can be safely identified as Craig Mervyn-Scott and Arron Freeman. As Aliyah invites the jury to turn to their bundles, she draws their attention to something else visible on the enhanced still of the point at which the boys turn to camera: the dark patches staining their clothing, and the flash of red across the face of Craig Mervyn-Scott.

'The jury will hear evidence tomorrow from the scientist who examined the clothing, but to give some context now, can you tell us, officer, what those stains are?'

Rose nods. 'That is the blood of Bernard Hooper.'

Aliyah thanks him, and resumes the footage. As the boys reach the top of the screen, they are prevented from running out of view by the wheels of a vehicle pulling up in front of them.

'This,' Aliyah asks DS Rose, 'is an attending police car, is that right?'

Rose nods, confirming with an entirely inappropriate grin that Craig Mervyn-Scott and Arron Freeman had run straight into the arms of the police.

'Now we don't see Jamal Lowton on that footage, do we?' Aliyah asks. I sit up straight.

'Indeed we do not,' Rose says, looking confidently at the jury. 'And the reason – can I say the reason?'

'Please do.'

'The reason is that the camera from the pawn shop only covers Rowe Street as you turn left out of Garth Yard. So Mervyn-Scott and Freeman, taking a left and running up Rowe Street – we can see them. But Jamal Lowton took a right out of Garth Yard, and so his exit wasn't seen by the camera. If you follow.'

Several nods from the jury box indicate that they do indeed follow.

'You have told us,' Aliyah says, 'that Jamal Lowton took a right out of Garth Yard. If he wasn't caught on camera, how do you know that?'

'Because,' Rose replies, 'he was found hiding in a bush on a nearby cul-de-sac a few minutes after. And if you look at your maps . . .'

Aliyah motions for a pause while the jurors flick to the document. She then beckons him to continue.

'So, ladies and gents, if you look at your maps, you can see Morgan Close marked with a purple sticker. In the front garden of number thirteen, that's where the arresting officers found Master Lowton at 00:08.'

'And what is the most direct route from Garth Yard to Morgan Close?'

'It's marked here on the map. You take the right out of Garth Yard, down Rowe Street, over the mini roundabout, then first left, then first right. Boom. You're on Morgan Close. We've retraced the route, and it's about a four-minute walk. One or two minutes if you're running.'

For the jurors who haven't yet conducted the arithmetic, Aliyah invites Rose to spell out that these timings would fit with the prosecution theory that Jamal had run out of Garth Yard when he heard the police sirens, around the same time as his co-defendants. All three had run following the murder. Meaning that all three had been present in Garth Yard when it happened. It's a theory which may not be bolstered by any CCTV, but has an audible ring of common sense to a jury, especially when corroborated – at least to some extent – by the testimony of Paul Bell and Farid Suhail.

By contrast, Jamal's case, that he had fled Garth Yard before any violence broke out, may not be disproved by CCTV, but is very much not helped by his decision to run and hide in a stranger's front garden. That behaviour, a jury *may* think, is not the behaviour of somebody who has done nothing wrong. It is behaviour which, if Jamal gives evidence, he is going to need to provide a pretty convincing explanation for.

I open a document on my laptop and remind myself of Jamal's instructions on this point, as distilled in his defence statement: *'The Accused was walking home when he heard the police sirens.*

He suspected that the sirens may have something to do with his co-accused, and he hid from the police out of panic.'

Parsed by lawyers, it is a passable excuse. Young, scared, stupid. Panicked. But innocent. A jury might buy it. It is not beyond credulity that somebody like Jamal would react to police sirens in that way, in these circumstances, even though he had nothing to do with the events in Garth Yard.

It just doesn't explain why, when the police found Jamal cowering in the bushes, he had discarded his jacket and shoes.

CHAPTER 20

HHJ Jeremy Letts (the judge)

Ten years ago today. When the clock strikes 2 p.m., it will be a decade since I entered the Royal Courts of Justice and strode its labyrinthine corridors as a barrister for the final time.

Aside from a smattering of oak panelling, the room allocated to my swearing-in was surprisingly modest, even underwhelming in contrast to the majesty of the building and the constitutional magnitude of the occasion. The Master of the Rolls was the (truthfully, slightly disappointing) judicial bigwig dragged out of his chambers to preside over the ceremony, who stood in his regalia behind a large mahogany desk while some officiant or celebrant or somesuch functionary invited me to repeat my oaths after her, line by line, like I was a remedial simpleton instead of one of Her Majesty's judges.

After I had successfully read out my oath of allegiance and my judicial oath without dribbling or soiling myself, the Master of the Rolls walked round to the front of the desk and clasped my hand between his clammy palms, asking to be introduced to my 'retinue'. While Amanda, at the time still my wife, could not truthfully be described as 'company', three would certainly have been a crowd, and so my retinue was a party of one, which at least made the ceremonial photographs quicker than they might have been.

As I now sit at my desk and look around me at the serenity of my chambers, the absence of clutter, the minimalist straight edges and the priceless reliability of the Jura Z10 Bean-to-Cup coffee machine, my answer – were I to give it today – is that I absolutely do not miss the Bar. I do not miss its petty politics, or its so-called 'characters', or the daily frustrations caused by the lack of basic competence of those supposed colleagues. But more than that, I am, it has been said more than once, ideally suited to the Bench. I do not chase popularity (although 'juries love you' is, again, something that has been said to me on multiple occasions), but I do demand – and command – respect. I always have done. And ten years on, although the hair beneath the wig may be, in places, a little thinner, the judgecraft on display has only improved with seniority.

I swore an oath to *do right to all manner of people after the laws and usages of this realm, without fear or favour, affection or ill will*, and I do. Independence forbids me from attaching too much, or indeed any, importance to how I am perceived by the public. But the newspaper clippings affixed to the wall of my chambers speak for themselves. (I presume that 'clippings' is still the correct terminology for printouts of stories from newspaper websites.)

A knock at my door startles me. It is Andrew Warner.

'Afternoon, Jeremy,' he smiles, closing the door behind him. 'Enjoying the reviews?'

I realise that, in my reverie, my eyes are fixed on the large pinboard erected just to the left of the window. I do not dignify his weak taunt with a response.

'Good morrow, Andrew. Welcome back. What grave and weighty matters does the Honorary Recorder have in his court today?'

He knows that I have seen his list, and that, due to a quirk of listing, the most senior judge in the building will be spending the next two days presiding over a two-day piffling sexual assault trial, while I sit on the murder that has all the nationals salivating.

He smiles. 'The perils of sitting at the Court of Appeal, I'm afraid. You spend a fortnight in London and return home to find you're the whipping boy for Ableford's list office. How is the People's Judge enjoying the delights of the New Year's Eve Massacre?'

'The People's Judge' is a reference to a headline printed in the *Ableford Mercury* a few years ago, after I sentenced a gang of seven teenage burglars to fourteen years, the maximum allowed by law and, I was later told, the only such sentence ever passed for that type of offence. The liberals at the Court of Appeal later knocked it down, of course, but as I recall the sentence made something of a splash in the press. For my part, I take no interest in such headlines whatsoever. Were the article not on my pinboard, I would have forgotten about it entirely.

I offer Andrew a quick rundown of the highlights of the trial so far, but his interest is superficial. There is, we both know, another purpose to his visit. He helps himself to the chair opposite mine.

'And, er, how is Jennifer getting on?'

Now we get to the meat of it. The real reason the Recorder of Ableford is knocking on my door like a wet schoolboy at the headmaster's office.

'She's fine,' I reply. 'For the most part, riding the coat-tails of the big boys, but no issues so far.'

He nods thoughtfully. 'And is she, er . . .?'

'Sober? As far as I can tell.'

'I was surprised to hear that she accepted this brief,' he eventually says. 'As far as I was aware, her clerks were quietly refusing anything to do with teenagers and knives.'

'It doesn't seem to have influenced the cases you sit on,' I observe.

'Well,' he says quietly, fiddling with a button on his sleeve, 'it is probably fair to say that losing Oliver hit Jennifer even harder than it did me. When she returned to the Bar after she moved away, she let it be known that she didn't feel able to act independently in such cases. Some of us, I suppose, just find it that bit easier to separate the personal from the professional.'

'Those who have been sentenced for carrying knives in your court might beg to differ.'

I intended that as a joke, but I am not convinced that it landed. In any case, Andrew moves the conversation on.

'And tell me this: how is disclosure?'

There is a mischievous glint in his eye. Alas, I have to disappoint him.

'No problems as yet. No complaints about missing material. No last-minute Section 8 applications. Not a peep from the defence to suggest that the Crown has acted in any way slovenly or improperly in discharging its duties of disclosure. All tremendously . . . unexciting.'

Andrew raises his eyebrows in an affectation of surprise. I nod agreeably.

'I know.'

'Particularly,' Andrew begins. 'Particularly given . . .'

I finish his sentence for him. 'Particularly given who is prosecuting.'

DAY 5 OF TRIAL – TUESDAY

CHAPTER 21

Aliyah (the prosecutor)

Mutilated corpses are ten a penny. Not so much an occupational hazard as an occupational raison d'être.

If that is not verbatim how Dr James Nicholls, my forensic pathologist, introduces himself to the jury, it is at least the vibe detectable from the slightly bored tone in which he talks about the business of examining the dead.

'My specialty is post-mortems in cases involving suspicious circumstances, in particular violent homicides,' he tells the jurors with the airy casualness of describing his preferred cheese.

It is less than ideal.

While the prosecution should not seek to titillate, nor to gratuitously excite the jurors' emotions, basic empathy still matters. There is a line between respectful neutrality and sociopathic indifference, and anybody who appears to lean towards the latter is unlikely to endear themselves to a jury.

And also: this is the exciting bit! The evidence of how Bernard Hooper died, and what conclusions the jury can draw from the way that his body was torn apart – this is the dream ticket for any juror. They could have found themselves seconded to an eight-week VAT fraud, listening to forensic accountants talking about input and output tax. We're giving them what they came for – blood and death. Let's try to at least act interested ourselves.

When I was briefed to defend in my first murder, being led by a silk at five years' call, I remember dashing home and telling Sasha. His level of interest in my work was already waning, his then-excuse being the stresses of ninety-hour weeks trying to make partner in a London-based US corporate law firm. But even his eyes widened when I told him the details: the history of intra-familial honour violence; the fire officer's expert report; the pathology cataloguing the fatal injuries. The photograph of a burned woman prone in a blackened double bed. The two tiny charred bodies cradled in her arms. Sasha didn't even make his boiler-plate quip about legal aid not paying the mortgage.

Lay people are fascinated by murder. You don't win a case by overlooking that fact.

Lay people are also, however, squeamish. And that is why, as I lead Dr Nicholls through the findings of Bernard Hooper's post-mortem, the jurors are directed in their bundles not to photographs, but to 'poser images': three-dimensional computer rendered recreations of the head, torso and lower body of Bernard Hooper, depicting the injuries inflicted.

I detect a mixture of relief and disappointment when I tell the jurors that they are to be spared the photographs of Bernard Hooper as he was found in Garth Yard, and as he was subsequently opened in the examination room. I of course have seen them – the shaky recordings from the body-worn cameras of the first responders, treading on tiptoes around the glistening pools of crimson; the hundred CSI photographs showing every angle of the bloodied disfiguration of something that was once, one would suppose, a human being. But the jurors, buffered by the computer reimagination, are kept a step removed from the immediate violence of the night's images.

There is no sanitising the words, however. Dr Nicholls's clinical précis of the cause of death – 'Multiple sharp force injuries and blunt force trauma to the head and body' – is swiftly followed by the detail that cannot be euphemised. I lead him through the distinctions that the jury will need before we examine each of the sixty-four separate injuries: stab wounds ('a wound caused by a sharp point, shorter on the surface of the skin than it is deep') versus incised, or slash, wounds ('caused by a cutting edge – say a knife – where the surface wound is longer than it is deep'). A chop wound, he tells the jurors, cleanly divides the tissue, whereas a laceration is a blunt force injury, where the tissue is divided raggedly, such as where a blow to a bony part of the body causes the overlying skin to split.

We then put the jurors' new-found knowledge into practice, methodically taking them through each of the injuries represented on their poser pictures. Dr Nicholls starts with the seventeen incised wounds to the arms, nine of which were shallow and eight of which had cut into the bone – 'requiring really quite heavy force'. He moves to the six stab wounds to the abdomen, penetrating to 5 centimetres and piercing the vital organs beneath. 'You can see,' he tells the jurors, 'the irregular overlapping incisions on the left flank. Those could be the result of multiple separate blows, or they could represent movement of a weapon while inside the body.'

I throw him a look. 'Movement of a weapon *inside* the body?'

Somewhat surprisingly, he takes the hint and offers a little colour. 'Yes. For instance, those injuries could have been caused by the assailant trying to withdraw the blade as the victim writhed in agony.'

The many injuries to Bernard Hooper's thighs were mostly chop wounds, the deepest of which had severed the femoral vessels and cut into the sciatic nerve.

'Meaning,' Dr Nicholls looks up at the jury, 'that he would have immediately lost the use of the muscles in the back of his leg.'

'So,' I clarify, 'had Bernard Hooper tried to . . .'

Nicholls finishes my thought. 'He would not have been able to run away.'

I nod for him to continue.

'It may be that it was at this point in the attack that Mr Hooper raised his hands in a defensive motion, because at numbers fifty-four and fifty-five . . .' he flicks forward in his binder to the poser images showing magnified renderings of two disembodied hands, 'we can see an incised wound approximately 7 centimetres on the left forearm, damaging the underlying tendons, and a vertical chop wound to the right hand which cleaved the palm in two.'

I ask him about the twelve wounds to the face; he describes them as a combination of chops and stabs, which cut into the nasal septum, exposing the bone. 'There were also lacerations to the back of the head overlaying a skull fracture,' he says. 'You perhaps do not need me to tell you, members of the jury, that it takes significant force to fracture a human skull.'

The jurors are then directed to a horizontal chop-type injury to the right side of the neck, which had penetrated over 4 centimetres.

'This is not an easy feat to accomplish,' Dr Nicholls says. 'Certainly not when a person is standing up.'

'So what conclusions can you draw from that?'

'The deceased was most likely positioned laterally when this blow was delivered.'

I spell it out for the jury. 'Bernard Hooper was lying on the ground?'

'I'd say that is overwhelmingly likely. It looks like . . .' He catches my eye and raises his inflexion, apparently seeking permission. I nod. 'The injury is consistent with a deliberate attempt to decapitate.'

Fifty-seven, fifty-eight, fifty-nine . . . Over the course of the morning, beyond the lunch hour – although I imagine few in the jury box have any appetite – and into the lower reaches of the afternoon, Dr Nicholls endures. He reaches the blunt force injuries, those inflicted by means other than a sharp object. Fractures, bruises and lacerations which could have been caused by other weapons, or could have been caused by heavy, sustained punches or kicks. Sixty-one, sixty-two, sixty-three, all the way up to sixty-four, an injury which I have decided justifies its own page in the bundle.

'This,' the doctor offers, 'is likely to have been the final injury inflicted with the blade.'

Letts harrumphs from the bench.

'*Likely?* It's certain, isn't it?'

'Well, Your Honour, yes. Because as we can see in the poser,' Dr Nicholls says, 'the weapon was still embedded in the chest cavity when the body was found. It had been driven in with very significant force, fracturing the ribs and penetrating the heart.'

I nod and close my jury bundle, a cue to the jurors that we are nearly there.

'Finally, doctor,' I say, stressing the *finally*. I need to keep the jury with me for this flourish. 'What conclusions, if any, are you able to draw from the distribution of the injuries taken as a whole?'

Nicholls looks directly at the jurors. 'The number and distribution of the injuries were such that, in my opinion, they were unlikely to have been inflicted by just one person. Or even two.'

I let the words bloom and swell in the silence.

'In your professional opinion, doctor . . .'

He has already begun answering. His nose twitches as his eyes dart to the dock, before returning to the jury. 'In my professional opinion, these injuries are what I would expect to see if Bernard Hooper had been subjected to a frenzied attack involving multiple participants.'

'And by "multiple", you mean . . .?'

'I would say at least three people were involved.'

I try not to let the pleasure show on my face.

'Thank you. Please wait there. There will be further questions from my learned friends.'

As I gently close my laptop and sit, Baxter Wyatt rises next to me. He, by contrast, is unencumbered by a laptop – or, at least, the one he has with him has yet to be liberated from its monogramed brown leather case. Nor for him the traditional A4 blue workbook, which he leaves unopened next to him. He appears to be operating entirely from memory.

'Bernard Hooper was five foot eleven and weighed fifteen-and-a-half stone.'

Wyatt fixes Dr Nicholls with his pale blue eyes and crooks his eyebrows, signalling expectation of a response. That Wyatt has not in fact asked a question does not appear, in his world, to be a hindrance to it being answered. To emphasise, he repeats the statement.

'Bernard Hooper was five foot eleven and weighed fifteen-and-a-half stone.'

Dr Nicholls holds Wyatt's gaze, appearing to contemplate whether to play nice with the defence, or whether to fight fire with shithousery. After several seconds, he seems to settle on the former.

'Yes, as I said in my report.'

'Right,' Wyatt agrees, breaking eye contact and directing his next statement towards the jury. 'And, from your examination and from consideration of Mr Hooper's medical records, there were no obvious physical ailments.'

Dr Nicholls considers. 'Well, he *was* dead.'

A snort from the jury box heralds the victory for shithousery. Nice one, doc.

'Thank you, doctor,' Wyatt smiles humourlessly, moving quickly on. 'No *prior* physical ailments. Nothing that would have impaired Bernard Hooper's mobility, for instance.'

Satisfied at having drawn first blood, Nicholls relaxes into a more amenable rhythm. 'No, nothing of significance.'

'There was nothing in his records suggesting any impairment in cognitive functioning.'

'That is correct.'

'Bernard Hooper, as far as the records show, was a man with all his faculties.'

'That's not necessarily a medical diagnosis, but I take your point.'

'You agree with it, don't you? You agree that Bernard Hooper was a large, well-built man in good health.'

'I agree that I have not seen anything that would indicate otherwise.'

'Bernard Hooper,' Baxter Wyatt turns back to the jury again, 'was not some frail, doddering old pensioner, confused and adrift on the streets.'

Dr Nicholls shrugs. 'Again, those are not medical terms. But I take your point.'

Wyatt nods, happy to agree with himself. 'Now, I am not interested in rehashing the findings of your post-mortem, but you will agree with this, I am sure: it is not possible for you to say, with any certainty, in which order the injuries to Bernard Hooper were inflicted.'

'Not with certainty, no. It is likely, as I have said, that the attempt to sever the head took place once Mr Hooper was on the ground, and the insertion of the knife into his chest would appear to be the final wound inflicted using that particular weapon. But as for the other injuries, no.'

'No. Now, in the course of these proceedings, you have also been provided with medical records relating to my lay client, Craig Mervyn-Scott, have you not?'

'I have.'

'Good,' says Wyatt, drawing out the vowels. He reaches with his right hand for the dormant blue workbook, slowly placing it flat on the lectern in front of him and spreading the pages. He mouths as he turns – one, two, three, four – and then with a flick of his left index finger knocks his copper-rimmed Gucci spectacles an inch down his nose. He peers intently at the contents of the page.

'Because I now want to ask you about the injuries to Craig Mervyn-Scott on the night of his arrest.'

CHAPTER 22

Jennifer (counsel for the third defendant)

Juror six, sitting closest to Baxter Wyatt, raises herself in her seat at that bit, lifting her chin and trying to catch a glimpse of whatever spells Wyatt has written in his magic blue notebook.

It's nothing, really. By which I mean, it really is nothing. I, and everybody else sitting on counsel's row, can see the blank pages which Wyatt is dramatically pausing to study, and the empty white lines towards which he occasionally jabs a finger for emphasis. It is pure am-dram, intended to highlight the part of the evidence upon which Craig Mervyn Scott's defence is being gradually built.

Wyatt has much more to play with than I do when it comes to the pathology. I have problems rather than opportunities with this witness. Chief among those is the expert opinion as to how many people were involved in the infliction of Bernard Hooper's injuries. *Multiple participants* – that I was expecting. That I could just about have lived with. I could have exploited the ambiguity and invited the jury to conclude that 'multiple' means simply 'more than one'. That would have been enough for Jamal.

But in leaping on Aliyah's invitation to refine his definition, Dr Nicholls has knowingly rammed a sizeable thorn into our case. *I would say at least three people were involved*. That added extra was not in his original report, a point not lost on Caz, whose reaction arrived piecemeal in a blizzard of emails no sooner had the words dropped.

AT LEAST THREE PEOPLE???!!! Where's that in your fucking statement you cheeky bearded twat???

Multiple = more than one, right? Show me where in the fucking OED it means more than two, wtaf.

Fuming! Cheeky, cheeky fuck. He's blatantly been ripped off by the prosecution.

Tipped off. FFS.

I am slightly more sanguine than my instructing solicitor. Dr Nicholls's aggressive pivot impacts not just upon Jamal, but Arron Freeman too, and Bob Evans is already thoughtfully tapping away on his keyboard. I am hopeful that between the two of us, we can put the good doctor back in his box.

Wyatt clicks his finger towards the young usher. Barking '*Garçon!*' as he does so makes the gesture more obnoxious, not less, despite Wyatt's evident belief to the contrary, demonstrated by the ironic grin he flashes towards the jury. Thrusting a pile of colour printouts into the lad's arms, Wyatt does not wait for the pages to be distributed before he resumes his cross-examination.

'These images show the hands of Craig Mervyn-Scott, as they appeared when he was inspected by a forensic medical examiner in custody on 1 January. You have seen these, yes?'

Nicholls confirms that he has.

The jurors each take a thin stapled sheaf of images from the heavy pile and pass the remainder down the row. The photographs show a series of cuts and scratches, of various lengths and depths, running in all directions across the palms of Craig Mervyn-Scott. These are real images, not posers. The sight of bloody injuries over teenaged hands jerks something within me, and I quickly swallow to stop the rise I feel in my throat.

'In total,' Wyatt tells the witness, 'there were thirteen separate scratch or cut-type injuries to the hands of my lay client. Correct?'

'There were thirteen mostly superficial cuts to the left and right hand, yes.'

'You say "superficial", but three were deep enough to require closure with medical glue, were they not?'

'As I said, *mostly* superficial. Four required minor treatment, yes.'

'Considering the locations and directions of these injuries to the hands, would you agree that they are consistent with defensive injuries?'

'They appear to be, yes.'

Wyatt removes his glasses, and holds them by the right arm of the frame, suspended in the air. He stares directly at Dr Nicholls.

'You have already told this jury that the wounds you observed on Bernard Hooper could all have been caused by the large so-called "zombie knife" that was found embedded in his chest.'

'Yes.'

'Were the injuries to Craig Mervyn-Scott's hands consistent with having been inflicted by that same weapon?'

The pathologist replies with confidence, 'No. In my opinion, they have been caused by a smaller sharp implement, likely of a more conventional shape.'

The assertiveness in his tone is born, I suspect, of a suspicion that this reply is not what Baxter Wyatt was expecting, much less wanting. But if that is the case, the witness is wrong.

'A more conventional shape? Something like a kitchen knife, for instance?'

'Yes, that could be it.'

Wyatt smiles joylessly and clicks again at the usher. 'There is a second photograph to be handed out.'

As a further pile of pages is separated out and distributed, Wyatt rebalances his glasses on the edge of his nose and ramps up the pace.

'Among many items you were asked to examine in the course of preparing your report was a photograph of an exhibit with a reference GD/2. Yes?'

Dr Nicholls nods slowly as he familiarises himself with the image now being passed to him. 'Yes.'

'This photograph shows Exhibit GD/2, yes?'

'It does.'

'And you agree, don't you,' Wyatt states, his tone absent of doubt, 'that the scratch and cut injuries to Craig Mervyn-Scott could have been caused by this item.'

'Yes, it's possible.'

'And to assist the jury with putting this into context, Exhibit GD/2 is described as a six-inch kitchen knife.'

'Yes.'

Wyatt closes his empty blue book, and turns to the jury. Pure fucking am-dram.

'A six-inch kitchen knife, which was recovered next to the body of Bernard Hooper in Garth Yard.'

CHAPTER 23

Craig (the first defendant)

Even when I don't know why Mr Wyatt is asking the questions he's asking, I can usually tell if he thinks it's gone well. His nose wrinkles and he pulls this little smile, like he's smelled something rank but at the same time he likes it. Like he's sniffed his own fart.

He's doing that face now, as he sits on his flippy chair and swivels his head round to whisper to my brief. And this time I can tell even without the face that this is good for me. When he said the thing about Hooper and the knife and all my cuts, the woman juror at the far end looked at us in the dock, and I swear it was like she was seeing us all over again, from the start. Like she was asking herself, *Have I got this all wrong? Maybe Hooper's not everything the prosecution are pretending he is?* I dunno, maybe I'm just mugging myself off coz I want her to be thinking those things. But I do reckon Mr Wyatt is making them think.

When Usher gave the jury the photos of my hands – the ones they took at the station when the nurse was looking at me – I don't think the jury was expecting that. They look proper fucked up. Even though by that time most of the blood had dried and gone hard and dark, and a lot of it had cracked and rubbed off, it's still obvious that someone's had a proper go.

It did make me wonder though, like why has Mr Wyatt not given them everything? If that is how the jury's faces go when they see just my hands, what would they think if they saw the photos of my face? My squashed nose and the black eye and the giant lump to my head where I was thrown to the floor. Or the way my back turned black all the way across, from when I was stamped on. Mr Wyatt did say before we started why he didn't want to tell the jury those things, and I thought I understood, but Mr Wyatt is not an easy man to follow. In my head, it's like, *Why wouldn't you tell the jury?* If I'm saying that the old man went for me, does it not make sense to say, yeah, look at how crazy he went, look at all these injuries. Not just a few of them.

I remember the nurse asking me when she was sticking the cuts together and writing down all the injuries. Because to begin with I think the feds thought that all the blood on me was Hooper's, not mine, and they hadn't pieced everything together. I started to tell her, coz in that moment it's like you're just talking to a nurse, but then I remembered that she's a fed and all.

They asked again when I was pulled into the interview room. Obviously, because of what I was being interviewed for, I went no comment to everything, like my brief said. But they kept pressing and pressing, and one of them even went, *Did Hooper do that to you?* They was all, *Tell us now if he did that to you or if you don't it will look bare bad when this gets to court.* But I just remembered what I'd been told.

And I do trust him. And I trust Mr Wyatt. A part of me just doesn't get why we can't tell the jury things which could really help my case.

'Dr Nicholls, I wonder if I might trouble you to revisit paragraph 9.1 of your report?'

Arron's barrister is having a go now. Although it's not so much like he's having a go. He's always so polite, even when you can tell that he's basically saying that someone is chatting shit. It makes me glad to have Mr Wyatt. He's a killer, my brief says. But Mr Evans, I just don't see him having that instinct, you feel me?

'I'd like to ask you about your conclusions in this segment of your report, in light of the evidence you gave to my learned friend concerning the number of participants in the infliction of the injuries.'

The doctor doesn't say anything, but his eyes are like he's been expecting to be asked this. He straightens his back and tries to make himself taller, which is jokes because he's shorter even than me.

'In your report, you offer the opinion that the distribution of injuries is consistent with an assault by multiple participants from different angles. Those are your words, is that fair?'

'It is.'

'You deliberately chose the word "multiple" – meaning "more than one" – rather than attempting to attach a precise number, didn't you?'

'I did.'

'In response to a question by my learned friend who prosecutes, you went a little further in your evidence, and suggested that "at least three people were involved". Now I'm sure you can appreciate the question I'm moving towards . . .'

'I think I can, yes.'

'Because while the distribution of injuries may be *consistent* with having been inflicted by three people or more, it is also consistent with having been inflicted by four people.'

'Could have been, yes.'

'And also consistent with having been inflicted by two people.'

'Well, I'm not sure I—'

'Sorry to cut across you, doctor, but perhaps I can put it in this way. Sixty separate injuries, give or take. Consistent, as you say, with a group attack involving many participants. But whether it was four people inflicting fifteen injuries each, three people inflicting twenty injuries each, or two people inflicting thirty injuries each, or any other combination – that's not something that you can be sure of, is it?'

'Well, not *sure*, no, but—'

'And, again, sorry to cut across you. But the point is that based on the pathological findings alone, you are not able to help the jury with whether all three of these defendants were involved . . .' Mr Evans then waves his arm towards us in the dock, and the jurors' heads all turn to look, 'or whether, for instance, Craig Mervyn-Scott and Jamal Lowton inflicted the injuries while Arron Freeman played no part at all.'

When the doctor agrees with him, I see four of the jury scribbling hard on their pads.

DAY 6 OF TRIAL – WEDNESDAY

CHAPTER 24

Aliyah (the prosecutor)

I had barely finished helping Clara, our nanny, corral the girls into her poky little Tiguan this morning when my clerks called with dreadful news. They had been in tentative discussions with the Deputy Chief Crown Prosecutor about my being lined up to prosecute a horrendous serial rapist – six women snatched on the street, all driven to an industrial estate and brutalised for days on end. Devastatingly, the defendant's solicitor has this morning confirmed that he will be pleading guilty. Which means no trial, and £30k – which I had already allocated to paying off the Amex – gone in a puff of smoke. The selfishness of these sex offenders knows no bounds.

My limited consolation, as I rise for Jeremy Letts's entrance, is that the pathology evidence yesterday went as well as I could have hoped – the defence extracted the cheap points I had expected, but nothing too detrimental – and today's biology lesson should run equally smoothly. The interpretation of DNA profiles and bloodstain patterns is today's swampy field of expertise; Dr Seamus Redmond the scientist strapping on the waders and beckoning the jury in.

He introduces himself as a forensic scientist with an MSc in applied biology and fifteen years on the clock. The length of his service is surprising in both directions. He looks both too young and too old; an unblemished babyface with a cropped horseshoe of hair disclosing the shoots of male pattern baldness. His maroon blazer is obviously high street, but I trust the jurors not to hold that against him.

'Deoxyribonucleic acid,' he begins unprompted, 'is what you all probably know as DNA.'

I raise a hand. 'Dr Redmond, I am going to ask please that you take this slowly. Imagine you are explaining this to me as somebody who has no idea what DNA is, or blood pattern interpretation. Feel free to make it, please, as basic as you can.'

'Of course. Put simply, we each have a DNA profile. Think of it a bit like a barcode. It's in all the cells in our body. Now, as human beings, we are great shedders of DNA. Have any of you ever met an Old English Sheepdog? Magnificent beasts. But good Lord, they shed hair like nobody's beeswax. Leave it absolutely everywhere, and on everything. That's a bit like humans with DNA. Whenever we touch or interact with somebody or something, there's an opportunity for our DNA to transfer onto that other person or thing. So when we find a DNA profile on an object, we can compare it to a DNA sample from a specific person, and work out the likelihood of that person being the one who has deposited it.'

Notwithstanding the slightly awkward forced chumminess, Redmond seems to be holding the jury's attention, so I invite him to continue.

'Now, 99.9 per cent of our DNA profile is the same as everybody else's, but the remaining bit is different. That's what we are looking at when we are comparing DNA profiles. The profiles are fed into a computer and represented in a graph, with a number of peaks. Those peaks are then given numbers – as I say, like a barcode – and we then see how many numbers present in that profile match the numbers in another one. The greater the series of numbers that match between a DNA profile and a sample from an individual, the greater the likelihood that the individual is the source of that DNA.

'So in this case, I was specifically asked to examine clothing for the presence of bloodstaining. Where we found a stain, we would sample it for the presence of DNA, and compare any profile we found to the profiles of various named individuals, to see if there was a match.'

'And whose profiles, in particular, were you considering?'

'We had four – Bernard Hooper, Craig Mervyn-Scott, Arron Freeman and Jamal Lowton.'

'What might you expect to see,' I ask, 'if more than one person deposited DNA on an object or a surface?'

'In that circumstance, we might get what's called a "mixed profile" – where multiple people have contributed. So, for example . . .' He points to juror number five. 'Let's say I cut my finger and then touched the sleeve of that very nice Iron Maiden sweatshirt you are wearing, sir, leaving a very unfortunate bloodstain. If we sampled the bloodstain, we might obtain a mixed DNA profile containing your DNA and my DNA. Possibly some more – maybe the gentleman sitting next to you, maybe the DNA of the jolly charity collector who brushed against you on the street. Does that make sense?'

Slow nods from the jury box suggests that it just about does.

'Bringing the theoretical back to the specifics of this case,' I steer, 'bloodstaining was another aspect that you were asked to consider. What can an eminent expert such as yourself glean from bloodstaining?'

Redmond does not realise that my flattery was aimed at impressing the jury, and visibly swells with pride at the description. An incongruent smile breaks out across his face as he enthuses about blood patterns and the various ways in which blood can be transferred.

'You've got your contact bloodstaining,' he grins, 'where wet blood comes into contact with a surface or an item. So that mess I'm leaving on your shirt, sir, with my bloody finger – that's contact bloodstaining. There are dripping bloodstains – where blood falls onto a surface due to gravity. Sometimes the pattern tells us the direction. You've got airborne blood, which lands on a surface or an item. Where force is applied into wet blood – say a bleeding area is repeatedly struck – blood droplets are projected outwards, creating spots on wherever they land. This is what we in the business call "spatter".'

'Thank you. I am now going to ask you to take us through the findings from your examination.'

I take the jury to a selection of photos in their bundles: twenty-four pages of disembodied jackets, tops, trousers and trainers, with areas of significance denoted by yellow circles and annotations.

Craig Mervyn-Scott's clothes are up first. I lead Redmond through the heavy contact bloodstaining on Mervyn-Scott's black Berghaus jacket and navy Nike trainers and the extensive spatter down the legs of his North Face joggers, which, Redmond confirms, 'place the wearer in contact with wet blood and in the vicinity when blood was propelled with force'.

'Whose blood,' I ask, emphasising the plosives, 'was *propelled* with force onto Craig Mervyn-Scott's trousers?'

'A complete DNA profile was recovered from the blood sampled, matching the profile of Bernard Hooper. The likelihood of the blood originating from somebody other than, and unrelated to, Bernard Hooper, was one in a billion.'

As we turn to Arron Freeman's street attire, Dr Redmond offers the same conclusions for the presence of contact stains coating the soles and upper aspects of Freeman's cheap trainers, the widespread spatter over the arms of his Primark coat and the directional airborne blood all down the front of his unbranded bottoms.

When we reach Jamal Lowton, I point out the absence of any jacket or shoes, taking the opportunity to remind the jury that Jamal Lowton had seen fit to discard these by the time the police found him hiding in a bush. 'However,' I suggest to Dr Redmond, 'you did examine the Adidas sweatshirt that Mr Lowton was wearing upon his arrest?'

'Yes. The cuff of the sweatshirt bore a contact bloodstain containing a mixed DNA profile with two contributors: Bernard Hooper and Jamal Lowton.'

'And the odds of the DNA originating from somebody else?'

'One in a billion.'

Clothing dealt with, I draw Redmond's attention to a large close-up photograph of the zombie knife. A fingerprint mark can just be made out in the blood on the blade. Although not Redmond's specialism, the fingerprint evidence is not disputed, so I take the chance to tie some threads together.

'The fingerprint in blood, on the blade of the weapon, matched the fingerprint of Arron Freeman?'

'Yes, it did.'

'And – and the jury will receive this evidence in formal admissions later, Your Honour – but to complete the picture, as it were, is it right that there were a number of prints on the handle of the knife?'

'So I understand, yes.'

'And most were insufficient for the purposes of comparison?'

'Yes.'

'Save for one – which showed a match for Craig Mervyn-Scott.'

Threads now grasped, I begin to weave. My questions are open, but the answers are no less predetermined. The jury have doubtless made the deductions for themselves, but it does not hurt my case to have common-sense inference endorsed by men in white coats (or, more accurately, a maroon blazer and high-street gingham shirt).

The findings are, Dr Redmond confirms, all consistent with each defendant having been involved in a sustained, bloodied assault on Bernard Hooper. These are the results that an expert such as himself would expect to see, if Craig Mervyn-Scott, Arron Freeman and Jamal Lowton had each taken it in turn to strike Bernard Hooper with the zombie knife, over and over and over, until he fell to the ground whereupon they had continued to strike him over and over and over, and had beaten him with fists or feet or miscellaneous blunt weapons, until the last glimmer of life had been extinguished.

CHAPTER 25

Craig (the first defendant)

I was ten years old the first time I got a blade pulled on me. Kayla, walking alongside me, was eight.

We had been to the park by the old library. It was one of those with a little play area for the small kids, with your swings and a roundabout and a tiny climbing frame with a slide, and then there was a bigger play area for the olders. The small one was covered in dog shit and needles and the chains on the swings were broken, and there was this little gang of three or four skagheads who would sit on the roundabout for basically all day, so the only mums who ever took their toddlers there were the ones shotting or the ones looking to score.

Kayla liked the big park though, even though she was too small for it. When she was three, she'd make me lift her onto my shoulders, and I'd then stand at the bottom of the really tall wooden climbing frame and she'd pull herself onto the bars and scrabble all the way to the top. It was as high as a house, but she wasn't scared at all. There was this little hut with a roof that you could sit in, with different shapes cut into the sides like windows, and Kayla would stick her little head through and shout to me, with the biggest smile you'd ever seen. When she got older, she'd still go just by herself; like when she needed to get out of the house if MJ was on one, or when shit was going down at school, she'd climb to the top and sit in that wooden hut, and shut herself away from the world. She used to say it was the place where she felt safe.

So anyway, this day I had taken her after school. It was the week after Kayla's birthday, and the sun was beating it down, and we were just leaving and walking along the path that leads from the tyre swing to the canal, when these two roadmen on BMXs came up from behind and swerved in front of us. One was proper ballied up, and the other had something dark – either a scarf or a snood – pulled up over his face. The bigger one, he was wearing the ballie, lifted up his top so we could see his waistband, and I knew straight away what was going down. Kayla didn't. She just thought these wasters were two of my mates, and even when they pulled out this mean blade – in the moment, I don't know if it was a chet or a Rambo, but it was about as long as my whole arm – I still don't think Kayla thought it was real. When I told her we had to give them our phones, she looked at me like I was making a joke she didn't get. She just said, 'It's my birthday present,' and I was like, 'I know, but this is just the way it is. Trust me.' And when she realised I was serious, her eyes were blinking away tears, but thank God she did as she was told, coz it was only a week later that some other fucker was wasted in that same park, and I'll bet it was those same two on the bikes.

Afterwards, I made Kayla swear not to tell our mum, coz if MJ found out that we had lost Kayla's birthday present, I knew it would be Mum who paid for it, and not with money if you get what I mean. So instead I sold my Nikes to this kid in my ends – I'd only had them a few months and they were basically like new – and then I bought Kayla the same phone, so nobody ever had to know.

'Dr Redmond, the jury have heard evidence from a pathologist that there were over fifty wounds. There would plainly have been significant blood loss?'

Mr Wyatt is asking the questions again. He's still not mentioned my other injuries, but right now, it sounds like he's trying to explain how come I've got so much blood on me if I wasn't actually involved.

'If somebody were to be at the scene at the time, it is quite possible that blood could have transferred to that person's shoes, yes?'

'Well, in the case of your client, Mr Wyatt – and in the case of Arron Freeman – there was not only contact staining on the soles, which I agree could be caused by walking through wet blood, but contact staining on the upper aspects of the shoe.'

Before Mr Wyatt can say anything, the judge is butting in. 'What might explain those stains?'

'One explanation,' the doctor says, 'is that Craig Mervyn-Scott and Arron Freeman kicked Bernard Hooper while he was bleeding.'

'Well, with respect,' says Mr Wyatt loudly, but there is no respect in his voice at all and his face has gone red, 'that is pure speculation, isn't it? Because is it not also possible that those stains could have been caused by Craig Mervyn-Scott leaning over the body while it was losing blood?'

'He'd have to be very close.'

'So we agree – it's possible. And leaning over the body during heavy blood loss could also explain the contact staining on Craig Mervyn-Scott's jacket, right?'

'It could, yes.'

'And if Craig Mervyn-Scott was standing nearby when Arron Freeman repeatedly stabbed Mr Hooper, it is also possible that blood might have been propelled onto Craig Mervyn-Scott? And that might explain the spatter on his jogging bottoms?'

'Again, that is possible.'

'And Arron Freeman repeatedly stabbing Bernard Hooper would, you have said, explain all of the bloodstains on *his* clothing?'

'Yes.'

'Now when it comes to Jamal Lowton, you had less to work with, but then you were never provided with his jacket or his shoes, were you?'

'No, I was told that those had not been recovered.'

'No. And as far as his trousers are concerned, it is possible for somebody to be involved in an assault like this, and for no blood to actually be transferred?'

'Yes, it is not certain that blood will transfer to every participant.'

'Likewise, when it comes to the so-called zombie knife, it is quite possible for somebody to have touched the hilt – to have held the weapon – and not to have transferred any recoverable DNA or fingerprints.'

'Yes. An absence of DNA on an item does not mean that somebody has not been in contact with it. Absence of evidence is not evidence of absence.'

'So the point, Dr Redmond, as I am sure you appreciate, is this: while you have confidently told this jury that the blood found on Craig Mervyn-Scott's clothing is consistent with him having been involved in the attack on Bernard Hooper, there is another explanation for your findings, isn't there?'

Before he can answer, Mr Wyatt carries on, not even looking at the man. Not even taking a breath. 'The other explanation for your findings is that Craig Mervyn-Scott was simply present. Very close by, but not actually involved. A bystander, while Arron Freeman and Jamal Lowton wielded the weapon and inflicted the injuries.'

The doctor has to agree. And he does. And Mr Wyatt tugs his black gown straight and gives that little smile.

'Good. We got there at last. Now, the last thing I want to ask you about is Exhibit GD/2 – the kitchen knife recovered from Garth Yard.'

I know what Mr Wyatt is going to ask about this, because he's told me when he's seen me this morning. The prosecution are going to say that there's no evidence that Hooper attacked me with that knife. They are going to say that there is no blood on the blade in that photo, and that what I've done is basically come up with this story because that knife actually belonged to one of us. Mr Wyatt said he's going to get the doctor to agree that just because my blood isn't on the blade of that knife, it doesn't mean that it wasn't used to cut me. That is something that the doctor has got to agree with, Mr Wyatt says. And again, as some of the jury scribble down more writings on their pads, the doctor says yeah, that could all be true.

And as I'm listening to all this talk about knives, I can't help thinking about how feared I was that day in the park, when the guy on the bike pulled his Rambo out of his waistband. I wasn't feared for me, I was feared for Kayla, but at the end of the day it doesn't matter who you're feared for – it's the same feeling. Like everything in your stomach wants to rush up your throat, and your brain is going a million miles an hour thinking of the worst that could happen, and trying to work out how to stop it.

But the truth is I didn't feel any of that when I was with Hooper that night. I was like Kayla all those years ago, laughing and thinking this was all just jokes, just somebody pranking us or whatever. None of it felt serious and none of it seemed to matter.

Hooper didn't even look like he knew what he was doing. He was acting the big man, giving it all that with his demands and shouting his threats, but he was no killer. I could see it in his eyes that he was holding back. I could hear Jamal laughing behind me, and even though it obviously made Hooper angry, he still wasn't going to actually do anything. He was hesitating, waving that little vegetable knife in the air like he was fucking scared of it. I didn't for a moment think he was actually gonna swing for me.

Until he did.

CHAPTER 26

Jennifer (counsel for the third defendant)

I catch myself chewing on a stray pen – not even sure it's my own – as I scroll through my notes for this witness. My head feels like there's a family of bats living in it, and I am deeply regretting my life choices; specifically the one that saw off a second bottle of Sauvignon the night before I was due to cross-examine a DNA expert.

Bob Evans has already done his bit, extracting identical concessions for his own client as Wyatt achieved. *Yes*, Dr Whatshisface agrees with Bob, *although the bloodstain evidence could be explained by direct participation in bloody violence, it might also be accounted for by Arron Freeman being nearby but not involved.* 'NBNI,' Bob grins at the jury, straining to coin an acronym that might catch in their minds.

The NBNI possibility doesn't de-fang the DNA evidence – the science remains consistent with the prosecution's case – but it softens the edges. It allows for doubt. It means that, when Baxter Wyatt and Bob Evans address the jury in closing speeches, they do not have to challenge the reliability of the science, but can instead invite the jury to disregard it on the Crown's own terms. *Even the prosecution's own expert agrees that we might be right* is a nice deflection to deploy.

Sadly, it's not an approach I can just copy and paste. We are not jumping on the NBNI bandwagon, asking the nice man if he agrees that the blood on Jamal's clothing could be because he was an unwitting bystander to his co-accused's brutality. Nope. Because Jamal maintains that he was nowhere nearby when the first drop of blood was spilled. NNWTFDOBWS. Not as catchy, and difficult to reconcile with the evidence – confirmed by inquiries with a defence expert – which puts Bernard Hooper's DNA in blood on Jamal's top.

Our many, lengthy conferences have failed to prompt Jamal into offering any alternative explanations for this inconvenient feature. 'I wasn't there' is an instruction I have received almost as frequently and consistently as Jamal's other refrain of first resort, 'I ain't no snitch.' As Caz has gently reminded him on more than one occasion, 'You're not gonna win a fucking cut-throat trial unless you're prepared to cut some fucking throats.'

But on we soldier. There is something that Dr Redmond has said which I am hoping might give us an inch of wiggle room. As Jeremy Letts nods at me to begin, I rise and place both hands on the lectern for support, briefly closing my eyes to try and calm the flapping of the bats.

'Dr Redmond, I want to ask please about the mixed DNA profile recovered from the bloodstain on the cuff of Jamal Lowton's sweatshirt.'

'Please do.'

Something in his cocksure response irks me. I try not to let it show on my face.

'There are two terms that I'd like us to drill into, if we can. You've told us about a "mixed DNA profile" – this is where you have biological material from more than one person, mixed together in the same sample.'

'Correct.'

'The area sampled here was a bloodstain.'

'It was.'

'But you have been very careful not to refer to "Bernard Hooper's blood" – instead, you have said "Bernard Hooper's *DNA in blood*".'

'I have.'

'And that's because you can't say that Bernard Hooper was the person whose blood was transferred onto the sweatshirt. All you can say is that there is blood on the sweatshirt, and that the DNA of two people – Bernard Hooper and Jamal Lowton – is mixed together in that spot.'

'That's right.'

'To assist the jury,' I flash a smile at them, eager to ensure that they remain with me, 'you in fact gave an example earlier of a mixed DNA profile being caused by one member of the jury touching the sweatshirt of another?'

'Yes.'

'Well, let's say one member of the jury bled onto their sweatshirt, and another juror brushed against that area. That might create a mixed DNA profile in blood, right?'

'Yes.'

'But testing alone might not tell you whose blood it is, and whose "touch DNA" it is?'

'Correct. We cannot always identify the cellular material containing the DNA. That is the position we have here.'

'Well, precisely.' I speak deliberately, slowly counting beats in my head to ensure that what I say next is not lost on anybody. 'And DNA testing does not tell you *when*, or in what order, DNA has been deposited?'

'That is one of the limitations, yes.'

'So let's say that Jamal Lowton had at some point bled onto the cuff of his sweatshirt. If he was, at some later time, walking alongside Bernard Hooper, and that cuff brushed against Bernard Hooper, that might result in Bernard Hooper's "touch DNA" appearing along with Jamal Lowton's DNA in a mixed profile, if you were to sample that bloodstain.'

I pause before turning my assertion into a question. I need the jury to be with me for this. I need them to appreciate that the response I am about to receive is not a consolation goal; it is a potential game-changer.

'Dr Redmond, might that scenario explain these findings? Could this in fact be Jamal Lowton's own blood, and Bernard Hooper's "touch" DNA?'

He nods, but it still feels like an age before the words arrive. The bats are now flapping so aggressively that I barely hear when he eventually answers.

'Yes. Yes, theoretically it could.'

DAY 7 OF TRIAL – THURSDAY

CHAPTER 27

Arron (the second defendant)

I barely slept last night.

It was the first proper bad night I've had for months. Obviously when I first arrived at Twyford, I didn't sleep at night for like a week. I was just a kid. I knew literally nowt about prison, other than what the boys at Rosewoods used to tell us. Some of them had brothers and dads inside and carried on like they had done time themselves, but when I got here it was obvious that they didn't have a clue. Neither did I.

The first night I was in induction, so I had my own pad, with my own shower and shitter. There were holes in the wall and the pillow was covered in some kind of sticky yellow stuff, but it was quiet compared to what it would be like when I got to the wing, and because I'd not slept for two straight days at the cop shop, I basically crashed straight out.

When I moved onto the wing the next day, the only space was in a double. My first pad mate was Anthony. He was seventeen but looked like he was twenty, with arms the size of tree trunks, and he called me Fish. He had already been in for a year on an armed robbery and basically ran the wing. He had all this canteen piled up next to his bed, and showed me this toastie machine which he'd got one of the screws to smuggle in, so he could heat up the cheese butties they gave us for dinner. That first day on the wing, Anthony talked for hours, telling me how he was running protection for the

Croydon boys, and how he could basically get anything he wanted and nobody would touch him. But then on my second day there was drama in the mess hall when the Croydon boys found out that Anthony had nicked their toastie maker, and they took this metal temperature probe from the kitchen and stuck it through Anthony's eye. So for the rest of that week I kept my head down and just lay in my pad all day and mostly slept. Which meant I was then wide awake during the night.

But that's not what was going on yesterday. Maybe it's because today is the day the jury gets shown what is on our phones. Maybe that's why I'm feeling like it's all about to tip over the edge. I remember Mr Evans, the first time he visited me at Twyford, saying that this is going to be the worst bit. He was dead stern; he made this face like Graham used to when he wanted us to take him serious. He was all like, *The phone material is going to play very badly with the jury, and we just have to hope that you can turn it around when you give your explanation.*

We all stand up as the judge walks in. The police officer then comes and stands where he was the other day. The jury door opens and they all go to their seats.

'Sergeant, you are still under oath,' says the judge, and Miss Arshad then gets up and begins.

'DS Rose, were any mobile phones seized from the defendants upon their arrest?'

'Yes, ma'am. Craig Mervyn-Scott had a gold-coloured Samsung Galaxy device in his jacket pocket, and Arron Freeman had a silver iPhone 15S in his trousers.'

'What about Jamal Lowton?'

'There was no phone on him when he was located, but attending officers recovered a red Acer smartphone from Garth Yard. When we reviewed the contents, we were able to attribute that device to Jamal Lowton.'

He then starts going through what he found in the contacts of our phones. He starts with Craig's, because Craig obviously had me and Jamal's numbers saved.

'Craig Mervyn-Scott had Arron Freeman's number saved under the name Az. He had the number for Jamal Lowton's Acer phone – the one we found in Garth Yard – saved as J1.'

'Were there any other contacts of significance?'

'After J1, there was then a second number, ending '0788', saved under the name J2. This has also been attributed to Jamal Lowton. It is believed that he had his primary Acer smartphone, and then the J2 phone, which was a burner phone.'

'How did you attribute J2 to Jamal Lowton?'

'The data shows all three defendants' phones using a cell mast serving Craig Mervyn-Scott's home address on the afternoon of New Year's Eve. This suggests they were together. Jamal Lowton's J1 phone's data suggests that he then leaves at around 6 p.m. to go back to his home address, before heading out again at around 10 p.m. Then at 22:37, we have his J1 phone locating near Reggie's, while Jamal Lowton stands outside Reggie's sending that "meet outside Reggie's" text to Arron Freeman from his J2 phone.'

'So he was carrying both phones?'

'That's what the evidence suggests, yes.'

'Was the J2 handset ever recovered?'

'No. We believe Mr Lowton disposed of it after he fled from Garth Yard.'

I nod to myself. When I get my chance, I'll happily tell them all that yeah, it was Jamal's grafting phone, and yeah, he chucked it after he ran away.

'But we do know what kind of phone it was,' the cop goes on. 'Because when we obtained the call data records for the J2 number, they showed the IMEI that that SIM was using.'

I'm a bit lost now. Miss Arshad gets him to explain.

'It's something that not many people realise. Some of the jury probably know that our network providers – Three, O2, whatever – record all the activity on our phone numbers; our call history, our texts and so forth. So if the police get those records, we can see the times and dates and cell locations of what that SIM has been doing. But we can also identify the particular handset.

'Every mobile phone has a unique fifteen-digit identifying number, called an IMEI. It's like a fingerprint. Call data records show the IMEI of the handset that is being used. So, when we got the data for the J2 number, we could see that the 'J2' SIM card was in a handset with an IMEI which we were able to confirm as being a Nokia 6300 model.'

I'll be honest, I'm zoning out a bit. It's all going over my head, this. But then they start talking about me.

'Regarding Arron Freeman's phone, did he have any relevant contacts stored?'

'He had Craig Mervyn-Scott saved under CMS. He didn't have any numbers stored for Jamal Lowton, but there were messages from the J2 number on the phone.'

Like I say, Jamal was Craig's mate, not mine. What am I gonna want with his number in my phone? If I need to speak to him, I go through Craig.

'Thank you, officer. Now, I would like you to please help us with some of the material that was discovered when the police examined the contents of the defendants' phones.'

Miss Arshad probably thinks she's being dead calm, but I can sense the excitement in her voice. She's buzzing at what she knows is coming.

'Let us start with the mobile phone of Craig Mervyn-Scott. I wonder, Your Honour, whether this document might be handed to the members of the jury, for insertion behind divider thirteen?'

She waves pieces of paper in the air, which the little guy in the glasses collects and gives out to everyone. Copies are passed through the thin holes in the glass to me and my co-Ds. I knew this was going to be bad, but the way the prosecution have put this all together, with the pictures and everything – it is not good.

'At the top of the page, we can see tabulated a series of Google searches that were made on Craig Mervyn-Scott's phone. Can you please read those search entries into the record?'

'On 1 March 2023 at 23:52, there was a search for "zombie knife".'

'Next, please.'

'On 1 March 2023 at 23:55, there was a search for "where to get Rambo knife".'

'Continue.'

He reads them all out. There's twelve altogether. Between 1 March 2023 and 30 December 2023, Craig was searching for knives, and for websites selling knives, and for pictures of knives. Six of the searches actually mentioned 'zombies' or 'ZKs'. The rest were for hunting knives, chets and Rambos.

'Below those entries,' Miss Arshad says, 'we can see a series of WhatsApp messages dated 29 December 2023. Firstly, who were those messages between?'

'Those were all sent by Craig Mervyn-Scott's phone to a number ending 4140.'

'Do we know whose number that is?'

'No, it was unregistered.'

'And, again, for the record, what did the messages contain?'

'The first was just a photograph of a large hunting knife. This was immediately followed by a message saying, "U get this."'

'And next?'

'Over the next three-and-a-half minutes, Craig Mervyn-Scott sent five photographs of other weapons, all bladed articles of various lengths and types, followed by another message.'

'What did that message say?'

'It said, "Could do some sweet damage with this."'

I want to turn my head to see the look on Craig's face. He must know he's screwed. But before I can even look at him, I hear my name. And I know that now it's my turn. Because while Craig may be a dickhead for doing them searches and messages, he's not the biggest dickhead. He's not the one with the worst on his phone. He's not given the prosecution – what was it Mr Evans said? – their smoking gun.

That is all me.

'On 28 December 2023, the following messages, recovered from Arron Freeman's iPhone, were exchanged between him and Jamal Lowton, using the J2 number.'

- Jamal: *YouTube link SENT*
- *Arron: Wat dat?*
- Jamal: Bro, u wanna play a game?
- *Arron: Wat game G*
- Jamal: Need 3 2 play
- *Arron: K*
- Jamal: Basically we all bang sum1 out . . .
- *Arron: Ye?*
- Jamal: But only 1 at a time
- *Arron: Wat u mean?*
- Jamal: So like u hit him then I hit him and we go round circle til sum1 wins
- *Arron: How u win?*
- Jamal: Lol when he's dead u daft fuk
- *Arron: Sick bro*
- Jamal: Srsly, u up for that?
- *Arron: Haha yeman maybe*
- Jamal: NYE?
- Jamal: Ask Craigy 2

[END OF MESSAGES]

CHAPTER 28

Jennifer (counsel for the third defendant)

In many ways, there is little unusual in Jamal's history. Well, no. Little unusual in the context of cases of this type. Defendants of this type.

In the context of children generally, we can only pray that stories like these are outliers. But young men appearing before the courts charged with fatal violence frequently fit a profile. The lines may be etched in different strokes from case to case, the shading may vary in its hues of grey, but you don't need to squint hard for the images to blur and merge.

Events which one might expect, in isolation, to define a human life, are but one small, familiar beat among a hundred small, familiar beats. The extraordinary multiplied by the improbable, producing results that are statistically implausible yet entirely predictable. A bevy of black swans, fracturing a childhood with their wings.

At an early stage, Caz instructed a clinical psychologist to assess Jamal and help us establish what level of dysfunction we were working with. The family history revealed within, gleaned from Social Services, medical and school records, was shocking only in its predictability.

That Jamal bore witness to routine violence, emotional abuse and neglect for the three years that his father was itinerantly in his life? That much I had assumed before I even opened the psychological report. Admittedly, the circumstances that led to Lowton Senior's permanent removal from the family home were a little less predictable in their finer detail: a disagreement as to whether a taxi driver's tardy arrival should be compensated for by a reduction in fare, or whether such poor service was more appropriately acknowledged by dragging the man out onto the road and running him over with his own vehicle. Indefinite imprisonment for public protection followed a conviction for manslaughter, and Jamal's mum took the opportunity to cut ties by conveniently losing the visiting slips each time they were posted out from prison.

Life did not improve from there. Jamal was the youngest of four children. The eldest, Taylor, died aged seventeen, when seven-year-old Jamal opened the front door of their flat to two balaclava-clad figures raining a hail of bullets over his head and into his brother's. The nightmares and flashbacks that years later would be unsurprisingly confirmed as the symptoms of complex PTSD persist to the present day. Brothers two and three, sensing safety in gang numbers, chased drugs and guns to the same destination as their father, and are not due for release for another few years.

Jamal was already, at the time of his brother's murder, subject to a child protection plan with the local authority after he was spotted eating out of the bins at primary school. Following the home invasion, he spent eighteen months living away from the area with his aunt, sharing a single bedroom with his mother until they were able to be safely re-housed.

Jamal's experimentation with skunk began at the age of eight, although routine exposure technically began in utero. It quickly accelerated until he was smoking daily by the time he was ten. He resisted cocaine for another two years, which is when he also started drinking, developing a healthy tolerance for whole bottles of white rum, which, he told the clinical psychologist, made him feel connected to his dad.

As for education, I could again forecast from a template. Jamal was truanting from primary school aged six, with staff reporting a lack of concentration, poor emotional regulation and generally aggressive and defiant behaviour. There were multiple referrals to Child and Adolescent Mental Health Services, none of which was completed. Teachers offered informal diagnoses of autism and ADHD, but whatever the specific neurodivergence, a failing Pupil Referral Unit was deemed a better equipped environment than a failing mainstream school. Jamal was bounced to The Springs, a therapeutic unit which measured success by whether its attendees managed more than one hour a week without throwing furniture at the staff. A series of Educational, Health and Care (EHC) plans, notwithstanding the best intentions of their authors, succeeded in achieving for Jamal neither education nor health nor, in any meaningful sense, care, and certainly no qualifications.

The terms that are scattered throughout the conclusions of the psychological assessment and psychometric testing would therefore be startling if they were absent. A Full Scale IQ score in the 'extremely low' range, with a similar level for his verbal comprehension, processing speed, perceptual reason and working memory. Antisocial attitudes, immaturity and susceptibility to behave recklessly and impulsively. A high risk of self-harm. The profound and long-lasting effects of complex trauma, carved across every measurable aspect of his seventeen years.

Sometimes, as the early hours of the morning melt into dawn and the last drops of the bottle are drained, I can feel the hermetic seal that I have carefully hewn between parenthood and work fissure. I stare at these reports for hours, down to the bottom of a second or third bottle, engrossed in the professional exposition of most parents' worst nightmares; a testament to the irreversible damage it is possible to do to a life that you bring into the world.

Yet these cases are not the most frightening. If Jamal is guilty, there will at least be something which informs his downfall. There is almost a comfort in seeing the archetype fulfilled. Opening the reports and being able to readily identify the familiar deficits – poverty, neglect, abuse, mental ill health, lack of education, negative peer associations, drug misuse – offers a measure of reassurance. Something that allows the system, and those of us in it, to shrug sadly, but to quietly tell ourselves that something could have been done; it just *wasn't*. That such events are within our power, as a parent, to prevent.

No, I assure you that the most terrifying are those where there are no signs at all. Where evil is prefaced not by the tantara of a trumpet that society chooses not to hear, but by silence.

The photograph from the fridge – the dark, emotionless eyes of Finlay with his arm wrapped around Ollie's shoulders – flashes into view, and I banish it with a shudder.

I doubt that any of this would offer any comfort to Jamal's mother, of course. And I would not dream of sharing such thoughts with her. Jocelyn Lowton, whatever her parental shortcomings, stands to lose a fourth son. She has attended court stoically, every single day, to listen attentively and impassively to the evidence showing her youngest child to be a cold-blooded killer in the mould of his father. Whatever causative link I may silently draw between her decisions and her son's destiny, and whatever moral judgement I may in weaker moments be tempted to deliver, it is not her fault that Jamal's case stirs me in the way that it does. She does not need to navigate my history alongside her own. I accepted this case as a favour to Caz. Not because I am seeking salvation, or confronting demons, or any other cliché which might naturally be assumed of my decision. It is just a case, and I am simply here to do my professional duty.

But at the same time, I am finding, when I stride up the corridor each morning past Jocelyn Lowton sitting patiently outside court, and when I glance across the courtroom and see her with her head bowed in the public gallery, that I need to impose limits on that duty. I can do formalities – a good morning and good evening to top and tail the day. But any family care beyond that, any conversations of substance or words of comfort, I am leaving to Caz. Just as I told Caz it would have to be when I accepted the brief: I don't do knives. I don't do teenage stabbings. And, I am afraid to say, in a case of this type I cannot do empathy. I cannot shoulder Jocelyn's burden as well. I cannot carry another mother's loss.

'These,' DS Chris Rose says loudly, snapping me back into the room, 'are the titles of videos that were viewed on the internet, using Jamal Lowton's J1 phone between 17:01 and 17:29. That was the time at which all three defendants were together on the Rosewood estate.'

I know the titles only too well. I also know what lies behind the hyperlinks: the content which even Jeremy Letts has agreed is too graphic and too prejudicial to play to the jury. Instead, the prosecution and defence have approved a form of words that describes, as concisely and unemotively as possible, what these videos depict. As DS Rose begins to read out the words that I, on Jamal's behalf, have agreed reflect his viewing habits, I cannot shake the words that I have overheard his mother reciting to Caz on a loop over the past seven days:

He's easily led, but he's not a killer.

'Video one,' Rose says, 'is entitled "Somali pirate DECAPITATES naked prisoner!" The video is forty-two seconds long. It shows an unclothed male whose hands and feet are bound. He is sitting on a chair in front of a black backdrop. A male with a face covering, holding a sword, appears on the right of the screen. He speaks indistinctly before swinging the sword and decapitating the bound male.'

He's easily led, but he's not a killer.

'Video two,' Rose continues, 'is entitled "Psycho clown makes obese kid bleed out". The video is eighty-nine seconds long. It shows a person wearing a clown mask, holding a sharp metal implement resembling a poker, approximately fifty centimetres in length. A large male can also be seen. His top is being lifted up by persons unseen. The "clown" proceeds to insert the implement nine times into the torso of the male, causing heavy bleeding from the wounds. At the end of the clip, the male falls to the floor.'

He's easily led, but he's not a killer.

'Video three on Jamal Lowton's phone,' Rose says flatly, 'is titled "six newborn puppies and their momma meet my flamethrower".'

He's easily led. But he's not a killer.

Three further videos, each purporting to show the mutilation and killing of people or animals, are described in the same flat tone. To give the officer his credit, he is not overplaying this. He recognises the impact of the evidence. It needs no hype. No editorialising. He also knows, as do I, that there is one video which the jurors are going to have to watch.

'It's right, isn't it, that a video recording was recovered from Jamal Lowton's J1 Acer phone?' Aliyah asks.

'Yes,' says Rose. 'The metadata shows that it was created on the device at 00:04 on 1 January 2024. It is an eight-second video clip, which shows . . . well, I think we're going to play it, aren't we?'

Aliyah nods wordlessly, and motions to the clerk to switch on the plasma screens for the jury. She fiddles briefly with a cable on her laptop, until the monitors light up with a still image, the first frame in the video clip. She pauses for a few seconds before clicking 'play', to allow the jury to get their bearings. Again, no narration or editorialising is required. What can be seen speaks for itself.

We are shown Garth Yard in portrait orientation. Bernard Hooper is lying in a bloodied heap on his back. The lighting is low, but the sheen of the blood soaking the pavement is just visible. Nobody else is presently on screen. When the clip begins, the camera pans left, to Craig Mervyn-Scott. He is holding the zombie knife. His face and hands are painted red, like a child at Halloween who has got carried away with the food colouring. Inarticulate and confused as Paul Bell proved himself to be, his description of Craig Mervyn-Scott – *head to toe dripping with blood* – is faultless.

He is only visible for a second, as he runs across shot and away to the right. The camera then refocuses on Bernard Hooper and zooms in on his face. He appears still to be alive, inasmuch as his eyelids are fluttering and a faint sound of gargling is audible as bubbles of blood burst around his mouth. As the camera operator takes a good, hard look at the handiwork – a lingering shot that feels infinitely longer than three or four seconds – the knife returns to view, prodding Bernard Hooper's cheek, and somebody off-camera can be heard shouting.

The words are not immediately comprehensible. The judge interjects.

'Can we hear that part at the end again, please.'

The clip is replayed. The jurors lean forward, trying to confirm what they thought they heard the first time. The judge then nods.

'It's a matter for you, members of the jury, but that sounded to me like "How does it feel to die, you fucking paedo?"'

He looks at counsel. None of us demur. It is clearly what was said.

Aliyah disconnects the video and the eyes of the jurors return to the witness box.

'What other activity,' she asks slowly, 'was on Jamal Lowton's J1 device after it recorded that video clip?'

'The video file was immediately sent by WhatsApp to Jamal Lowton's J2 number.'

Aliyah nods. 'Thank you, officer.'

I look at the jurors, trying to gauge what they make of that part of the evidence. It is something which I have struggled with, and which Jamal, naturally, has been less than helpful in cutting through. We have had at least three conferences in which Caz and I have attempted to take instructions on the phones, and what Jamal has offered is infuriatingly insubstantial. He has admitted, from the outset, that he was the person using the J1 and J2 numbers that night. He has not volunteered a reason for having a second phone, but I can hazard a guess, and in any case it is immaterial why he had it. The point is, he did.

However, Jamal maintains that he had left the scene before the violence started, and, by extension, before the video was recorded on his J1 phone. Fine, I've said to him – you fled, you dropped your phone, somebody else (as Craig is on screen, it can only be Arron behind the camera) picked it up and used it to record. We can make that work. But the part that makes no sense – the question to which the jury are going to want an answer – is this: Why would Arron, having made this recording, send it from your J1 phone to your J2 phone? What is that all about? What would be the purpose in doing that?

I have asked the question a dozen times in a dozen ways. It is clear that Jamal understands it. But he does not want to answer it. And that, I have explained to him a dozen times, is a problem.

It suddenly occurs to me that Aliyah has not yet dealt with one of the earlier entries in the mobile phone events. For the briefest moment, I allow myself to fantasise that she has overlooked it. It is there in the sequence of events, but if the prosecution has omitted to draw it to the jury's attention, there's a chance that the jurors will also not realise its significance, and maybe . . . But of course Aliyah has not forgotten. She is, I realise just as quickly as the thought gathers steam, deliberately leaving it to the end of this section of the evidence, taking it out of turn to maximise its impact. And I do not blame her. Because if the rest of the mobile phone evidence has hammered nails into the casket of Jamal's case, this little nugget slides a boulder on top of it.

'Finally, officer, can we please go back to an earlier entry on our chart. At line two, we can see that a Google search was made on Jamal Lowton's J1 phone on New Year's Eve at 16:08.'

'That's correct.'

'This search was made at a time when, as we've established, the defendants were all together at or near Craig Mervyn-Scott's home address.'

'That's right.'

'And this would be approximately seven hours before the defendants headed into town and encountered Bernard Hooper?'

'Yes, it would.'

'Officer, can you please read this Google search into the record?'

DS Rose looks up at the jury. 'It reads, "How long do u get 4 murder?"'

DAY 8 OF TRIAL – FRIDAY

CHAPTER 29

Aliyah (the prosecutor)

I awoke this morning with a feeling of lightness that has been noticeably absent for the past nine days. It was helped by the fact that it is a Friday, and so one of the three days on which Clara does the school run, purchasing precious time during which I can get ready for court in peace and make my way in at my own pace, rather than the girls', and avoid any more interminable bickering about phones or surreptitious boyfriends. Sasha is also away on a 'team-building with a twist' long weekend with his charity, heralding three glorious days without any pointed mention of spiralling credit card interest or idle threats of downsizing.

More than that though is the sense of relief that the most potent evidence we have has now been adduced, and, if the noises off that I could hear as I examined Chris Rose are a reliable indicator, it has landed with the jury. Few murderers throughout history have been helpful enough to spell out their plans in writing for the police to stumble across. The mobile phone evidence in this case is probably as close as we can hope to get. After the disappointment of our eyewitnesses, and the points scored by the defence with the scientific evidence, our case is firmly back on track. Victory – not that victory matters – now feels significantly more tangible.

This morning's offerings for the jury are likely to prove less explosive. I have some agreed witness statements to read out – uncontroversial witnesses whose attendance at court the defence have agreed to waive. Then Chris Rose is back in the box for some tidying up, and to deal with the defendants' police interviews.

This afternoon, however, the jury can expect some blood sports. DS Rose will be cross-examined by three highly experienced defence counsel, and the errors and omissions for which he is responsible – and which have hitherto gone largely unmentioned in front of the jury – will be held up to the light and forensically dissected. There will be nowhere for Rose to run, and nowhere to hide. And while, in an ideal world, I would rather the prosecution not be in the position of having the police investigation kicked to pieces, if the universe will not deliver a competent OIC, it can at least book me front row seats to his undoing.

One thing which, to his credit, Rose has belatedly addressed – and which may, in some part, be contributing to my elevated spirits – is the counselling records. After what felt like the hundredth polite request from Bob Evans when I arrived at court this morning, Rose bustled over to us to confirm that he has nearly finished reviewing the records, and there is nothing disclosable so far. Quite why it has taken until day nine of trial for this to be done is a reasonable question, but not one to which I would have any faith in receiving a reasonable answer. I shall take the fact that it has finally been done – and that there is nothing in the records to support Arron Freeman's case – as a win.

Court is assembled and the jury are adjusting themselves in their seats. Jeremy Letts gives the jurors a brief explanation of agreed evidence, and directs them that the statements I am about to read carry just as much weight as if the witness had given the evidence live from the witness box. 'This is purely about convenience,' he smiles toothily at them. 'There is no point dragging to court somebody whose evidence is not going to be contested.'

I stand up and tilt my laptop so that I can see the screen without lowering my head.

'Ladies and gentlemen, there are two statements from Rita Hooper. The first is dated 3 January 2024.'

I read slowly, conscious that the author is sitting in the public gallery and anxious to do justice to the words she somehow, incredibly, composed herself to write only two days after her husband's murder. She has declined the option of giving the evidence herself – probably a wise decision, given that her choice of boot is a poor match for her dress. I try to strike the perfect balance between poise and pathos, and a tear on the back row of the jury box proves I have succeeded.

I allow a long pause before I move on to Rita Hooper's second statement. 'It is dated 31 May 2024,' I tell the jury. I do not tell them why the statement was taken; that much will become evident. Namely, to address the absurd suggestion by Craig Mervyn-Scott – already floated in front of the jury by Baxter Wyatt – that Bernard Hooper had gone out that night armed with a knife and looking for violence. I pity the officer who was tasked with troubling this grieving widow with what must, to her, have seemed an utterly ludicrous set of questions concerning her cutlery drawer. Fortunately, she did not slam the door in his face, and obliged as follows. I begin:

I am the above named person, and I reside at the address overleaf. I make this statement further to my statement dated 3 January 2024.

I have been shown a photograph of a kitchen knife, Exhibit GD/2, and have been asked if I recognise it. It looks like a knife we might have had in our kitchen, but I cannot be sure.

Given the passage of time, I can't say whether a knife went missing around New Year's Eve. I have since moved house and have replaced all of our crockery and cutlery, so I do not know what might have been missing.

I am not aware of any reason why Bernard would have taken a knife with him to go out to the shop. As far as I am concerned, this is not something that he would have done.

CHAPTER 30

Craig (the first defendant)

At the end of the day, it doesn't matter what you think, Mrs Hooper. Coz your husband *was* out with a knife. There's bare shit you don't know about your husband, Mrs Hooper. Shit he probably didn't even tell you. So maybe you should just wind your fucking neck in, yeah? I'm not being harsh. Or if I am, I don't mean to be. But listening to the way that Big Bird has been making out like Bernard Hooper was this nice old man who wouldn't hurt a fly, it's making me scratch my fingernails into my seat to stop me shouting out.

It's not Mrs Hooper's fault though, I do know that. I know that you don't always know people, even when you think you do. Some people are just good at hiding who they really are until it's too late. And by the time you realise, you can't do nothing about it. They've dug their claws in to your life, and you can shake and shake and shake, but there's no way you can get free.

I look at Arron sitting two seats down. He's got his back straight and is paying proper attention, like he's in school assembly or some shit. He's listening to Big Bird as she reads out more statements to the jury. At the start, they're all sitting straight and listening, like Arron, but after like the fourth or fifth one, some of them sort of slump in their seats and look a bit bored. There's statements from all the feds who turned up to nick us, and all the ambulance people who came after we was nicked, and then the doctors at the hospital who looked at Hooper and were like, yeah, obviously the man's dead.

Then there's the drugs.

When we got off the van at our police stations, all of us had our blood tested. The nurse who was looking at my injuries took out this needle, and what she got from me was then sent to a lab, and apparently it was the same for Arron and Jamal. When they looked at the blood, they could tell that we had all three of us been blazing, and that me and Jamal had also had flake. I don't know why that's supposed to make a difference to anything, but the way Big Bird reads out those statements, it's like she wants the jury to think something bad of it.

The clock on the wall says that she's been reading statements for more than an hour now. Finally she stops and says the jury is going to hear from the fed again, and the round little fucker waddles back into court and starts telling everyone about the pictures in their folders.

I pick up my folder from under my chair. The photos are all in different bits. There's the pictures from the yard, showing Hooper lying on the floor, although the way it's taken you can't see his face. He's just this lump on the ground, with the knife sticking out. There's other photos from the yard, not showing him but showing the stuff that was on the floor, and the yellow skip behind the black metal fire escape. Big Bird reads a statement from the feds who say they went to the top of the fire escape and found the door into the building was rusted and locked from the inside, so there's no way anyone was getting in or out of it, if that's what anyone's wondering. Mr Wyatt says that this is an important one for us, the skip. In the picture, you can see all these blue rubbish bags spilling out of the top. There's no photos of actually inside the skip. Again, Mr Wyatt says this is a good thing for us, given what I'm going to be telling the jury.

Now it's the photos they took of my bedroom when they searched the house. There's not really much in there: just a mattress with no sheets and an old wardrobe with a door that won't close. But it's still bare messy – my joggers and hoodies and bedsheets are all over the floor, and there's a pile of dirty plates next to the mattress. On my bed is an open pizza box full of crusts, which I must have had for breakfast that morning. The pot of garlic mayo has spilled and there's a close-up photo showing it leaked all over the bed. The older woman on the back row of the jury catches my eye, and I feel properly shamed. It's like, even though this is obviously not the worst thing she's heard about me, she's, like, really *disappointed* in me. There's a look, like my mum used to give me. Obviously my mum's not been in my room for years – well, five years, four months and thirteen days – but if she had been, she'd probably have pulled the same face as that lady, and this is how I would have felt.

It's not the mess that the prosecution are really interested in, though. It's the wardrobe. There's nothing much inside it, obviously. The wooden pole where you're supposed to hang clothes is missing, and it's not like we have any hangers anyway. There's one shelf, but that just has some old grey football socks that don't even match. But it's what's on top of the wardrobe that the prosecution are so excited about.

'Officer,' says Big Bird, 'what can we see on page thirty-two, on top of the wardrobe?'

'That,' he says, 'is a cow-hide sheath.'

'Was there anything inside that sheath?'

'Yes,' he says. 'The sheath contained a large hunting knife.'

I see one of the jurors write something down.

'And if we turn to page thirty-three,' the prosecutor says, and everybody flicks over the page, 'we can see a close-up image of that hunting knife, with the measurements detailed, yes?'

'Yes, ma'am. It had a 15 centimetre wooden handle, and a stainless steel blade, 25 centimetres in length and 5 millimetres thick, curved to a point.'

When Mr Wyatt first showed me these photos, I asked him

whether it would help if I said that the knife had only been there for a few days. I asked what about if I said it was Jamal's. *Jamal could have put it there,* I said to him. But Mr Wyatt said it basically doesn't matter how long it had been there, the point is that it shows I've got a thing for knives, and I know how and where to get hold of them. And the jury are going to ask why the fuck Jamal would hide a knife on top of my wardrobe – it doesn't really make sense, Mr Wyatt said, which is fair. I don't want to have to lie to the jury anyway. But then, at the same time, I don't think I can tell them the complete truth about this. I can't tell them why I got it. Coz that would then mean I'd have to tell them everything.

Big Bird says thank you, and that we can all close our folders. They've finished with the pictures now, and they're going to tell the jury all about our interviews.

'The wording of the caution,' the officer says, 'is: "You do not have to say anything, but it may harm your defence if you do not mention, when questioned, something you later rely on in court. Anything you do say may be given in evidence."'

'Was that caution administered when the defendants were each arrested?'

'Yes, it was, ma'am.'

'And was it given, and its meaning explained, at the start of each defendant's interview?'

'Yes, it was. Basically, members of the jury, we break the caution down into three parts. You don't have to say anything – that's the first bit. It's your right to remain silent. You don't have to answer our questions. Second bit: But it may harm your defence – it may come back to bite you at trial – if you don't tell us something, but later come to court and tell it to a jury. And the last bit, if you do say anything, it can form part of the evidence at your trial.'

'When Jamal Lowton was arrested, did he say anything in response to caution?'

'Yes. He said, "I wasn't there."'

'And when he was interviewed, did he offer any further information?'

'No, ma'am. He gave "no comment" to all questions asked.'

'Arron Freeman – same questions. Any comment upon arrest?'

'No.'

'And in interview?'

'No comment, ma'am.'

'And Craig Mervyn-Scott, did he give any comment upon arrest?'

'No, he did not.'

'And in interview?'

'No comment to all questions. But Mr Mervyn-Scott did provide a prepared statement, through his solicitor, at the outset of his police interview.'

When I sat down with my brief, he told me that I didn't have to say anything. He said that, because there was Arron and Jamal being interviewed, and because we didn't know what they were going to say or what the rest of the evidence might be, that I should just give the feds nothing at all. Just 'no comment, no comment', all the way through. Wait and see, he said.

But even though he obviously knows more about this than me, I didn't want to just say nothing at all. I wanted to get our story out there. Or at least some of it. And I already suspected that Arron wasn't going to have my back. So my brief agreed, although he wasn't happy about it, and he wrote out something.

In it, I said that this man attacked me and my mates on Rowe Street. I said he had a knife and was shouting about money. I said we were afraid for our lives, and that my mates just did what they did to try and protect us all. Only they took it too far.

And I said that I didn't touch the guy. I swore down, it was not me who did those injuries.

And my brief read it all out to me. And I signed it.

I thought I was doing the right thing for all of us.

CHAPTER 31

HHJ Jeremy Letts (the judge)

Small mercies, and all that. Had any of the defendants given an account in their interview, we would have all been treated to yet another dramatic reading from the Arshad School of Performing Harpies. When she was reciting that mawkish testimony of the widow, I had to restrain myself from asking if we were in the presence of Vivien Leigh. She was Indian actually, as it happens. And the way she kept staring at that juror with the conjunctivitis. Heaven save us.

'As the self-styled Officer in the Case, you are responsible for the overall conduct of the investigation, yes?'

Baxter's eyes are locked into the officer's. No mischievous grin on show for this cross-examination. He has the bit between his teeth, evidently. I pick up my pen to jot down the highlights for my summing-up, but I rarely remind jurors of every criticism levelled at the police by the defence. They do a damned difficult job. Not least, as in the case of this poor fellow, when they have to work with a hamstrung CPS and a succession of inept counsel. Arshad's predecessor in this case, Bill McMahon KC, was a famously lazy sod right up until the end, and when Arshad was parachuted in upon his cardiovascular departure from this mortal parish, it was not so much an upgrade as a relocation from frying pan to frying pan. Lord knows what sort of guidance this chap has had on disclosure from the understudy of last resort.

'And your duty as an investigator is to pursue all reasonable lines of inquiry, whether they point towards a suspect's guilt, or away from a suspect's guilt. Yes?'

The officer is nodding, and I politely remind him to respond verbally for the digital recording equipment.

'Because an incomplete investigation can have serious consequences, can't it, DS Rose?'

DS Rose finds his voice. 'Yes,' he says, the word carrying greater confidence than its delivery.

'An incomplete investigation can have *disastrous* consequences, can't it?'

'Well, I wouldn't say . . .'

'An incomplete investigation can result in a guilty person getting away with a serious crime, yes?'

'Well, yes . . .'

'Or an innocent person being convicted of a crime that they did not commit.'

There is no sensible argument with this proposition, so Rose says, 'In theory, yes.'

Wyatt lowers his voice. 'And as an officer of His Majesty's constabulary, charged with upholding the law of the land, you would surely describe an innocent person being convicted of a crime that they did not commit as *disastrous*?'

'I would, yes.'

'Right. Well, let us look, shall we, at the steps you took to ensure that this was a full and fair investigation. The steps that you took to avoid such disastrous consequences. Starting, please, with the knife.'

'The murder weapon?'

The chap freezes. Too late, he recognises the elephant trap into which he has obediently walked.

'No, officer. The jury have heard quite a lot about the zombie knife. What I would like to ask you about is the *other* knife that was recovered from Garth Yard. Exhibit GD/2. Do you remember that exhibit?'

'Yes. Right. Sorry. Of course I do.'

'Of course you do, yes. You recognised, as a *competent*, *careful* detective pursuing a full investigation, that a knife found at the scene of an apparent murder was obviously relevant, didn't you?'

'I did.'

'That's why it was photographed *in situ* by the crime scene investigators?'

'Yes.'

'And you also knew, as the officer in charge of this full and fair investigation, that in his police interview, Craig Mervyn-Scott had told the interviewing officers that he had been threatened with a knife by Bernard Hooper.'

'Yes.'

'So let us take stock. You have a suspect telling you that the deceased threatened him with a knife. And you find a knife next to the deceased's body. Presumably, the very first thing you do, in your full and competent investigation, is to have the knife scientifically examined. To see if it has Bernard Hooper's fingerprints on the hilt, or Craig Mervyn-Scott's blood on the blade, yes?'

'Not straight away, no.'

In an earlier cross-examination, the jury might have predicted Baxter Wyatt to turn towards them at this answer, his expression riven with feigned shock. But still he does not break eye contact with the officer.

'Why. Not. Straight. Away?'

'We were prioritising the forensic opportunities that might be available in respect of the primary weapon of interest, sir, that being namely the large implement protruding from the chest of the deceased.'

The words are delivered in a soup, apparently in the belief that haste conveys confidence. None of us is fooled.

'In plain English, do you mean you were too busy focusing on the zombie knife?'

'I wouldn't put it quite like that, what I would say—'

'Well, help us with this. You had the scientific results from the zombie knife within seven days. The Streamlined Forensic Report is dated 8 January 2024. So how soon after that did you submit Exhibit GD/2 for examination, to see if it supported what Craig Mervyn-Scott had told you?' The officer blinks and breaks eye contact. The effect is to leave a pause which, in reality, does not exceed two seconds, but is enough for Wyatt to jump back in. 'You appear to be having difficulty answering that question, officer. Is that because, in fact, you *never* had Exhibit GD/2 scientifically examined?'

'It was ultimately not submitted for examination, that is correct, sir.'

'No. It was the defence who had to ask to have this obviously relevant exhibit examined, wasn't it?'

'I believe there was a request from the defence solicitors in terms of the knife, yes, sir.'

'And what were the defence solicitors told when they asked for the knife to be released to a defence expert for inspection?'

This time Wyatt does not interrupt Rose's pause. He lets it balloon, allowing the witness to buckle under its weight. Eventually, DS Rose replies, 'I believe that by the time of the defence request, Exhibit GD/2 had been misplaced in storage.'

'By "misplaced in storage", do you mean "the police had lost it"?'

'Yes.'

'And so all that the experts have to work from, and all this jury have, are the photographs that we have seen. The knife itself, the knife that is central to Craig Mervyn-Scott's defence, was never examined by the police, and by the time the defence solicitors asked for it, the police had lost it. Is that the shape of things, officer?'

Rose confirms that it is.

'Aside from the scientific testing, there were other reasonable lines of inquiry obvious to you as the investigating officer, weren't there? For instance, making an inquiry of Rita Hooper to see if Exhibit GD/2 matched the knives that Bernard Hooper kept at home.'

'Yes.'

'The jury have heard that she gave her first statement on 3 January 2024. When that was taken, was she asked about the knives?'

'No.'

'No. We know that she was in fact not asked that obvious and reasonable question until four months later, in May 2024. By which time, she had replaced her cutlery set.'

'I believe so.'

'You *know* so, officer. This is your investigation, you've claimed.'

Another silence affords Wyatt the opportunity for a recap.

'So to summarise, the knife was never examined, it was then lost, and by the time you thought to ask the obvious question of the widow, it was too late.'

I step in. He has drawn enough blood on this topic. 'Mr Wyatt, I think perhaps . . .'

'I'll move on. Officer, let us look at the scene photographs . . .'

'Mistakes were made, I take full accountability.'

'I beg your pardon, officer?'

'I'm just agreeing, mistakes were made. Yes.'

'Yes. *You* made the mistakes, as the investigating officer, didn't you?'

'Mistakes were made.'

'By you.'

'They were made, and I take accountability.'

'Well, I'm sure that the jury,' Wyatt turns to them, 'can make up their own minds on that. But on the subject of mistakes, officer, can we please look at the scene photographs?'

'The knife?'

'No, no, not the knife that you lost, no. Other mistakes. Officer.'

The finest cross-examinations might sometimes be described in the language of a dance-off. Spontaneous choreography between a sharp witness and a sharp(er) interrogator. What follows in the remainder of Baxter Wyatt versus DS Chris Rose is rather more akin to a man quickstepping with a mop; dragging its inanimate form across the dance floor at whatever speed and in whichever formation he so chooses.

The scene photographs, the jury soon learn, are incomplete. Another set of digital photographs were taken and exhibited, but burned to a master disc which was thereafter corrupted beyond recoverability, losing one third of the originals showing the state and contents of Garth Yard. It follows, Wyatt suggests, that there may have been relevant evidence at the scene that has not been seized. It is another obvious trap, but the decreasingly impressive officer lumbers into it.

'I'm pretty sure that all relevant evidence was seized.'

'Really? What about the bag for life?' Wyatt says dangerously.

'Which . . .?'

'The bag for life that Bernard Hooper is seen carrying in the Co-op. He is shown on CCTV with it when he goes into Garth Yard, yet it doesn't feature on any exhibit list that we have seen, does it?'

Silence.

'And this is the point, officer. You cannot say that all relevant evidence has been seized, because there is at least one item you've missed, and we cannot see for ourselves what else might have been missed at the scene, because the police have lost a full third of the scene photographs.'

Round and round they spin, until Baxter Wyatt arrives at what will be his swansong for this cross-examination, although I doubt even he could predict the flourish that DS Rose generously sets up for him.

'The jury have been told that when Jamal Lowton was arrested, he was not wearing a jacket. And he was not wearing shoes.'

'That is correct.'

'He had discarded these between running from Garth Yard and his arrest in a nearby residential garden.'

'Yes.'

'That jacket, and those shoes, were never recovered by the police, is that right?'

Rose rolls back his shoulders and juts out his chin. 'That is the position, yes.'

'Knowing where Jamal Lowton had been, and where he had run to, what search was made of the area to locate this potentially crucial evidence?'

'We did not search the area at the time. We did not know that Mr Lowton had discarded any clothing until we obtained the CCTV footage showing how he was dressed earlier in the night. Our working assumption on the night was that he had gone out in the clothes he was wearing when he was arrested.'

Even now, Baxter Wyatt resists what must be a violent temptation to mug to the jury. His eyes widen, but they remain fixed on his prey.

'Officer, it was the middle of winter. Are you telling this jury that your working assumption was that Jamal Lowton had gone out that night not wearing any shoes?'

A snort from the jury box tells Wyatt that his work here is done. Now he can turn to the jury. Now, as he bends and lowers his gangly frame into his seat, he can break out that smile.

CHAPTER 32

Aliyah (the prosecutor)

I despise watching a police officer being unfairly criticised.

I assumed that it would follow that I would luxuriate in the dismantling of an officer like Chris Rose. I had expected to feel at least a warm spread of vindication as the infelicities that were privately obvious to me were paraded publicly, and humiliatingly, in front of a jury. But schadenfreude is giving way to concern. Even pity. Concern because, while there are many genuine errors in the investigation of this case, I had not – prior to today – considered them a serious threat to the prospects of securing convictions, and I am quickly re-evaluating whether I have allowed confidence to creep into complacency. And pity because – well. Just look at the state of him. The crumpled Moss Bros suit that he has brought out for the big occasion may have fit him at one time, but as of today it is serving only to squeeze his middle like a tube of toothpaste, doubtless contributing to the cartoonish beads of sweat that are quite literally rolling down his forehead.

Bob Evans has been coolly cross-examining for around fifteen minutes so far. Some has been gentle background probing, some has been riffing on the chord progression laid down by Baxter Wyatt. But as I hear the words, 'Officer, can we please take a moment to consider the mobile phone evidence?' I know – as I suspect does Rose – that the temperature is about to be ratcheted up again.

'The J2 phone – Jamal Lowton's burner, as it has been called. The handset using the J2 number was never found, is that right?'

'That's right, sir. Given that we know he was using it earlier in the evening, we believe he must have thrown it as he ran from the scene of the murder.'

'I see, thank you. Although—'

'And I should say,' Rose interrupts, anxious to forestall the criticism he surmises is around the corner, 'that we couldn't possibly have known Mr Lowton had a second phone before we saw the CCTV and started piecing the evidence together, so there was good reason why we didn't search the surrounding area for it on the night.'

His eyes dart towards Baxter Wyatt, who is smiling to himself, proud of the hyper-paranoia that his cross-examination has evidently induced.

'I was not for a moment going to suggest otherwise.' Bob smiles kindly, and Rose's shoulders relax. The idiot. 'No, what I would like to ask you, officer, is about the call data records.'

Rose's shoulders are back up.

'To summarise for the jury: mobile phone network providers keep call data records, which show various activity attributed to a particular number?'

'Yes.'

'If I make a call or send a text message, or use my mobile data to access the internet, that information is recorded and retained by the network provider.'

'That's correct, sir. The call data records don't include any content, but they show the date, time and duration of any such outgoing activity, and the numbers that are called or texted.'

'And, as you told the jury earlier, the records contain details of "IMEI"s associated to the phone number, allowing you to identify the handset used – a Nokia 6300 for the J2 number.'

'Yup.'

'Yes, thank you. So if I send a text message to you, the call data records for my number would show that a text message was sent to your number at whatever date and time, from whichever handset.'

'Exactly, sir.'

'The call data records also tell us the location of the cell mast to which the phone is connected for each of those calls or messages.'

'That's right.'

'And that is how what is known as "cell site" evidence is produced – by looking at the locations of the masts that a mobile phone is using over a period of time, it is possible to identify patterns that can show where a phone is, or the direction in which it is moving.'

'That's right.'

'It is potentially very powerful evidence.'

'It is indeed.'

'And that is why you obtained the call data records for Craig Mervyn-Scott's phone number?'

'Yes, sir.'

'And Arron Freeman's.'

'Yup.'

'And Jamal Lowton's J1 number.'

A pause. 'Yes.'

'But not, is this right, officer – not the J2 number?'

'Well, I did make the CycComms request, sir. I asked for that data. But there was a problem with the form.'

'What problem was that, officer?'

Rose looks towards me and I avoid meeting his gaze. 'I filled in the wrong date, sir. We obtained the data for a six-month period beginning 1 January 2024.'

'I see. But not – a wee bit unfortunately – the data for New Year's Eve, or the lead-up to New Year's Eve?'

'Right.'

'Was there anything of note on the J1 number after 1 January 2024?'

'No, sir. There was a text message sent from the J2 number to an unknown number just after midnight – that's how we got the IMEI. But the J2 obviously stopped being used after Jamal Lowton was arrested and remanded in custody.'

Bob nods understandingly, still smiling.

'When you realised your mistake, officer, did you then make a request for the J2 data for New Year's Eve and earlier?'

Rose looks again at me. I cannot look at him. He remembers our conference, when I was first instructed in November 2024, when I specifically raised the issue with the J2 call data – which had been missed by previous counsel – and told Rose that he needed to fix it. He remembers every email I sent to the CPS over the last two months, chasing and chasing and reminding and reminding of the need to obtain the J2 records for New Year's Eve.

'I didn't, sir. No. I forgot. It was an oversight on my part, sir. By the time I made the request it was too late.'

'An oversight? Oh, dearie me. You say it was "too late" – is that because call data records are only held by the network providers for a limited period of time?'

'Yes. Twelve months, sir.'

'And so your request for the correct dates was made after that period?'

'It was sir, yes."

Another snigger from the jury box – the second of the afternoon – which I could really do without. I silently practise the beats of my closing speech. *No police investigation is perfect. Officers are human beings doing their best in a straitened system. Errors – even multiple errors – are bound to creep in. What matters is whether the errors in this case actually affect anything. Yes, though not obtaining the J2 data is a fuck-up, nothing actually turns on it. And, as I will establish with Rose when I re-examine him, it is not as if any of the defence teams had applied for these records to be obtained. These attacks on the investigation are cheap attempts to distract from the real evidence in the case. Smoke and mirrors, members of the jury.*

'And so the effect of this is that we do not know what other activity Jamal Lowton was up to on the J2 number on the night leading up to the alleged murder?'

'We don't, no.'

'We can't say where the phone was, or who else Jamal Lowton may have been contacting on it?'

'No, I'm afraid not.'

Bob's delivery slows, not theatrically, but sufficiently to hint at the significance he wishes the jury to attach to his next question. 'Did you ever seize and examine Bernard Hooper's mobile phone?'

'No. It wasn't with his body. It seems that he lost it before encountering the defendants.'

Bob gives a pained smile. 'Or might this be one of those items which the police omitted to seize from the scene? Given the mistakes which you accept were made?'

Rose shrugs, defeated. 'I can't say.'

'What about Bernard Hooper's call data records? Did you obtain those?'

'No, that was not a line of inquiry we were asked to pursue.'

'So, we don't know, for example, whether there had been any telephone contact between Jamal, using the J2 number, and Bernard Hooper?'

'No,' concedes Rose. 'We don't know.'

Bob lets the answer settle, before going back in.

'And finally,' he says. 'You have told us about messages sent from Craig Mervyn-Scott's phone in which he appears to be making requests for weapons.'

'Yes, sir.'

'Who were those messages sent to?'

'It was an unregistered number, sir.'

'And, when you found that the number was unregistered, what

inquiries did you make to identify the person to whom Craig Mervyn-Scott was communicating? What did you do to establish the identity of the person who – on the face of the evidence you have – may well have supplied Craig Mervyn-Scott with the murder weapon?'

A third snigger. I look up expecting to see the same culprit – juror eight – as on the first two occasions. But that juror is studiously silent, considering Rose with curiosity. It must have been another. It doesn't matter. They are all certainly laughing inside. By now all twelve know the answer that Rose will give. Bob's questions are not merely prompts; they are spoilers.

'Nothing, sir. I hold up my hands. We did not follow up the number that Craig Mervyn-Scott was messaging about weapons.'

Something then occurs to me. I had reflexively assumed juror eight to be the offender, but the derisory snort did not, I realise, come from my right. It came from behind me.

I turn around as discreetly as I can and scan the dock.

Craig Mervyn-Scott is rocking in his seat. And he is smiling.

DAY 9 OF TRIAL – MONDAY

CHAPTER 33

Jennifer (counsel for the third defendant)

I could do without another hangover. Although today is only legal argument – so I don't need to worry about impressing a jury – and although there is only a limited aspect of it that affects Jamal, it would be easier without the feeling that somebody has parked a minibus behind my eyes. Whether this is an improvement on bats, I have yet to decide.

Maybe it was the judge's promise of a Monday off for the jury that sent mixed signals to my subconscious and subliminally green-lighted a three-day weekend. It seems unlikely; I am normally well-calibrated at keeping within the lines. Even when, on the difficult nights, I go beyond my limits, my brain usually pulls the emergency cord before I reach a state that is liable to impact upon the next morning's performance. But it is possible, my rational brain knows, that the exigencies of this case are taking their toll. The pretence that I am fine is harder than I have allowed myself to acknowledge. Truthfully, it is becoming exhausting.

The photographs of Craig Mervyn-Scott's bedroom, for instance. When I got home last night, I found myself staring into the emptiness of my spare room, visualising the squalor of that poor boy's existence. It took but minutes for my brain to then generate the inevitable contrast, summoning a vivid reconstruction of a space loved and adorned and occupied; guitars and scrappy *NME* posters hung across one wall, small golden rugby trophies lining the shelves opposite. Ollie's tall muscular body crumpling the duvet on the previously immaculate bed, shaking his dark curls out of his eyes to meet mine. The whole point of moving 200 miles away – apart from (unsuccessfully) putting distance between myself and Andrew – was to remove myself from a home in which I was converting Ollie's bedroom into a shrine, frozen in time. Yet my stupid masochistic brain insists on recreating one for me.

So it is that, while functional, I feel wretched this morning, and I am well aware that it shows. The hand tremors while applying my make-up did not help. Catching myself in the hallway mirror as I left the house, I saw Batman's nemesis staring back at me.

Jamal can tell. When I go down to the cells to see him first thing – alone, as thank fuckety Christ I don't have Caz with me today to see or smell me – he shuffles into the conference room and grins at me. 'Big weekend, miss?' he says, before I have even opened my mouth. I mumble something about not having slept well – not actually untrue – and divert him onto the business of the day.

'Today there is going to be a lot of lawyer-talk,' I say. 'Don't worry if you don't follow all of it. The important thing is that I do.'

He is still grinning, but thankfully does not – as he would be entirely within his rights to – query whether I am in a fit state to follow anything.

'We are going to be arguing about "bad character". The prosecution want to tell the jury about the times you've been in trouble before. And I am going to be saying that the judge shouldn't let them, as it's not fair. Does that make sense?'

He nods, grin dissipating and cogs evidently whirring. 'Are they going to tell the jury about the one on the bus?'

'That's part of the prosecution's application, yes.'

'But I was twelve! And that wasn't even my knife. I was told to hold it for like, a second. It's just that it looked bad on CCTV.'

'I know, and that's why you were only given a caution. And it's why I am going to be saying to the judge that it is completely different to the facts of this case. There was no suggestion that anybody used that knife for violence. I am going to say it would be unfair for the jury to hear about that.'

He nods, still troubled.

'Does it also mean,' he asks slowly, 'they're gonna bring up that time with me and Craig a few years back?'

'They want to, yes,' I reply calmly. 'And so does Arron's barrister. He is supporting the prosecution's application, because he thinks it will help Arron if he can show that you and Craig have been violent together before.'

'Fuck's sake, man.' He shakes his head. 'It was something and nothing. Just a little fucking bit of shoving in a pub.'

Well, it was an affray involving a lot of hefty punches and kicks, and half a dozen stools tossed at the bar staff. So the prosecution – and Bob Evans – are unsurprisingly submitting that this demonstrates a propensity for Craig and Jamal to use violence when intoxicated, which, together with Jamal's previous for carrying a knife in public, are issues lying at the heart of this case. But arguing the toss with Jamal now – and forcing my brain to parse the nuances of the Criminal Justice Act 2003 into Jamal-talk – is more than I can deal with at my present caffeine level, so I settle for a sympathetic nod.

'I know, Jamal. I know.'

An iMessage flashes up on my laptop.

Is everything ok?

I slam it shut. At some point I will probably have to offer an explanation for the half-dozen missed calls my ex-husband woke up to this morning, but now is not that time. As I gingerly rise and press the buzzer for security to open the door, Jamal pipes up.

'And what about Craig's other offence? Will the jury be told about that?'

'Oh, *that*,' I say, my eyes widening. 'Well, of course the prosecution *want* to tell the jury about that. But I don't think the judge will let them. I think he will say it is far too inflammatory.'

'What does that mean?'

'Sorry, Jamal. I mean, if the jurors hear about that, it will distract them from what this case is really about. If the judge lets the jury find out what else Craig did – they will convict him of murder without a second thought.'

CHAPTER 34

Craig (the first defendant)

I don't remember my first brief's name, but I remember her telling me I was lucky that I wasn't charged with violent disorder. We were in the duty room at the Youth Court, and she said that even though I was fourteen and it was my first offence, I'd got myself in a bad situation. If I went guilty to affray, I wouldn't go to prison, I'd just have to do some programme or some shit, and agree to go to these classes and talk about everything that had gone on.

I remember laughing at that, and she looked at me like I was taking the piss, and I had to say sorry, but no, I'm not laughing at you. I'm laughing because I'm like, seriously, where am I going to find the time to talk about everything that has been going on? And she started saying about how I'd go with my mum and meet this panel and they would come up with ideas and shit, and I was like, sorry, no. Like, literally – where am I going to find the time to do this? My mum can barely leave the house. I've got a little sister who depends on me, you know?

To be fair, she listened then, and when we went in court, she told the judge about what I had said, and how things had been for the past two years since my mum could no longer look after herself. And when the judge then gave me that order, for those six months all the different people who came into our lives – I could see they were trying to help. I did appreciate that. But at the end of the day, I was fourteen with a mum in a wheelchair who couldn't even get on the toilet by herself, and nobody else but me and K to be there. There's not nobody who is gonna suddenly come in and help my mum with what she needs, or do the shopping or make sure the electric is topped up, or lock Kayla in her room so she does her schoolwork instead of running around with some wasteman. That shit falls on me, now. So, yeah. Basically a few months after it had all kicked off, life carried on just the same as it had been.

Obviously I still saw Jamal. One of the things my offender manager said was that I should try to find different friends, because I'd told him how it had been Jamal's idea to go to the pub that night, and how Jamal had been the one to get us the flake, which at that time I'd never done before. And I said to my offender manager – Timothy, he was called – I said, 'Tim, on my mum's life, it wasn't actually Jamal's fault.' I said that shit had just been building and building, and I had been stressing and stressing and I had told Jamal that I needed to properly blow off some steam, not just blazing round his, but a proper night. I just needed to forget it all.

And I hold my hands up – by the time we got to the Lion, I was absolutely steaming. I was a mess. And I don't remember everything, but I know myself and I know I would have been chatting shit and causing beef. Jamal said the flake he had was like, basically import purity. He had got it from his brother – this was before Jamal started shotting for himself. Before he built his little empire. And so I was off my head, and whatever I said to those lads that made it all kick off, that's on me.

Respect to Jamal, though. He must have had as much to drink as me, but he was on point when it all went down. He proved that night why he is the guy you would want as your enforcer. And, to be fair to me, since that night – and it has been almost four years – I have not let myself get wrecked in that way. I don't like feeling like I'm not in control. I'd still score from time to time, obviously. But I know my limits. And while I am still mates with Jamal, I've not made the same choices as him. I'd never shot. Selling drugs always leads to problems. Just ask Bernard Hooper.

So in that way, maybe the judge's order did work. Apart from me ending up here, obviously. And apart from what happened earlier on New Year's Day.

They're talking about it now. Big Bird is telling the judge all about it, all the details, and then Mr Wyatt is saying how the jury shouldn't hear it. He's saying, 'It's wildly prejudicial!' over and over, his voice getting louder each time, and I have to look at my feet so the judge doesn't see me smiling.

And Arron's barrister is chipping in, saying that he wants the jury to know as well, and Mr Wyatt is basically telling him to shut the fuck up, but all lawyerly. And Jamal's lady stands up for a bit, but I swear down she looks like she's about to empty herself all over her computer and she then sits and puts her head in her hands. I'll tell you the truth, I can't follow what is going on, but eventually the judge makes them all stop talking, and now he's speaking.

He's saying, 'I refuse the bad character applications in relation to the first and third defendants. I will provide a full ruling later but, for now, I am satisfied that the earlier two matters are too old and too dissimilar to justify admission under the statutory gateways. In relation to the more recent matter relating to the first defendant, while a finely balanced exercise, I am satisfied that allowing it to go before the jury would have such an adverse effect on the fairness of proceedings that I ought not to allow it. This ruling is, of course, subject to anything that the defendants might say if and when they give evidence.'

I think that's good. Big Bird is sitting down and looking well vexed. Arron's barrister is smiling, but then the man is always smiling, you get me? He's like the happiest fucker I've ever met. Mr Wyatt swivels and winks at me, and I think that means we've won.

And now Arron's barrister is standing up again.

'Mr Evans,' the judge says, 'that deals, does it not, with the defendant bad character applications?'

'It does, Your Honour. But there is—'

'Yes, there is a separate application on behalf of your lay client. A non-defendant bad character application.'

'Yes, Your Honour,' Arron's barrister says to him. 'It is an application by the defence to adduce the bad character of Bernard Hooper.'

CHAPTER 35

Jennifer (Counsel for the Third Defendant)

I have no dog in this fight. The bad character of Bernard Hooper, while highly unlikely to endear the deceased to the jury, is not something that has any relevance to Jamal's defence. It means that, while Bob develops his submissions to a bored-looking Jeremy Letts, I will have a few minutes to recharge. I have already drained the water carafe in front of me, resisting the urge to dissolve an Alka-Seltzer in its tepid contents, and I ponder the reaction I would receive from the bench were I to fish under my seat to retrieve the still-steaming Americano that I didn't have time to finish before we kicked off.

I place my hand on my forehead as if concentrating on my laptop screen, and savour a delicious semi-second of shut-eye. It turns out not to be delicious; it in fact serves only to ratchet up the volume of the bassline in my head. Swallowing a sudden wave of nausea, I realise that distraction may offer the safest route, and focus on the Word doc in front of me. It is titled 'Closing Speech Thoughts', and acts as a disordered log of the snippets of evidence and half-formed rhetoric that strike me as potentially usable as we go. It is not a long document. Nor, at present, does it augur a particularly compelling narrative for Jamal's case.

My lay client, if he gives evidence, can tell the jury that he had left Garth Yard before the violence began. But he can't – won't? – give any explanation for why the three of them were out together that night, or how they ended up alone in an alleyway with Bernard Hooper. He won't comment on the allegations made by his co-defendants, other than to repeat his insistence of his own non-involvement. And as for what the jury have heard about the damning material on his phone, Jamal can only offer a pseudo-philosophical, 'It is what it is.'

Even this morning, when I made a final attempt at discussing the subject of Bob Evans's application, and the allegations that underpin Arron Freeman's case, in the hope that something new would emerge in his instructions, all Jamal would give me was avoidant eye contact and an unenthusiastic, 'I don't know anything about that.'

Inevitably in my conferences with Jamal, I have had to guard fiercely against regression. Caz's presence has helped. But on the rare days that she has not been able to attend, and it has been just me and Jamal, sitting across from each other over a screwed-down trestle table, I cannot stop it. The second I take off my wig, I am no longer counsel, but Mum, sitting over our breakfast bar and administering advice no less robust and no less empathetic, but just as scarcely received.

There is little physical resemblance between Jamal and Ollie. If there had been, I think it would have made this impossible. That they are the opposites in build, colouring and – obviously – background has been what I have clung to. The victim in this case being a pensioner rather than a teenage boy, also. But there is something in Jamal's manner – the way in which, when I am telling him things he does not want to hear, he narrows and lowers his eyes and folds his arms tightly across his chest with his thumbs pointing to the sky – that is so infuriatingly Oliverish that I want to reach across and shake him. I want to shake him out of his teenage stupidity, shake him back in time to before he made decisions that could not now be unmade. And when I've finished shaking him free from his stupidity, I want to pull him against me, and feel the heat of his body spread through mine. I want to hug him like I should have hugged him every single day, not because I idealistically believe that more hugs – more love – could have stopped what, in hindsight, would come to look inevitable, but because, given what I could see unfolding, I should have allowed for the possibility, however unthinkable, that there might come a day when the world stopped.

The decisions were stupid, but then so were the arguments. So were my efforts at turning him around. However competent I might consider myself at persuading juries, my bag of rhetorical tricks did little to convince my own child. Too often and too quickly, cajoling turned into shouting and logic was jettisoned for hyperbole. The compassionate and pragmatic handling of immature, scared young men which, according to my chambers website, was my professional hallmark, deserted me in my own home. When the youthful scrapes that Finlay routinely got himself into threatened in adolescence to morph into something more intractable, and to drag Ollie into a world which I knew all too well but for which, as a mother, I had ill-prepared him, I was no match for whatever arguments were being made by the other side. I had no answer to it.

The factual distinction, obviously, is that my advice to my clients is post-facto. There is no fear that the worst might happen, because it already has. There is no use in telling Jamal, however calmly or hysterically, of the stupidity of hanging out with people who carry knives. There is no use in reminding him that people like that, who would expose you to the risk of solicited violence, are not friends in any real sense. Or that just because you are not the one holding the knife, that does not mean you can't be harmed by it. Once a blade has been unsheathed, you have little control over where it is plunged. Into whom it is plunged.

However much I regress when with Jamal, I have not yet chased him out of a house onto a moonlit suburban street screaming that his decisions, and his stupid fucking friendships, will be the death of him.

Bob is now speaking.

'Your Honour has read our written submissions. The application in respect of Bernard Hooper is made under Section 100(1)(d) of the Criminal Justice Act 2003. We submit that the jury ought to be entitled to hear about Mr Hooper's previous conviction.'

'This is the matter from 1978, yes?'

'Your Honour, it is. And I make plain at the outset, I recognise that it is a conviction of some antiquity. However, given the nature of that offence, we submit that it carries substantial probative value in relation to an issue of substantial importance in the context of this case. Your Honour knows from Arron Freeman's Defence Statement how, he says, the violence came about. And what, in particular, provoked it. This conviction lends significant weight to the credibility of Mr Freeman's defence.'

'I see. Of course, at this stage the jury have not heard anything that is in the Defence Statement. And nor will they, unless and until your lay client chooses to give evidence.'

'Your Honour, I can say with confidence that, given the nature of the evidence that he faces, this is a case in which Arron Freeman will be stepping into the witness box. So the jury will hear about this issue. The question is whether, in Your Honour's judgement, the previous conviction is admissible to assist the jury's determination of that issue.'

Letts considers this.

'Very well. I'll hear your submissions. Remind me – where will I find Mr Hooper's antecedent record?'

'It's on the Digital Case System at Section Q, Your Honour. The conviction was recorded against his alias: his former name, Bernard Hopper. If you look at page two, you can see . . .'

'Yes, I have it. August 1978. A single conviction. Indecent assault of a female child.'

CHAPTER 36

Arron (the second defendant)

Funny how Craigy's statement in his interview doesn't mention anything about revenge.

I don't even know what he was playing at, putting that in. Saying something that he's then stuck with, which was snide to me and Jamal, and which was always going to look like bullshit once other stuff started to come out. He knew they had our phones. He knew that the stuff about Hooper was gonna come out, even if the prosecution don't want to see what's under their own noses. And now, what? He's gonna get in the box and try to stick to what he said to the police? When he knows what the jury have heard, and what else I'm gonna tell them?

I was always going to go no comment, even before my solicitor gave me the advice. Obviously I panicked a bit when I was arrested, when all I could hear were a hundred sirens, and all I could see was a sky full of flashing blue lights, and then crowds of cops in black, spilling out of their cars and charging towards us with their sticks held high. This bird went for me – she was small, but my God did she have some power behind her. She knocked us clean to the floor, and to be fair, yeah, I panicked. I almost said something I shouldn't have. But once they'd put the cuffs on and thrown me in the van, once everything started to get a bit quieter and I had space to think, it was all a bit clearer.

'Give yourself time to breathe, and time to think,' was what

Graham used to say. Before making an important decision, you have to let yourself take time. Because there's no point trying to take that time after the decision's been made. Anyone can make a quick decision, he'd say. The trick is making a good decision.

So I took my time in my interview. I went no comment, and decided I wouldn't say anything official until we knew what the evidence was. And it was a relief – because, although lots of it looks dead bad, there is a lot which we can show the jury that helps. They haven't seen it all yet – Mr Evans says we have to wait until the defence case for most of it – but in the prosecution's own evidence there are things we can point to and be like, 'Look, Arron Freeman is telling the truth.'

It was a good decision. To be fair, Graham knew a lot about good decisions. That's why he had a good job and a decent car and had never been in trouble. While obviously we are very different people – I don't think he'd last five minutes where I grew up – the things he'd done with his life were the things I wanted to do with mine. And the mad part is, when all this went down, it was all falling into place. I had a girlfriend. We had money coming in. We were looking to get our own place once I left Rosewoods. She was getting ready to tell her mam about us.

And then, bam. I find myself here. Spending six months in Twyford waiting for the trial, then another six months coz the prosecution barrister has a heart attack and there's nobody else. A year of my life away from all of it. I'm not mithered about being away from Rosewoods, to be fair – in many ways, it's better in here than it is out there. Better food, anyway. The gym is sound. The other lads are basically the same, only they don't chat shit pretending to be hard like at Rosewoods, because they are properly hard. So you know where you stand. I only have to share the shitter with one pad mate, not twenty filthy scruffs, so it stays cleaner, even if we've not had a toilet seat for eight months.

But going no comment was a good decision. Coz it means that

now I'm able to say to the jury, this is the truth, and look at all of this evidence that shows it's the truth. I can say that what happened in the ginnel was nothing to do with me. I can show the jury that Bernard Hooper taught piano or singing or something at Ableford Primary School a few years back. I can talk about the conversation Craig and me had a few weeks before New Year's, when he told me how Hooper had taught his little sister, Kayla, when she was about six or seven. I can say that, according to Craig, Bernard Hooper used to keep Kayla back after lessons to show her how to do special breathing for singing. And that he'd help her by making her stand on this little plastic chair, and then putting his hand under her skirt and down her knickers, but that it was a special way of breathing that she shouldn't tell anybody else about, because otherwise they'd sound as good as she did. And she never told, until that day in November when Craig found out.

I can say that from the day Craig told me this, he became obsessed with finding this man, and making him pay. And that, on New Year's Eve, when we rolled into town and Craig saw Bernard Hooper, he and Jamal spied their chance to do just that.

I'll tell them all of it.

And it'll be obvious I'm telling the truth.

Because, as Mr Evans is telling the judge right now, it turns out that Bernard Hooper has done this kind of thing before.

CHAPTER 37

HHJ Jeremy Letts (the judge)

You just can't go around slicing up nonces. That is what it boils down to.

I imagine I will refine the phrasing before I hand down my ruling. The nonce's widow is in court, for one. But the point remains: this application appears to me to be an overtly egregious attempt to sling mud at the deceased. I cannot in good conscience say that the fact that Hooper many moons ago received a fine for popping his hand down a teenager's blouse for a cheeky squeeze has *substantial probative value in relation to a matter in issue of substantial importance in the context of the case as a whole.* There is also a question of sauce and geese and ganders: if I am not allowing the jury to know that two of the defendants have convictions for violence, I am not minded to let the defence tell the jury that Hooper is a convicted sex offender.

Freeman is of course at liberty to put his defence before the jury. He can say that the murder was instigated by Mervyn-Scott, due to Mervyn-Scott believing that Hooper had diddled his little sister. And Mervyn-Scott can – as Baxter Wyatt tells me he will – deny any such thing and tell the jury that Freeman is off on a frolic, inventing some cockamamie tale for his own ends.

But an historic conviction, factually different from the much more serious abuse supposedly alleged by the sister, cannot sensibly assist the jury in determining who is telling the truth on this point.

As Baxter Wyatt points out, the old conviction was disclosed to Freeman's team *before* he first raised this defence. If Freeman had volunteered this defence in interview, and Hooper's previous sexual offending was *then* disclosed, it would provide some support for the truth of Freeman's account. But in the absence of any independent evidence to show that Mervyn-Scott's sister ever made a sexual complaint against Hooper – neither side, it seems, is going to be calling her as a witness – then it is all too easy to suggest that Freeman has invented this defence upon learning about the conviction. In which case there is little value in the conviction going before the jury at all.

Bob Evans is having a good go. He says that these are all arguments that can be made to the jury in closing speeches if the previous conviction goes in. He points out that the school records suggest that Hooper did spend some time at the school of Kayla Scott, and relies on the fact that somebody called Hooper a 'paedo' on the snuff home video – but I am not persuaded. In a town like Ableford, a music teacher like Bernard Hooper would have overlapped with almost every child in state education. It doesn't mean that he diddled all, or any, of them. And 'paedo' is the epithet *du jour* of today's youth, irrespective of the recipient's sexual leanings.

No. The fact of Hooper's previous conviction has minimal bearing on the questions of whether Craig Mervyn-Scott knew that his sister had made an allegation against Hooper, and whether that was the motive for the murder. It is muck-raking. Nothing more. I am quite satisfied that Baxter Wyatt, and the prosecution, are correct, and that the jury should not be told anything about this.

I credit the prosecution as a courtesy, but the legwork in that legal argument was all Baxter Wyatt's. Arshad sat there rolling her eyes while Bob Evans was on his feet, and then got up and squawked two sentences which added absolutely nothing to Wyatt's submissions. If that was her at full pelt, Christ help the Crown.

Maybe her lack of bite is an overcorrection. Even disclosing this previous conviction was a pretty generous application of the test. I suppose I have to allow the possibility that inviting this application and all but conceding that the jury should know that her sympathetic victim is a kiddie fiddler is all part of her efforts at rehabilitation. Time was, you found yourself in the eye of a disclosure scandal like hers, and you would never prosecute again.

I was discussing this with Andrew Warner over lunch last week. While I was aware of the nature of Aliyah Arshad's claim to ignominy, I was not previously acquainted with the detail. It was five years ago, Andrew told me. A case called George Burrows. Some poor chap accused of rape. Bog standard relationship fare, he-said-she-said, man of good character, consent in issue, the usual. The chap had replaced his mobile phone since the relationship ended, but was adamant that there would be material on the girl's that would assist him. Nothing to disclose, came the reply from CPS RASSO. At trial, defence counsel asked Arshad to personally review the phone records to confirm that there was nothing disclosable, and was assured that she had.

The chap was potted and given eight years. Fast forward nine months, and his house has been sold to fund his legal fees, and his sister is packing up his belongings when she finds his old phone in a shoebox or some such. Turns out the thing is full to the gills with messages between defendant and complainant, casting an entirely different complexion on the relationship. And when new prosecution counsel then reviews the complainant's phone download from the original trial, they find three hundred pages of texts, Facebook messages, and so forth, all disclosable, including messages in which she boasts to her girlfriends about having stitched up her ex. All missed by the police, the CPS and Arshad.

Andrew emailed me the Court of Appeal judgment, and it was brutal. '*We find it inconceivable that any prosecutor reviewing this material would not have immediately recognised its significance. We do not make any finding as to whether this is due to lack of competence or bad faith; it suffices simply to observe that a more flagrant failing in disclosure is difficult to imagine. We have no hesitation in concluding that the conviction is unsafe.*' Stick that on your chambers profile and smoke it, eh?

The story was all over the front pages of the broadsheets for a week or so, and there was some excited chatter from certain MPs making all sorts of hollow declarations. An internal investigation followed, and I don't know the ins and outs, but it seems that the axe swung heaviest on the CPS lawyer and the disclosure officer. Whatever Arshad said to the investigators – the waving of the diversity card, perhaps – it resulted in her evading any sanction. She was *persona non grata* at the Crown Prosecution Service for a few years, until a lack of alternatives meant she was handed this trial as a return. But she persevered with a moderately successful defence practice, and the whole business was evidently no impediment to her taking silk.

Still, I muse to myself as I start to read out my ruling, I would not relish the thought of being prosecuted by her.

Certainly not if I were innocent.

CHAPTER 38

Aliyah (the prosecutor)

I slam the boot of my Discovery and tug my Tumi 19 Degree cabin suitcase up the pebbled drive and towards the house, instinctively looking back over my shoulder to check that the electronic gates have properly shut.

There is one remaining bottle of Fattoria Le Pupille which has been sitting patiently, counting down the days until I close my case, and it would be rude to keep her waiting any longer than is strictly necessary. I nudge open the front door, kick off my pumps and head straight to the drawing room, plucking a Bordeaux glass from the dresser. I hurry through the hallway, dragging the soles of my feet through the plush grey pile which snakes through to the top of the dusted oak staircase that we had designed when we renovated the wine cellar four years ago. I glide down, retrieve my prize, and within minutes am curled on the midnight blue sofa in the snug, under the dimmed spotlights, slugging a generous quarter of the bottle into my glass. As the first drop hits my tongue I close my eyes, and the tumult of the past two weeks feels – at last – as if it may just have been worth it.

The grandmother clock chimes six, and I know that I have less than half an hour before Clara returns home with the girls. What I really do not want to do is to spend those precious minutes thinking about the trial, but detachment eludes me. The edited highlights of today's proceedings loop in my head, although it is not a wholly unflattering reel. My submissions on the admissibility of Bernard Hooper's bad character were poised, succinct and, evidently, highly persuasive.

Too persuasive, if anything. A part of me was hoping that Letts would rule against us, and allow Bernard Hooper's previous to go before the jury. I could never have conceded the application – the CPS would have plenty to say if I agreed that the defence could parade a murder victim's irrelevant historic offending. But I would not have been heartbroken to lose the argument. While it would have meant sacrificing the jury's sympathy for Bernard Hooper, losing would also have allowed me to demonstrate to the jury the manipulative cynicism of Arron Freeman. It would have exposed the evolution of his defence. First, he gives a no comment interview. Next, the prosecution dutifully discloses Bernard Hooper's previous convictions. And then, in his defence statement, Arron Freeman offers, for the very first time, a fantastical story artfully constructed around those convictions.

It would have been an enjoyable line of cross-examination. But not to be. I will just have to confront Mr Freeman's lies on their own terms.

Setting my glass on a Mulberry leather coaster and lighting a Jo Malone candle, I pause and breathe deeply as the space around me suffuses with Pomegranate Noir. The action replays persist: me, standing before the jury and self-assuredly reading out the final piece of the prosecution case; five pages of 'agreed facts' – a summary of uncontentious evidence, mostly filling continuity gaps or confirming matters to which allusion has already been made by counsel earlier in the trial. The unchallenged scientific evidence, the identification procedures attended by the eyewitnesses, and so forth. A terminally dull exercise, but a necessary formality. It would have been livened up somewhat if the judge had allowed me to tell the jury about the previous convictions of Craig Mervyn-Scott and Jamal Lowton, but following Letts's ruling I had to delete the draft agreed facts I had devised telling the jury about their previous orgy of drunken, coke-fuelled violence. It's a pity. It would have been a satisfying note on which to close my case. Even more so if I had been allowed to throw into the mix Craig Mervyn-Scott's other offence as well. That really would have been curtains. That said, it is not as if I am otherwise short of evidence demonstrating their proclivities. If I were a juror, I would already be more than satisfied that I had the measure of these youths. The phone material alone would convince me.

Winning, plainly, is not important to me. That is not how I judge myself. I present the case fairly and scrupulously to the best of my ability, and what happens thereafter is in the lap of the jury. That is how justice is done. But at the same time, losing this trial is unthinkable. There is more than enough evidence already – before the defendants lumber into the witness box to convict themselves – for the jury to be sure of guilt. Whatever knocks the prosecution has sustained over the past weeks, the structural integrity of our case remains intact. I have been measured and adaptable in how I have approached the evidence, in a way that, I hope, has softened the blows landed by the defence. I have not overreached. My case theory is as solid now I have closed my case as it was when I opened it to the jury. There is simply no other explanation that fits the evidence the jury have heard.

It has long been my practice to draft my closing speech before I deliver my opening. The habit is inculcated at Bar school, where you are taught that every question asked of a witness should be with a view to establishing your case theory; the interpretation of the facts that you will ultimately be asking the court to accept. You cannot successfully navigate without knowing your destination. Most of my peers jettisoned the advice no sooner than they had passed their finals and bought their wigs. Speeches tardily bullet-pointed over the court lunch break, or even delivered improvised *sans* notes, became almost a badge of honour. The robing room equivalent of a student's humblebrag of barely having revised for an exam.

Whereas I, knowing intimately the strengths and weaknesses of the evidence, committed my closing arguments to polished prose a month before this trial began. Truly unforeseen events may call for tweaks as the trial unfolds, but if you understand your case, there should be few surprises. So it is that, while the vagaries of Paul Bell and Farid Suhail have precipitated a modest revision, the scientific evidence remains precisely where I expected it to be when I clicked save on 'Closing v1.1a' four weeks ago.

I knew the concessions that the defence would extract. I knew that the experts would have to, in good faith, agree the propositions put to them; agree that there *could* be innocent explanations for their findings. And I expected that one or two jurors would excitedly murmur and take notes as the defence, with all the subtlety of a rhinoceros performing a root canal, extracted alternative rationalisations and bandied them in the jurors' faces. But, as the relevant paragraph of my speech will remind them, anybody can invent a story after the event, to fit conveniently around the established evidence.

These three defendants murdered Bernard Hooper. That, I announce to Nala, our rotund British shorthair as she hops onto the cushion next to me, is all there is to it. Everything else is smoke, mirrors and red herrings.

That being undoubtedly true, there are still curious features to this case. Particularly regarding Bernard Hooper, né Hopper. It is not only his apparent predilection for young girls, nor how, troublingly, he managed to evade the DBS and obtain work with children simply by changing one letter in his name. No, there were other curious facets to this man.

His finances, for one. In the early stages of the investigation, when the police were trying to establish Bernard Hooper's movements on the night, DS Chris Rose had an uncharacteristic fit of productivity and obtained Hooper's bank statements. This was how we were able to place him making a purchase in the Co-op shortly before he met the defendants. What the statements also showed, however, was several large withdrawals in December – in the thousands – running his account overdrawn. Given what his widow said in her statement about visiting family in Australia, I had assumed this was just a pre-Christmas splurge, but the cynic in me wonders if there isn't something else.

Ultimately, it does not matter. Class A, prostitutes, mail-order kiddie pics – his secret has gone with him, wherever he has ended up. The speculation is mildly titillating, and something I might share with defence counsel over a bottle once the trial is over, but Hooper's financial activities have no relevance to his murder. The information cannot reasonably assist the defences that are being run, so the bank statements have not been disclosed. Craig Mervyn-Scott's defence alludes to some kind of botched robbery by Hooper, but even if Hooper was cash-poor, he was asset-rich, and being a few grand overdrawn is hardly likely to be solved by robbing some teen wastrels on the street. No. This information cannot help.

I am sure.

Every time I have made a decision on disclosure in this trial, I have double- and triple-checked my working. It is not that I doubt my judgement; merely that I can feel the glare of the spotlight, given everything that happened five years ago. The truth – not that the gossipmongers would care to hear it – is that the awful disclosure failings in the case of George Burrows had nothing to do with me. I was indeed asked at the eleventh hour by defence counsel to do the CPS lawyer's job for her and re-review the complainant's mobile phone download. But the truth is that I did not. Could not. The ridiculous pressures of time, of my other cases and of single-handedly orchestrating childcare for two primary schoolers simply did not allow for it. I should not have given the defence the assurance that it had been checked, I know. But I took on trust – idiotically – that the police and CPS combined could not have missed anything *that* obvious. It was a lesson learned the hard way, through a year of embarrassing Court of Appeal proceedings and an eighteen-month Bar Standards Board investigation. But, as the BSB eventually accepted, the error was not my fault. It was not the case, contrary to vile rumour, that I had seen the exculpatory text messages and covered them up. That is not how I have ever operated. Would ever operate.

I float back upstairs to fetch my laptop. One of the consequences of my ordeal is that I am now, if anything, too diligent. Every square inch of every document is scrutinised twice. Which is why, as I return with my MacBook Pro to my sacred spot, I will be spending the rest of my evening rereading Craig Mervyn-Scott's phone records, ahead of his giving evidence tomorrow.

Chris assures me that the original disclosure officer – the one who conveniently threw a sickie prior to my instruction – has been through these with 'a fine tooth cone'. But – lesson learned – I want to be able to truthfully say that I have checked it for myself. As the screen whirrs into life, my inbox springs up, and I swiftly minimise the cacophony of unread emails. One screams *Urgent Message About Your Latest Credit Card Statement* and there is a new one from Sasha, with the subject header *Check out this 1-bedroom studio for sale on Rightmove!* In the body of the message, he has written: *In case your trial goes tits up . . .*

Fucking hilarious. Maybe I should reply with a link to Ableford comprehensive. That would save us £40k a year. See how much of a sense of humour he has about the girls going state.

I click on Adobe and wait for the phone records to load: 4,632 pages, of which I have read just over half. Having already isolated the activity for the seventy-two hours up to New Year's Eve, I am satisfied that there is nothing over that period that the jury have not already been told about, and I am now scanning through the dozens of illiterate WhatsApp chats and thousands of irrelevant

YouTube searches that occupied Craig Mervyn-Scott's life over the preceding months.

Nothing, nothing, nothing. I reach for my glass, and Nala skitters over my lap and off the sofa, pressing a stray paw on the keyboard as she goes, which sends the PDF skipping. Cursing her, I replace my glass and try to re-find my place. And then I see it.

That entry *cannot* be right. I blink, waiting for the illusion to disappear. It doesn't. I stare at the date stamp. This does not make sense. Yet, as I scroll down, there it is on the next page, too. I scroll back up. It is still there.

I compute the ramifications. Whichever way this is looked at, it has the potential to change everything. It tosses my entire case theory up in the air. Everything I have told the jury – everything in my pre-drafted closing speech! Yes, it probably hammers a nail into one defendant. But it leaves the prosecution case against another in tatters.

Shit. Shit shit shit a fucking brick.

My mind fizzes. There are also the reputational considerations. My name attached to late disclosure of crucial material which should have been spotted months ago – the robing room whispers will go into overdrive. Few will care about the mitigation: that the investigation has been conducted by a buffoon; that the disclosure officer pulled a sickie; that the CPS reviewing lawyer has a hundred and fifty other cases on her desk; that CPS management refused to authorise two counsel for this case, depriving me of a junior to review the unused material. The headline will be 'Aliyah Arshad: Disclosure Fuck-up'. Again.

This is my reward for diligence, is it? I shout at Nala. *This is what I get for caring more about my job than other people do theirs?* If I had just left my laptop upstairs in my bag, settled in for a deserved night off, this would never even have come to light. If I hadn't seen it, it wouldn't be disclosable. And if it wasn't disclosable, then perhaps the most important trial of my career – the trial on which so, so much depends – would not be about to implode before the jury's eyes.

I exhale. The irony is exquisitely bitter. Screwed in George Burrows for not having the time to read the phone download. Screwed in my first prosecution murder trial for making the time to read the phone download.

I empty my glass.

Of course, there is another possibility, I say to Nala jokingly. It is possible, I suppose, that maybe I did leave my laptop in my bag tonight.

It's not a particularly funny joke. But it's also not . . . implausible? It is possible – reasonable, even – that, as with George Burrows, I have not had time in this case to do everybody else's job for them. It is possible that I have not conducted my own review. That I have not seen anything. And, if asked, this time I would be upfront and say that I have made no checks myself, and that any decisions on disclosure have been made by the CPS. And if there is nothing further to be disclosed, then we are exactly where we were twenty minutes ago, when I sat down and uncorked my Fattoria Le Pupille, and celebrated a case expertly navigated on a course to convictions, and toasted the success-to-be of my first murder in silk, prosecuted fairly and scrupulously, to the best of my ability, ensuring that justice, for all concerned, is done.

Another email pings through. I close the laptop and refuel my glass.

PART II

THE DEFENCE CASES

DAY 10 OF TRIAL – TUESDAY

CHAPTER 39

Craig (the first defendant)

I'm vexed today. I needed to get some proper shut-eye last night. It wasn't even the flashbacks this time. The van got back to the prison at fucking half past eight, so I missed dinner, and my stomach was making noises all night. Then at around midnight, the little spicehead in the pad next door was having one of his fucking episodes, losing his shit about literally nothing, and when Danielle – who to be fair is one of the decent screws – when she came and opened his hatch and told him to shut the fuck up, he potted her. The stench of piss and shit made me gag from where I was sitting, so fuck knows how Danielle felt. And so then it bare kicked off, and all the screws piled in and the kid got a proper bending-up and was dragged off to the block. And after that drama I'm just lying there, wide awake, not getting a wink of sleep. Then we got knocked on at half-five to get on the van, before they'd handed out the breakfast packs, so I've not had jack shit to eat since yesterday lunchtime.

So yeah, basically, I'm not happy. My eyes hurt and I can't string a sentence together. I keep losing my thoughts before I've got them out.

And today matters.

The jury's gonna decide what they're gonna decide based on what I say today. That's what Mr Wyatt reckons. He was all, *You don't have to give evidence, but the judge will tell the jury they can hold that against you. And it would mean the jury not getting to hear your side of the story.* And I need them to hear my story. I need them to understand why it went down the way it did. I need the jury to see that the prosecution don't know what the fuck they're talking about.

So even though Mr Wyatt says I have a choice, I really don't.

When he came down to see me this morning, I was struggling to keep up with what he was saying. To be fair, I often don't follow many of the words he uses, but today my brain was just not clicking with any of it. I wanted to ask him to say bits of it again, but before I could think of the question, he was talking about something else, so I just allowed it.

Parts of it I got, coz I've heard it before. Telling me that giving evidence means being cross-examined by three barristers all trying to trip me up and make it look like I'm lying. Mr Wyatt was like, *They're all going to try to get under your skin, to provoke a reaction.* Well, so what? At the end of the day, it's about taking responsibility. I've never pussied out of a fight. I have been through enough shit with Mum and with Kayla, and I've proved that I will stand my ground and do what I know is right. So some pussyhole in a wig is gonna try to take a shot? Good luck to them, you feel me? New Year's Eve shows that nobody fucks with me or my family. Just fucking try it and see what happens.

I'm rubbing my eyes and trying not to yawn as the judge walks in and sits down. I look around me at Arron and Jamal, but they're staring forward. Even just the way Jamal is sitting winds me up, slouching back with his hands in his joggers. Mr Wyatt says that if I kick off when the other barristers are having a go, it will be the worst thing I could do, but right now I feel like every little thing is getting to me.

The jury are coming in, and I'm trying hard not to watch them in case they look back at me and see that I'm on edge. I can feel my heart banging in my chest, so loud that I swear the jury must be able to hear. I close my eyes and breathe deep. Not so deep that it shows, but just enough to steady myself. It's what Kayla's therapist showed her for her panic attacks, and what Kayla showed me when she was trying to talk me out of what she guessed I was planning to do. It didn't work then, obviously. But right now, it is helping. Everything is slowing. The rattling in my ribs is getting quieter with every deep breath.

It is all right, I say to myself. I can do this. Just tell them what I need to tell them. Don't lose my temper. And breathe. There's nothing to it. Breathe. Breathe. Breathe.

'Mr Wyatt?' says the judge, when all the jurors have sat down.

'Your Honour,' Mr Wyatt says, sticking his chest out and making himself big. 'On behalf of the defence for Craig Mervyn-Scott, I call Craig Mervyn-Scott.'

CHAPTER 40

Aliyah (the prosecutor)

'Your full name, please.'

'Craig Mervyn-Scott.'

The youth in the witness box jerks his head to flick his lank, greasy hair out of his eyes and moves his body ninety degrees to face the jury. His gaze is attached to Baxter Wyatt, awaiting the first question, which allows me a moment to study him. The grey encircling his eyes adds a few years, but the acne running down his sallow cheeks, inflamed by razor burn, takes them off again. Today he has forsaken the pale grey sweatshirt and joggers combo that has hitherto served as his uniform, and somebody – his sister? – has issued him with a box-creased, long-sleeved white polyester shirt, which he has buttoned up to the neck. The bagginess on the arms has the effect of semi-swallowing his upper half, but not so much that the broadness of his frame is disguised. He still looks like he could pack a punch. Which very much suits my purposes.

'Now, you have seen how other witnesses give evidence,' Baxter Wyatt says sharply, dispelling any doubt that the jurors might have been entertaining as to whether Wyatt would adopt a fluffier tone of examination with his own client. 'And the same rules apply to you. Look at the jury when speaking, and ensure that you keep your voice loud enough for them to hear. Got it?'

Mervyn-Scott offers a grunt of comprehension.

'Let us start,' Baxter Wyatt says slowly, 'with an easy one. How old are you?'

The inaudible reply provokes an immediate rebuke.

'No. What did I just say? Nobody will hear you if you mumble. Try again, please. How old are you?'

'Seventeen.'

'Better. And how old were you at the time that this jury is concerned with, that is, New Year's Eve 2023 and New Year's Day 2024?'

'I would have been sixteen.'

Wyatt bowls some further softballs, acclimatising his client to the rhythm of the questioning and the required volume of the replies. Every drop in levels elicits an elongated 'Nooo!', a method of conditioning which swiftly yields results, as by the time Wyatt is ready to move on to matters of substance, the jurors are no longer leaning forward to hear and have eased back in their seats.

I have reflected overnight on what I might have found had I reviewed Craig Mervyn-Scott's phone records, which, of course, it transpires I did not. And it seems to me that not reviewing them is, in many ways, the fairest course. It avoids messiness and undue complexity, neither of which benefits any of the parties. And there is also the point, it occurs to me, that the disclosure officer has already signed off this material as *clearly not disclosable*. Who am I, after all, to question the judgement of an experienced disclosure officer? Even if I had seen something, which of course I have not.

I softly type Craig Mervyn-Scott's answers as, with Wyatt's help, he begins his autobiography. The more he talks, the more he looks at the jurors, not making eye contact with any one, but giving a passable impression of addressing the collective.

'My mum died giving birth to me,' he says. 'Obviously I didn't know her, so she's just a name to me. Sheena Mervyn.'

'What about your father?' Wyatt asks. Mervyn-Scott explains, periodically apologising for his incautious language, that Craig Scott Senior had assumed the burden of parenthood for a full two years before walking out, leaving his girlfriend Paula to raise his son and their newborn daughter, Kayla.

'Paula was basically my mum,' Mervyn-Scott says. 'She did the whole adoption thing after my dad fucked off, and to be fair, she did her best. But she had her own thing going on, you get me?'

In case the jurors did not 'get him', he is encouraged to spell out Paula's thing.

'It was drinking, basically. Like, she would have these boyfriends, and they . . .' He looks at Wyatt, who nods. 'Like, no offence, but they were just wastemen. And they would always, like, hit her and stuff. And when it first happened, she would fight back, but then they would just give me or K a slap instead, and so she just allowed it. Y'know, like, it was better for them to smack her than to smack us. And maybe she reckoned that it would hurt less if she was wasted, I dunno. Maybe it just made it easier for her to forget about all that shit. But whatever it was, she was basically downing half a bottle of voddy, easy, before breakfast, and that was most days. And that made it hard for her to hold down a job, which pissed off her boyfriends even more when she wasn't bringing in any doe . . .'

The words start to coagulate as his pace increases. Wyatt holds up a palm.

'Right,' he says. 'And is it correct that – and we do not need to descend into the details – but is it correct that around 2018 there came a time when Paula became very unwell, and required care and support with everyday living?'

Wyatt is being deliberately circumspect. He knows that this is a potential landmine. His choice of language is intended to steer Mervyn-Scott away from the finer details of his mother's health, in case the boy says something stupid that gives me a chance to renew my bad character application.

Mervyn-Scott nods. 'Yeah.'

'And who provided that care and support?'

'Well, me. And Kayla a bit. The Social were in and out. But it was mostly me.'

'And how old were you when you started to care for your mother?'

He thinks. 'I was eleven.'

Further questions establish that this remained the position until December 2023. As of that year, the family were living in a three-bed ground-floor flat on the Rosewoods Estate – the local authority having eventually relocated them to accommodation adjusted for his mother's mobility needs. Mervyn-Scott would handle the shopping and most of the cooking (by which I assume he means the collection of takeaways). He claims that he would also take responsibility for maintaining a baseline of cleanliness, although given the visible standard of his personal hygiene, I imagine this line to be subterranean.

Pushing hard on the sympathy button, Wyatt lingers on the topic of the family routine. When she was not at school, Kayla would be on hand for the toileting and bathing duties, but the defendant, allegedly anxious that his sister enjoy a more fruitful education than his own, discouraged her from staying at home on his account. Monday to Friday, therefore, he juggled his reduced timetable at his Pupil Referral Unit around his mother's, taking her to doctors' appointments, physical therapy and the community centre, and organising his own social life around her sleeping patterns, rendering him virtually nocturnal.

Family portrait coloured, Wyatt moves on to something new.

'Now, how do you know Arron Freeman?'

I note several jurors instinctively looking at the dock, where Arron Freeman is sitting and staring at the floor. I hit return to start a new paragraph.

'He's just a mate.'

'I think we can do a little better than that. How and when did you first meet Arron Freeman?'

He says that he first met Freeman when they were fourteen or fifteen, after the latter moved into the Rosewoods Family Centre, the children's home located two streets down from *chez* Mervyn-Scott. Mervyn-Scott knocked around with some of the boys from the home, and they had introduced him to 'Manchestaaah', as the residents had christened their new arrival. The youths soon realised they shared common interests, and became good friends.

'What interests in particular did you and Mr Freeman share?' asks Wyatt.

'Just chilling, basically.' Wyatt corkscrews an eyebrow, and the hint is taken. 'Yeah, I'll be honest with you, it was mostly blazing and that. That was, like, what we'd do in the evenings. Basically skin up and just . . . yeah.'

His face devoid of reaction, Wyatt continues. 'And what about Jamal Lowton?'

'Yeah, he blazes too.'

'Well, let's take things step by step. How did you meet Mr Lowton?'

Mervyn-Scott tells the jury that he and Jamal Lowton have known each other since they were nine. They had briefly spent time in the same class at the same unit, before Jamal was transferred elsewhere, and they learned that they lived in adjacent towers. Again, the nature of their relationship is succinctly summarised as 'chilling', and Baxter Wyatt takes the opportunity to spell out, 'for the benefit of any jurors not accustomed to your vernacular', that his client is talking about smoking cannabis.

'Most nights I'd chill with those boys. We were tight.' He stops short at the sound of a throat being cleared in the dock. Arron Freeman is still staring at his feet, but his head is slowly shaking. Uncertainty flushes over Mervyn-Scott's face, but he quickly recovers and completes his thought. 'Yeah, we were tight. We basically did everything together. I think, y'know . . . that's why they did what they did when it all went down in the alley.'

Wyatt nods solemnly. 'Well, let us look at that now. I am going to ask you to take us – slowly, please – through everything that happened on the evening of New Year's Eve 2023.'

CHAPTER 41

Craig (the first defendant)

So I tell them. All of it, basically. Everything that I've been wanting to say.

I tell them that on New Year's, my mum had been at the centre for the afternoon, having this little party where they'd put on sandwiches on a table and leftover Christmas crackers and played shit music from the 2000s that old people like, and so me and Arron and Jamal had been blazing together for basically the whole day. Kayla had said she'd pick Mum up after and take her home – she'd spent New Year's last year with some boy she was seeing, so this year was my turn to chill with my mates.

Nothing else happened that afternoon. We were literally just chilling round mine, coz I don't often get the place to myself. There was no plan, nothing. Me and Az played FIFA on Xbox, this tournament thing that we'd set up, while Jamal was dicking about on his phone. There was no aggro. Yeah, we were drinking, of course. It was New Year's. We don't keep anything at home given how my mum used to be, so Jamal had nicked – sorry, he'd got – two bottles of Sourz from the offy on the corner, and we had about a bottle between us.

Jamal had to go home for his dinner, but we said we'd meet up again after, to go into town. At midnight they do these fireworks at the rugby club which are usually hype, so we thought we'd go in and watch. Also, we needed more drink, so it made sense to walk into town. It only takes ten minutes.

The CCTV shows us meeting up at Reggie's, yeah. I can't remember what we bought, but it was a bottle of something – could have been Sourz again. We wanted to find somewhere we could sit and drink it, and Arron said we should go to the park. There's a kids' play area there, with a climbing frame and swings and that, he said. But the thing is, by this time we was all feeling a bit, y'know, because of what we'd been drinking and the haze, and I didn't really know my way to this park, and so we ended up getting a bit lost. Not completely lost, but we must have taken a wrong turn or something because we ended up near these flats, which Arron said wasn't right.

And so, yeah, Mr Wyatt, and members of the jury, that whole video which shows us walking around Ableford after we've been to Reggie's, that's what that was.

Mr Wyatt then asks me straight, he says, 'The prosecution suggest that you are following a male stranger in this footage – "stalking" him, is how it has been described. What do you say about that?'

I can't help myself but laugh. Not a full-on belly laugh, but a little snort comes out of my nose and it sprays, and although it's not funny, it also sort of is, given how mad it sounds. And I keep looking at the jury, and I say, *No.* I say, *On my mum's life, I didn't even notice the guy in front of us. We were literally just trying to find our way to the park, and when we reached those flats, we realised that we were going wrong, and we just turned around. That's what we were talking about. That is it, I swear.*

So we then walked back the way we came, and then we reached the town centre, but by now we had wasted all that time getting lost, so there was no point in going to the park. We were just going to go to the rugby club.

'The CCTV shows, at 23:40, the three of you running along

Dalston Street in the direction of Rowe Street. Why were you running?' Mr Wyatt asks.

And I say it's because it was getting close to midnight, and we didn't want to miss the fireworks. There's always a massive queue to get in, so we were in a hurry. It was when we got to where Dalston Street meets Rowe Street that we saw the old man.

'Did you know or recognise him?' Mr Wyatt says, and again, I look straight at the jury – I choose one of the ladies on the front row and stare her right in the eyes – and I say, *No. I had literally no idea who he was. He was just some random old man who walked over to us and started talking.*

'What was he saying?' asks Mr Wyatt. I tell him that I actually don't know, like, I wasn't really paying attention at that point. I'm not gonna lie, he could have said anything. It was probably, *All right, what you up to?* sort of thing. He looked a bit wild in his eyes, but he was friendly, he wasn't having a go or anything. It was Jamal who went over to him first, coz he was mashed out of his head and me and Arron were like, *What are you up to, you mad fuck?* But then we all just got chatting as we were walking together, and that was basically it.

'Help us with two points,' Mr Wyatt says. 'First, we can see on the footage that you are clearly wearing a backpack. What was in the backpack?' And again, I smile, and straight away I start worrying that I shouldn't have smiled, and I say sorry to the jury. I tell them that I'm not finding this funny, obviously, but that it is sort of funny that the prosecution think there was a weapon in my bag. It was literally just some skins and my keys, I say, and a scarf because of how cold it was.

'Secondly, it has been suggested that you were "luring" Bernard Hooper in a certain direction. What do you say about that?'

I say it's fucking bullshit. And I don't say sorry this time, because I'm not. The jury need to hear this and they need to believe it. We were all just walking together, I say, and I feel my voice wobbling in my throat. The three of us were vibing, we'd had some drinks, we were just chatting to this guy, that was it. We weren't trying to hurt him, or to take him anywhere. We were just feeling chill and having a good time, and there was no drama until we got near the alley.

What happened when we got near Garth Yard? Well, when we were at the corner, next to the offy which is all boarded up, the man, Mr Hooper, told me to step into the alley with him. He said he wanted to show me something. Yeah, this probably *was* strange, I agree with Mr Wyatt, but my head wasn't really with it coz of the Sourz and the weed, so I just went along.

When I walked into the alley, I could see there was this big skip at the end, behind this black metal staircase that went all the way up to the top of the building.

'A fire escape?' Mr Wyatt says, and I say that I think it was, but obviously I didn't go up it so I don't know. All I remember is that the skip had all these metal things sticking out, these objects that I could see shining even though it was dark. But even then, I wasn't really paying attention, coz Mr Hooper was pulling on my sleeve and trying to take me deeper into the alley, and I was thinking, *What is going on?* Then all of a sudden he turns round and he's holding this sharp kitchen knife. Yeah, it's the one the scientist was asked about, which the police lost.

'Did Bernard Hooper say anything?' Mr Wyatt asks.

I say yeah, he did. He was shouting about money, telling me to hand over whatever I've got in my pockets. It was all . . . I dunno, like he'd planned it. Looking back, I think to myself – did he take us down Rowe Street to the alley because he'd decided to rob us as soon as he'd seen us? I suppose it doesn't matter, I tell the jury, but the thing is, he is actually – or was – a big man. Like, I'm only five foot nine or something and he was literally towering over me, holding this knife and coming at me. I'm not gonna lie, I was shitting my pants.

One of the woman jurors on the front row, who looks a bit like a teacher with frizzy hair and big red glasses, pulls a face when I say this, and I say straight back to her, 'I'm sorry, miss, but that's how it was, yeah? Man pulls a shank on you and you shit your pants, I'm sorry.' Then I see that Mr Wyatt is giving me a look, like *Just chill, allow it*, and I take a breath.

'Did you give him any money?'

'No,' I say, 'I didn't have any on me.' And Mr Hooper did not like that. He started swinging for me with the knife, cutting me on my hands, shouting, *Give me the fucking money*, and I swear to God, I thought he was going to kill me. 'That's why,' I say to the jury, 'I had the cuts to my hands, and also those other—'

But Mr Wyatt jumps in and stops me saying what I was about to say. 'Where were Arron and Jamal when this was happening?'

I say that I don't know for sure, but as soon as Mr Hooper started cutting me, they both rushed in and tried to get the knife off him, but I think he was probably slashing at them too, and then Arron grabbed something from out of the skip. I couldn't see what it was at first, but he was using it to try and defend us from Hooper. 'That's what that man – Mr Bell – saw when he says one of us was waving a knife at the beginning. That was Arron. What he'd got from the skip was that zombie.'

'What did Arron do with the knife?' Mr Wyatt asks.

I say to the jury – and I am finding it hard to keep calm when I'm saying this – I say that on my mum's life, it was all moving so fast I don't know exactly what happened when, but the next thing I know I can feel something warm spraying on my face, and when I wipe my cheek I see that it's blood. I thought, *What the fuck is going on?* and looked around and saw Hooper on the ground, struggling to get to his feet. Arron was holding the knife and also had blood all over him. Jamal was kicking Hooper to his stomach and face, proper nasty kicks, trying to knock the knife out of his hand and making sure he couldn't get up and go for us again.

'Did you touch the zombie knife at any point?' Mr Wyatt asks me.

Yeah, I say. When I realised what it was, and when I saw the state of Mr Hooper, I panicked. I grabbed the knife out of Arron's hand and ran out of the alley with it. My head was all over the place, and then I started thinking to myself, *What if Hooper goes for my friends again?* And in that moment – I know it probably doesn't make much sense but on my mum's life, this is what I was thinking – I was saying to myself, *I've got to go back*, and so I did. That's what Mr Bell saw, me running out of the alley with the knife, and then going back in. And that's what's on Jamal's video – the bit you can see is me taking the knife away. That's what that was about.

When I went back in the alley, everything was blurring. I don't know if it was the weed or the adrenaline or both, but I was struggling to work out what was what. All I know is that one of the other two – I don't know which one – took the knife from me and then it ended up in his chest. Like you see in the pictures. But that wasn't me.

'Apart from removing the knife from Arron Freeman, did you touch the knife?'

No, I say.

'Specifically, did you at any stage use the knife to inflict injury on Bernard Hooper?'

I reply slowly, begging the jury with my eyes to believe me. No, I say to them. I did not.

Mr Wyatt then asks about the video, and I tell them all that I didn't even know Jamal was recording. Obviously if I'd known, I'd have told him to stop. What happened next is mixed up in my head, but I know that Jamal ran away first when we heard the sirens. He turned right out of the alley. Me and Arron, we were a few seconds behind him, and I'll tell you the truth, I panicked. We tried running to the left, back up Rowe Street where we'd come from, but the cop cars came whizzing round and nicked us.

I feel like I've been talking for hours and hours, and I'm trying to tell from the jury's faces what they're thinking, but it's impossible.

My thoughts are swimming, and to tell you the truth I could do with a break, but Mr Wyatt obviously wants to carry on. He says, 'Just a few more questions,' and I take a deep breath, because I can guess what he wants to ask about.

'The jury have heard evidence of activity and searches made on mobile phones. Starting with Jamal Lowton's J1 phone, the jury have heard descriptions of violent videos that were viewed on the afternoon of New Year's Eve, at a time when you were with him. What do you know about those?'

Nothing, I say, shaking my head. As I already told the jury, I was basically on Xbox all afternoon with Arron. I didn't have a clue what Jamal was up to on his phone. The same with that search he made about 'How long do u get 4 murder?' or whatever it was. That's just Jamal, he does fucked-up shit sometimes. It was nothing to do with me.

'Tell us,' Mr Wyatt says next, 'what you know about the "game" that the jury have seen discussed in messages between Arron Freeman and Jamal Lowton.'

Again, literally nothing, I say. The messages were between them, not me, and nobody mentioned anything like that to me. If they had said anything like that, I'd have thought it was just banter.

Mr Wyatt then starts asking about what the police found on my phone. It's not what it looks like, I tell the jury. I don't even really remember googling for knives. It was probably just boredom or because someone had mentioned zombies and I wanted to see what one looked like. It definitely wasn't because I was trying to get hold of one.

'The prosecution suggest that the messages sent by you on 29 December to an unattributed number – for instance, the message "U get this" sent with an image of a knife – is a request, by you, for this other person to obtain a knife for you. What do you say?'

I shake my head. It's just banter, I say. That's just some lad I know who's well into all that stuff. None of it was serious. I promise, that wasn't me trying to get my hands on a knife.

'The jury may note the similarity between the hunting knife recovered from on top of your wardrobe, and the knife in the photograph in that message. Is that because you received that hunting knife after requesting it in that message?'

No, no, no. No. Everything's getting twisted, I tell him. On my mum's life. That hunting knife was just something that was left by one of my mum's old boyfriends. Yeah, I sent a photo of it to my mate in that message, but that was just me showing him what I had. It wasn't me asking him to get me something like that, do you get me? I swear, I am telling you all the truth. This is just the prosecution twisting things to make it fit their story.

I am not the person they are saying I am. I did not murder Bernard Hooper.

Those last words echo around the room, and Mr Wyatt goes quiet to make sure they sink in with the jury. Finally he asks me, 'Have you told this jury the truth?' and I say yes, I swear I have. *I have, members of the jury. I promise you all, all twelve of you, I can look into your eyes and swear on my mum's life, on my sister's life, that I am telling you the truth.*

And now I do look at each of them, in the eyes, one by one. This, my eyes are saying as well as my words, is the truth. The whole truth. And I need you to believe me.

And even though deep, deep down, I know, obviously, it's not the *whole* truth, I hope it's close enough for them to believe it.

CHAPTER 42

Jennifer (counsel for the third defendant)

I am glad of Caz's company today. Her Youth Court rape trial has finished and so she is back in the sidecar, although I would never say those words to her face. *Sidecar? I'm the driver of the fucking bulldozer, love,* I can hear her howl. Whatever the acceptable vehicular metaphor, Caz has resumed her post behind me in court, the aggressive drumbeat of her keyboard oddly reassuring.

We spoke on the phone before and after court yesterday, but her absence has felt longer, somehow. I've not said as much to her; her guilt at having left me by myself has been expressed more times, and in more self-flagellating terms, than is warranted, and does not need exacerbating. There is also the point that I am technically an adult woman, and so theoretically capable of surviving a day doing my job without somebody stroking my head, and illusions must be maintained. Although that horse has probably bolted. The root of Caz's chest-beating is almost certainly her recognition that I am struggling, more than either of us had anticipated.

In the far corner of the robing room, I sit typing at a wobbling desk, taking care not to catch my sleeves on its splintered edges. Caz, heeding the 'DO NOT SIT' warning handwritten on a scrap of paper balanced on the only other available chair, is standing over me, commentating on the morning's evidence. My lunch is rarely in solid form – 1 p.m. to 2 p.m. is just another working hour – but Caz has had the foresight to bring in a tupperware filled with a home-made Korean salad, which she is prodding with a fork, unapologetically dispersing the odour of fish sauce across the room as she talks. Meanwhile, I nod intermittently as I make notes for my cross-examination of Craig Mervyn-Scott.

Bob, as second defendant on the indictment, gets the first go. Then me, as D3. Finally it is the turn of the prosecution, although often by the time the Crown cross-examines in a cut-throat, most of the damage has been done. Prosecuting counsel is like a Western gunslinger swinging open the saloon doors only to find the furniture overturned and everyone inside fatally wounded. Sometimes all you need to do is discharge a few rounds into the bodies for show, and help yourself to a drink from the bar.

Caz has not mentioned the word 'drink', but I suspect it is not far from her mind. Today, I am confident that I am not exhibiting any observable evidence of my choice of breakfast, nor the period of time over which I drank it (3 a.m. to 6 a.m., if we are being candid, 2 a.m. to 8 a.m. if we are being even more so). I definitely feel a greater equilibrium than yesterday. The deal I struck with myself – and raucously toasted for its brilliance a few hours ago – is that I am allowed to manage by whatever means necessary for the duration of the defence cases, when the evidence is likely to be particularly raw, subject to two conditions. First, that the cabinet is firmly locked as soon as we are onto closing speeches. Second, that my management style does not affect my performance in court, nor how I handle Jamal. Ten hours into this agreement, I am satisfied that I am complying.

'Do you reckon it's tactical, or is he just a dick?'

A fugitive strip of sesame-soaked lettuce lands on my keyboard and I look up.

'Sorry,' Caz says, swiftly removing the offending object. 'But what do you reckon? The way Wyatt speaks to his boy in front of the jury – what's that about?'

'I'm not sure,' I tell her. 'Possibly both.' I smile to soften the brusqueness of my reply and return to my screen. I have seen this style of examination-in-chief before. The theory is that juries do not like barristers being too pally with an unappealing defendant. By distancing yourself from your client through aloofness – or, in Wyatt's case, active hostility – you lend credence to the arguments you will later ask the jury to accept in closing. *I don't like this guy either, members of the jury, but let's look objectively . . .* As with all pet theories about jury persuasion, nobody really knows.

The crackle of the tannoy distorts the usher's message, but the words 'Court 11' are sufficiently distinct for us to pick up our belongings and trudge back for the afternoon session. Once we are all reinstalled in our positions, Bob Evans rises and addresses a nervous-looking Craig Mervyn-Scott.

'Mr Mervyn-Scott, as you know, I represent Arron Freeman. And you also know, don't you, that Arron's account of what happened on New Year's Eve is very different to yours?'

'Yeah,' comes the quiet reply.

'I am going to be suggesting that your accounts are different because you have not been telling this jury the truth. And I have to put Arron's case to you to give you a fair opportunity to respond to it. Do you understand?'

A nod. 'OK.'

Bob's manner has altered slightly. He is still unfailingly polite, there remains the faint trace of a smile, but there is a steel behind the eyes that was not present when he cross-examined during the prosecution case. Bob knows that this time he is not going to be able to draw out helpful concessions from the witness by dripping honey and moonbeams. He is going to have to destroy him.

'You have told the jury that you did not know Bernard Hooper until you randomly encountered him on New Year's Eve.'

'That's right.'

'Well, that's *not* right, is it, Mr Mervyn-Scott?'

Twelve backs straighten to attention in the jury box, like a

Mexican wave of meerkats. This is the very first the jury have heard of Arron Freeman's madcap defence, and I am fascinated to see how they react to it.

'The truth is that you *did* know Bernard Hooper, didn't you, Mr Mervyn-Scott?'

'Umm, no.'

'Bernard Hooper taught music lessons at the primary school attended by your younger sister, Kayla.'

'Did he?'

'We know he did, the jury will see the school records. And *you* knew that too, didn't you?'

'No idea what you're talking about, mate.'

'And you came to believe that Bernard Hooper had sexually abused your sister.'

I catch the expression on the face of the young, balding juror on the front row, whose eyes have widened to Manga-style proportions. He is not alone. A ripple moves through the jury as the new information is processed.

'You told Arron Freeman, didn't you, that you believed a teacher called Bernard Hooper had abused your sister?'

'Did I fuck, mate. You're chatting shit.'

'And you became obsessed with taking revenge on Bernard Hooper, didn't you?'

'Is this what he's told you? That prick over there – you believe what he says, do you?'

'Mr Mervyn-Scott,' intervenes HHJ Letts. 'This isn't about what Mr Evans believes. His job is to ask questions on behalf of his client. Your job is to answer those questions. Now, did you tell Arron Freeman that you wanted to take revenge against Bernard Hooper?'

Craig's face is a grim line. His right hand is resting on the witness box, and I can see his tendons straining as he tries not to clench his fist. He is making it only too obvious how difficult he is finding it to regulate his temper. Which is, of course, precisely the effect that Bob is artfully aiming for.

'No. I didn't.'

'And when you bumped into Bernard Hooper on 31 December 2023, you saw your opportunity for revenge, and you took it.'

'No fucking way. No way.'

'Well, I hear what you say. Can we perhaps look at some of the detail you have given in your evidence?'

Scene now set, Bob rewinds to the beginning. His tone remains cordial, the reasonableness of his manner serving only to emphasise the ruthlessness of the questions. He is expecting indignant denials, and so can afford to accelerate his cross-examination to a speed below rapid-fire, but with enough momentum to create the effect of railroading; of a witness being trafficked to an unavoidable narrative destination.

Do you have a fascination with knives, Mr Mervyn-Scott?

Is that why your mobile phone was full of internet searches for knives?

Is that why you sent pictures of knives to your associates?

Is that why you were requesting knives?

Is that why you kept a hunting knife on top of your wardrobe?

Were you carrying a knife in your backpack when you went out on New Year's Eve?

Were you carrying the zombie knife?

When you saw Bernard Hooper in the street, did you run after him?

Did you and Jamal Lowton decide to take revenge against him?

Is that why you sent Jamal Lowton over to talk to Bernard Hooper?

Did you encourage Bernard Hooper to accompany you?

When you reached Garth Yard, did you produce the zombie knife from your backpack?

Are you really suggesting that you just happened to find this weapon lying conveniently in a skip?

Did you shout threats and abuse towards Bernard Hooper?

Did Arron Freeman try to step between you, to keep the peace?

Did you push past Arron Freeman and strike Bernard Hooper with the knife?

Did you repeatedly hit Bernard Hooper with the knife?

Did Jamal Lowton help you by punching and kicking Bernard Hooper?

Did Jamal Lowton pick up an object from the ground – maybe a metal bar – and use it to hit Bernard Hooper?

Was Arron Freeman begging you to stop?

Did Arron Freeman try to grab the knife from you?

The first half-dozen 'No's are loud and defiant, but gradually the energy starts to drop. By the time Bob Evans is addressing the events in Garth Yard, the replies have plateaued to a low monotone, which – to my ear, at least – gives off an impression of tedium unlikely to play well with the jurors. That is until Bob raises the topic of the video.

'When Bernard Hooper was dying, being filmed by Jamal Lowton, somebody – I suggest Mr Lowton – called him a "paedo", didn't they?'

'It wasn't me.'

'No, we agree. But he was called a paedo because you thought he *was*, didn't you? That remark was a reference to what you and Jamal Lowton believed Bernard Hooper had done to your sister?'

'No. Just no.'

'The violence, Mr Mervyn-Scott, was not sparked by Bernard Hooper trying to rob you, but by your thirst for vengeance. Do you agree?'

'Of course I fucking don't.'

'Bernard Hooper didn't attack you with a knife, did he?'

'He absolutely fucking did. How else do you think I got all these cuts to my hands?'

'I suggest those very small cuts could have been caused by many things, but they were not caused by a frenzied assault by Bernard Hooper, Mr Mervyn-Scott.'

The tether snaps. For the first time in his evidence, Craig stands up. The raised platform of the witness box makes him appear much taller, and far more imposing, than he presumably realises, as he lifts his voice. 'He did! On my mum's life, the fucking cunt absolutely went for me, and it wasn't just the cuts with the knife, but there's also all that bruising that the jury haven't seen yet. All the marks to my chest and face in them other photos that my barrister is hiding from the jury!'

I gasp, and quickly dip my head in the hope that it wasn't noticed by a juror. Did he really just say that? The tap-tap from behind me heralds an imminent email from Caz. It is characteristically pithy.

FUCK. ME.

Bob Evans turns and addresses the bench. 'Your Honour, might I raise a matter of law in the absence of the jury?'

As the judge assents and the jurors are led out, confusion creased across several faces, I try to make sense of what I have just heard. I didn't mishear. Obviously. Bob and Caz heard it too. I look across at Baxter Wyatt, who looks thoroughly displeased with his lay client, which tells me absolutely nothing. I replay the answer Craig Mervyn-Scott has just given. I can't quite believe it.

The stupid, stupid boy has done it. He's gone and torpedoed his own case.

DAY 11 OF TRIAL – WEDNESDAY

CHAPTER 43

Craig (the first defendant)

I didn't sleep again.

This time it had nothing to do with the noise. The kid in the next pad was in the block after potting Danielle, so for once it was quiet. It wasn't even how bad things had gone in court, and all those things the judge said, that was making my head spin.

It was the flashbacks.

They began literally the day after New Year. At first it was every single night, but then after a few months they stopped for a bit, and then started again, and then stopped. I've had them a few times while the trial's been going on, but I've learned how to shake things up in my mind so I can distract my brain and make it think about something else, so at least they don't keep me awake for too long.

But not last night. Last night it was as bad as it's ever been. Literally every single time I tried to close my eyes, I was there. Right back on New Year's Eve. All the sights and sounds and smells. And my body was acting like it did on that day, with all the feelings rushing through my arms and my legs, burning and tingling and *surging*. My fists kept screwing up into tight little balls, shaking and shaking, not because I was scared, but because of how *good* it felt. It was like the thought of the violence, of making him hurt, had just built and built until I felt like it was going to burst out of my skin, and then the relief I felt when it finally did . . . it was like nothing I can describe.

All the pain felt like it was flowing out of me and into him, and the more I hurt him, the less pain I was feeling myself. And when his blood started to spurt, and I could feel the warm spray on my face as he was screaming – *screaming* like the sick little cunt he is – and begging and begging for his life, I was all of a sudden not feeling pain at all, but like a rush of happiness. And when I realised he wasn't fighting back, and I could then slow down and take my sweet time making sure he felt every single blow, I swear I could have done that for ever. If I'd had longer, if I hadn't had to run from the sirens, I'd have chopped him into fucking pieces.

I wish I'd recorded the whole thing. I'd give anything to see that look again, that fear on his mashed-up face as I swung down on him. And the part when he realised who I was, and what was going down. When I told him, 'This is for what you did to her.'

CHAPTER 44

In the Crown Court at Ableford

RULING ON BAD CHARACTER APPLICATION

HHJ LETTS: Mr Evans, I indicated yesterday when granting the bad character application in principle that I would hand down a full ruling of my decision this morning before we resume with the jury.

This is a renewed application made on behalf of the second defendant, Arron Freeman, and supported by the prosecution. It arises out of assertions made by the first defendant, Craig Mervyn-Scott, in the course of his evidence yesterday.

The first defendant's case is that the deceased, Bernard Hooper, was killed by the second and third defendants after Mr Hooper attacked the first defendant with a knife. In support of his case, the first defendant has adduced photographs of injuries to his hands which, the prosecution expert agrees, are consistent with cuts caused by a blade. The second defendant's case is that the first and third defendant lured Mr Hooper to Garth Yard and killed him in an act of revenge.

In cross-examination of Mr Mervyn-Scott, Mr Evans put to him that his account of events in Garth Yard was untrue. Specifically, it was put to Craig Mervyn-Scott that the cuts to his hands had not been caused by Bernard Hooper wielding a knife. Mr Mervyn-Scott retorted that not only were the cuts to his hands caused by Bernard Hooper, but that he had sustained other injuries, namely bruising to his face and body, which appeared in photographs that the jury had not seen, and which had been suppressed or hidden from the jury.

That, it is agreed between all parties, is not true. The reason that Mr Wyatt had quite properly not shown the jury any photographs of the injuries to Craig Mervyn-Scott's face and body, was because those injuries, as Mr Mervyn-Scott well knows, had nothing to do with the events concerning Bernard Hooper. Those injuries had instead been sustained in the course of an entirely separate incident that had occurred earlier on New Year's Eve. The circumstances of that earlier incident have already been the subject of a bad character application, which I refused at the close of the prosecution case, on the grounds that to admit that evidence would have such an adverse effect on the fairness of the proceedings that I ought not to admit it. However, in so ruling, I made clear that it was a finely balanced decision, and one which was capable of being revisited should anything said by a defendant in his evidence so require.

I have no doubt that this would have been explained to Mr Mervyn-Scott by his representatives before he gave evidence. But even had it not been, it matters little. It was explained by me, and Mr Mervyn-Scott knew full well, when giving his evidence yesterday, that he was misleading the jury as to the cause of his injuries. It can therefore come as no surprise to him that Mr Evans and Miss Arshad both re-apply to adduce the details of that earlier incident under the bad character provisions, Section 101(1)(f), in order to correct the false impression given by Craig Mervyn-Scott.

Mr Wyatt sensibly concedes that a false impression has been given and that it cannot be left uncorrected, but submits that the correction can be made in a way less prejudicial to his lay client's case. For instance, he suggests that the jury can be told that the injuries to which Mr Mervyn-Scott has referred were caused in another way, without specifying the detail. The detail, Mr Wyatt submits, remains too prejudicial to go before the jury. I do not agree. The scales have now tipped. This was not merely a slip of the tongue by Mr Mervyn-Scott. It was a deliberate attempt to bolster his case with an untruth. Credibility is the central matter in issue as between the defendants in this trial. In my judgement, ensuring fairness to all parties requires that the full detail of the earlier incident go before the jury.

I turn now to the details of that incident, which as a result of this ruling will be put before the jury.

Matthew Jamieson is a male now in his early forties who was for some years in a relationship with Paula Sheppard, the adoptive mother of Craig Mervyn-Scott. On 1 December 2018, Mr Jamieson committed a serious assault on Paula Sheppard in the family home, as a result of which she sustained life-changing injuries. He was consequently convicted of inflicting grievous bodily harm with intent, and sentenced to ten years' imprisonment.

Mr Jamieson was released from that sentence, on licence, in early December 2023. Craig Mervyn-Scott became aware of this, and, on the morning of 31 December 2023, at around 10 o'clock, attended Mr Jamieson's flat. He forced his way into the flat and, finding Matthew Jamieson asleep in the bedroom, embarked upon a sustained revenge attack, using his fists and his feet to inflict numerous and serious injuries, including a fractured jaw, two broken arms and a bleed on the brain. A neighbour heard the commotion and called the police, but Mr Mervyn-Scott had left by the time officers arrived to find Matthew Jamieson unconscious. Mr Jamieson also had bruising to his knuckles, consistent with having landed at least some blows defending himself against Craig Mervyn-Scott.

None of these facts are disputed. Craig Mervyn-Scott made full admissions in his police interview, after he was swiftly identified as the assailant from CCTV footage, and has pleaded guilty to inflicting grievous bodily harm with intent. He stands to be sentenced for that offence at the conclusion of this trial.

The point, as is understood by all, is that the bruising to Craig Mervyn-Scott's face and body is not fairly attributable to Bernard Hooper. Those injuries were caused by the defensive actions of Matthew Jamieson. The only way to correct the false impression that Mr Mervyn-Scott has created is to give the jury the full picture.

My earlier ruling in relation to the rest of Craig Mervyn-Scott's bad character remains. The jury will not hear about his previous drunken violence with Jamal Lowton. The gratuitous violence he inflicted upon his stepfather, however, is now – as a result of Mr Mervyn-Scott's own decision to mislead – something that can be kept from the jury no longer.

Can we have the jury in, please.

[INAUDIBLE]

Oh, hang on, Sandra. Yes, Miss Arshad? What is it now?

CHAPTER 45

Aliyah (the prosecutor)

My left foot searches for the side panel of the bench as I stand. Finding it, I push outwards, straightening my back and inhaling deeply.

'Your Honour,' I say. 'A matter has arisen overnight which I need to raise with my learned friends.'

He stares at me, his amphibious jowly face drooping with displeasure.

'And am I, as the lowly judge in this trial, to be told what this matter is?'

'Your Honour, of course . . .' I begin.

'Oh, goody. Lucky me.'

I take a second to prepare myself, even though I know what his reaction will be the moment the next sentence leaves my lips. 'It's a matter of disclosure, Your Honour.'

Letts performatively widens his eyes and offers a poor affectation of not having heard me. 'I'm so sorry – *disclosure*, Miss Arshad?'

I nod.

'Oh, dearie me. At this late stage? Oh, dearie, dearie me. Well, we know that juries don't like to have their time wasted, don't we, Miss Arshad? So how about this: you take however long you need – up to a maximum of, say, five minutes – to address this with the defence. And then perhaps when we resume, you can start with a little apology to the jury for the delay.'

There is no point in arguing or explaining. For one, I do not care what he thinks. With other judges, I am conscientious to preserve good terms. But when it comes to Jeremy Letts, I do not – and I choose my words carefully – give two shiny shits. What is about to happen is not aimed at pleasing him. It is about justice.

I push my way out of court, tailed by Wyatt, with Evans and Rennie a step behind, and motion for them to follow me. When I nudge open the conference room door, I am expecting to have to eject Chris Rose, but he has disappeared, abandoning his whirring laptop on the desk and apparently omitting to lock the door. It is just as well that this isn't a building filled with criminals, or that might constitute a poor policing decision.

We crowd in and Bob tugs the door shut behind him. There are still only two chairs in the room. Wyatt sinks into one and leans back, legs intertwined, with an expectant grin on his face. Jennifer declines Bob's effusive insistence that she take the remaining seat, and they stand awkwardly as I rest my backside on the table.

'Overnight,' I begin, 'I conducted a further review of Craig Mervyn-Scott's mobile phone download, to triple-check that there was nothing disclosable.'

This has the advantage of being technically not untrue. Twenty-four hours bought me some much-needed perspective, as a result of which I dug out my MacBook at 1 a.m. this morning and isolated the disclosable records. Perspective, I realised, is the key. Because while there may be a cynical, unfair perspective – *Aliyah Arshad, Disclosure Fuck-up* – there is another, potentially transformative one: *Aliyah Arshad, Disclosure Saviour*. The selfless prosecutor, working into the night for free, uncovering and dutifully disclosing critical material, saving the CPS's blushes and, without reaching for a word quite as on-the-nose as 'redemption', reaffirming a deserved reputation for fairness.

Who wouldn't want to instruct that silk?

Disclosing the phone material now is also probably safer than risking the material emerging in eighteen months, post-conviction, and sparking a rerun of the George Burrows fiasco. And, of course, it ensures a fair trial. Which is my undimmed priority.

Nobody need ever know the unserious thoughts that flashed through my mind the other evening when I first saw the material. Nobody need even know that I saw anything at that time. My laptop still, officially, remained in my bag on Monday night.

'Is this the download that the CPS repeatedly told our solicitors they were not allowed to see because it had been *extensively* reviewed and nothing further fell to be disclosed?' Wyatt polishes the lenses of his glasses with his pocket square and props them back on with a maddening smirk.

'As I say, Baxter, triple-check. I wanted to satisfy myself that there was nothing which, in light of your lay client's evidence yesterday, should be disclosed to the co-accused.'

'And do I infer from this impromptu ménage à trois that you found something?'

'Fuck's sake, Baxter.' Jennifer Rennie's eye catches mine. 'Can you just let her talk? Go on, Aliyah.'

I thank her silently and resume. 'There were two Google searches on Mervyn-Scott's phone. Both in November 2023.'

I am interrupted by a knock at the door, and Bob squeezes enough of himself aside to allow the caseworker to half-enter and hand me a thin sheaf of photocopies. I dismiss her and disseminate a leaf to each defence counsel. 'It is of greater assistance to you, Bob, than it is to the others. Certainly it won't help your boy's cause this morning, Baxter. But you're of course entitled to see it.'

Notwithstanding my own discomfort, I am able to savour a small shiver of pleasure as Wyatt absorbs the contents and the light in his eyes starts to dim. Craig Mervyn-Scott is in the middle of giving evidence, which means that he is not allowed to talk to his lawyers. There is no way for Baxter to take his client's instructions, or to warn him about what lies ahead.

First Google search, made on 8 November 2023 at 22:49:
'Bernard Hooper teacher ableford.'

Second Google search, same date, one minute later.
'Bernard Hooper address ableford.'

Jennifer Rennie's laugh cracks the silence. 'Well, fuck a duck. Your lad's toast, isn't he, Baxter? Manna from heaven, eh, Bob? Other bread-related metaphors are obviously available.'

There's a wildness to her manner which feels slightly out of place, but she isn't wrong. Wyatt knows it. And, although he is far too decent to crow, Bob Evans knows it too. What I am still weighing up is how this material affects my own case. I was catastrophising when I first saw it, I am at least confident of that. The searches assist Arron Freeman's case, but they do not prove it. There could be other reasons why Craig Mervyn-Scott made those searches, entirely unconnected to Hooper abusing Kayla Scott. Just because I cannot immediately see what those reasons are, does not mean that Arron Freeman is telling the truth. Despite the temptation to pivot, to lean closer to Freeman's case and agree that there may have been a revenge motive, for Mervyn-Scott at least, I am minded to stay the course. Stick to my theory: a random attack, as born out by the messages. After all, there is still no evidence at all to support the claim of Hooper abusing Kayla Scott. Kayla herself has refused to give any account to the police, and is similarly unwilling, it seems, to come to court on behalf of any of the defendants.

'Any other late surprises?' Wyatt's lip is still curled as he tosses the records onto the desk.

'No,' I smile sweetly. 'There is nothing else to disclose. Everything has been checked and checked again. You have the Aliyah Arshad seal of approval on that.'

My reverie is broken by another knock at the door.

'We're coming,' I say, expecting to see a hassled usher as the door opens. But it is DS Chris Rose. He does not look well, even for a man who, I assume, subsists on a diet entirely supplied by Just Eat. He lets the others file past him, and then, when we are alone, he leans in to me, his eyes red and his breath a putrid plume of stale coffee.

'Aliyah,' he says quietly, 'can I have a quick word?'

I notice that his clammy hand is clutching a bundle of papers, and can just about make out a faded NHS logo within. 'It's about those counselling records.'

CHAPTER 46

HHJ Jeremy Letts (the judge)

It is not an impressive apology. Arshad shrieks at the jury for a good thirty seconds about the 'inconvenience caused', and I demonstrate characteristic restraint by not adding aloud the words *by you*.

The jurors look a little perplexed. I doubt that they give a hoot about the half-hour delay in starting. But it was not the jurors' feelings that were uppermost in the judicial mind when I ordered the apology. It was scene-setting. Before Craig Mervyn-Scott's cross-examination resumes, the jurors now know that something of significance has transpired since last they were in court. They know that new material has only just been provided to the defence, and that, in my eyes at least, the prosecution are at fault.

Juries, in my experience, do not like it when a judge appears to be favouring the prosecution. That sort of perception can provoke a rebellion in the retiring room, with acquittal-shaped ramifications. It is important that I am seen, at least occasionally, to be bearing down hard on the Crown. Such even-handedness makes it more likely that the jury will be receptive when I sum up and invite them to convict.

Plus – and this is important, as Arshad's grovel splutters to an end – it is funny.

The jury were absent for my observation when I was told the nature of the two pieces of material disclosed this morning. 'Not only are these disclosable to the second defendant,' I suggested, 'but I would have thought them pertinent evidence that forms a crucial part of the Crown's case against the first defendant.' The jurors did not see Arshad's panicked freeze as her little brain clicked and whirred. Eventually, she shakily assured me that the Crown 'was considering carefully how best to frame its case in light of these developments'.

Well, I was good enough not to say in response, *you know where the drawing board is, dear.*

Craig Mervyn-Scott is escorted once more from the dock to the witness box, and tubby little Bob Evans rises to resume. This should be entertaining.

'Mr Mervyn-Scott,' he begins. 'When we paused yesterday, I was asking you about the altercation you had with Bernard Hooper. And you said this: "On my mum's life, the fucking cunt absolutely went for me, and it wasn't just the cuts with the knife, but there's also all that bruising that the jury haven't seen yet. All the marks to my chest and face in them other photos."' Bob pauses. 'Do you remember saying that?'

'Something like that, yeah.'

Bob nods. 'Well, it's right that you had bruising to your face and chest, isn't it?'

'Yeah.'

'And it's correct that there are photographs of that bruising, which the jury have not been shown.'

'Yeah.'

'But the reason those photographs have not been shown to the jury, is that the bruises were not caused by Bernard Hooper. Were they, Mr Mervyn-Scott?'

'Probably.'

'You know that the bruises were caused by somebody else, and you lied to the jury yesterday, didn't you?'

'No.'

'Well, respectfully, Mr Mervyn-Scott, you did. You knew that the bruises were sustained earlier in the day on 31 December 2023, when you committed a sustained and violent attack on a man called Matthew Jamieson.'

I carefully watch the jury box. Confusion envelops them. Juror eight whispers in the ear of juror seven, who returns a shake of the head and passes the query to his left. Four jurors start sifting their notes, as if searching for a paragraph they had skimmed over which would lend meaning to what they were now hearing.

Exactly the effect that I expect Bob Evans was hoping for. The little drama queen.

'On the morning of New Year's Eve 2023, you broke into Matthew Jamieson's flat and punched and kicked him as he lay in bed, using such force that you broke his jaw and his arms, and caused a bleed on his brain. You agree, don't you?'

There is no response. There doesn't need to be. Bob Evans slowly and emotionlessly takes the jury through the details of the assault – and of Craig Mervyn-Scott's confessions – which I have ruled are now admissible. They require no emphasis; the unadorned facts speak for themselves. And even this young dullard, with his apparent gift for making the worst of a bad situation, recognises that the only thing he can do – the only option he has – is to quietly agree with each and every one. Including, inevitably, the kicker: *And it was in the course of that assault, as Mr Jamieson defended himself from you, that you sustained the bruises to your face.*

'So,' Bob Evans says with a theatrical sigh, 'I'll ask you again, Mr Mervyn-Scott: You lied to this jury yesterday, didn't you?'

'Hooper fucking went for me.' He drops his voice and inspects his hands, before looking his inquisitor in the eye. 'He went for me. All right, yeah, fine, maybe not all the bruising. But he fucking . . . he did.'

'I see,' says Bob Evans, swiping the trackpad on his laptop. 'Well, perhaps we can look at something else. Yesterday I asked you whether you knew Bernard Hooper before you encountered him on New Year's Eve. And you said no, do you remember?'

'Yeah.'

'I put Arron Freeman's case to you – I suggested that you believed Bernard Hooper to have abused your sister, Kayla, and that this was the motive for you killing him.'

'Bullshit, mate.'

'Well, quite. That is what you said yesterday, in equally colourful terms, and is that still your evidence today? You had never previously heard of Bernard Hooper?'

'That's right.'

Bob reaches down to his left and produces a pile of exhibits. 'Now, the jury are already aware – as are you – that this morning the prosecution disclosed some material to the defence. I am going to ask that copies of this be handed to the jury, and a copy for yourself. To assist everybody, what we see here are two Google searches which were conducted on Craig Mervyn-Scott's mobile phone late in the evening on 8 November 2023. On your timeline, Mr Mervyn-Scott, this is just over seven weeks before you have ever heard of Bernard Hooper.'

The usher collects and distributes the printouts, and as a copy is placed in the witness box, Craig Mervyn-Scott picks it up, stares at it, and keeps staring.

'Do you need any help with your reading?' I ask helpfully. He shakes his head.

'Mr Mervyn-Scott,' Bob continues, 'could you please read out the first Google search?'

'I . . . I didn't . . . this isn't me.'

'Just read it out, please.'

'"Bernard Hooper teacher ableford".'

'And the next one, please.'

'"Bernard Hooper address ableford".'

Juror one puts her hand over her mouth. If Bob Evans looked

to his right, he would see the remaining eleven crossing their arms tightly in near-perfect unison, but his focus does not waver from his quarry.

'So, seven weeks before you've ever heard of the retired teacher, Bernard Hooper, here you are searching online for Bernard Hooper's address.'

Mervyn-Scott shakes his head furiously. 'Nah. Nah nah nah. It wasn't me.'

'It is your mobile phone, isn't it?'

'Yeah, but so what? Everyone uses everyone's phones, don't they? I'm always lending my phone to mates and that.'

'I see. So can you help us with which mate might have been using your phone, at 11 o'clock at night on 8 November 2023, to Google search Bernard Hooper?'

'Could have been anyone.'

'Anyone?'

'Yeah.'

'But definitely not you?'

'Definitely not.'

Bob nods thoughtfully and rubs the arm of his spectacles. He then reaches down, and returns with a further, single sheet of paper. 'There was a second disclosure made to the defence this morning – even later than the Google searches – and so I'm afraid I don't have copies for everybody.' He smiles at the jury. 'But it may be that we don't need them.'

Mervyn-Scott's eyes flit towards his counsel, but Baxter Wyatt is leaning back and keeping his sight trained on Bob Evans, his face suggestive of having a lemon in his mouth and a lime up his bottom.

'Mr Mervyn-Scott,' Bob continues. 'Do you know a Charlotte Taylor?'

The boy's face is blank.

'Maybe this will help. Charlotte Taylor is a counsellor, who works in NHS Ableford Talking Therapies. She specialises in helping young people with depression and anxiety. Ringing any bells?'

Still no reaction.

'From October 2023, one of the young people she supported was Kayla Scott. Your sister.'

Still nothing.

'Charlotte Taylor's notes indicate that you would sometimes accompany Kayla to her counselling sessions at Ableford and would collect her afterwards. Do you agree?'

Mervyn-Scott gives a moment's consideration to his options, before recognising that there are none. 'Yeah.'

'In her counselling sessions, Kayla spoke about the difficulties you had both experienced growing up. The pressures brought about by your mother's health. But she also mentioned something else. Something specific. And she agreed that Charlotte Taylor could talk to you about it. Do you remember a conversation with Charlotte Taylor on 15 November 2023?'

There is no immediate answer. Bob does not wait.

'Well, I can perhaps help, because we have Ms Taylor's notes of her conversation with Kayla, and her conversation with you. Let me ask you this: Do you remember a discussion, on 15 November 2023, in which Charlotte Taylor told you that Kayla had revealed that she had been abused by a teacher when she was in primary school?'

A snort is stifled in the dock, which buys Craig Mervyn-Scott a second's thinking time, but it is not enough. Again, Bob carries straight on, holding the record up to his nose and reading from it.

'In that conversation, did you tell Charlotte Taylor that you were already aware that Kayla had made these allegations as she had told you the previous week?'

'I can't remember.' It's all he has.

'And that is why, a week before, you were googling Bernard Hooper. Isn't it?'

'I don't know.'

'Mr Mervyn-Scott,' Bob says, lowering his voice and decelerating his delivery. 'I'll ask you one final time. You knew, didn't you, that your sister, Kayla Scott, had made an allegation of sexual abuse against her former teacher, Bernard Hooper?'

Every juror is staring at the witness box.

CHAPTER 47

Jennifer (counsel for the third defendant)

A wise person once said, *There is little more pleasurable in life than watching a co-defendant self-immolate in an inferno of his own lies.*

That wise person was me. And I said it just now, to myself, and found it so amusing and perceptive that I emailed it immediately to Caz, and am still staring at my inbox waiting for her confirmation that I am, indeed, both amusing and perceptive, when I realise that Bob has sat down and everybody is waiting for me to begin.

'Sorry, Your Honour,' I mumble as I stand up, balancing my laptop carefully on the lectern and frenetically opening and closing browser windows in search of my bullet-point list of questions for Craig Mervyn-Scott. 'Sorry, members of the jury. Technological hiccup!' After what feels like a decade, I finally locate the pissing Word document, and beam at the jury with a wattage which I immediately realise is disproportionate to the achievement, and overcorrect by fixing my mouth into a stern pout.

It is possible, I concede, that somewhere around 3 a.m. I might have misjudged precisely how much was required to take the edge off. But then, it occurs to me, perhaps not. Standing here right now, breathing in and surveying my domain, I realise that I have, if anything, the perfect amount of edge. Goldilocks quantities, in fact.

I also realise that I am still not saying anything.

'Members of the jury,' Jeremy Letts interjects, 'we will take a short break before Miss Rennie cross-examines.' After the jury have trotted out he raises an eyebrow at me and asks, 'Will fifteen minutes be enough for you to, ahem, ready yourself?'

I am already ready, but have no mind to engage with the daft little badger's riddles, so I politely agree, asking if, in fact, he would allow a little longer so that I can go to the cells and take Jamal's instructions following this morning's hoopla. I am pretty sure I do not say the word 'hoopla' out loud – or 'daft little badger' – but Caz's face as we walk out of court causes me to doubt myself.

'Is everything OK?' She touches my arm and guides me to the side of the corridor. The absence of foul language in her question is troubling. I smile at her and look her in the eyes, reassuring her that I am absolutely tickety-boo fine.

'Are you sleeping?' she asks quietly. 'Is it . . . y'know. Is it Ollie stuff?'

Not at all, I soothe, waving my hand. No no no. That's honestly not an issue. It's truthfully the furthest thing from my mind. No, it's a drugs case that I've got coming up after this trial. I was up late last night drafting a skeleton argument, and I'm just waiting for the coffee to kick in. That's honestly all there is to it. There's no need to worry. There's no self-medicating, if that's what you're thinking. I am entirely in the horse and on the saddle. On the horse. In the saddle.

Caz allows me to run out of steam. She then suggests – and I think this is a great idea, actually – that I take the opportunity to step outside and get some air, while she nips downstairs to speak to Jamal. We part ways, and I pad down the stairs, doing my best to manoeuvre a cigarette out of my handbag without making the rest of its contents clink. Once outside the building, I light up, take a drag and then hold my face upwards, closing my eyes and letting the warm breeze wash over me as I exhale. As I tip my head backwards, I feel my wig sliding and clutch the back of my head to keep it in place. I remain in this position, drinking in the air for a good few minutes, long enough for my fingers to alert me to the cigarette having burned out.

I decide against a second, and make my way back through security and along the ground-floor corridor. As I reach the bottom of the grand staircase, I bump into Caz emerging up the steps from the cells.

'Better?' she asks.

'Muchos,' I reply.

'We've got a little extra something,' she says as we climb the stairs. 'He's actually given some fucking instructions. It's about the search on his phone.'

'Jamal's phone? The "How long do u get 4 murder?" search?'

'Yeah.' Caz's breathing deepens as we reach the second flight and I stride ahead of her. 'When I went down, first thing he said to me was, "I don't want to be a snitch, but as it's all coming out anyway, I need to tell you something."'

I stop at the next floor for her to catch up. 'Go on.'

'He says Craig was messing around on his phone that afternoon, and that it was Craig who made the Google search.'

I consider this. 'Well, that's something. The jury will think we're just jumping up and down on a corpse, but I'll put it to him in cross-examination. See what he says.'

Court reassembles, and Craig Mervyn-Scott trudges back to the witness box. This time I have my questions ready, and in truth I do feel slightly more together for the fresh air. Not that it necessarily matters for the purpose of this exercise. A man already convicted of brutal violence who has been shown to have repeatedly lied under oath – there's no coming back from that. My cross-examination is ornamental; a formulaic putting of Jamal's no-frills case, which Mervyn-Scott will deny, and which could be conducted by anybody capable of reading words on a screen.

My limited instructions as to the events earlier in the night mean there is little I need to deal with, save for Jamal's brand-new assertion that it was Craig Mervyn-Scott making reckless searches on Jamal's phone. Privately, I think that Jamal would have been best off not trying to throw this particular stone, and it lands as ineffectively as I'd expected. Mervyn-Scott laughs at the suggestion, informing me that my lay client is 'a fucking clown', and asking (not unreasonably), 'Why the fuck would I want to use his fucking phone when I had my own? This is just Jamal stirring shit coz he can see I'm in trouble.'

But it is when I move to the events in Garth Yard that Craig Mervyn-Scott really starts to go for Jamal. I had expected him to scratch and spit and dig hard into his position, but his antagonism towards Jamal borders on the gratuitous. It is as if he has surmised that I am a softer touch than Bob Evans, or that I at least have less ammunition with which to hurt him. Or maybe he has just decided that, if he is going down, he is taking us with him. Nothing more dangerous than a man with nothing to lose, and all that.

So when I put to him, firmly but not provocatively, that Jamal Lowton walked out of Garth Yard before any of the violence started, it is not enough for Craig Mervyn-Scott to disagree, or to tell me Jamal is a liar, or to give the jury a reprise of his own defence. Jamal not only remained in Garth Yard, he angrily insists, he was acting 'like a fucking psycho'. He was 'going for the man, again and again and again, as he lay on the floor, trying to kick the shit out of him'. I ask him if he is lying again, just as he lied to the jury yesterday and this morning, but far from dampening his confidence, this ignites it. Jamal, he says, pointing furiously, found the whole thing so hilarious that he took out his phone and 'videoed this man fucking dying on the floor'.

His levels are rising, and he is either unable or unwilling to hear Jeremy Letts's warnings as he frays, and unravels, and, finally, splits. 'Do not be fooled by this man, I'm telling youse all,' he stands and shouts, banging his hands on the side of the witness box, and pointing towards the dock. 'Jamal Lowton may look like shit wouldn't melt, but he is a stone-cold killer.'

As Letts shouts him down, I decide to leave the battlefield here. Anything further I ask is only going to invite further potshots at Jamal. There will be enough to say in my closing speech about Craig Mervyn-Scott's wholesale lack of credibility and, given what they have heard, the jurors will hopefully see his performance as the unreliable histrionics of a desperately guilty liar.

However, as I sit down and begin typing up my notes, highlighting the responses that I might want to refer to in my closing speech, I start to second-guess. I revisualise the events of the last few minutes. I mustn't be complacent. While his credibility is shot, there was nevertheless something in that final paroxysm which was, well, not *persuasive*. But compelling, perhaps, in its rawness. While I do not for a moment expect the jury to believe Craig Mervyn-Scott's defence, he is more than capable of dragging Jamal down with him. The jury may well conclude that that vivid description of Jamal's behaviour, his character, has not been plucked from thin air. Craig Mervyn-Scott may be many things, but a creative narrative force does not seem to be among them.

Aliyah is now sweeping up for the prosecution, picking apart the granular detail of his evidence.

Why take such a big rucksack if it only contained your keys, cigarette skins and a scarf?

It was in fact because you were carrying the zombie knife, wasn't it?

I beg your pardon, are you seriously suggesting that Arron just happened to find the zombie knife lying conveniently on top of a skip?

You have lived in Ableford your whole life, and you say that you got lost in the town centre?

You told us that you were walking to the rugby club for the fireworks, yet you were walking down Rowe Street away from the rugby club?

You were in such a hurry for the fireworks that you were running on the CCTV, yet you suddenly decided to take a stroll with a complete stranger?

Why did you take your rucksack off in Garth Yard?

Why did you not give any of the detail that you've given to the jury to the police when you were interviewed?

'I don't know' is the default rejoinder right up until Aliyah asks why, if Craig's purpose in taking hold of the knife was to disarm Arron, Craig then ran back into Garth Yard still holding the knife. 'I panicked, I thought Hooper was going to go for my mates again,' he replies.

'But, on your account,' Aliyah says innocently, 'by this point Hooper is lying on the ground, in a pool of his own blood, unable to move.' There is no answer to that.

Finally, Aliyah asks, 'Do you now accept that you recognised Bernard Hooper when you saw him that night?'

'I don't,' Craig insists. 'I didn't know what he looked like.'

This is interesting. I was unsure how Aliyah proposed to square today's revelations with her case theory that this was all a random encounter with a complete stranger.

'The man who you suspected had abused your sister, whom you had been googling online – you came face-to-face with him and had no idea? Is that your evidence?'

'Yeah, that's the truth.'

'Isn't the truth that you knew full well who he was when you happened to bump into him, and that cemented in your mind the plan you had already made to kill?'

There is a shake of the head but no audible response to this. Craig has reverted to defeatism; the flurry of bravado he managed to summon while jousting with me has dissipated. At least I assume it is defeatism. Again, scouring the jury box for clues, I wonder if there is a more dangerous interpretation that the jurors might reach. Might the contrast between his anaemic answers to Aliyah, and his forcefulness when sermonising about Jamal the 'stone-cold killer', be explained not by a drop in energy as he absorbed blow after blow after blow, but by the fact that, when talking about Jamal, Craig was telling the truth?

As Aliyah sits down, I turn and cast a glance towards Jamal in the dock. There is something in the way he is staring at Craig that makes my blood freeze.

CHAPTER 48

Craig (the first defendant)

I know when I fuck up. And I've fucked up.

I get it now. I should've listened better when Mr Wyatt was talking, although to be fair he doesn't always make it easy. I thought that because the judge had already said that nobody was allowed to tell the jury about MJ that it was safe. That I could say what I said about the bruises. And yeah, now I obviously know it was fucking stupid, but in that moment, when you're standing up there and you've got all those questions coming at you – *bam bam bam* – it's like, where do you turn? And I panicked, didn't I? Basically, I panicked.

But the rest of it – fuck me, man. How was I supposed to know they'd go to Kayla's fucking therapist? I didn't mention that to anyone. How would they even know that she was having therapy? Or that her therapist had talked to me? It makes no sense. That is some fucked-up bad luck right there.

I just hope the jury see that it's not how it looks. Fair play to Big Bird, she's good at her job. The questions she was asking – it was like there was nothing I could say that didn't sound bad, that didn't let her call me a liar. Even when I wasn't lying, she was making me stop and question myself. Absolute head fuck.

After she was done, Mr Wyatt did his best to try and fix things. He gave me a chance to tell the jury why I had said what I said. And by that point, I've basically got nothing to lose so I was just straight with them. I said, this is how it is. I'm a fucking idiot for saying that Hooper caused the bruises. I only said that because on my mum's life, he *did* go for me with that knife. I was just trying to get you all to believe that. And I know how it looks with Kayla and what she says Hooper did to her. If I'd said that I knew about all of that, it basically plays into Arron's hands. Even though – and this bit I said to the jury really slow so that they could not miss it – even though Arron is lying. I said to them, he is taking a little thing which he knows and twisting it into a big thing to make a story that you will all fucking believe, because he thinks he's clever. But he is a fucking snake, I said to them. I promise you all, I said: revenge for what Hooper did to Kayla is not why what happened, happened.

At that point I was basically shouting at the jury, and I was going for Arron just like I went for Jamal with his barrister. It was just like a survival instinct.

I don't know if any of them believed me. They were listening, I think. Most of them had their arms folded when I was talking, but they were at least looking towards me, and the posh-looking woman on the front in the stripy jumper wrote down something, so maybe that's a good thing.

There were still things I had to lie about, obviously. Some big things, but mostly little things. Stupid little things which I can't believe the prosecution hasn't put together. Like the WhatsApps saying *'U get this'* and *'Could do some sweet damage with this'*, with the pictures of the knives. Even when she was cross-examining me, Big Bird kept going on and on about this being me asking a mate to help get me a blade. It's like, one – as if I need any help. But, two – if your fat fucker of a fed had done his fucking job properly, you would know that that number isn't any mate of mine. It's fucking MJ. And I was not asking him to get me anything; I was telling him what was coming to him. What had been coming to him for the past five years. What I had been dreaming about doing ever since that fucking piece of shit fucked up my mum's life. My whole family's life.

Obviously I didn't say that to Big Bird. If they knew how long I had been planning, waiting for the day he got out on licence, and if they knew that I'd taken my hunting knife with me when I went to his flat, they'd have charged me with fucking attempted murder, not GBH. It's the same with that search on Jamal's phone. On my mum's life, I thought I had killed him that morning. When I felt my foot go deep into his face with this squishy, cracking feeling, I knew there was some serious damage. Like the bones of his face going into his brain, maybe, I don't know. But when I heard the sirens and I ran – before I'd even had a chance to use the knife – he wasn't moving and there was bare blood pouring out of his ears, so later when we were chilling and my phone was on charge, I borrowed Jamal's to look up how long you get for murder. Coz I was sure as I could be that that cunt was dead. And while MJ had enemies, it wouldn't take long before the feds came knocking for me.

But again, I'm not going to say that to the prosecution, am I? I'm not gonna give them a chance to make things any worse for me on the MJ charge. So I had no choice, basically. I just had to keep saying that all my WhatsApps were just banter with a mate, and the other thing is on Jamal's phone and I don't know why that dickhead is searching for that shit.

Maybe that was the wrong thing to say. I dunno. When Mr Wyatt and my brief came down to see me after I'd finished my evidence, it was pretty fucking clear that they thought I'd said the wrong things. Mr Wyatt stood in the corner of the room while my brief and I sat at the table, and then he took off his wig and said with a grin, 'Well, that was a shitshow, wasn't it?' And even though it wasn't funny, and there was no reason for us to be smiling, I laughed at him, and then he just shrugged, like a *What the fuck am I supposed to do now?* kind of shrug.

It's too late, obviously. But now, as the bus takes us back and I'm leaning my face on the window and feeling the *bump-bump-bump* as I shut my eyes, I'm thinking to myself, should I have gone a different way with the jury? Maybe I should have just told them about Arron and the drugs going missing. And how I'd never seen Jamal so worked up. And how one thing leads to another and then here we all are. Would that have been any better?

It probably wouldn't, to be fair. Because one thing *does* lead to another. And the reality is that if I was to start going into all of that, to start telling whole truths, then somebody else is gonna end up dead.

DAY 12 OF TRIAL – THURSDAY

CHAPTER 49

Arron (the second defendant)

I don't really get nervous. My nails are bitten all the way down, but that's just habit. I stopped when I was living with my nana coz she would mither non-stop about it, but ever since she passed I've found myself just chewing when I'm not really concentrating. I'm not giving it all that, saying like I'm a hard man or anything, it's not like, *Oh, I never get scared, me*; it's just that I think maybe because of the things that have happened, to my mam and my nan and that, that I sort of expect bad things anyway. So it's like, why bother stressing about it?

Today though is as close as it gets. Today is the day that is gonna basically decide everything. I can already hear the shouting from the landing and the slamming of doors, and I know it's only minutes before the screws knock on for the van to court.

Bang. Bang. Bang.

Lying on my bed, I squash a pillow over my face and try to think about other things. There's no point getting worked up, or thinking about the different ways it might go. Craigy had a plan when he got up to tell his story, and look how that went for him. 'Zen' was a word that Graham said once, which I'd never heard of before. It basically means just chill the fuck out mate, and that is me right now. I'm zenning.

Bang. Bang. Bang.

The screws are at the pad next to mine. There's some kind of beef, coz I can hear the Somali kid who doesn't speak English yelling something, and there's a sound of something breaking and then everything goes quiet. There's no more sound for a minute, and then it starts up again. They're outside my pad. The noise is getting louder.

Bang. Bang. Bang.

I wait for them to shout my name.

CHAPTER 50

In the Crown Court at Ableford

DISCUSSION RE ABSENCE OF DEFENDANT

CLERK: All persons having anything to do with His Majesty's Crown Court, draw near and give your attendance.

HHJ LETTS: Give me a moment. Right. I see from the dock that we are one defendant down this morning.

MR EVANS KC: Indeed, Your Honour. When I went downstairs fifteen minutes ago, I was told by the cells staff that Mr Freeman has not been produced from HMYOI Twyford Park.

HHJ LETTS: Why not?

MR EVANS KC: The official line is that Arron Freeman refused to come out of his cell and get on the prison bus this morning. My solicitor has not been able to speak to our lay client directly, nor is anybody at the prison picking up the phone, but I must say that this strikes me as peculiar. Mr Freeman knows he is due to give evidence today and was most keen to do so.

HHJ LETTS: I see. So we are faced, are we, with yet another inglorious episode of a prison claiming that a defendant has refused to travel to court, when the truth is more likely that the prison has either forgotten or simply not bothered to put him on the van?

MR EVANS KC: I could not say for sure, Your Honour. But, as I have indicated, it is a little odd. This is not a defendant who has hitherto caused any difficulties or shown any disinclination to attend from custody.

HHJ LETTS: Well, once again, the court finds itself dancing to the prison's tune, but I don't see that we have much option other than to send the jury home. As I said at the start of the week, I have a judicial training day tomorrow and so the trial won't sit. A nice long weekend for the jurors.

MR EVANS KC: Very good, Your Honour.

HHJ LETTS: I'll break the good news. Jury in, Sandra.

DAY 13 OF TRIAL – MONDAY

CHAPTER 51

Aliyah (the prosecutor)

The long weekend has been an unexpected blessing. Professionally, if not domestically.

On the home front, it has been three days of Sasha at his housebound worst. On Friday, my inability to instantly summon £4,750 for Esme's school skiing trip to St Moritz sparked the predictable teen hysteria. The howls of 'But you never *used* to say no!' were raw enough; Sasha's patronising reassurance that 'Mummy is trying her best' made me want to throw a kettle at him.

My response – admittedly not my finest parenting moment – was to explain to Esme how we all need to make little sacrifices now, as it is important that her father gets to enjoy his hobby. I knew I would be punished, but the opportunity for a callback to how Sasha used to – oh, so ironically – describe my publicly funded criminal law practice back when he was bringing in £400k, was just too sweet to pass up.

The weekend has thus been seventy-two hours of silence punctuated by the occasional micro-aggression: Sasha pretending not to hear me and then chiding me for raising my voice; pretending to mishear me to provoke a petty squabble that he feels he can win; correcting me mid-sentence on trivial non-sequiturs. The whole toolkit of casual misogyny, forged in the furnace of corporate law, which, as Sasha's manhood adapts to becoming a secondary earner, I have noticed him reaching for with increasing frequency.

As a result of my being punished, I have however been able to spend a full thirty hours in my study, picking through the sensitive and non-sensitive disclosure schedules, reviewing each page line-by-line and cross-referencing with my own notes, quadruple-checking that there is nothing in the unused material which should be disclosed and which hasn't been. I have been back through all the mobile phone downloads, confirming that there are no more surprises. And I have compiled a list of queries to fire at Chris Rose, aimed at filling small holes and ironing out ambiguities in some of the schedules.

I am satisfied that, unseemly as the series of tardy disclosures this week has been, the evidence is still tilted in our favour. I had a telephone call on Friday afternoon with the anxious-sounding CPS reviewing lawyer, ringing for a progress update, and I reassured her that while there have been developments, we are still on course for a clean sweep of convictions. *So if you have any more murder briefs coming through . . .* I considered adding in jest, but did not. Aggressive touting has never been my style. I prefer to let my results speak for themselves.

The need for a result was also impressed upon Chris Rose before he left court on Thursday, my finger jabbing into his pudgy chest with a little more force than I had intended as I whispered, 'No More Fuck-Ups.' To be fair, there has been an instant reaction. Rose even took to working on a Sunday. When his email landed yesterday morning, subject header *'Ugrent'*, rather than asking aloud how the spelling of such a simple word had eluded him, I silently applauded him for giving me some notice, and not just springing the email's contents on me as I walked into court. I then listened to the audio file attached, and, taking deep breaths and reminding myself that I am prone to catastrophising, replied, *'Thanks, Chris. Please add to sensitive schedule and remind me tomorrow to decide whether disclosable.'* It is almost as if we are a functioning team.

So it is that now, as the time creeps towards 09:45, Rose sits across from me in our poky room, his left arm resting on a stack of printed MG6C and D disclosure schedules, his right hand jotting as I rapidly fire through the final points of my three-page to-do list.

'Forensics – continuity statements all appear to have been scheduled, but can you please double-check?'

Rose grunts.

'Third-party material, now all obtained and reviewed, and nothing further to disclose in medical, Social Services or school records?'

'Correcto,' he says.

'The CCTV trawl – as far as I can see, the logs and statements from the officers who seized and reviewed the CCTV have all been scheduled, but again, can I ask you, Chris, to do a full review on police systems to double-check?'

'Roger that.'

'And that . . .' I say with hesitant finality, 'I think covers everything.'

Rose shifts in his seat and stretches his elbows backwards, a gape in his shirt revealing more than anybody needs to see.

'You've seen the bank statements, right? Do we need to—'

'No. Those are not disclosable.'

There was a sharpness in my voice that I had not intended, but it does not seem to have cut through Rose's hide. He continues without blinking.

'Fairy do's. And what about yesterday's email?' he asks. 'The OPT4 call. You're the expert, obviously. But are we not disclosing that? Doesn't that . . . change things? Like, a hell of a lot?'

I think for a moment. 'Not yet,' I tell him. 'I'm still mulling it over. Schedule it as sensitive, and I'll decide later today whether the defence need to know about it. Given that we've only just had this recording, I'm not worried if it reaches them a little late.'

He looks at me uncertainly, but wisely thinks better of contradicting me.

I gather my laptop and my bag, and stand up to leave. 'Now let's see what Arron Freeman has to say for himself,' I announce as I open the conference room door, and Rose walks out stiffly.

We will not have any more disclosure failures, I assure myself. But – and not that winning matters – we will also get ourselves that result. I am going to deliver a clean sweep.

CHAPTER 52

Arron (the second defendant)

There's no mirror in my pad, obviously, but as the screws are taking us up to court, I catch a look at myself in the glass panel in one of the doors.

Craig looked dead smart in the box, with his white shirt and pants. I'm basically wearing the same, but it's not right. I don't feel like I look proper; like when I was interviewing at Maccy's and Graham put me in a shirt and tie and dark grey pants instead of trackies. It's like someone is wanting me to be somebody I'm not. I'm looking at this kid in the glass and thinking to myself, *Who even is that? Who do you think you're trying to be?*

My fingernails look minging too. I had a proper shower yesterday and everything, but tea last night was some kind of cold microwave curry with bits of what was supposed to be chicken, but the bits had all gone rock hard so you couldn't eat them. So I had to pick them out with my fingers, and now my fingers have gone yellow from whatever they put in the sauce and it won't come off. And my nails were bitten basically all the way down anyway, so with all the yellow my hands look like I've got some kind of disease. When Mr Evans was down here before, he looked at them and was all like, 'Maybe just keep your hands out of view when you're talking to the jury.'

Mr Evans was dead sound about Thursday. Even though obviously I told him that it wasn't my fault, that Twyford screwed up their list and didn't put me on the van, I wasn't sure anyone would actually believe my word against theirs. But he was like, 'This happens all the time,' and did this daft laugh and said the jurors would be happy for having a really long weekend, and that I shouldn't worry about it. Just focus on what's ahead today.

When we get up into court and they take off my cuffs, I don't look at Craig to my left. I sit down and stare dead ahead. It's not coz I'm arsed by what he said about me last week – that's just the game. I get it. I'm just focused on what I've got to do. If anything, I feel shit on the kid. I don't want to have to cause grief for him. He's basically family to me. But, like I say, I've got priorities now. There's too much on the line for it to all end like this.

There's a noise from behind me. Someone's coming into court. Without thinking I turn my head to the left, and I catch Craig's eye. There's this brief moment when we're staring at each other, but then he puts his head down and I crane my neck to see who's coming through the doors. It's one of the barristers, obviously. Jamal's. But even though it's stupid, for a minute there was this little part of me that thought, maybe . . . But obviously not. And even now, without really thinking about it, I'm looking over at where the members of the public sit, and looking dead slowly at all the faces, like there might be someone there for me.

It's mad. I don't know why my head is going there. I don't need anybody here watching me. But I can't stop my brain thinking it would be nice to know there's somebody here rooting for me when I'm up there. Jamal's mam has been in court every day, waving at him when he's brought in each morning and blowing kisses to the dock when the judge isn't looking. Mine would have been here too, I know that. My nan as well, if she wasn't, y'know. And Graham too, if *he* wasn't, y'know.

I shake my head, trying to get rid of the pictures that are forming. My heart is racing and my eyes feel full all of a sudden, which is the last thing I need, and I try to think about something else. Anything else. My brain is still fighting against me though. It's showing me

Graham's last day at Rosewoods. With me sitting in the front seat of his car and asking him not to go. Begging him, basically. Not crying exactly, but just saying things – anything – to try and get him to stay. And he was saying he had to go, and that I'd be fine at Rosewoods without him. And that I was gonna make something of myself, and how I was a fighter and he was proud of how far I'd come already.

I need to get a grip of myself, I'm thinking, as I'm dragged to my feet and the judge walks in. Graham was right. I am a fucking fighter. I whisper this to myself, and I feel a jolt, a little burst of energy, and I realise my heartbeat is slowing down. As the jury are all brought in and go to their seats, I keep whispering, and Craig and Jamal can probably hear me, but I don't care. It's working.

I am a fucking fighter.

I'm still whispering as Mr Evans stands up and says, 'Your Honour, members of the jury, I call Arron Freeman to give evidence.'

And I'm barely moving my lips as they take me from my seat in the dock and walk me past the benches with the barristers and into the witness box, but I'm still saying it, getting funny looks from the screws who can hear that I'm whispering, but can't tell what I'm saying.

I am a fucking fighter.

And then I'm reading out the oath and promising to tell the truth, but inside my head, I'm repeating it over and over. It's my mantra, and it is what's gonna get me through what's about to happen.

I am a fucking fighter.

I am a fucking fighter.

I am a fucking fighter.

And then it begins.

CHAPTER 53

HHJ Jeremy Letts (the judge)

With his shoulders hunched and his hands balled up in his trouser pockets, Arron Freeman cuts a smaller figure than the preceding defendant. Whereas the stocky outline of Craig Mervyn-Scott was perceptible even through his ill-fitting formalwear, the effect of a shirt on Arron Freeman is envelopment: a thin, rodent-like face poking through an amorphous white sheet as he reads out the oath. What is it about the underclasses that generates that ubiquitous ratty quality? NHS dentistry probably plays a part, I suppose.

'I swear by Almighty God that the evidence I shall give shall be the truth, the whole truth, and nothing but the truth.'

The boy runs his tongue over his protruding eye teeth – a tic which, I soon learn, recurs whenever there is a pause in his speech. It does not help with the rat thing.

'Now, Arron,' Bob Evans says, with an unseemly smile. 'Can you please start by telling the jury your full name?'

'Arron Freeman.'

'And your date of birth, please?'

'24 November 2007.'

'Is this your first time giving evidence in a courtroom?'

'Yeah.'

'The jury have already heard this, in the agreed facts read as part of the prosecution case, but can I ask you to confirm: You have no criminal convictions, do you?'

'That's right, yeah.'

'And no cautions, warnings or reprimands?'

'None of them, no.'

'Prior to the early hours of 1 January 2024, had you ever had any dealings with the police at all?'

Freeman shakes his head. 'Nah. I mean, when I was little, like, my mam had the social in and out, but I don't think there was actual police, do you know what I mean?'

Bob Evans frowns sympathetically. 'Well, let's see if we can help the jury a little with your background, and life growing up with your mum.'

Another sorry history unfolds.

Arron Freeman was born in Wythenshawe, which is 'basically in Manchester', we are enlightened. His father – name unknown – did not hang around long enough to ever meet his son, but long enough to bequeath mother, Zara Freeman, a raging crack cocaine habit, which attracted the attention of South Manchester Children's Services. The Pre-Birth Protection Conference ('loads of social workers chatting with my mam before I were born') resulted in the inevitable application for an interim care order at two days old, and, with the grandmother living at the other end of the country and unable to take in a newborn, Arron Freeman's first months on earth were spent in foster care. Zara Freeman was able to sufficiently clean up – at least outwardly – to persuade the court making the full care order that Arron could safely remain with her, but the years to follow would see Arron periodically removed and re-fostered, his home and his schooling at the mercy of the vagaries of his mother's 'illness', as Bob Evans terms her weakness.

'How many foster placements did you have?'

'To be honest, I've lost count. At least ten, I reckon. Some of them were for only a few days, while I were waiting for ones who could take me for longer.'

'And how many schools did you go to?'

He thinks. 'I had five primary schools, although to be fair one of those I went to twice, once when I was six and then again when I was nine. And three secondary schools. But one of them was when I moved to my nana's.'

The move to his grandmother's is explored, and I note down the lowlights, although I don't intend to remind the jury in detail of this sob story, artistically drawn by Bob Evans as it may be. At the age of twelve, Freeman returned to his mother's care. She had, with the assistance of a local drugs charity, taken 'meaningful ownership of her addiction', mustering abstinence and securing part-time work at a centre which specialised in helping smack addict prostitutes (or 'sex workers with substance misuse' – heaven help us). An income above universal credit had enabled her to escape the unpleasant-sounding Mossfields tower estate with its crack dealers on every landing, and to secure a private tenancy for a one-bed flat, in a quiet development within walking distance to 'the Metrolink', whatever that is.

'It had taken over a decade,' Bob Evans says, 'but it sounds as if stability for you and your mum had finally begun to crystallise.'

When Stage 4 ovarian cancer was diagnosed eight months later, Zara Freeman put her faith in the statistics, hoping that a 30 per cent chance at a five-year survival rate gave a reasonable chance of seeing her son safely past his sixteenth birthday. Her body gave her four months. Arron Freeman, aged thirteen and a half, was uprooted to the West Midlands to the care of his maternal grandmother.

'It was a mint year,' the boy says. 'My nana was dead sound – she wasn't soft, but she just made everything work, do you know what I mean? It was like, you don't mess with her, but she was also dead kind and just sorted out everyone's problems for them. She made sure I did my schoolwork, and I could have my mates round but they all knew the rules. You didn't mess with Nana. You know?'

Genetics being the bastards that they are wont to be, and fate being the bastard it had already proved itself to be, Nana's diagnosis granted her a little longer than her daughter, but not by much. Arron Freeman was not yet fifteen when his life was upturned once again, back in the hands of a local authority shorn of ideas and short of capacity in an overflowing care system. The only option identified was a move eighty miles away to Ableford, where the Rosewoods Family Centre (most recent Ofsted rating: Inadequate) had several vacancies after six of their intake had graduated to youth detention following an arson attack at a local petrol station.

'How did you get on at Rosewoods Family Centre?'

Freeman shrugs. 'Yeah, y'know. It's . . .'

He stops and clears his throat. His voice cracks as he asks for some water, and he pulls his face into a scowl, staring sternly as he gathers a response. 'It was OK.'

'Just OK?'

'Quite a lot of the lads . . .' He stops again. He scratches the back of his neck and inhales deeply.

'I think quite a few of the olders had been, like, in trouble before. And there wasn't much that most of the staff could do to get them to . . . stop. Do you know what I mean?'

Bob Evans nods. 'What sort of trouble did they cause?'

'Just . . . there was a lot of bullying, I think.'

'Of you, or in general?'

'Just in general. And of me, I guess, yeah. Just coz I sound different and that.'

'What did they do, these other boys?'

'Just banter and stuff, but they'd, like, take it too far. Like, beats where they'd take it in turns to try to make my arms bruise. Weeing in my drinks. Once, they, one of them pooed in my bed. There were these photos of my nana that I'd got, basically the last ones I had, and they drew cocks all over them with pen. I know it doesn't sound like much, but . . .'

He tails off, and Bob Evans, doubtless sensing that the jury have had enough of a flavour of this pity porn, moves to wrap up this segment. 'But despite these difficulties, what these older boys were doing, you still – as you've already told us – you still didn't get into any trouble yourself, did you?'

The youth shakes his head. 'I didn't, no.'

He looks at the jurors, and then turns his head to the dock.

'Not until I met Craig.'

CHAPTER 54

Arron (the second defendant)

I first met Craig on the Rosewoods estate, I say to the jury. It was only a few weeks after I moved to Ableford, so around the summer of 2022. Craig's home was a five- or maybe ten-minute walk from the centre, and we got talking one day when I was waiting for a bus. It turned out he knew some of the kids at the centre, and we realised we both went to the same school. Although different classes.

From then, we would spend our time just chilling round his or down the rec. Yeah, we'd sometimes smoke weed, I'm not gonna lie. Although to be fair, that was mostly Craig and Jamal. Oh, yeah, I met Jamal through Craig. I don't really have much to do with him, to be honest. He'd often be hanging around Craig's, but it wasn't like me and Jamal were tight or anything like that. He was just someone I knew to let on to.

Mr Evans then asks me when I first heard the name 'Bernard Hooper'. And I say, it was probably a few weeks before New Year's Eve. Craig was pissed out his head, and said he had just found out that this guy, this teacher, had done something to his little sister. Touched her up or something.

'What was your reaction upon learning that?'

I shrug. 'Dunno, nothing. It's like, obviously it's bad, but I barely know Craig's sister. It's not like I'm gonna say anything to her about it. I think I just said something like, "Oh, that's shit, bro", or summat.'

'And was that the only time Craig discussed Bernard Hooper with you?'

I shake my head. No, I say to the jury. No. He kept talking about it. It became like this obsession. He was googling him, and trying to find out where he lived, and basically it became all that he wanted to talk about. How he was going to find Bernard Hooper. And what he was going to do when he did.

I keep facing the jury, trying not to turn my head to look at Craig.

'How did that obsession, as you've described it, make you feel?'

'I said to him, I said, "Mate, you know what it is, you're gonna have to just let this go, all right?" I said, "Basically, if you're not gonna go to the police, there's nothing more you can do. So just . . . chill, yeah?"'

Mr Evans is nodding like he understands. I'm looking over towards the jury, trying to get a read of what them jurors are thinking, but it's hard as I also need to concentrate on what I'm saying, and also what Mr Evans is saying.

'You said a moment ago that Craig would tell you how he was going to find Bernard Hooper, and "what he was going to do when he did". What did Craig say he wanted to do?'

And I tell the jury straight. No point in dressing it up. Craig said that he was going to fuck that man up. He was talking about knives, and the things he knew to do with them from what he'd seen on TikTok and that.

'Did you believe him?' Mr Evans says. And I shake my head again and tell the jury, no. I didn't. I knew Craig liked knives, coz he'd shown me that hunting knife he kept on top of his wardrobe, but I thought he was just chatting shit, sorry for the language, members of the jury. That's Craig, always making out he's the big man. I didn't think he'd actually ever do anything. And no, Mr Evans. I had no idea that Craig had taken to carrying a knife.

Mr Evans then asks about New Year's Eve. And I say that yeah, some of what Craig has said is true. We were all three of us round his that afternoon, and I was playing Xbox. I got there just after dinner, maybe two o'clock. I didn't have a clue what Craig had done earlier that morning, going round to his stepdad's and battering him. He didn't say anything to us about that. Obviously he was a bit bashed up, but that's Craig. He's always getting in scraps.

We had our tea at Craig's – me and Craig, Jamal went home for a bit – and then went into town. Jamal said there was this new bar that was doing cheap shots for New Year, so our plan was to go there. I don't know the name of the bar, because we never found it. As you can see on the CCTV, I tell the jury, we were walking around in circles looking for it, because Jamal was mashed out of his head and didn't know where he was taking us. To be honest, I don't even know if that bar even existed.

We then all found ourselves back in the town centre. I'll be honest, I say to the jury, I can't remember what our plan was by that point. We'd had quite a lot to drink, we'd wasted half an hour looking for Jamal's imaginary bar. But then Craig saw someone on the street, and pointed and shouted, 'That's fucking him!'

Mr Evans pulls a face when I say that. Not a big one, not long enough for the jury to see, but I notice it: he stops and blinks like he's suddenly lost. But then he's talking again, and I'm wondering whether I've imagined it.

'Take us from there,' he says, and I tell the jury how Jamal then says to me, 'That's him. That's Bernard Hooper.' And I didn't recognise him, of course, because I've never met the man, but Craig has seen his picture online or whatever, and must have shown Jamal, because Jamal is suddenly walking over and talking to this guy. At this stage, I say to the jury, I don't know what's going on. I don't know why this man is here, or what's about to happen.

'To your knowledge, was there any plan to meet Bernard Hooper that night?'

Not to my knowledge, I promise the jury. But I obviously don't know what Craig and Jamal were up to, whether they'd made some plan to meet him. They could have done that and just not told me.

What did I think was going to happen when they started talking to him? I swear down, I had no idea. But I thought the best thing was to stay close in case Craig tried to do anything stupid. I know what he's like with his temper – everyone now knows what Craig is like with his temper – and I just thought, if I'm here, I can maybe stop something from happening.

We all walked down Rowe Street, as you can see. I can't remember what we were talking about, I say. I wasn't really saying anything, just keeping my wits about me in case anything happened. It was when we got to the ginnel that everything went mad.

'When you refer to the ginnel, do you mean Garth Yard?'

Yeah, I say, that's when Craig took off his rucksack and got out the knife. I swear down – Mr Evans starts to talk over me but I've already started to answer the question that I know is in his mouth – I swear down I did not know he had that in his bag. I don't even know where he got it from. I guess maybe them people he was messaging about getting hold of weapons? I don't know. Anyway, Craig was waving it around, and was shouting the odds at Mr Hooper, and I did the only thing I could, and I stood between them.

From there, I just listen carefully to what Mr Evans asks me. I don't want to get myself mixed up, so I let him ask what he needs to ask to help me tell the story. I look straight at the jury for all of this part, making sure they can hear me loud and clear. I tell them how Craig pushed past me and went for Hooper, cutting him deep with the first hit, sending blood spraying over us like a fountain.

I describe the look on Jamal's face – this wild, unhinged howl he gave as he jumped in and started punching and kicking as Craig set about Hooper with the knife. I admit that when this started, yeah, I froze. I should have done more to help but I just couldn't believe what was going on. It was just mad, like a bad dream where you're just thinking you'll let the dream do its thing, and it's OK because soon you'll be awake and it will all be over.

I was begging, I tell the jury, and I hear my voice cracking again. I was begging Craig and Jamal to stop what they were doing, but they either didn't hear me or they didn't care. I think I even grabbed the knife at one point, touched the blade, but they just carried on. And the more they hit him, the more the blood spilled and sprayed and coated us all.

And even though I'm supposed to be listening to Mr Evans's questions, my words are coming too quick for me to stop, and as I'm getting them out I realise that my voice isn't cracking any more, it's broken, and there's tears – actual fucking tears – on my cheeks as I tell them how, as the old man is literally lying on the floor choking up blood, bubbles spilling out of his mouth, Jamal is getting out his phone and calling the guy a paedo and laughing about this being one for his stories – y'know, on his Snapchat – and I'm screaming at him, at least I think I'm screaming. By this point, I'm finding it hard to know what's real.

The sirens are what makes me sure. When we hear them, it's like somebody has switched on the lights at the end of a party – obviously it's not a party, members of the jury, but you know what I mean. It just makes everything real again. Jamal legged it straight away, dropping his phone he was running so fast. I was left with Craig in the ginnel, and I didn't know what to do, so yeah, I ran too. I shouldn't have – I hadn't done anything wrong. But I panicked, didn't I?

Mr Evans then asks me about the police station, and how it was my first time in a police cell, and my first time speaking to a solicitor, and then my first time being interviewed by police, for hours and hours and hours.

'Why did you decide to answer "no comment" to questions?' Mr Evans asks. And I say to the jury, I was in shock. Proper, actual, literal shock. I'd literally witnessed a murder. And I had this brief telling me that the best thing to do was go no comment. What would you do? You're sixteen years old, you've never been in a police station before, and you've got a lawyer telling you to go "no comment" – what, am I supposed to just ignore him? I just did what I was advised. Tell me you wouldn't do the exact same thing.

My pulse is racing, and Mr Evans gives me a minute and waits for my breathing to slow down. He asks if I'm OK to carry on, and I wipe the back of my hand across my face and I nod. 'I just want to get this over with,' I tell him.

'I want,' he says slowly, 'to ask you about something the jury have seen. The messages between your phone and Jamal Lowton's J2. The "u wanna play a game?" messages.'

I say that, yeah, I know the ones. And it's not how it looks. Not even a bit.

'Well, let's take things in turn,' he says. 'Do you accept sending those messages?'

Of course, I say. I'm not gonna lie about it. That was Jamal dicking around. That's what he's like. He's a weird kid. He's always watching them sick videos on his phone, and always coming out with the maddest shit, and we're always like, 'Yeah, yeah, Jamal. Sure. Whatever.' That's all that was.

'In the messages,' Mr Evans says, 'Jamal describes a "game" in which participants take turns to hit somebody until they are dead. Have you ever played such a game?"

No! Of course I haven't! None of that was serious, I tell them, my voice getting louder until I realise I'm almost shouting. Look at what I actually say in them messages – I don't agree to anything. That's because it was just stupid banter. Listen to what I'm telling you – it had nothing at all to do with what happened to Mr Hooper. It's the prosecution taking something completely the wrong way and twisting it to fit what they want this jury to believe.

There was no game, I promise the jurors.

You cannot believe what the prosecution are telling you.

CHAPTER 55

Jennifer (counsel for the third defendant)

It is possible my perception is skewed by this morning's medicine, but for a youth who has not given evidence before, Arron Freeman is acquitting himself well. Potentially to the point of actually acquitting himself, which does not augur favourably for Jamal. His explanation for the messages with Jamal is by some distance the least convincing part of his testimony, but given our mutual interest in it being true, I don't expect either Wyatt or I to touch it in cross-examination. We will have to find other ways to break him.

'Do you think you are clever?'

Baxter Wyatt's opening salvo is delivered with his head bent down in his notes. Or, at least, his note*book*; once again, from my vantage point I can see the blank page exposing the affectation. His refusal to meet Arron's eye, and the pained silence that follows, has the desired effect of immediately knocking the kid off his stride. He looks towards Bob, and then the judge, then me, and finally says shakily, 'You what?'

Wyatt slides his glasses up the bridge of his nose and meets the boy's confused stare.

'Do. You. Think. You. Are. Clever. Mr. Freeman?'

I try to shut out the *Dad's Army* theme tune which inconveniently springs into my head. Arron looks around again for an answer. Bob, correctly, avoids his gaze.

'I dunno,' he eventually offers. 'Not really. Maybe.'

'You see, I suggest that you *do* think you are clever, Mr Freeman. You have given the jury an exceptionally detailed account of what you claim took place. But what you have done, I suggest, is you have taken strands of the evidence, and snippets of information that you have gleaned from others, and have constructed an elaborate fiction around it.'

It is, once again, not a question but a speech. But Letts appears content to allow Wyatt free rein. And despite the absence of a question mark, Arron Freeman is willing to answer.

'No, I've told the truth.'

'Because, despite the *extraordinary* detail you are now able to provide – a year after the event – when you were arrested and interviewed by the police you did not say *any* of this, did you?'

'Like I said, my solicitor told me to go no comment.'

'There was no prepared statement summarising even the bare bones of your defence,' Wyatt enunciates for emphasis, reminding the jury that his lay client, whatever the deficits in his interview, did at least partially set out his stall beforehand. 'No mention at all of Craig Mervyn-Scott having a vendetta against Bernard Hooper, was there?'

'It was on legal advice.'

'No mention whatsoever of Craig Mervyn-Scott having told you of his desire to exact vengeance on Mr Hooper?'

'It was on legal advice.'

'Not even a hint of a suggestion that you had been frantically trying to pull Craig Mervyn-Scott away as he showered you all in Bernard Hooper's blood.'

'I'm not a grass.'

'Ah,' Wyatt's lips twist. 'So which is it – did you refuse to answer questions because of legal advice, or are you now saying it is because you have a moral code which precludes you from telling the police the truth?'

Arron's muttered answer escapes me, but Wyatt booms over him in any event. 'The point, Mr Freeman, is that despite having been cautioned – despite having been told that this was your chance to tell the police your story, and that it could be held against you at court if you failed to do so – you did not mention *anything* that you now ask this jury to accept. And the reason for that, is that you were biding your time, waiting to see what evidence emerged, and contriving to concoct a clever little story around it.'

'No.'

'Because the truth, as you well know, is that you panicked when Bernard Hooper pulled out a knife on Craig, and you and Jamal Lowton completely lost control. And your elaborate fabrication is designed to distract this jury from that very simple truth.'

With those foundations aggressively laid, Wyatt systematically hacks away at each aspect of Arron Freeman's testimony which contradicts Craig Mervyn-Scott's. For the most part, he draws little blood; it is a procession of assertions and denials which, as with many cross-examinations, risks becoming repetitive. Happily for the jury, Wyatt has another explosive up his sleeve, as he reaches Arron Freeman's account of the rendezvous with Bernard Hooper.

'In your evidence today, you told the jury that Craig Mervyn-Scott saw Bernard Hooper on Dalston Street, pointed at him and shouted, "That's fucking him." And that Jamal Lowton then said to you, "That's Bernard Hooper." Were you telling the jury the truth about that, or were you lying?'

'Telling the truth,' Arron replies.

'Well, perhaps you can help us then with this.' Wyatt theatrically waves a stapled document in the air. 'Your defence statement, served on the court and setting out your defence. Signed and approved by you, yes?'

As the usher shuffles a copy up to the witness box, Arron nods uncertainly. 'Yeah.'

Trying to decide whether the grin on Wyatt's face would be classified as impish or wolfish, I bring up Arron's defence statement on my laptop. Paragraphs ten and eleven are where I expect Wyatt to go. And he does.

'Read those paragraphs to the jury, please.'

Arron blinks and begins reading. '*At around 23:45, as the defendants travelled along Dalston Street, by chance they encountered Bernard Hooper. At this stage, Arron Freeman did not know Mr Hooper's identity, but Craig Mervyn-Scott and Jamal Lowton appeared to recognise him, and approached him to engage him in conversation. Arron Freeman was not party to what was being said, but followed his co-accused and Bernard Hooper as they made their way down Rowe Street. When they arrived at Garth Yard, Arron Freeman realised that the male was Bernard Hooper . . .*'

'Stop,' Wyatt barks. 'Now, nowhere in that statement do you say that Craig Mervyn-Scott shouted, "That's fucking him." Do you agree?'

Arron's eyes dart over the page. He nods slowly.

'Nor do you say that Jamal Lowton told you, "That's Bernard Hooper."'

'I must have forgot that when this was written.'

'Well, no, because in fact you say the complete opposite: in this document, you say that you had no idea that the man was Bernard Hooper until you were at Garth Yard.'

'Right.'

'Those versions cannot exist in the same world, can they? So were you lying to the court in your defence statement, or lying to the ladies and gentlemen of the jury?'

Something moves behind Arron's eyes. It is indefinable, but instantly evocative. I shut my own eyes and try to stifle the image that is re-forming. A teenaged boy trapped in a lie, desperately computing his escape routes and finding each one blocked off. An incredulous prosecutor privately hoping that the jury shares in the disbelief. A public gallery holding its breath.

Eventually: 'I wasn't lying. I think I just got confused.'

'You got confused, Mr Freeman, because you are not telling the truth. This is yet another example of you trying to twist the knife – excuse the expression – into Craig Mervyn-Scott. Another example of you bolstering your own fictitious claim that Mr Hooper's death was about revenge. Only this time, you have tripped over your own lies.'

They joust a little more, Arron Freeman maintaining innocent mistake, Wyatt pounding at dishonesty on oath. The sparring continues as they roll into Garth Yard, and there is a temporary cessation as they find common ground – the (for me) unhelpful involvement of Jamal Lowton throughout – before they lock arms once more over the mechanics of the killing, and who was doing what with the zombie knife.

Fatigue is setting in by the time it is my turn to cross-examine, and Jeremy Letts generously offers the jury five minutes to empty their legs and stretch their bladders, the lack of reaction to his unintended transposition an indicator of just how shattered everybody is. I decide to take the time to audit my questions, intending to delete anything that is not absolutely necessary, but find that by the time the jury are being brought back in, I have in fact simply sat stationary at my laptop.

Like Baxter Wyatt, I take a few moments to set the context for my questions. However, no sooner have I started reminding Arron Freeman of Jamal's case, than I am interrupted.

'Lies.'

'I beg your pardon?' I smile over-politely.

'Sorry, miss,' Arron Freeman says, looking over at the jury box, 'but everything Jamal Lowton is telling you – everything he is telling youse all –' he points at the jurors – 'it's just lies.'

'Mr Freeman . . .' I start, but he appears reinvigorated for the break, and I decide that there is more to be gained by letting him tire himself out than trying to talk over him.

'Sorry, miss, but it is. Jamal was more involved than any of us. If the police had found his jacket, you'd have seen all the blood.'

'Well, Mr Freeman,' I say. 'I am going to suggest that this is another example of what Mr Wyatt described. This is you seizing on a detail – in this case, the police's failure to seize Jamal's clothing – and exploiting it to support your lies.'

'They're not lies, miss,' he says, his confidence growing. 'Why did Jamal get rid of his jacket if there was nothing on there? How did Mr Hooper's blood get on his top? Why was he hiding when the police arrived? Like them guys watching told you all, there was three of us in the alley. We was all there. And Jamal was the one, with Craig, who was laying into Mr Hooper. I know you don't want to hear it, coz you're trying to help Jamal, but that is just the way it is.'

His confidence is encroaching on arrogance, and I am tempted to see whether, if given a little more time, it will begin to grate on the jurors. But instead I decide to wrest control back, mindful of the need for brevity. 'But that is not "the way it is", is it, Mr Freeman?'

'What do you mean?'

'Again, you are twisting the evidence and fitting your story around it.' Surrendering to the double act with Wyatt, I do not pause for breath. 'You are only putting Jamal at the scene, because you have seen the pathology evidence showing that more than one person was involved in inflicting the injuries.'

'Nah—' he begins, but this time I am not letting him finish.

'Because, if you told this jury the truth and admitted that Jamal was not involved in the infliction of the fatal injuries –' I pause just long enough for the jurors to complete the sentence in their heads, before doing so for them – 'then it would have had to be *you*. Wouldn't it?'

I expect an immediate denial. But there is something else. That look *again*. Behind the eyes. And this time, I allow my mind to build the image, a million pixels swirling into focus and settling into place, transporting me to a different courtroom, in a different time. Another young face staring out from the witness box, another flash perceptible only to those who know to look for it. Another boy accused of murder, pleading his innocence, but his mind diverted; his attention straying past the barrister examining him, and out towards a face in the public gallery.

A face voided of expression by rage, by grief, by fear and by bargaining and by depression and by every fractional consequence of loss, every conceivable product of having had something you loved with everything you ever had and everything you ever were, and of standing only metres across from the person who took it all away.

My face.

The hollow shell in this gallery, the apparition of mourning shaking her head as she locks into the dark eyes of the boy in the witness box – it is me. Too weak, too defeated, too emptied to stand up or shout out, to make known in any coherent or incoherent fashion the torrents raging within me. But capable still, with that shake of the head, of making one thing clear: I know what you did. Whatever verdict this jury renders, I know what you have taken.

I wrap up my questions as quickly as I can, before running out of court and vomiting all over the concourse.

CHAPTER 56

Aliyah (the prosecutor)

The early lunch break prompted by Jennifer Rennie's dramatic dart out of court gave me an unexpected hour to hone my questions for Arron Freeman. Again, much of the meat has been picked off by counsel for the co-Ds, but there's still enough left to make a tasty snackette for the jury.

The 'murder game' messages are where Arron Freeman is weakest. Unsurprisingly, neither Baxter Wyatt nor Jennifer Rennie went near those. Equally unsurprisingly, it is where I intend to begin. Mr Freeman's holier-than-thou, poor-little-poor-boy act might have distracted one or two of the more credulous jurors, but the defence cross-examination has hopefully yanked their focus back. I am quietly pleased with the flow of my questions, neatly set out in double-spaced bullet points, size 22 font, and the extended lunch break has allowed me to perfect the phrasing. The best cross-examinations drag a witness to a pre-ordained destination along the precise route of the questioner's choosing, not merely anticipating the answers, but ensuring, through skilful composition, that there is only one answer a witness can sensibly give.

While not so immodest as to consider this the *best* example of my work, I do think it comes close. With Craig Mervyn-Scott already in the bag, and with Jamal Lowton not yet confirmed as giving evidence, Arron Freeman is my big game kill. And I am very much looking forward to the chase.

'All sorted, Miss Rennie?'

Letts does not even attempt to feign concern as he strides onto the bench, leaving no doubt that, whatever has happened, it'd better damn well be sorted. I wonder whether he heard the same rumour that blew through the robing room – that a pool of sick was found next to the broken water cooler on the third floor – and whether he has connected it to her.

'Thank you, Your Honour. I do apologise – I suddenly felt faint and needed some air. That's all. Much better now.'

He nods, either unconvinced or unimpressed, but waves at his usher.

'Fine. Well, let's get the jury back in and see if we can conclude the second defendant's evidence this afternoon.'

Once we are all reassembled, I smooth my collarette and rise, fixing Arron Freeman in my sight. A shiver ricochets through me as I allow the anticipation to build, and then, 'Do you believe in coincidences, Mr Freeman?'

He looks unsteady. Exactly as I had planned. 'What do you mean?'

I do not break my stare. 'Is it just a coincidence that, on 28 December 2023, Jamal Lowton invited you and Craig to murder somebody on New Year's Eve, and then on New Year's Eve, you, Craig and Jamal were present when Bernard Hooper was brutally murdered?'

He searches for the right answer. He will eventually realise that there isn't one. 'It's . . . I'm . . . Jamal didn't invite me to murder anybody. It's like I've said.'

Marvellous. He has invited a dissection of the message, and I am only too happy to remind the jury, again, of precisely what was said.

'Let's look together, shall we,' I suggest, directing the jury to the messages in their bundles. 'Jamal starts by sending you a link to a YouTube video. The video now cannot be traced, but you can presumably help us? What was it?'

'I can't remember.'

'Seriously? You must have *some* idea, Mr Freeman. Given the importance of this evidence to your case. Given what you've told this jury, you must have *pored* over these messages, frantically wracking your brain to recall the true context. Can you really not remember what that video was?'

'No, miss, I can't.'

'Oh, dear. Was it violent? Did it show, perhaps, somebody being killed?'

He doesn't reply.

'Well, you do remember Jamal asking you to play a game in which "we all bang sum1 out". Yes?'

'Yeah. But it was bants.'

'And "bang sum1 out" – you understood that to mean killing somebody?'

'It was bants.'

'Bang out means kill, yes?'

'Yeah, but it was a joke.'

'Jamal tells you that he needs three people to play this game. Remind the jury, how many of you were there in Garth Yard?' My smile has evaporated, and out of the corner of my eye I can see rows of folded arms in the jury box. They are with me. 'How many, Mr Freeman?'

'Three, as you know, but that has nothing to do with them messages.'

'Jamal says, "u hit him then I hit him and we go round circle til sum1 wins". I stop, and pick up a hard copy of the pathology report which I have had printed as a prop. "Bernard Hooper had injuries all over his body, consistent with multiple blows from multiple individuals, didn't he, Mr Freeman?'

'Yeah, but it had nothing to do with that.'

'You were interested in the game though, weren't you? Asking Jamal, "How u win?"'

'No, it was banter. I've told you, I never thought Jamal was being serious.'

'Not even when he said, "Srsly, u up for that?"'

'No, not even then. Because it was just Jamal being Jamal.'

'Your response is interesting, isn't it, Mr Freeman? "Yeman maybe". You *were* up for Jamal's game, weren't you?'

'No. I was just . . . I wasn't taking him seriously.' His voice is hardening. His temper is fraying.

'And when Jamal suggested "NYE", and told you to "Ask Craigy 2", that is exactly what you did, isn't it?'

'No.'

'And that is why the three of you were out on New Year's Eve, armed with a deadly weapon, looking for somebody to kill.'

I whizz my index finger over my trackpad to bring up my next page, resisting the temptation to stare for too long at the jurors, or to smile too broadly. My quarry is stunned; uncertain how to get back to his feet, uncertain whether to struggle and prolong the pain, or to lie down and hope that it is all over quickly.

'Can I just say something?'

'Wait for a question,' Letts tells him.

'Yeah, this is my answer to what the prosecutor just said, judge.'

Letts relents. 'Go on then, be quick.'

'The thing is, right, you've got this theory, miss, and yeah, I get it. Them messages don't look good. But the thing is, you've had your little theories from the very start, and you've been calling me a liar and saying I'm making it all up, but actually, the jury now know I'm right.'

The delay in processing his accent means I am too slow to interrupt.

'So I have said from the start, yeah, that this all happened because of what Mr Hooper did to Craig's little sister. And you told this jury that no, it's nothing to do with that, there's no link between these kids and the old man. And then what happens? Them counselling records come out, and all that stuff that Craig was looking for on his phone, and it turns out I'm telling the truth. And your little theory was wrong.'

Although the words are coming fast, Arron Freeman is not losing control. I wonder whether he has prepared this little speech, and I look pointedly at the bench for Jeremy Letts to step in. But he is avoiding my eye.

'It's the same with these messages, miss. You think I'm making this up because it's your job to think like that. But I swear down, I am telling you, all of youse, the truth. And you can keep going on about the messages, but basically, that's all you've got now. The rest of your case has basically gone to shit, yeah? And so you're hammering me on these messages, hoping that the jurors don't see that you're wrong about this, just like you were wrong about Kayla.'

"This is—" I start.

"I mean, no offence, miss, but isn't this sort of thing – all these bits you keep getting wrong – isn't this the reason everyone says you're not supposed to be prosecuting?"

A gasp from Jennifer Rennie behind me is swallowed by a growl from the bench. 'Mr Freeman. This is not an opportunity for you to give little speeches. You are being asked entirely proper questions by the prosecution. Just. Answer. Them.'

A glance to my right confirms that several of the jurors are smiling. Whether it is because they are amused by Freeman's cockiness or impressed by the soliloquy does not matter; what is important is that the tension artfully hewn by my questions has disintegrated. I feel like a teacher tearing off a 'Kick me' sign pinned to her back and trying to recapture her authority.

I was prepared for the argument, of course. This was always the danger caused by the Google searches and the counselling records. I was going to have to make a concession in Arron Freeman's direction, and I have amended my closing speech accordingly. But I was not prepared for the jury's reaction. Their smiling along as this gobby street rat *mocks* me.

Face still burning, I stiffly re-mount my horse. 'Again, Mr Freeman, this is you taking a detail and building a false account around it. Whatever history there may have been between Craig and Bernard Hooper, you agree that your encounter with him that night was by chance, yes?'

'Yeah.'

'Exactly. And your motivations, when you came across him, are made clear in those messages.'

Before he can answer, I pick up my next line of questioning, but the remainder of my cross-examination proves perfunctory at best. I get him looking shifty once or twice when pressing him on his no-comment interview, but Wyatt's giant footprints are already over that part of the evidence, and I don't linger in case I look like a desperate tribute act. Through it all, I feel the anger knotting in my chest, at the injustice that I – and the jury – have been deprived of what could have been and should have been an irresistible dismantling of a plainly guilty defendant.

When I eventually sit down, the feeling burns hotter and harder, and the more I try not to dwell, the greater grows my paranoia that I have let Arron Freeman's conviction slip through my fingers, with all the consequences that such a result would entail.

Before I have a chance to overthink, I open Outlook and bash out an email to Chris Rose.

Chris, Do not disclose the OPT4 call. Mark as non-disclosable. List on sensitive schedule so defence are not made aware of it. AA

DAY 14 OF TRIAL – TUESDAY

CHAPTER 57

Jennifer (counsel for the third defendant)

'He's got to, hasn't he?'

Caz extracts the last drag from her cigarette and drops it the ground, crushing the butt with the heel of her Doc Marten. I have been lost in thought long enough for mine to have burned down to the filter, and it is only the heat threatening my fingertips that jolts me back.

'I honestly don't know,' I reply. 'Yes, he does. But at the same time . . .'

I shrug at her blankly. Caz rolls her tongue over her teeth and frowns. She is not used to uncertainty; my default mode is to decide first, regret later. I am increasingly aware that recent days have exposed my longest-standing professional friend to a side of me that, but for the extenuating context, would justify immediate removal of all instructions and, as Caz has delicately put it, a one-way ticket to the funny farm.

If I am permitted further mitigation, the decision as to whether a client gives evidence is always significant, and seldom straightforward. If Jamal declines to get into the witness box, the jury will not hear his version, and will be directed by the judge that they can hold Jamal's silence against him. If he does give evidence, he will be cross-examined by three silks in a battle of wits in which Jamal will be completely unarmed. Even with the intermediary helping to ensure he understands the questions – a process which always blunts the efficacy of cross-examination – the odds of Jamal giving a coherent and persuasive account of himself would be resisted by even the most optimistic gambler.

But there's the other thing, too. The lurking fear that is making me second-, third- and fourth-guess myself. While Caz has assured me – repeatedly, and at all hours of the night – that my client care with Jamal has not been affected by what happened to Ollie, the cruel whispers in my subconscious have not subsided. I am constantly and increasingly paranoid that my advice to Jamal is being infiltrated, even shaped, by dormant emotions bubbling ever closer towards eruption. That however much I kid myself, there is no way to separate Ollie's fate from my ability to act independently for Jamal.

'It's the gaps,' I finally say, walking slowly towards the revolving door. 'The jury are not going to accept that the holes in his account are just the product of him being off his face. He is going to be pressed and pressed and pressed for answers, and we still have no idea what he's going to blurt out. We've already had a drip-feed of instructions during the trial – such as Craig being responsible for the "How long do u get 4 murder?" search – and I just dread to imagine what contortions he will get himself into over three cross-examinations.'

I lower my voice as we join the security queue, checking around me for stray jurors.

'And there's something else.'

'Go on.'

'I went back over the phone material last night. And I think I've spotted a discrepancy in the time stamps in the SOE. I can't make sense of it. I'll show you when we get inside, before we go down to see him.'

Caz nods. 'OK. But if you're struggling to make sense of it, I doubt our hero is going to be able to shed any light.'

Once through security, we drag ourselves to the robing room. I hurriedly put on my robes and swipe a stray rucksack off a table to make space for my laptop. Caz leans over my shoulder, and I point out what I have noticed. It takes my fuzzy brain a couple of goes to made myself understood, but the significance, once made clear, is not lost on Caz.

'Well, fuck me,' she offers. 'We'd better go and see what Mr Chatterbox says about it.'

Jeremy Letts, in a rare fit of charity, has given the jury a late start this morning, to allow me and Caz time with Jamal before Jamal makes his decision. We knock on the heavy security door to the cells and wait for the jangle of the keys heralding the arrival of a sullen Serco officer. He unlocks and leads us in silence through two more sets of fortified doors and into the conference area, where we surrender our phones and are directed to the smallest of the offensively small legal rooms, with one screwed-down chair and a narrow wooden bench fixed to the back wall. I squeeze onto the bench and balance my laptop and the printed sequence of events on my knees. Caz patrols the perimeter like a wild bird planning a breakout.

Jamal is brought in, his handcuffs are released and he drops into the chair. He looks exhausted.

'Jamal,' I begin slowly, dispensing with pleasantries. 'We need to decide today whether you are going to give evidence. But before we do that, there's something I need to discuss with you. Does that make sense?'

He grunts confirmation that it does, staring at his fingernails. I wave my hand gently to divert his gaze and lock eyes.

'We need to talk about the meeting at Reggie's,' I tell him.

He looks lost already. 'You mean when it all kicked off?'

'No,' I smile and shake my head, already prepared to repeat every sentence to ensure his understanding. 'I mean the meeting at Reggie's, the off-licence, where you, Craig and Arron first met that night. You sent a message to Arron at 22:37 which said, "*Meet outside Reggie's*", and then Craig and Arron are on CCTV meeting you there at 23:12. Do you remember?'

He says nothing for a good ten seconds, and then slowly nods.

'Now, you have always agreed that you sent that message to Arron—' I start, but am interrupted by a low grumble.

'I said *maybe* I sent it,' Jamal says, breaking eye contact. 'I dunno. Can't remember. I was battered.'

I share a look with Caz, and she stands and leans over him.

'Jamal,' she says. 'You told us that you had your red Acer, what the prosecution are calling the J1 phone, and then there's a second, burner phone, which you threw away as you ran from the police, because – we're all adults here – it had drug messages on it. Right?' He does not reply. Caz continues. 'And our understanding of your instructions is that the J2 number – the one ending 0788, which sent the "Meet at Reggie's" message to Arron – was your burner. Is that right?'

He considers this. 'Yeah.'

'Right.' I pick up the baton. 'This is what we need to talk about. Because I have looked again at the raw data on Arron Freeman's phone download, and compared it with the call data records from O2. And there is something the prosecution have missed.'

'What?'

'The times on Arron's phone handset are all out by one hour. It's to do with the internal clock settings – we see this sometimes. It should have been spotted and adjusted in the SOE, but it hasn't. Anyway, the point is that that message to Arron Freeman, which the sequence of events says he received at 22:37 – that was actually an hour later.'

He doesn't react. To illustrate the point, I tear off a page from my SOE and hand it to him.

He stares at it. 'Now that,' I say, 'doesn't make sense, does it? Because by 23:37, the real time that Arron received that WhatsApp, you were with him. You had *already* met him at Reggie's. So why would you be sending that message at 23:37?'

I try to regain eye contact, but he is still staring at the SOE.

'If you say so,' he says eventually.

'Do you see the point?' I ask. He doesn't react. I purse my lips and exhale. 'I mean, did you get separated at some point? Or did somebody else send that message to Arron from your phone? And, if so, why would it be saying to meet back at Reggie's?'

'Nah,' he says immediately. I raise my eyebrow at him. He gives a pained smile. 'You look bare shifty when you pull that face, miss. Nah, I've already told you that's my number. I sent that WhatsApp. I dunno, maybe it's like . . . maybe the message just took a long time to get through. It's New Year, innit?'

That is a possibility, I concede. I vividly recall one New Year's Eve when my frustrated efforts to text 'Happy New Year! Lots of love, Mum xxx' resulted in fourteen-year-old Ollie receiving the message thirty-one times the following morning, to the high amusement of his mates at the sleepover.

'Miss,' Jamal says. 'I think you're overthinking this. Are you OK?'

Caz is grinning at me, and I shake my head, smiling back. 'I am fine, thank you, Jamal. Well, let's put that to one side for now. More importantly, moving on, are you giving evidence? That is what we really need to talk about. There are pros and cons, and—'

'I want to give evidence.' His certitude takes me by surprise.

"Okaaay,' I say warily. 'Let's take a few minutes to talk through the options, because—'

'Miss, I ain't done this,' he says. 'And I need to say that. My mum's here.' He holds up his palms, as if the conclusive logic of his argument speaks for itself.

'Jamal—'

'No, miss, I know what you're saying – I might not be the best at speaking. But I've got Janine to help me say the right things—'

'Jamal,' I cut across him. 'The intermediary does not tell you what to say, she's—'

'Yeah yeah yeah. But look, thing is I don't need to talk about it with you any more, because I can answer all their questions. I can do it. I need to tell them my truth. I need my mum to hear my truth.'

I feel my voice rising in volume and pitch, and a growing powerlessness to stop myself.

'I'm afraid we *do* need to talk about it, Jamal. Because it *isn't* that simple. Can I tell you my fear, Jamal? Honestly – no bullshit? My worry is that if you step into that witness box, you will be torn limb from limb. You haven't even answered all of *our* questions – and we're the ones on your side. You say that giving evidence is as easy as telling the truth, but you've already told us different things during the course of this trial to what you were telling us beforehand. You contradict yourself in the witness box and . . . well, you've already seen what happened to Craig. He fucking torched his own case! And – I say this with respect, Jamal – I don't have much faith in your ability to charm your way past Baxter Wyatt, Bob Evans and Aliyah Arshad, each of whom is, for the few hours you are in the witness box, going to make it their life's mission to show that jury how utterly, indescribably guilty you are.'

Caz looks worried. I allow a minute of silence, for my pulse to settle and the air to cool, counting the seconds in my head, and scrutinising Jamal's blank expression for signs of reaction. Acutely conscious of the optics of a robed legal professional looming over a vulnerable teenaged boy and shouting in his face – a scene redolent of a Bar Standards Board professional misconduct training video – I prepare to soften my tone, and perch back on the bench. Caz speaks first.

'Jamal,' she says slowly, 'what Miss Rennie is saying is that it's going to be difficult if you give evidence. But if you want to, that is your right. We're not saying you will definitely be convicted if you give evidence. We don't know what the jury are thinking. There's always fucking hope, isn't there, Jen?'

I nod. 'Look. It's your call, Jamal,' I say, striving to keep my tone conciliatory. 'As Caz says, all we can do as your lawyers is advise you.'

Before he can respond, a cells officer knocks on the door. I shout back without turning round. 'No, we're not finished – the judge has given us until eleven.'

The knocking persists. I stand up and walk over. But the face peering through the cracked, translucent panel does not belong to a Serco guard.

'Bob,' I say, opening the door and stepping out.

'Good morning,' he says, with much less *joie de vivre* than I am used to. Perhaps the strain is getting to him too. Maybe we'll all crack, in unison, and the jury will have to be discharged on the grounds that all counsel involved have lost their collective shit.

'I assume,' Bob says, still not smiling, 'that you haven't got any WiFi down here, so I thought I'd pop in to just let you know about a little development.'

'Go on.'

'It's more disclosure. Late again – although, to be fair, it only happened over the weekend, so the prosecution haven't had it long.'

My mind is still bowing under the permutations of Jamal giving evidence, and I'm struggling to keep up. 'Sorry, what happened? What have they got?'

Bob's face hardens. He looks as tense and as sombre as I have seen him all trial.

'A prison call. Between your lay client and one of his mates. In which your client confesses to the murder.'

CHAPTER 58

Aliyah (the prosecutor)

I am not prone to outbursts or rash decisions. My ability to maintain composure in even the most tumultuous conditions has been remarked upon by opponents and judges alike, and while the metaphor of a swan has been overused to the point of cliché, I have overheard more than one opponent whispering avian comparisons.

Dividing sentiment from the duties of a prosecutor has always come easily to me. I do not rile quickly, if ever, and prioritising – as I always do – fairness of the proceedings over the substantive outcome avoids any unwarranted emotional investment in my work. The question for me is always, What does justice require?

So it is that I reflected with care over the question of the OPT4 call. At the time I sent the email to DS Rose, my considered opinion was that it did not meet the disclosure test, and so could not properly be given to the defence. Nor, at that time, was I minded to rely upon it for the prosecution's purposes. But overnight I had the opportunity to cogitate further. And I can see that there is a way in which the content of that telephone call is capable reasonably of assisting Arron Freeman, and undermining the prosecution case against him. So, entirely properly, I emailed Chris Rose and the reviewing lawyer this morning, informing them of my revised opinion. They both readily agreed, a testament, one might think, to the correctness of my judgement.

I have the transcript in my hand now. All telecommunications from prison are automatically recorded. Prisoners know this, yet can be surprisingly incautious, presumably on the assumption that the vast majority of phone calls made by prisoners are mundane and of little interest to the authorities, and so unlikely to be monitored with any vigour. Category A prisoners, however, are of course different. The authorities are often extremely interested in what people convicted – or, in our case, accused – of murder might be saying when their guard is down.

The outgoing calls by all three defendants, made using the prison PIN system, have been monitored since their remands into custody, with some poor sod responsible for listening to the interminable, incoherent ramblings. Nothing of any significance has emerged, at any stage. Whatever secrets the defendants may be storing, they have been sufficiently self-aware to avoid spilling over the phone.

Until Sunday morning.

Three days ago, Jamal Lowton placed a call to a contact called Jared Grimes. The necessary checks were conducted when Mr Grimes was added to Lowton's contacts list over the weekend, and no trace came back. It transpires that, contrary to popular belief, the Lowton family have at least one associate who is not a wholesale scumbag. Or, at the very least, a scumbag savvy enough to evade the attentions of the Police National Computer.

The bulk of the three-minute call is inconsequential, with Lowton mostly moaning about the food options at his state-run hotel. However, at the two-minute-and-forty-second mark, the following exchange takes place:

JAMAL: Anyways man, Az is in tomorrow, innit.

JARED: He's going in the box?

JAMAL: Yeah, man. Fucked up, innit. Funny thing is, bro, man didn't even do nothing, you feel me?

JARED: What do you mean, bro?

JAMAL: Az didn't even touch the guy. I swear down. (LAUGHS)

It is by no means fatal to my case against Arron. After all, I do not need to prove that Arron 'touched' Bernard Hooper to secure a conviction for murder. If he was at least actively encouraging the others, that will suffice for a joint enterprise conviction. However, Bob Evans will undoubtedly wish to apply to put this conversation before the jury, and they can make of it what they will.

And it is an application which, on balance, I have decided the prosecution will support.

For the call does *not* show that Arron Freeman was not involved. But, unhappily for Jamal Lowton, it is a pretty conclusive admission that he was.

CHAPTER 59

Jennifer (counsel for the third defendant)

It is not a confession. At least, not in the way that most people would think of a confession.

But it is nevertheless fatal.

Taking the transcript from Bob, I thank him quietly and slip back into the conference room. My eyes are glued to the page as I stand in the corner, reading and rereading, feeling the blood draining from my face.

'What is it?' Caz asks, striding over and snatching the sheet out of my hand. I don't reply. I don't know what to say. Fortunately, Caz is willing to begin the diplomatic dispensing of difficult advice.

'You fucking idiot,' she murmurs.

Jamal stares, genuinely shocked. He has not, to date, been the recipient of Caz's tough love approach to client care, which she tends to reserve for gnarly old lags or self-deluding sex offenders.

'You know that they record prison calls, don't you? You know that everything you say as a Cat A on remand for murder is going to be pored over?'

'Yeah,' he replies quietly. 'Of course. I'm not stupid.'

I am grateful for the deep breath she opts to take instead of verbalising her instinctive response to that, as I sense we are one barked barb away from our client shutting down completely. I lift the transcript out of her hand and place it in front of Jamal. I trust neither of us to say anything further at this stage, so leave him in silence to digest the contents.

'Can you . . .' I start to check.

'Course I can fucking read it.'

Minutes pass, Jamal's eyes criss-crossing the page, the information slowly seeping in. Finally, he speaks.

'Is that it? Have they got anything else?'

Caz puts her head in her hands. 'I can't, Jen. You tell him.'

I sit back down on the bench.

'They haven't, Jamal, but they don't need anything else,' I explain, trying to keep my voice level. 'This is enough. For one, the pathology evidence shows that at least two people inflicted the injuries. This phone call has you stating that Arron Freeman was not one of them. Therefore it must have been *you*, Jamal. But more to the point, how would you know what Arron did or did not do *unless you were there?*'

Jamal leans back in his chair. A look I haven't seen before sweeps over his face. I can't quite compute it: at first, there is a flush of what looks like a childlike fear of the unknown, but it is quickly replaced by something more knowing, more worldly. As if he has suddenly acquired an understanding, or a clarity of perspective, which has cast off a lifetime of misapprehensions. And then he is laughing. A deep, throaty chuckle that echoes around our tiny box, bouncing off the walls.

'Fuck, man,' he grins. 'Fuck. Me. They proper got me, didn't they?'

I look over at Caz. We both wait for an explanation. There isn't one. Jamal doesn't even try.

'It is what it is, innit?' he laughs, clapping his hands slowly. 'Game over.'

At the end of the afternoon, I return to court and tell the judge, my colleagues and the members of the jury that Jamal Lowton will not be giving evidence in his defence.

PART III

DIRECTIONS OF LAW, CLOSING SPEECHES AND SUMMING-UP

DAY 15 OF TRIAL – WEDNESDAY

CHAPTER 60

HHJ Jeremy Letts (the judge)

'Come.'

It has taken the best part of three weeks, but the effeminate agency boy, whose name is apparently (and implausibly) Barnaby, has acquired the ability to knock before entering my chambers. As he prances through the door, his black gown askew, he grins like a hound, as if anticipating a congratulatory biscuit for mastering rudimentary social skills.

'Heel,' I say to him without looking up from my *Spectator*.

'Umm, I'm sorry, judge?' he quivers.

'I said good morning,' I say, folding the magazine away and standing up. Barnaby retrieves my trousers from the press and passes them to me, another trick he has successfully learned under my tutelage.

'I assume we are good to go?' I ask, as I slip on the trousers and walk over to the back of my door, where my robes are hanging. The boy nods, and stands in awkward silence while I gather my wig, laptop and charger. Awkward silence is good. There is no mindless wittering with awkward silence. He really is learning. Maybe I was too hasty in sending that email to the agency. Still. He will find other work, I am sure.

I follow 'Barnaby' along the corridors, and he knocks on the court door – surprisingly firmly – to portend my arrival. I am relieved to see that court is fully assembled, and, having confirmed that counsel have no issues to raise, direct that the jury be brought in to commence the directions of law. Then we will have closing speeches, followed by my summing-up of the evidence.

It is a delicate art, the summing-up. Too long, and you risk losing the jury (plus it takes a fucking age to type). Too short, however, and you risk missing out important points, particularly those which counsel have overlooked in their speeches, omissions which, out of fairness, I am always happy to highlight to the jury. There is also the question of balance. In a case such as this, where guilt is obvious to a blind/deaf mute, the summing-up provides an opportunity to give the jury a careful steer towards their verdict. Juries do not, general wisdom holds, like feeling as if they are being leaned on by their judge, and so subtlety is the byword. A gentle emphasis on this piece of prosecution evidence, a deft undermining of that part of a defendant's case; with practice you pick up the calibration.

I also find the summing-up to be a helpful way of delivering constructive feedback to counsel. I well remember from practice how rarely one receives input on one's court performance, and it feels unnecessarily direct to call counsel into chambers to tell them face-to-face. So as part of my summing-up, I might remind the jury of an argument which they may – and I always emphasise 'may' – find compelling. Or of a submission which the jury may – again, *may* – think utterly devoid of merit, the rambling non sequitur of a midwit. Part of that I obviously don't say aloud.

In this case, Aliyah Arshad has enhanced her reputation as a diligent collector of disclosure fuck-ups, which would ordinarily merit an honourable mention, but I may swerve away lest it lends grist to the defence mills. I am minded to say something about the slick charms of defence counsel – 'oily' is a bit too on the nose – and will certainly repeat the Crown's caution about smoke and mirrors for the benefit of any credulous jurors.

I could, if I were feeling particularly mischievous, make some reference to Jennifer Rennie appearing half-cut at various times – maybe weave various synonyms for booze into my summary – but I shall behave. Having spoken to Andrew Warner at some length last Friday evening about this trial, and about his ex-wife in particular, I am not completely without sympathy, although why on earth the silly girl agreed to take on this case is beyond me.

My meet-up with Andrew followed on from some of my own research into their family history, although many of the search engine results seem to have been expunged. I obviously knew the basics. I knew about their boy, Oliver, the stabbing and the subsequent murder trial. I knew their marriage had hit the buffers as a result, and that Jennifer had then moved to Ableford ten years ago or so to make a clean break, only for her ex-husband to nab the Recorder of Ableford gig last year. That much is general knowledge. But I had not quite appreciated the finer details of the case.

'Oliver was fifteen, a high attainer, at a solid grammar school,' Andrew Warner told me as he threw back his third Scotch. 'Fee-paying,' he added hastily. He and I were the only patrons in the VIP area of the Pomeranian, the lounge/bar attached to the golf club, but Andrew nevertheless checked over his shoulder as he spoke.

'Ollie's downfall began when he encountered this so-called friend, Finlay. Local comp lad, whom Ollie met through the Scouts, but who a few years later inveigled his way onto some sort of assistance scheme for Ollie's grammar. He lured Ollie away from the decent friends he had made at prep school, and into the association of some of the scholarship boys from south of the river.

'What started as the occasional crafty joint behind the bike sheds – or whatever – led to debts being accrued, and arguments about those debts, and then . . .'

He paused to receive his fourth drink from a youth with an unpressed waistcoat and an unacceptable number of pimples. Young Spot made a slow job of leaving, and by the time he had finished fucking off, Andrew had tailed off. I took it upon myself to pick up his thread.

'And then it transpired that one of these yobbos was in the habit of packing a shiv in his satchel?' I offered. Andrew nodded sluggishly, eyes fixed towards the bottom of his tumbler. Not having all night to spare, but also intrigued to secure the inside track, I continued for him. 'And young Oliver Warner-Rennie then found himself in the wrong playground at very much the wrong time, I presume?'

Andrew gave a weighty sigh.

'Finlay and Oliver had been growing apart over the months leading up to it. Different factions within the same group. Oliver had foolishly agreed to "persuade" Finlay to repay a debt that was owed by one faction to the other, and there were some fairly aggressive WhatsApp messages exchanged – just idiot boys playing to the gallery. But when a meet at the rugby field was called to straighten this out, somebody brought something along for enforcement, and it all . . . well. It played out as we know these things play out.

'Oliver was only on the periphery of the group when the knife went into Finlay's heart. But eight boys, along with the knifeman, were charged. Joint enterprise murder. And the jury were satisfied that Ollie had assisted or encouraged with the necessary intent.'

Goodnight, Vienna, I thought. Hello, life sentence with a minimum term of fifteen years.

'Jennifer and I were in court throughout,' he resumed after another hefty chug. 'It was obvious to us both that it was a pretty thin prosecution case. But the turning point . . .' Andrew shook his head and picked at his upper lip, 'was when Oliver gave evidence.'

'Oh?' I asked innocently.

'It was not pretty, Jeremy. He went to pieces. The Crown's silk kicked him around the courtroom for a whole day. And Oliver was one of five convicted. The three who were acquitted did not give evidence.'

I leaned back in my armchair and did my best impression of a sympathetic listener.

'I imagine,' I said, 'that there were pretty ugly recriminations for counsel who had advised Oliver to get in the box?'

'Abso-fucking-lutely. Jennifer had found this chap on a recommendation from her Head of Chambers. Some media-whoring silk with a flash website. She complained to anybody she could – his chambers, the Bar Standards Board, the Court of Appeal. All at enormous expense and to zero effect. We'd have been better off representing Ollie ourselves. We'd never have let him get within a hundred yards of the witness box on the evidence they had. He'd given a full-comment interview to the police – there was just no need to take the risk. The decision was an absolute gift to the prosecution.'

I said nothing further to Andrew about it, but knowing this now, it does rather make me question whether the advice Jamal Lowton has received has been entirely objective, or whether it has been filtered through a certain lens. Considering the strength of the case against him and the absence of any positive defence having been advanced in his interview, he really needed to get in the box. The jury have heard floated the idea of Jamal Lowton not being at the scene, but there is no evidence to support this. Not even an 'I wasn't there, guv' prepared statement in interview. And no explanation for what he said in that prison call. I rather thought that my allowing that to go before the jury would force Lowton's hand, but no. His story is absent from this trial. And it shouldn't be. This is not, Rennie is apparently in need of reminding, a comparable scenario to ten years ago.

I am a sympathetic man, and appreciate that emotional wobbles may have prevailed over sound judgement. But Jamal Lowton's failure to give evidence is something that the jurors are entitled to hold against him when determining his guilt. And, while it gives me no pleasure, I shall be emphatically inviting them to do so.

Barnaby leads the jury from their pen into the courtroom. I beam at them as they take their seats, and thank them for their promptness. Paper copies of my legal directions are disseminated as I tell the jurors that we are entering the final stages of the process.

Now let's get ourselves some convictions.

CHAPTER 61

Legal directions

FUNCTIONS OF JUDGE AND JURY

1. Members of the jury, when this trial began, I told you that you and I try this case together, but we have different roles. I am the judge of the law. What I say about the law, you must accept. It has been discussed and argued with counsel and you must apply the law as per my directions.

2. You twelve, however, are the judges of the facts. You decide what evidence you accept, what evidence you reject, and what conclusions you can safely draw. When I sum up the evidence after counsel's closing speeches, it is only my summary. If I appear to emphasise something that you do not think is import ant, then ignore it, because it is not important. If I do not mention something that you think *is* important, then take it into account, because it *is* important. Likewise, you are free to accept or reject any of the arguments that counsel make to you in their speeches. They are only arguments. Your view is what matters.

3. Witnesses in this case have given conflicting evidence. Most significantly, as to exactly what happened in Garth Yard at the

time that Bernard Hooper was killed. Different witnesses have told you different things. How do you resolve that? It is up to you, but you may want to ask yourselves how honest each witness is, how accurate they are, and how reliable they are. Parts of a witness's evidence may be truthful, accurate or reliable, while others might not be. Common sense and experience of real life will be your guide. When assessing a witness, you must apply the same fair standards to all witnesses, whether they are witnesses for the prosecution or witnesses for the defence.

4. You do not have to decide every single issue that has arisen in this case, only the issues that are necessary for you to return your verdicts. There will be no more evidence. Please do not guess or speculate about what might have been said by people from whom you have not heard.

5. It is entirely natural to feel emotion or sympathy in a case such as this, but emotion and sympathy have no part to play in your deliberations. Put them aside. A cool and dispassionate consideration of the evidence is what is required.

BURDEN AND STANDARD OF PROOF

6. The prosecution bear the burden of proving the guilt of each defendant. None of the defendants has to prove his innocence. This is the burden of proof.

7. The prosecution prove guilt if they make you sure of every ingredient of the offence charged (see 'Route to Verdict' below). This is the standard of proof. If having considered all of the evidence, you are sure that a defendant is guilty, then your verdict is guilty. If you are not sure, your verdict will be not guilty.

8. You must consider each defendant separately. You may reach the same verdicts or different verdicts in respect of the different defendants.

THE INDICTMENT

Count 1 – Murder

9. Murder is the unlawful killing of another with the intention of causing death or really serious harm. A person may be guilty either by inflicting the fatal injuries themselves, or by intentionally assisting or encouraging somebody else to do so.

10. The prosecution allege that these three defendants took part in a planned attack upon Bernard Hooper, using a zombie knife taken to the scene for that purpose. It is not in dispute that Bernard Hooper received multiple stab wounds which caused his death, as well as other blunt force injuries. The prosecution say that each defendant either joined in the attack, using violence towards Mr Hooper intending to cause him death or really serious harm, or that he intentionally assisted and/or encouraged his co-defendant(s) in the attack, intending that death or really serious harm would result.

11. Craig Mervyn-Scott and Arron Freeman each admits presence at the scene, but denies being involved in the violence.

12. Craig Mervyn-Scott says that Arron Freeman and Jamal Lowton overreacted when Bernard Hooper threatened them with a kitchen knife, and used weapons they found nearby to inflict fatal injury. Let me make it clear at this stage – there is no suggestion that, if that is what happened, the actions of AF

and JL would amount to the use of reasonable force in lawful self-defence. That is not an issue for you to worry about.

13. Arron Freeman says that Craig Mervyn-Scott and Jamal Lowton lured Bernard Hooper to Garth Yard for a revenge attack, which he attempted unsuccessfully to stop.

14. Jamal Lowton has not given evidence, but you have heard it suggested to other witnesses that he had left the scene before the violence began.

15. Mere presence at the scene during the violence is not enough. The prosecution must prove either that the defendant took part in the violence, or that he intentionally assisted or encouraged another defendant to take part.

16. If you are sure that a defendant took part in the violence with the necessary intent, or that he intentionally assisted or encouraged another defendant to take part in the violence with the necessary intent, then it would not matter who actually inflicted the injury from which death resulted.

17. Intention is not the same as pre-meditation or planning. Intention may be formed on the spur of the moment.

ROUTE TO VERDICT

Question 1

Are we sure that the defendant whose case we are considering *either* took part in the attack on Bernard Hooper *or* intentionally assisted/encouraged one of his co-accused in the attack on Bernard Hooper?

- If yes, go on to consider Question 2
- If no, your verdict is not guilty

Question 2

Are we sure that the defendant whose case we are considering intended that Bernard Hooper should be caused death or really serious injury?

- If yes, your verdict is guilty of murder
- If no, go on to consider Question 3

Question 3

Are we sure that a reasonable and sober person would have realised that as a result of the attack, Bernard Hooper might suffer some, but not necessarily serious, harm?

- If yes, your verdict will be not guilty of murder but guilty of manslaughter
- If no, your verdict will be not guilty

I will give further legal directions in relation to other matters, including:

i. The good character of Arron Freeman
ii. The previous conviction of Craig Mervyn-Scott
iii. How to approach lies told by a defendant
iv. How to approach a failure to mention facts in a police interview
v. How to approach Jamal Lowton's decision not to give evidence
vi. How to approach Jamal Lowton's 'confession'

in the course of my summing-up of the facts, following counsel's closing speeches.

CHAPTER 62

Aliyah (the prosecutor)

'Members of the jury, it falls to me to address you in closing on behalf of the Crown.

'I start by echoing, respectfully, what is set out in His Honour's written directions, and what I set out when I opened the case to you: the prosecution bear the burden of proving this case. And we do so by making you sure of guilt. Nothing less will do.'

As ever, calmness and measure are my signature as I take the time to make eye contact with each of the twelve jurors in turn. This, they already know and will be told time and time again, is one of the most important decisions that they will ever be asked to make. I am asking them to return a verdict that will permanently define the lives of the three young men in the dock. As with my opening, I will do so not by hectoring, but by gentle guiding. Even-handedness and fairness have characterised my prosecution of this case. They will see me through to the result that justice requires.

'I also wish to thank you, members of the jury, for the careful attention you have clearly paid throughout this trial. This has not been an easy case to listen to. The subject matter is of course distressing. You have multiple versions and contradictory explanations for how and why Bernard Hooper met his fate in Garth Yard on New Year's Eve 2023. But that does not mean, the prosecution say, that there isn't a very simple route through this case. There is. And it is a route that becomes clear by applying good, old-fashioned, British common sense.

'That, after all, is why you are here. You – the jury – are the cornerstone of the English and Welsh criminal justice system. There is a reason we do not leave decisions of this magnitude to lawyers, but to ordinary people, selected at random. You are real people with experience of the real world, and you apply that knowledge and experience to the evidence you hear. You know, from everyday life, how people behave. You are experts at weighing up when somebody is lying to you. You are experts at spotting red herrings, cutting through the smoke and mirrors and digging out the truth.'

Obligatory flattery dispensed and early hints fired about defence trickery, I can slowly increase the temperature.

'And the truth in this case, the prosecution say, lies in the obvious, common-sense explanations. The explanations which fit the evidence, and which were set out for you right at the start of this trial, when I first addressed you.

'These three defendants murdered Bernard Hooper. They did so for reasons ultimately known only to them, but which, the prosecution say, you can safely infer from the wealth of evidence that you have heard about them, their interests and their motivations.'

I ready myself for the next paragraph.

'Now the prosecution accept that, as evidence has emerged in the course of the trial, it has become apparent that Bernard Hooper was known to at least one of the defendants. But that, the prosecution say, is by-the-by. A distraction. There is no evidence to suggest that there was any reason for Bernard Hooper to cross paths with these three defendants on that night beyond sheer grim misfortune. But for Mr and Mrs Hooper's New Year's Eve plans being affected by the weather, he would not have been out on the streets at all. There may well, the prosecution agree, have been an extra frisson of excitement for Craig Mervyn-Scott when he realised that the group's chosen victim was a man against whom his sister had made a – completely unproven – allegation.

'But the motive, and the intention, linking these defendants is far simpler. Far baser. It was the exhilaration of killing. The thrill of taking a life.'

It's done. A swift and graceful glide over the evidential turbulence. Confess, avoid and move nimbly on.

'And that much you know from the "murder game" messages, exchanged between Jamal Lowton and Arron Freeman on 28 December 2023. Again – you will apply common sense. They spell out in these messages precisely what they intend to do, and what they go on to do.

'When? "NYE" – New Year's Eve.

'Who? Arron Freeman, Jamal Lowton and "ask Craigy too".

'What? A game. Go round in a circle. Take it in turns to strike the victim. Until he is dead.

'Arron Freeman invites you to believe that this was banter. If so, it is, you may think, the mother of all coincidences, the most spectacular twist of bad luck, that days after this "banter", Arron Freeman is with Craig and Jamal, covered in the blood of a man who has been killed in just this fashion.

'It's not bad luck, the prosecution say. It is the carrying out of a plan.

'Just as Craig Mervyn-Scott's messages to the 4140 number – on 29 December – in which he sends pictures of knives, asking his contact, "U get this" – those are not unlucky coincidences. They are part of the plan. He is sourcing the weapon they will go on to use.

'He even, you have heard, was searching online for "zombie knife". Is it just bad luck that his fingerprints end up on the handle of the zombie knife used to murder Bernard Hooper? No. It was part of the plan.

'What then happened on New Year's Eve? Again, the evidence tells you.'

I take a sip of water and check on my predicted foreperson. Number seven. He is engaged. I check the remaining eleven – no wandering eyes or distracted stretching. All good. On we go.

'The three defendants spent the afternoon together – after Craig Mervyn-Scott's violent attack on his stepfather, which we will return to later – drinking, smoking cannabis and taking cocaine. They were getting in the mood, watching online videos depicting the most extreme, sadistic violence. And, lest there be any doubt as to what was at the forefront of their minds, Jamal Lowton even had the foresight to google, "How long do u get 4 murder?"

'The sequence of events and CCTV footage then tell the tale. Jamal arrives outside Reggie's just after 22:30, and sends a message to Arron Freeman. Arron and Craig meet him at Reggie's at 23:12. And then the hunt for a victim begins.

'Again, common sense is your guide. It is obvious, isn't it, that they are following that stranger? Stalking their initial target for ten minutes, only to be foiled when their prey enters a flat block, at which point they turn around and retrace their steps.

'Craig Mervyn-Scott and Arron Freeman have both told you that they were simply lost, innocently and aimlessly wandering the streets of Ableford. You may have found the suggestion that they were lost in their own home town utterly risible. They could not even get their stories straight on what they were doing – Craig told you that they were looking for the park, at Arron's suggestion, while Arron told you they got lost searching for a bar recommended by Jamal. Again, ignore the smoke and mirrors, the prosecution say. Look at what is obvious.

'Look on the CCTV at the way they ran down Dalston Street when they saw Bernard Hooper. Look at their desperation to catch up with a lone, vulnerable man, who they then – we know from the footage – managed to lure down Rowe Street and towards Garth Yard.

'As for what happened inside Garth Yard, we have no cameras, but Farid Suhail and Paul Bell help you fill in the gaps. Their memories were, understandably, imperfect, but they were clear on the essentials. They have no reason to lie about what they saw and heard.

'Paul Bell saw the three defendants guide Bernard Hooper towards Garth Yard. You have heard in the agreed facts that Paul Bell did not pick out Jamal Lowton on the identification procedure, but there is no suggestion that it wasn't these three defendants. The CCTV footage is clear. Paul Bell told you how, having looked away, he heard Bernard Hooper shouting, and looked out of his window to see "the blond kid, Male 1," – Craig – waving a giant machete, which had obviously been taken from his backpack. Mr Bell heard the "whooping and hollering"; the "egging each other on", the screams, and the pleas from Bernard Hooper for the violence to stop. He saw Craig Mervyn-Scott run out of Garth Yard carrying the knife. And, despite what may be suggested on behalf of Jamal Lowton, he confirmed that all three males remained in Garth Yard throughout the violence.

'Farid Suhail likewise confirmed when cross-examined by Ms Rennie that "all three of them was there. And they was all laying into the old man."'

I deepen my voice an octave.

'All three of them were there. All of them were laying into the old man.'

I see juror two making a note, and stop to allow it to be completed. We then catch each other's eye, and I nod. Good juror.

'And that explains, doesn't it, the scientific evidence? It explains why Bernard Hooper's blood was all over Craig Mervyn-Scott and Arron Freeman's shoes and clothing. It explains Jamal Lowton's decision to run from the police, discarding his outer clothing and shoes as he went, and depriving you of knowing what was on that clothing. Although of course, Bernard Hooper's DNA in blood was nevertheless found on Jamal Lowton's sweatshirt. It supports what

Dr Nicholls, the pathology expert, told you about the number and distribution of injuries being consistent with having been inflicted by multiple assailants from different angles. All of the evidence points towards all three defendants being involved. "Laying into" Bernard Hooper, or at the very, very least, each actively assisting and encouraging the others.

'As I say, common sense. The obvious answer is usually the right one.

'The graphic video recorded by Jamal Lowton on his mobile phone, and then immediately forwarded to his other phone, shows Craig Mervyn-Scott with the knife. Wild. Out of control. It shows Bernard Hooper dying on the ground. You can hear a voice – Arron Freeman or Jamal Lowton – taunting him as his life ebbs away.

'The prosecution evidence proves the active involvement of all three defendants in the murder of Bernard Hooper.

'But you of course don't only have the prosecution evidence. You have the defence evidence to consider. And you will I know treat the defendants fairly, applying the same fair standards to assessing their evidence as you do to all witnesses. You may well have sympathy for the difficulties that Mr Mervyn-Scott and Mr Freeman encountered growing up. But, as you know, you put sympathy and emotion to one side. Analyse coldly and clinically what they tell you.

'And when you do, it is crystal clear that what these two defendants have told you, is arrant, self-serving nonsense.

'Craig Mervyn-Scott is not only, as you now know, a dangerously violent young man, but a proven liar. He lied to you on oath, over and over and over. He lied about the cause of his injuries. He lied about knowing Bernard Hooper. He lied until he could not lie any more, thinking that he would not be caught out.

'But he was.

'And this liar, this man who has perjured himself before you, still asks you to believe that he was the victim of an attempted robbery by Bernard Hooper, and that the zombie knife miraculously appeared in a skip and was used by Arron and Jamal to fend off the seventy-four-year-old armed robber? That, you may think, is an insult to your intelligence.

'Nothing about his account stands up to scrutiny. Why take out a rucksack if all he was carrying was keys and cigarettes? Why, if they were running to get to the midnight fireworks at the rugby club – look at your map – was he walking down Rowe Street, away from the rugby club? Why stop and talk to Bernard Hooper if he was in such a hurry? Why, if his purpose in grabbing the knife in the alley was to disarm Arron and Jamal, did he then go *back* into Garth Yard with the knife? "I thought Hooper was going to go for my mates again," he claims. Yet we know from the video that Bernard Hooper was lying motionless in a torrent of his own blood. Absurd from beginning to end, say the prosecution. You can be sure that Craig Mervyn-Scott's evidence is untrue.

'Arron Freeman's evidence fares little better under the spotlight. As you know, his explanation to you is one that he did not give to the police when interviewed, and as His Honour will direct you, you can hold that against him. You can ask why it is that he didn't mention any of the facts upon which he now relies. The prosecution say that it is because he had not yet decided which fictitious defence to run. He was biding his time, waiting to see what evidence emerged, before fitting a defence around it.

'But even with the benefit of time, he still struggles to present a coherent account to you. If he is telling the truth, he knew that Craig Mervyn-Scott was obsessed with exacting vengeance against Bernard Hooper, yet Arron Freeman willingly accompanied his co-defendants as they lured Bernard Hooper along Rowe Street. He willingly followed them into the darkness of Garth Yard. What exactly did he think was going to happen? A friendly chat? It makes no sense at all for Arron Freeman to have involved himself in this way – unless he *wanted* to be involved.

'And that takes us back to the messages. "Banter," he says to you.

Balderdash, say the prosecution. Those messages mean exactly what they say. They show his interests, and they show his motivations. They show exactly what he intended, and what he did, when he entered Garth Yard with Bernard Hooper. Arron Freeman was no innocent bystander. Even if those off-the-cuff remarks by Jamal Lowton in the prison phone call are correct – and you've not heard any evidence from Jamal Lowton to back them up – and even if Arron Freeman did not join in with the violence, he was at least actively encouraging the others, which, as you know from the route to verdict, is all that is required. His spiteful, degrading words to Bernard Hooper on the video recording – "How does it feel to die, you fucking paedo?" – make that clear.'

I hope that the jury do not pay too close attention to the somewhat inelegant revision of my case against Arron Freeman; the sidestep from certain direct involvement to potentially just encouraging. I was left with little choice once I had disclosed the Jared prison call, but I think I have styled it out. At the very least, I am not seeing any facial expressions in the jury box that cause me concern. Time to deftly move on to firmer ground.

'Finally, Jamal Lowton. This will not take long, because he has not even deigned to give you an explanation for the prosecution evidence against him.

'And the reason for that is the same reason that he ran from the police, discarding his clothing. The same reason Bernard Hooper's blood was on his sweatshirt. The same reason the prosecution witnesses put three men in the alley, laying into Bernard Hooper. And the same reason that Jamal told his mate Jared that "Az didn't even touch the guy" – implying not only that Jamal was present throughout, but that he, Jamal, very much did "touch the guy". That reason? Jamal was there. He was involved. And he knows that, if he subjected himself to cross-examination in front of the twelve of you, his guilt would become even more obvious.'

There are a couple of nods on the front row when I make

eye contact, but whether that is genuine agreement or reflexive will remain to be seen. I do not engage in the tea-leaf science of jury-reading. What will, I am sure, be met with genuine appreciation is my cue that we are reaching the end. I close my laptop and turn my body away from my lectern, loosening my posture and letting my hands fall by my side. I have memorised the last part to allow the impression of spontaneous sincerity. *I am one of you. Trust me, friends, on what I am telling you.*

'Members of the jury, please do not be distracted in your task. My learned friends will suggest to you that there is too much confusion in this case for you to be sure of guilt. There is not. There have been attempts to sow confusion, but that is because the truth is so plain from the evidence.

'I am not going to pretend that every question has been answered by the evidence, just as I am not going to pretend that this was a flawless police investigation. Obviously there are gaps. But as you have been directed, you do not have to decide every single issue. Only those that you need to decide in order to reach your verdicts.

'And on those central issues – what was each defendant doing, and what was his intention – the evidence is overwhelming.

'None of the defendants can explain away the evidence against him. And that is because the only explanation that fits the evidence is that all three defendants were involved in the murder.

'Common sense is the key, members of the jury. Ignore the distractions.

'The prosecution invite you to return a verdict of guilty against each defendant.'

DAY 16 OF TRIAL – THURSDAY

CHAPTER 63

In the Crown Court at Ableford

CLOSING SPEECH ON BEHALF OF CRAIG MERVYN-SCOTT

MR WYATT KC: Ladies and gentlemen of the jury. It has become rather fashionable in recent years to talk our country down. To denigrate or mock our heritage and traditions. To downplay our nation's achievements. To tell us that we should be ashamed of our history. To minimise what Great Britain has given to the world.

Well, you will forgive me for not hoisting myself up onto that bandwagon. I am afraid you will not find me apologising for the actions of our forebears. To the contrary, I am going to invite you to celebrate them. Because amidst all the doom-mongering, there are many virtues that I happen to think have not only made our country great, but continue to keep it so.

And chief among those is the system of criminal justice that we have successfully exported throughout the Commonwealth and beyond. Principles of justice which were born in the community courts of our Saxon kings, honed in the *Curia Regis* of Westminster, codified in Magna Carta and judiciously developed over many centuries through our common law – these now underpin judicial systems across the globe.

And perhaps the most sacrosanct of all those noble principles, is the presumption of innocence: the golden ideal that no man in this land can be convicted of a crime unless a jury of his peers – twelve men and women good and true – are sure of his guilt.

It is a burning flame of liberty that lights up the skies above all of us. We are all entitled to its protection. From princes to paupers, from aristocrats to the likes of Craig Mervyn-Scott, each and every one of us enjoys that right. If the state knocks on your door while you're eating your porridge and accuses you of a crime, the state bally well has to prove it, to the satisfaction of the rest of us, before it can insert itself between you and your oats.

So throughout your deliberations, keep that, please, at the forefront of your minds. Ask yourselves, at every juncture, not, 'Do we think the state *might* have proved guilt?' but, 'Are we *sure* that it has?'

Now, in the case to which you have dutifully listened, the issues have been well established. You know what the prosecution say. And you know what Craig Mervyn-Scott says. He tells you that Bernard Hooper was the aggressor. That it was Bernard Hooper who, following a chance encounter with the defendants, took Craig into Garth Yard, whereupon Hooper produced a kitchen knife and demanded money. The violence directed against Hooper was a reaction by the co-accused, Messrs Freeman and Lowton, who seized what they found to hand, and set about their work. Terrified of what was unfolding, Craig Mervyn-Scott wrested the blade from the hands of his co-accused, and we know from Mr Lowton's video recording, and the eyewitnesses, that Craig did indeed run out of the alley carrying the knife. The only mistake he made was returning to the alley, out of concern for his friends, at which point the weapon was snatched off him, and the bloody assault continued.

And here's the thing, ladies and gentlemen: the prosecution evidence is – when you analyse it – consistent with Craig Mervyn-Scott's account.

Somebody was shouting about money, says Farid Suhail.

The old man was shouting, it could have been threats, says Paul Bell.

The voice begging 'Stop!' could have belonged to one of the younger men, says Paul Bell.

The injuries *could* be accounted for by only two assailants, says Dr Nicholls.

The bloodstaining on Craig and Arron's clothing is consistent with Craig standing close by, as an innocent bystander, while the other two carry out the assault, says Dr Redmond.

The scientific evidence does not exclude Arron or Jamal having handled the knife, says Dr Redmond.

And, says Dr Nicholls, the injuries to Craig's hands are consistent with Bernard Hooper having slashed at Craig using the kitchen knife found in Garth Yard.

And this is the crucial part, members of the jury: you can now be sure – although the prosecution did not choose to tell you about this when the case began – you can be quite sure that Bernard Hooper did have a knife. But for the incompetence of the police investigation, we might have been able to say with certainty that it had been taken from Hooper's home address, but at the very least you have the evidence of his widow, who confirmed that it 'looked like' a knife from their kitchen. But for the police losing the knife – *losing the knife*, would you credit it? – we may well have had the DNA evidence to boot.

Now why, you will ask yourselves, would Bernard Hooper be wandering the streets armed with a knife? The prosecution cannot offer you an explanation. Not a single one. Arron Freeman and Jamal Lowton cannot offer you an explanation. Only the account given by Craig Mervyn-Scott – an account which he volunteered to the police right from the very start – can explain that feature of the evidence.

The prosecution invite you to dismiss it out of hand. 'Absurd,' says Miss Arshad, to suggest that a senior citizen would be looking to commit a robbery. Well, we do not know what desires, what madness and daemons, lurk inside the minds of other men, do we? We do not know what difficulties might have been preying on Bernard Hooper, what might have come over him to cause him to act in such a way, and we must not speculate. But you may suspect that something was amiss. Because Bernard Hooper did not tell his wife that he had gone out armed with a knife. And when he met the defendants, he was not walking home – he was walking in the opposite direction, to who knows where? It is not enough for the prosecution to wave away such an important piece of this puzzle. If they cannot explain it, their theory cannot be right.

So on the one hand, we have the abundant evidence consistent with what Craig Mervyn-Scott has told you. What then do the prosecution rely upon not only to contradict his account, but to make you *sure* of his guilt?

Well, they rely upon Paul Bell and Farid Suhail. Paul Bell, a drunkard, two storeys high and three sheets to the wind, who hid from the police initially, who gave an incomplete account later that day, then another, longer account a week after that, and who, in evidence before you, eventually admitted, 'I don't know what effing happened in the effing alley.' He began by telling you that he saw Craig Mervyn-Scott waving the knife at the start of the incident and hitting Bernard Hooper with it – compelling evidence, you must have thought when the prosecution elicited it. But as soon as he was pressed to any degree, he started to crumble. 'I got only a fleeting glance,' he agreed. 'Yes,' he conceded, 'I assumed that the male with the knife at the beginning was the blond kid because I got a good look at him with the knife at the end.' Well, assumptions are not good enough, are they?

By the end of it, he agreed that it could well have been Arron Freeman, not Craig, who was brandishing the knife at the start. Again, take him at his word: 'I don't know what effing happened in the effing alley.' His evidence has no value whatsoever.

And then there's Farid Suhail. You will doubtless recall the state of him. The prosecution place enormous weight on what he blurted out at the very end of his evidence, almost as an afterthought, about there being three people 'laying into' Bernard Hooper. But consider him as a witness. He was a mess, wasn't he? Utterly incoherent. In evidence in chief he suggested that there may well only have been *two* people involved in the violence. The man doesn't even know his own mind. Can you convict a teenage boy on the strength, the reliability and the accuracy of his evidence? Would you be happy for a jury to convict *your* son of murder on the confused, addled testimony of a man like Farid Suhail?

The minute you start to prod at the prosecution's 'overwhelming' case, as Miss Arshad put it yesterday, it begins to fall to pieces. There's nothing there. Not a single shred of direct, reliable evidence that Craig Mervyn-Scott laid a finger on Bernard Hooper.

What else do the prosecution cling to? They invite disbelief that Craig Mervyn-Scott might have got lost, as he told you accounts for his movements on the CCTV. Is it really so 'risible' that some teenage lads, a little the worse for wear, might take the wrong turn? I don't know whether my learned friend drinks, I don't like to make assumptions, but many of you members of the jury may have had that experience. We're not always the best navigator after a sherry.

'The knife was obviously taken from his backpack!' they claim. No evidence for this at all. Nobody sees it. This is pure guesswork, precisely the type of speculation that the learned judge has told you to avoid.

What else? The fact that Craig assaulted his stepfather, the man who paralysed his mother, using his fists and his feet. Does that in any way demonstrate a tendency to involve himself in random, frenzied knife attacks? This is truly desperate stuff from the prosecution.

'They were watching unpleasant videos the same day,' the Crown tells you. Well, no – Jamal Lowton was watching those videos. No evidence that Craig Mervyn-Scott was even aware of them.

As for the material on Craig's phone – there is no evidence that the messages concerning knives were ever anything more than bluster. Teenage boys say and do stupid things. Bad taste and prurience do not a killer make. A child who plays with water pistols is not a gangster. A boy who likes Action Man is not a soldier.

The prosecution case is a Jenga tower of speculation and guesswork. They think that if they say words like 'absurd' enough times, you will accept it, and not apply your minds. Don't fall for that, members of the jury. There may well be smoke and mirrors at play, but they are not being erected by Craig Mervyn-Scott.

I suppose I should say something about Arron Freeman. The prosecution, unsurprisingly, do not invite you to place any weight at all on his evidence, and here I agree with the Crown. Arron Freeman's account has clearly been carefully constructed to fit around the evidence, which is why he did not offer it to the police.

It does not make sense on its own terms. All three defendants' phones have been fully interrogated, and there is no evidence of any pre-arranged meeting with Bernard Hooper. So whatever the background between Craig's family and Bernard Hooper, their encounter on that night can only have been by chance. This business about allegations by the sister is a smokescreen from Mr Freeman.

In any event, Mr Freeman's case is fatally compromised, is it not, by the 'murder game' messages he exchanged with Jamal? Are those messages not entirely in keeping with Arron and Jamal's reactions when the opportunity for violence presented itself? Messages with which, let us not forget, Craig Mervyn-Scott had no involvement at all.

Now, we know that Craig Mervyn-Scott has not been entirely truthful in his evidence to you. He is young. He is scared. He is scrapping for his life. Sometimes – as the learned judge will direct you – people lie for innocent reasons, including to bolster a true defence. Panicking in the witness box and saying something untrue does not make somebody guilty of murder. You may very well have some sympathy with why he felt he had to say what he said. As he told you, he is doing his best to combat the cynical, manipulative lies of Mr Freeman. Fighting fire with fire. He shouldn't, of course. But you can understand why a youth of his background and apparent intellect might fall into error. That the prosecution seek to make so much of this young man's misstep is a sign, I submit, of how flimsy they recognise the rest of the evidence against him to be.

Ladies and gentlemen. The burden, as you have been directed, lies on the prosecution. They have to make you sure of guilt. Not merely suspicious.

How, given the way that the central planks of the prosecution case crumble upon inspection, and how, given that everything that remains is consistent with Craig Mervyn-Scott's account, can you possibly be sure of his guilt?

I submit you cannot. Not safely. Not being true to your oaths.

The only verdict in respect of my lay client, I submit, is a verdict of not guilty.

DAY 17 OF TRIAL – FRIDAY

CHAPTER 64

In the Crown Court at Ableford

CLOSING SPEECH ON BEHALF OF ARRON FREEMAN

MR EVANS KC: Good morning, members of the jury. I hope you all had a pleasant evening and were able to take a deserved break from this case. I was supposed to be out at the theatre last night with my wife and daughter, but had to tell them that, unfortunately, while they were enjoying a cheeky Nando's and a night of Pinter, I would be locking myself in my study to write a speech to deliver to you. My wife was full of sympathy. 'That poor jury,' she said. 'Have they not suffered enough?'

Well, I shan't sour the atmosphere by asking you to say whether or not you agree with her. But I will make this promise: I can keep my closing remarks to you relatively brief. And I can make that promise because we have all noticed the care and attention that you have paid throughout this trial, and how closely you have been following the evidence. Jury service, as I know you recognise, is one of the most important civic duties we as members of a society ask of each other. Every case in these courts matters, every case is serious, and can define the lives of the people involved. But trials such as this, where the subject matter is so serious and where young lives are in your hands, can feel like a particularly weighty burden for a jury to carry. And I know I speak for all the barristers in this case when I say thank you for the way in which you have done that.

I have promised you a succinct speech, so I had better get on with it. And I'm going to start by mentioning a name. It's a name that hasn't been mentioned by either of my learned friends. But it is important. Because it is the key to unlocking and understanding this entire case.

Kayla.

Kayla Scott is someone you haven't heard from, but whom you have heard a lot about. The younger sister of Craig Mervyn-Scott. Who made a serious allegation against her former music teacher Bernard Hooper. An allegation which, Arron Freeman has told you, explains what happened on New Year's Eve in Garth Yard.

And you almost didn't hear anything about Kayla Scott, and her allegation to her counsellor and to her brother. Because, as you know, this information was only disclosed to the defence at the very last moment.

My learned friend who prosecutes, in her closing speech casually told you that 'evidence has emerged in the course of the trial'. As if it appeared from nowhere, in a puff of smoke. As if this daily drip-drip-drip of relevant, crucial information is an entirely normal way for a serious trial to be conducted. As if this 'emerging evidence' is not material much of which the Crown has had in its possession for almost a year, and which has only been disclosed at the eleventh hour and fifty-ninth minute.

With respect to my learned friend, and appreciating that it is not her fault, this is not the way for a serious trial to be conducted.

And what is remarkable about all of that 'emerging evidence' – and this is why I place it front and centre of my speech to you – is how every single piece of it supports what Arron Freeman has told you. Every single piece makes it less likely that the prosecution case is correct, and more likely that Arron Freeman is right.

When this trial began three weeks ago, you were told that this was a chance encounter between Bernard Hooper and three defendants hunting for prey. The only person telling you otherwise was Arron Freeman. He had told the prosecution in his defence statement that Bernard Hooper was not merely known to Craig, but had become an *obsession* for him. Because Craig had learned what Bernard Hooper had allegedly done to his younger sister, Kayla. Craig Mervyn-Scott denied that he knew anything about such an allegation. The prosecution dismissed it as a red herring. As Arron having constructed an entire defence around something he had made up.

That was until that 'emerging evidence', the late disclosure of Kayla's counselling records, in which we – you – learned the truth. The truth that not only had allegations been made by Kayla, but that Craig knew full well about those allegations. That was swiftly followed by the 'emerging evidence' showing the Google searches on Craig's phone for 'Bernard Hooper'. The truth that Arron Freeman was trying to tell you, while the prosecution were blithely complacent that he was making it all up, is a truth that the prosecution are now forced to accept.

Before that 'emerging evidence', we had been told by the prosecution that the counselling records had been reviewed and that there was nothing to disclose. That was not correct. We were told there was nothing disclosable on Craig's phone. This was not correct. And the list of mistakes and errors does not end there.

You know from the cross-examination of the officer in charge of this investigation, DS Chris Rose, that the prosecution failed to obtain the call data records for Jamal's J2 phone number over the relevant dates. You know that they failed to seize and examine Bernard Hooper's mobile phone, or to obtain his call records. So we do not know whether there might have been previous contact between the J2 phone and Bernard Hooper. That, you may think, is an important gap. My learned friend Mr Wyatt KC made the point to you that there was nothing on the phones to show any prior meeting had been arranged between Craig Mervyn-Scott and Bernard Hooper. But we don't have all of the phones, do we? Who knows what Jamal Lowton might have been discussing with Bernard Hooper?

You also know that the prosecution made no effort to trace the people behind the numbers to which Craig sent those messages requesting weapons. Again, perhaps important. Such a line of inquiry might have been able to establish who provided Craig with the zombie knife. We will never know.

The list continues. The police firstly failed to forensically examine the kitchen knife found at the scene, and then lost the knife completely. The police failed to search Bernard Hooper's address to establish whether that knife matched those he kept in his kitchen. Half of the photographs of the murder scene have been lost. We know that the police failed to recover the carrier bag that Bernard Hooper was seen carrying on CCTV, so we do not know what was in it. And, perhaps most egregiously given the issues that you have to decide, the police did not bother to search for the jacket and shoes which Jamal had discarded as he ran away. Clothing which may have helped establish whether Jamal Lowton was as involved as Arron Freeman has told you he was.

So you have an incomplete picture. Hole after hole after hole. And yet the prosecution have the temerity to say that you can be *sure* of what happened here?

A point which I invite you to consider on behalf of Arron, but one which applies to all three defendants: Has this been a competent investigation? And, more importantly, are you sure that this has been a fair investigation? If this were your son on trial for murder, would you be happy to endorse the way that the police and the prosecution have acted? Because if this investigation would not be good enough for your son, it is not good enough for Arron Freeman. How, I respectfully ask, can you possibly be sure of guilt when the prosecution's own investigation has thrown up so much doubt?

What then of the evidence that we do have? Paul Bell agreed that, when he first saw the group, Arron was hanging back, not really showing an interest. Mr Bell agreed that the old man was shouting, that there was an argument. What might there have been to argue about, given they had apparently just met? It only makes sense if you accept there was some history here. Something between one of the young men and Bernard Hooper. And, we now know, there was. We know that Bernard Hooper had been accused of abusing Craig's sister. And we know that Craig Mervyn-Scott is a violent man. Somebody who barely twelve hours earlier had committed a serious assault on his stepfather. Out of revenge. For his family.

It appears that Bernard Hooper was carrying a knife. We don't know why, but, again, the reason might have been revealed had the police bothered to obtain and interrogate his mobile phone. There might have been all manner of messages between Hooper and Jamal Lowton on his J2 number. All manner of threats of what was to come, should their paths cross. We just don't know, do we? The prosecution haven't bothered to fill in the gaps.

The CCTV does not capture precisely what happened in the alley. But you know that, as Arron told you, Craig had the knife to begin with. That was what Paul Bell first told the police in his witness statement, whatever he might have said in his admittedly confused evidence to you. Paul Bell agreed that it could have been Male 2 – Arron – pleading for the violence to stop. Farid Suhail could barely remember his own name – he blurted out at the end of his evidence that all three males were involved, but for the reasons Mr Wyatt has explained, you will please treat Mr Suhail's unclear and contradictory evidence with extreme caution. The pathologist agreed that it was possible that the injuries could have been inflicted by only two people. The blood and DNA makes it no more likely that Arron was involved than that he was simply nearby when the blood was spilled.

There is nothing here on which the prosecution can rely to make you sure that Arron Freeman was a participant to the murder, or encouraging the murder.

You may by now be confident that the prosecution theory that these boys went out looking for a random person to kill is nonsense. You may already be sure that the key to this case lies in the history between Craig and Bernard Hooper. But let's briefly deal with the messages between Arron and Jamal. Arron has been frank with you – this was 'bants'. Nothing more. But look at what is actually said by Arron. Does he commit to anything? Does he even give a word of approval? No. To suggest that this is evidence of an agreement is yet another error by the prosecution. It an overreach. What is significant, you may think, is that there was nothing of relevance on Arron's phone, unlike Craig and Jamal. They are the ones with a particular interest in death and weapons. It is not Arron who is googling, 'How long do u get 4 murder?'

Another important point is that Arron has never been in trouble before. He has no convictions. Nothing at all, despite what you might think has been an extremely difficult upbringing. As His Honour the learned judge will direct you, this 'good character' is relevant. It makes it less likely that Arron committed the offence. And it may make it more likely that he is telling you the truth. You can use that in his favour. I respectfully urge you to do so.

Finally, as if all of that were not enough to bring the prosecution theory crashing to the ground, you have the phone call made by Jamal Lowton to Jared Grimes. The prosecution in their speech invited you to rely on this as an admission of guilt by Jamal Lowton. They argue that, by saying that Arron 'didn't even do nothing' and 'didn't even touch the guy', Jamal was tacitly admitting that *he* did do something. Fine. We agree! But the prosecution are then stuck, aren't they? Because they can't get around the fact that this phone call, this 'admission', completely undermines the prosecution case against Arron! They can't have their cake and eat it. If they tell you that you can rely on this comment by Jamal as true, then their case against Arron collapses. They are gracelessly pivoting and saying, 'Actually, even if Arron *didn't* touch Bernard Hooper, you should convict him on the basis that he was assisting or encouraging.' That wasn't how they originally put the case against Arron Freeman. The prosecution told you, with confidence, that the defendants had taken turns with weapons, that they had acted out this supposed 'game'. Now, in the final throes, they say to you that, maybe, actually, Arron Freeman didn't do that at all, but that you must still find him guilty?

You may be left with the feeling that the prosecution are thrashing around, desperately reaching for ways to salvage their case against my lay client.

The truth, I respectfully submit, is what is stated candidly and unguardedly by Jamal to Jared. It is what Arron has told you himself: that he was nearby but not involved – NBNI. Standing shocked, stunned and helpless as Craig and Jamal, for reasons now clear on the evidence, killed Bernard Hooper.

I will end by repeating what you have heard many times already, and that is because its importance cannot be overstated. Your verdict is determined by the burden and standard of proof. Arron does not have to prove his version is correct. The burden of disproving it is on the prosecution. They have to make you sure of his guilt.

I suggest that they can't possibly do that.

Thank you very much for your time.

CHAPTER 65

Jennifer (counsel for the third defendant)

'Members of the jury, I have nothing to say.

'This is not the first time in my career, but it is the first time in a case of this gravity. There is no explanation from my client in evidence, and a shitload of shit in need of explanation. Which I cannot explain either.

'But – and please don't ask me why – I don't actually think he's guilty. At least, I don't think I'm sure he is. So neither should you be.'

Let's call that 'Version 1', I told myself last night, depressing the backspace button until I was left with a blank Word document and a taunting flashing cursor. Tempting as it would be to see Jeremy Letts's face if I said that and just sat straight back down. I once heard an urban rumour about a silk in London who in his closing speech in a murder simply stood up, shrugged and asked the jury, 'Is that it?' By comparison, offering the jury my baseless hunch appears orthodox.

Of course, my hunches have been wrong before.

Sitting in the public gallery at Chelmsford Crown Court, squeezing Andrew's hand until the bones cracked and avoiding looking directly at the tear-streaked faces of Finlay's parents to our left, the hardest part of watching Ollie's cross-examination was not that, as a lawyer, I recognised it as effective. I wasn't afraid of the jury being hoodwinked by the art of the advocate; but the unmooring of my own certainties. As Ollie tripped and stumbled into elephant trap after elephant trap, getting caught in lie after lie, and giving stupid answer after stupid answer, it was not only the jury who could see through the facade. By the end of the exercise, my greatest fear – that the jury system to which I had devoted my life would fail to do its job – had been replaced by another: that it would work.

Maybe, if Jamal had gone into the box, it would have been a similar story.

As it is, we will never know what he might have said, and what hits might or might not have been landed by our opponents. I of course can't give evidence for him, and so the piecemeal instructions that he has actually provided – such as Craig being the one using Jamal's phone to search 'How long u get 4 murder?' – will never be heard by the jury. The only fragment they have is what he told the police upon arrest: *I wasn't there.*

So that is what I must work with.

I watch the jurors returning to their seats after their break, and wait for Letts to give me the nod.

'Good afternoon, members of the jury.

'This is a truly awful case, which will stir every human emotion. Bernard Hooper was murdered in the most brutal and unthinkable way. You would need a heart of stone not to be moved for his family. None of us could begin to put ourselves in their position, and, God willing, none of us will ever have to.

'But as the judge has directed, you must put all emotion, however understandable, however human, to one side. Your task – the oath or affirmation that you have each sworn – is to faithfully try this case, and these three defendants, on the evidence.

'I'm not going to tell you what happened on the night of 31 December. None of us knows, none of us was there. But I do want to say something about assumptions. And how one assumption can lead to another.

'If you assume that somebody is a murderer, then when you see him walking behind a stranger in the street, it is easy to assume that he has evil intentions.

'If you assume he is a murderer, then *of course* blood on his clothes is evidence of his guilt. *Of course* evidence that his phone has been used to search for "How long do u get 4 murder?" means that he has committed a murder. *Of course* text messages appearing to glorify violence become not simply distasteful, but evidence of murderous intent. Of course, when he says to a mate, "So-and-so wasn't involved," it is a tacit admission that he himself *was* involved.

'When you start from the assumption that somebody is a murderer, almost any evidence can be interpreted to support that assumption.

'But those sorts of assumptions are so, so dangerous. Because they are the very opposite of how our system of justice is built. We do not start from the assumption that the prosecution case is right, and interpret all of the evidence in light of that assumption. That may be the prosecution's job. But it's not yours, members of the jury. You start from the presumption of innocence. And from there, you have to analyse the evidence coolly, critically and without any preconceptions. And you don't ask yourselves, "Does the prosecution case have *some* evidence to support it?" because the answer to that question will always be, "Yes." That, after all, is why we are here. That is why we have a trial. There is always some evidence to support the prosecution case. No, instead, the question is, "Have the prosecution presented us with evidence so compelling, of such high quality, that we can be sure of guilt?"

'And when you conduct that exercise and ask yourselves that question, I suggest that the evidence – not the assumptions, but the evidence – against Jamal Lowton is nothing like as strong as the prosecution would have you believe.

'I'd like to illustrate this in ten short points. And let's start, not with a presumption of guilt, but a presumption of innocence. A presumption that – as Jamal told the police immediately when he was arrested – he was not involved in the violence. Let us presume that, instead of being part of a pack of would-be killers hunting for prey, Jamal was simply a teenage boy out for a night with his friends, and played no part in what his friends then did. If we start there, where does the evidence take us?

'One. The CCTV shows Jamal's body language as the three boys walk through town that night. He appears relaxed. He is, at most times, lagging behind the two others. He is not a leader. This is not a young man on a mission, prowling for a kill. His demeanour is mild and passive. After the group encounter Bernard Hooper, there is still, on the witness evidence and the CCTV, no hint of threat or aggression displayed by Jamal, all the way along Rowe Street and up to Garth Yard.

'Two. We know that Jamal left Garth Yard before the police arrived. The key question is: Did he leave before or after the violence started? You have two witnesses overlooking the alleyway. First, Paul Bell. Other counsel have highlighted the weaknesses in his evidence. I'll add two points. One, that his view was so poor that he failed to identify Jamal in an identification procedure, even though we know Jamal was on the street. Two, Paul Bell *insisted* that he was watching the entrance to the alleyway the whole time and insisted – told you he was "def-i-nightly one hundred per cent sure" that he saw all three young males run out of the alleyway into the waiting arms of the police. *This is wrong.* This is how Craig and Arron were arrested, but we know that Jamal was arrested several hundred yards away. Paul Bell cannot have seen what he swore on oath he did. He said he was just as sure – "def-i-nightly one hundred per cent sure" of the number of people in Garth Yard. Paul Bell perfectly illustrates the real danger of a confident, but mistaken, witness. You cannot safely rely on him. If you think he might be wrong, his evidence does not help the prosecution case.

'Three. We then have Farid Suhail. Again, my learned friends have highlighted how Mr Suhail's evidence was vague, inconsistent and unclear. Right at the end, he blurted out that he had definitely seen three people attacking Bernard Hooper. This was moments after he had confirmed the number as "two or three". His outburst, you may have thought, was born of spite, designed to hurt the defendants because of something he thought he had heard said by one of my learned friends. Farid Suhail only started watching once the knife had been produced. Is it not entirely possible, on his evidence, that when he looked out he saw two people – Craig and Arron – in Garth Yard with Bernard Hooper, and that Jamal had left before the violence began?

'Four. The video recording made on Jamal's phone immediately after the attack only shows the faces of Bernard Hooper and Craig Mervyn-Scott, the latter wielding the knife. You do not see Jamal on the footage. You also do not see Arron on the footage. Could he, in fact, have been the camera operator? Could Jamal's phone have been dropped at the scene when Jamal left? Jamal has not given evidence, and I can't create evidence for him, but you are entitled to ask yourselves this question: Why on earth would Jamal take a video on his J1 phone, send it to his J2 phone, and then abandon his J1 phone in the alleyway? Is this not the most bizarre thing to do? Is it not equally, or more, likely that his phone was used by somebody else, *after* Jamal had left Garth Yard? And that the reason it was sent to the J2 number, is because *that is the phone that the absent Jamal had with him*?

'Five. The scientific evidence does not link Jamal in any way to the zombie knife. The only scientific evidence relates to Bernard Hooper's DNA in a bloodstain on the cuff of Jamal's sweatshirt. Which, the scientist confirmed, could be explained by it being Jamal's blood, with Bernard Hooper's DNA having been transferred onto the stain by touch, at an earlier point, perhaps when they were walking together down Rowe Street. The scientific evidence all fits with – there is nothing there to contradict – Jamal not being present during the attack.

'Six. The pathologist agreed that the distribution of injuries might be accounted for by two assailants.

'Seven. The "murder game" messages on Arron's phone, sent from the J2 number, and the web searches on the J1 phone. I repeat what previous counsel have said. There is a world of difference between bad taste teenage bravado and a sincere intention to commit murder. From these messages alone, the latter is no more likely than the former. Anybody who has had teenage boys, or known a teenage boy, knows the gulf, the chasm, that exists between the things they brag about to their mates, and reality.

'Eight. Jamal has not given evidence. You will be directed by His Honour about this. You can use his silence as *some* support for the prosecution case. But that's all. You first have to be sure that the prosecution case is so strong that it calls for an answer. And secondly, you must be sure that the true reason for not giving evidence is that he did not have an answer that he believed would stand up to questioning. We, each of us, have the right to remain silent. We don't have a Fifth Amendment in this country, but we still have that right. You know that Jamal is a seventeen-year-old boy who has sat through this trial with the assistance of an intermediary. I leave it to your fair judgement whether you decide that his silence supports the prosecution case. But it doesn't prove it. It is certainly not inconsistent with innocence.

'Nine. You have heard evidence from Craig and Arron. Both point the finger at Jamal. But both would, wouldn't they? We know that more than one person inflicted the injuries. Each of them *has* to blame Jamal. But how reliable are they? They also blame each other, so you know that at least one of them is lying. Can you place any weight at all on what they say about Jamal? Or is their evidence really just white noise?

'Ten. Finally, the so-called confession. Is that a confession? Is it really? The prosecution say that the fact that Jamal didn't say, "Oh, and I didn't do anything either" during that conversation with

Jared means that he was admitting to murder. Is that a fair interpretation? If I say, "You, juror number four, have not stolen a car," does that mean that *I* have stolen the car? Are we required, in our every unguarded moment, to keep a running denial of every crime we *haven't* committed? Is that the world the prosecution suggest we live in? And, anyway, just imagine Jamal *had* denied his own involvement in that call to Jared. Would the prosecution simply accept it? Of course they wouldn't. They will always spin this to their advantage. Heads the prosecution wins, tails Jamal loses.

'Now I am not for a minute suggesting that any of this evidence "proves" Jamal's innocence. Of course it doesn't. But the point is that it doesn't prove guilt, either. All of the evidence can be interpreted either way, depending on viewpoint. And that is not enough. Not sure equals not guilty.

'If you think Jamal might be guilty, your verdict has to be not guilty. If you think he is *probably* guilty, your verdict is not guilty. If you are *almost sure* he is guilty, your verdict is not guilty.

'There is doubt in this case, members of the jury. The prosecution have not done enough.

'Thank you for listening.'

DAY 18 OF TRIAL – MONDAY

CHAPTER 66

Aliyah (the prosecutor)

I feel as refreshed today as I have done for weeks. The effect of evidence and speeches being completed and of disclosure, for all its trivial hiccups, having been successfully navigated, is a tonic which I have richly earned.

The finishing line heaving into view over the horizon brings with it not only the promise of whatever professional rewards accrue to a successful debut murder prosecution, but, crucially, the guarantee of unshackling myself from DS Chris Rose, whose absence from our conference room this morning can be counted as his most welcome contribution to date. I am able to sip my almond milk latte in glorious silence as I scroll through the sale items on mytheresa.com, luxuriating in every one of the ten minutes I have to myself until Jeremy Letts begins his summing-up.

My serenity is spoiled by a knock at the door. Chris Rose shoves it open and waves at me like a fool, Greggs paper bag in his hand.

'Morning!' he beams.

I smile winningly in return. 'Chris, I rather expected you might have had other duties to attend to now that we're on the home straight.'

'No, no, Aliyah. I'm not jumping ship just yet. No woman left behind, and all that. No, in fact Derek, my SIO, is popping down later, just to see how we're all ticking along.'

The prospect of giving the Senior Investigating Officer a frank and thorough debrief on Chris Rose's performance propels a delicious shiver down my spine, but I need to think tactically. MIT officers often have input into which silks the CPS instruct for their murders, and, while I have no desire to cross paths with Chris Rose again, I don't want to unnecessarily alienate his team.

'I also thought you'd like to know that I've now completed the review of the unused material,' Rose says proudly.

'I confess, Chris,' I say, 'I had rather understood that that review had already been completed before we finished the evidence last week. But that may be my misunderstanding, premised – and this is my fault entirely – on you telling me last week that you had completed the review of the unused material.'

He grins infuriatingly. 'Yeah, I thought I had, but then I remembered what you said about the continuity statements from the officers who seized the CCTV, and I just wanted to make sure everything added up.'

'I presume it does,' I say, closing my laptop, 'because if there is anything further to be disclosed, it's a bit too late now.'

'No, no. It's all tickety-gravy.' He sits down as I stand up to leave. 'The only statement missing was from the officer who reviewed the footage from the camera in Garth Yard.'

The words swirl unobtrusively in the air, like a gentle waft of air freshener, and it takes a moment for my senses to register. When they do, I instinctively grasp the desk for support, causing the laptop to slide out of my hand and crash to the floor. I don't even move to retrieve it. 'The what, Chris?'

'The CCTV camera at the end of Garth Yard. Above the fire escape.'

I scour his face desperately for signs that this is a deeply unfunny joke.

'There was a camera *in Garth Yard*?' I stress the final three words, hoping that saying them with emphasis will somehow trigger a different response. It does not.

'Yeah, but—'

'Why the fuck am I only hearing about this now, Chris?' I can't raise my voice above a whisper. The room is spinning and I squat on my haunches and close my eyes, preparing for the indignity of being the second barrister to empty herself in the course of this trial.

'It's one of the dozens of local authority cameras – number fifty-four or some such. The footage and the viewing log is listed on the unused schedule, but it wasn't until I was chasing the exhibiting statement that the officer who seized it told me that camera fifty-four was actually in Garth Yard.'

I shake my head. 'Please, please, please, Chris – tell me that somebody has now viewed that footage.' My mind races with the permutations, straining for a plan. 'The jury have not yet retired. It's unconventional, and hugely embarrassing, but we could theoretically still apply to reopen our case and play it to the jury. Although the defence would doubtless object. Unless of course it *helped* them, in which case . . . although it can't help *all* of them, so they won't all agree. Which means we may have to recall defendants to comment on the footage. Which I don't think we can do at this stage. So that means . . . what? Discharging the jury? A retrial? Fucking hell, Chris. Fucking, fucking, fucking hell.'

Breaking for breath, I realise that Rose has been muttering something through a mouthful of sausage roll. He is shaking his head. 'Nmmmm pmmt, Aliyah.'

'What?'

'Sorry.' He swallows, a large flake of pastry clinging to his chin. 'No point. The footage had already been viewed. There's nothing on it. That's why it was scheduled as unused. It's not been disclosed, because it's doesn't help anybody.'

It takes a second for the information to trickle in. 'So we *haven't* missed anything?'

'No.' He looks confused. 'Like I said, disclosure's all tickety-boo.'

I leap to my feet, ball up my fists and thump on his chest. 'Oh, thank fuck. You fucker. You absolute fucker, Chris. Thank fuck. Oh my God. Why the fuck did you not lead with that?'

He grins like a baboon and, as the tension floods out of me, I am torn between weeping with relief and body-slamming him through the table.

'You didn't give me a chance. No, the camera in Garth Yard was malfunctioning. It was pointing in the wrong direction and covered by foliage – not even visible to the naked eye. All you can see on the footage is the top of the fire escape. It doesn't record any of what is happening on the ground. It's no use to anyone.'

Wiping my eyes, I kneel back down to pick up my computer, which has fortuitously survived the fall unscratched, and loop my Birkin over my shoulder.

'That,' I say to Rose, 'would have been . . .' I don't need to complete the thought. I leave it hanging. The suffocating syrupy air of the conference room is now pickled by the steaming bean-and-cheese melt Rose is greedily undressing. I straighten my wig and stride out, slamming the door behind me.

CHAPTER 67

Craig (the first defendant)

A little part of me thought that now everything's out there, now I've told the jury all about MJ and I've said what I've said about Hooper, that the nightmares would stop. But last night was the worst yet.

My pad mate Kieron was shaking me by the shoulders and literally slapping my face to wake me up, because apparently I was shouting loud enough to wake up the whole wing. He says my arms and legs were thrashing like I was having some kind of fit, and he had to basically pull me off the bed.

What I was dreaming is hard to describe exactly, now I'm properly awake. It's basically the same as it always is, only each time it gets more real. More colourful. And this was the most real yet. I was back in the alley, standing and watching the slashing, over and over and over, and the bright, wet redness splattering all around. I remember the knife being in my hand, and then torn out of my hand again. I remember it being plunged into Bernard Hooper. And I remember the shrieking, the laughing and the goading. The shouts of 'Come on, Craigy!' and the urge growing inside me to join in.

Then my head thumped on the floor as Kieron yanked me off the bed and it took me like a minute to realise what was going on, and I swung for him because in that moment my brain was still stuck in the dream, and I couldn't make out what was real and what wasn't.

Thank fuck he didn't swing back. He's a big fucker and the last thing I need is another nicking for fighting if the screws walk in. Instead, Kieron was bare calm, he just pinned me to the floor and shouted, 'Wake the fuck up, dickhead!' again and again until I did.

So I'm tired again, obviously. Struggling to keep my eyes open as the judge fucking goes on about what the evidence was, and how strong it is or whatever. Mr Wyatt says that it doesn't actually matter if I pay attention today or not. He says I probably wouldn't understand even if I listened, so basically not to worry. Friday was what's important, he says. When Mr Wyatt got to properly say to the jury, this is why Craig is not guilty. 'I was good, wasn't I?' he said to me after he'd done speaking.

I trust Mr Wyatt. My brief said that Mr Wyatt is basically the best in the business, and I know he knows what's doing. But I also know I've not made it easy for him. I'm not stupid. I was listening when he was talking to the jury and most of the time I'm thinking, yeah, this makes sense, but then there's also the bits where I know he's wrong because I've not told the complete truth, and I'm trying to work out whether the jury have figured that out.

That thing he said about why I lied though – that is the truth. If I had admitted that I'd told Arron about Kayla, it would have just helped him out, which then would have gone bad on me. So I had to say I didn't know. Obviously that was wrong. But at the time, I just didn't see how else I could get the jury to see my side.

I've not seen Kayla for a couple of weeks now, not since that last visit when she bare lost her shit and was crying and crying when she had to go. I was worried when it all kicked off with her therapy records that what if she suddenly decided to turn up at court that day, and have to watch it all being raked over? But she hasn't been here at all, obviously. Not with everything she's now got going on with Mum and the baby. Thing is, she's not been picking up my calls neither, which isn't like her. Maybe she's tracked down that wasteman and he's finally doing right by her. She wouldn't tell me his name – she says I don't know him so what's the point – but it is some fucked-up shit to get a kid like that knocked up and then pussy out of being a father.

If I do get out of here, I can actually be some help to her. I can be an actual uncle to that kid, you feel me? It's not fucking right for her to have to do all of that on her own. But getting out of here, that's obviously out of my hands. I'm praying that Mr Wyatt has said what needs to be said to make the jury listen, to make them see that none of this is how it looks.

But I also know the reality. And the reality is that I'm probably gonna go down for something that's not my fault.

CHAPTER 68

Arron (the second defendant)

I don't want to get my hopes up. There's still a long way to go, I do know. But it's gone as well as it could have, Mr Evans told me this morning. He says that Jamal's phone call was 'a gift from heaven', giving me this big daft smile from behind his bushy beard. 'You couldn't have planned it better,' he said, and I was like, *Mate, have you met Jamal? There's no way I could make that kid do anything, you know what I mean?* 'Nah,' I said to Mr Evans. 'That is just Jamal being Jamal. He's dozy as fuck, sometimes.' Thank God.

The prosecution were always gonna put their own spin on the phone call, he said. They've obviously told the jury that even if Jamal was telling the truth, it doesn't mean I wasn't involved in some way, but like Mr Evans said in his speech: they can't have it both ways. They can't be all, *Jamal is telling the truth when he suggests that he's guilty, but not telling the truth when he says Az is innocent*, basically. Mr Evans thinks the jury will see through that. I dunno. I hope so.

There's obviously things the prosecution have still got. The messages about the game don't look good, I do appreciate that. And while I got the chance to tell the jury that it was just mates dicking about, Mr Evans says it's the thing that he'd be hitting hard if he was prosecuting this case. 'And the jury of course haven't heard from Jamal – he hasn't given the same explanation as you for those messages,' he said. But I said to him, I said, 'Mate, you know what it is? Even if he had stood up there, I don't think Jamal would have helped us.' And Mr Evans laughed his high little laugh and said I was probably right.

The judge is finishing his summing-up now. He's telling the jury that they've all got to agree, all twelve of them – either all of them saying guilty, or all of them saying not guilty. And then I'm watching them going out to have their little chat, and with some of them it's like they're buzzing, like this is what they've been waiting for. I asked Mr Evans how long it's gonna take them to decide, and he said it could be anything. Could be an hour, could be a week. Or more. Just depends, he said.

'A fighting chance', them's the words Mr Evans used. 'You've done well – you've given yourself a fighting chance.'

And I know I need to stop thinking about the way things were, and the way things could have been, and that I just need to focus on what's right here in front of us. But it's words like that that make me think about all those times with my nana when she'd tell me how proud of me she was, for basically going through all I'd gone through with my mam and that. And also how it was with Graham, telling me how well I'd done, how I was such a hard grafter, how I could achieve everything that he had achieved, and more. It's like I've had all these people – first my mam, then my nana, then Graham – all doing their best to keep me straight, to stop me ending up in the places where kids like me usually end up.

And it makes me think, for what?

For me to get so far, to do what I'm told, to get everything in place. To become a fucking dad, to actually have a family for the first time in my fucking life – and for somebody else's shit to drag me down.

I was having these thoughts last night when I was on the phone. I love her, but my head is up my arse at the moment. I'm not thinking right, and I know that it makes it harder for her. I know I'm not giving her what she needs. I mean, literally, as I'm in here. But also in the way that I know she wants to talk about the future, and every time she calls she's so positive and, like, hopeful. Making plans and thinking of what we'll do when I get out – where we'll live and what we'll do for money. And I try, I really do. But I can't pretend it's all going to be fine. It's been a year already, and she says she'll wait however long it takes, whatever happens, she keeps saying that she's chosen me and she's standing by me no matter what anyone else thinks – but it's things like this that remind me that she's just a kid.

It's easy to forget because she's been through so much, and she's got this air about her where it's like she knows things beyond her years. Even though I'm a couple of years older, from the very beginning it's been like she's the one with her head screwed on. That was one of the things that stood out when I met her. The girls at Rosewoods were all scruffs and she was proper fit, which was one thing, obviously. But more than that, it was how she understood. The shit she's had in her life, OK, it wasn't the same as me. But it was close enough. Just chilling with her was like nothing else. I could tell her things that I hadn't even told my nan. Things I hadn't told Graham. The good and the bad. And, whatever it was, she would just listen calmly, and even if it wasn't anything that could be fixed, what she would say would still make me feel better.

And in all of her letters, which she writes me every week with photos stuck in the envelope, and whenever she visits – although that is getting harder because of everything – she still does it, still tries to make it seem like it's all going to be OK. I just worry that I'm not being as good for her. Graham used to say, 'The woman you want is one who will still be there when life is at its lowest,' and I swear down, that might be the truest advice I ever got. I've got to get out and be with her.

That's why I've had to do what I've done. I'm not a grass, and if it were my choice, course I wouldn't be dropping Craigy in it. Like I say, the kid's basically family. I mean literally, now. Even if he doesn't know it.

Kayla understands, she says. She knows that I'm doing what's best for us. For our baby. She understands that there's no way that Craig and I both get out of this. And she's made her choice. If she hadn't told me about them records and what she'd been telling her counsellor, and if she hadn't pushed me to get my lawyers to ask for them, there would have been no way to prove to the jury that I've been telling the truth. If I get a not guilty, it will be because of her. Because she's made a choice I never wanted her to have to make. I don't know how I can ever properly repay her for that, how to show her what she means to me. But if this jury gives me the chance, I'll spend the rest of my life trying.

I don't want to get my hopes up, but I also know if I don't stay positive, I'll just keep thinking about the worst. And that's not something I can face.

The next twenty years spent banged up in a cell, with the life I've made for myself carrying on outside without me.

DAY 20 OF TRIAL – WEDNESDAY

CHAPTER 69

Jennifer (counsel for the third defendant)

For the first time since I met Jamal, the pressure seems to have lifted. He appears almost at peace with himself. I would not say relaxed, or content, but, I don't know . . . liberated? No longer the surly, brooding enigma quietly fizzing with tension, it's as if the inevitability of his fate has relieved him of the need to make any further decisions. Resignation, I suppose, but worn almost lightly.

From the minute that the implications of his prison phone call were spelled out, there has been a clarity of comprehension and firmness in his own mind that would have been helpful when we started out. We spent two hours going back and forth in the cells after the call emerged, ignoring the furious tannoys demanding our return to court, Caz and I taking turns at good and bad cop, covering every angle, emphasising every risk and pitfall of giving evidence and of remaining silent.

We must have asked Jamal a hundred times whether he was content with his decision, before he endorsed my brief to confirm that he was. Even then, with his signature on the dotted line, we checked and double-checked and triple-checked that he fully understood the ramifications.

I think the role reversal took us both by surprise. Up until Bob Evans knocked on the conference room door to deliver the phone call, I could not see a way in which Jamal could improve his case by giving evidence.

But following that knock on the door, once Jamal realised the implications of what he had said to Jared, a switch was flicked. The guard came down, the smile came out. And all of a sudden, it was Caz and I jointly urging him, 'You *have* to explain this to the jury,' and Jamal point-blank refusing to countenance saying a word.

'There's no point, is there?' he said. 'Like what you were saying before, I ain't got no good answer to any of this. I ain't gonna waste anybody's time.'

And then all of the fears of Jamal being cross-examined, all of the logic and the tactics and whatever emotional ghosts from Ollie's trial had burrowed into the cracks in my judgement were exorcised. Gone. No, Jamal would *not* make a good witness. But he needed to explain this call. He *needed* to say *something* to the jury. And to his mum! Even if it was as blunt and as inchoate and as unsatisfying as the explanation he had given me and Caz: *It's not how it looks.*

But as I argued my new-born conviction – like a pupillage interview exercise in which I was given sixty seconds to make an argument in favour of a proposition, and then immediately told to advocate the opposite – all of the points that I had reasonably and painstakingly made earlier were politely reformulated and tossed back in my face.

I won't speak well for myself, miss. Those other barristers will absolutely ruin me. There's no way of making this look better. I can say nothing, and you can do all the talking in your speech.

And it turns out it's very difficult to win an argument against yourself.

Back upstairs, we trooped into court and, following an optimistic – and naturally unsuccessful – application by me to exclude Jamal's prison call, the jury were brought in and the damning extract was played.

When the recording was over, and its import had been absorbed by everyone in court, there was a scream from the public gallery. A visceral howl, only the word 'No!' intelligible amid the raging, gulping sobs. Caz ran over and swiftly escorted Jamal's mother out of the door, but her cries still pierced the thin walls of the courtroom. Had the significance of the phone call not already been obvious to the jury, it surely was now. Even Jocelyn Lowton realised that there could only, realistically, be one verdict now for her son.

And yet.

I hate trying to read juries, especially when addressing them. More times than I care to remember have I successfully conducted twelve nodding heads with the power of my oratory, only to have a unanimous adverse verdict an hour later. A barrister who claims to read jurors is as scientifically reliable as beachside fortune-teller.

But something about two jurors in particular stood out when I was giving my closing speech on Friday. It could have been fatigue, could have been indigestion. But as I was reading out my ten points, the ten key features of the evidence which, I suggested, viewed fairly through a presumption of innocence, might just create enough space for doubt, I saw eye contact. Juror three – the thirty-something woman in the blue and white stripy top – and juror four – the fifty-something man in a faded salmon shirt – looked at each other as I was talking, and then simultaneously turned and looked at me. Something was being shared. Something I said was going in.

It is possibly nothing. Probably nothing. I'm almost sure that it's nothing.

But maybe there's hope.

Court is now fully re-assembled, Caz and I having scrambled back inside the building at the sound of the tannoy, me wafting the tobacco smoke off my gown as I took the stairs two at a time. Bereaved Hoopers, fatalistic Lowtons and fascinated press reporters crowd the galleries, and in the well of the court our merry band – the odd assortment of damaged individuals randomly thrown together to make sense of this most senseless of events – reunite for, I hope, one last song.

I turn to the dock and mouth at Jamal, *Verdicts.*

The courtroom falls silent as the clerk asks the foreperson to stand.

'Madam Foreperson, will you please answer my first question "Yes" or "No". Have the jury reached verdicts in respect of all defendants upon which you are all agreed?'

'Yes.'

There's always fucking hope.

PART IV

POST-TRIAL

DAY 32, POST-TRIAL – FRIDAY

CHAPTER 70

Aliyah

As I feel the soles of my Louboutins squelch on the damp linoleum, I reflect that I have possibly misjudged my attire for the Frog and Frangipane. The choice of venue was of course Chris Rose's, not mine, and in mitigation this looked from the website to be a gastropub in which, even if the food is unlikely to excite, one can safely slip in for an Aperol. As it happens, the risk of slipping anywhere is minimal given the adhesiveness of the floor. And they are apparently out of Aperol.

There is something fitting about Chris Rose's preferred meeting point being somewhere aesthetically hideous and barely fit for purpose. As he sees me treading past the neon-lit bar, he rises from his seat and waves his arm apishly over his head.

I have absolutely no desire to be here tonight, let me make that plain. Given the option, I would much rather be at home, spending quality family time staring in silence at our phones. But, given the success of R v. Mervyn-Scott and Others, I have accepted Chris's offer of a celebratory drink with the aim of nudging his Senior Investigating Officer to send another Major Investigation Team murder to the CPS with my name on it. Regrettably, it soon becomes clear, the SIO will not be joining us, and I am instead facing an evening alone with Chris Rose. Or however long it takes me to down a single measure and fake a domestic emergency.

I evade Rose's attempted bear hug and sit down opposite him.

I am about to complain about the dreadful table service when he advises that we are expected to place drinks orders at the bar. He does not offer to buy mine, and I would not let him in any event. Once I have returned cradling an anaemic-looking pink gin and tonic, Chris begins his reminiscence of 'a bloody good job done bloody well'. I am content to let him babble as I suck on my cheap plastic straw.

Life with minimum terms of thirty years for each of Craig Mervyn-Scott and Jamal Lowton represents a heck of an outcome, considering their age, but, as I predicted at the time, the applications for leave to appeal against those sentences were lodged within days, and are likely in time to be granted. Jeremy Letts desired the headlines generated by a whacking great sentence, which he duly got, but I expect the Court of Appeal to shave a few years off.

Arron Freeman's acquittal still rankles, but once Jamal Lowton's confession to Jared emerged, a conviction for Freeman was always going to be tricky, not helped, of course, by the way in which our dirty disclosure laundry was aired in front of the jury. All things considered, it is a commendable result, I feel, for a first murder prosecution, and my reputation at the CPS, and with MIT, can only have been improved.

I realise that I have not taken in a single word that Rose has said, but my lack of reaction does not seem to faze him. He is already onto a new story about a different case: a murder linked to an OCG involved in pumping multi-kilos' worth of crack cocaine and heroin around Ableford.

'Funnily enough,' he says, 'it features an old haunt of ours – Garth Yard!'

'Really?' I say, wondering if a tenuous geographical connection might be enough to secure me the trial brief.

'Well, not in Garth Yard itself – it's the derelict premises on the corner with Rowe Street. The front door's on Rowe Street, but the side of the unit runs along Garth Yard.'

'Sure,' I say, bored already.

'Division have recently had some issues there with skagheads breaking in and using it as a dosshouse. It used to be a commercial storage unit, back in the days when businesses in Ableford had anything worth storing, and then it was converted and rented as a shop premises – it was the original Reggie's, in fact. Before Reggie lost his licence and opened up a phoenix store on Horcross Road with his brother's name above the door. Anyway, the leaseholder's not been able to rent it since then, so it's just sat empty. But – and this is what I'm coming to – turns out that it's not just been a squat for users, but some pretty serious gear has been kept there by this OCG. Drugs, weapons, the lot. Seems that somebody was putting their hand in the till and ended up with a bullet to the back of the head.'

Something at the back of my mind is burning, but I attribute it to the gin. I ignore it and drain the glass. 'Well,' I say, pointedly brandishing my empty, 'I should probably make tracks. But if you're asked for recommendations for counsel for that case, somebody with a one hundred per cent success rate in prosecuting murders . . .'

'Oh, don't worry,' Rose beams, tearing open a bag of Mini Cheddars. 'You're the ladywoman of first choice, Aliyah. It's been lovely to see you.'

I force a grimace, hoping that it will suffice as a substitute for returning a compliment I don't intend.

'Actually, before you go, the other thing I wanted to tell you – see what you make of this.'

I stop in the act of fastening the clasp on my Mulberry clutch. I have heard this Columbo routine too many times over the past month. Rose is as bad a bluffer as he is a detective. This, clearly, is the main purpose of this rendezvous. He wants to get my read on something. Which, if history is any indicator, does not augur well.

'You know how we identified the J2 number as being used in a Nokia handset through the IMEI on the call data records?'

'The otherwise utterly pointless records that you obtained for the wrong dates? Those ones, Chris?'

He has the decency to blush. 'Yeah. Well, you remember – obviously – that the data showed no activity on the J2 number after New Year's Day. But the thing is – and it's a funny one really – we've discovered that the IMEI has actually been used since. Quite recently, in fact.'

I stare at him.

'It seems that the J2 phone is still active.'

CHAPTER 71

Aliyah

Rose is still playing dumb. I think. I briefly allow the possibility that I am giving him too much credit, and he really is as thick as he is affecting, but dismiss it just as swiftly. Of course there was an ulterior motive, a reason that Rose was so keen to meet me away from our respective professional environments. The panic behind the piggy eyes indicates that he knows this new information is potentially important. And he needs me either to reassure him that it is not; or, if it is, to make whatever problem it creates go away.

I lower myself back into the seat. 'Take it from the beginning, Chris.'

'Well, as you know, from the data set we obtained for the J2 number—'

'That was the data for 1 January 2024 to 30 June 2024, right?'

'Right. As you know, that showed nothing. No activity at all on that number. Which is what we expected, given that Jamal was arrested and remanded on 1 January.'

'But you said it's now active?'

'Well, the number isn't. But the handset is. That Nokia's IMEI has recently been associated with another number, one which hadn't previously featured in this case.'

'So somebody has put a new SIM in the J2 handset?'

'Precisely.'

'Well,' I suggest, 'is the answer that Jamal has somehow smuggled that handset into prison? Or, given that our belief has always been that Jamal discarded the phone on the night, that some random has simply found it and decided to use it?'

'Well, those would both be fair assumptions,' Rose says, producing a packet of Scampi Fries from under the table. 'But.'

He shovels in a fistful of bright yellow crisps, and I wait patiently until he recaptures command of his mouth.

'But we know it can't be Jamal.'

And then something he said moments ago catches in my brain.

'What do you mean *hadn't* featured, Chris?'

'Eh?'

'You said that the new number associated with the Nokia's IMEI *hadn't previously* featured in our case. Previous to what? How did you even come across it?'

He clears his throat.

'We put in a CycComms request for subscriber details and call data records for a number which came to our attention in the last few days of the trial. The records showed that number to be using the same IMEI as the J2.'

I can feel the bile rising in my throat as possibilities start to build in my imagination. One suddenly lodges, painfully, as I spot the missing fragment that Rose has not yet revealed to me.

'Chris. The only new number that cropped up during the trial was the one that Jamal called from prison. His confession call.'

Rose nods at me, his joviality exhumed, his mouth a tight, grim line. He knows – he *knows* – what this means.

'Chris,' I whisper. 'This means that we got the whole thing wrong. The J2 number wasn't Jamal.'

Rose has done the workings too. But he lets me give the answer.

'It was Jared.'

CHAPTER 72

Arron

I rock the buggy and wave at Kayla as she has a go on the swings, her legs flying up into the air, higher and higher. Then my phone buzzes in my coat pocket and I take it out to check my Snapchat. I've missed my Snap. Thing about prison burners is they're so fucking small, you can text but nowt else.

Telling the Croydon boys that Anthony had thieved their toastie maker was the smart move. OK, so Anthony lost an eye, but I got me guaranteed protection in Twyford right from the start. And a burner. I swear down, that changed everything. Without my burner, there's no way I could have kept speaking to Jared. And no way we would have come up with the plan.

We need four clear days, Jared had said. So I've pretended to be asleep when the screws knocked on for the van that Thursday during the trial, and because they're fucking lazy as shit they didn't ask twice, like I knew they wouldn't. They just told court I'd refused, and that was that. The judge had already said right at the beginning that we wouldn't be in court that Friday coz he'd got some course or some shit, so we'd now got ourselves a four-day weekend. Which was the time that Jared reckoned he needed to lay the groundwork.

Fucking Jamal, man. Honest to God, that kid is the thickest fucking cunt I've ever met. He just does whatever he's told, doesn't think for a minute about the consequences. I swear down, you tell that kid to fucking shoot himself in the kneecap and his reply would be, 'Which leg?'

To be fair, that's what made him a good grafter. He just did it. As long as he didn't have to use his fucking brain, he was sound. He'd already done a bit of shotting for himself, but he was fucking useless at chasing dough, remembering who was holding for him. Working for me just made sense – I've actually got a head on my fucking shoulders. So I ran the lines and Jamal did the runs like I told him, and everything was sound. The dough just kept coming.

That was until Jamal went and lost half a kilo of fucking white. Twenty-five grand. I'd literally done everything for him – set up the switch, booked his taxi there and back, sent another soldier in another car with the dough – basically, everything except wipe his arse. All he had to do was get out the taxi, pick up the bag, get back in the fucking taxi, and come home. Too hard for Jamal, that. Went and fucking left it in the taxi, didn't he? Like I say – thick as fuck.

Everything that happened can then be traced back to that. All Jamal's fucking fault.

I should probably be grateful, in a way. If Jamal wasn't so fucking thick, he wouldn't have been so perfect for Jared's plan.

When you think about it, Jamal really only had himself to blame for what was coming.

CHAPTER 73

Aliyah

Jared was using the J2 phone.

J2 was Jared.

These fragments repeat in my head, gathering speed and volume until I feel my balance shifting, and have to push my hands onto the sticky table to steady myself. I close my eyes and swallow, trying to quell the rising nausea.

Rose speaks. 'In fairness to us both, Aliyah, we had no reason to doubt that J2 was Jamal. He never denied it – not in his defence statement, not at trial. The attribution of that number was never challenged by his barrister – why would we think to question it?'

I am torn between my desire to pin myself to Rose's ready-made – and not entirely unreasonable – excuse, and my innate masochistic need for self-flagellation. But then a third possibility creeps into my mind.

'Chris, isn't it possible that J2 *was* Jamal at the time of the murder, but that he discarded that phone on the night – as we know he must have – and it has subsequently been found or adopted by Jared?'

He stares at me. Christ, if I can't even convince Chris Rose, it must be a bum point.

'The alternative, Chris . . .' I can barely bring myself to articulate the alternative. 'The alternative is that J2 was Jared all along. Which means that it was Jared who messaged Arron to tell him to meet at Reggie's. It was Jared to whom the video of the murder was sent from Jamal's phone. Oh, fuck – Jared who was messaging Arron about the murder game. And then . . .'

Rose finishes for me. 'And then Jared who Jamal confessed to, exonerating Arron.'

We both fall silent as we process the implications. I try to shake myself free of the shock of the paradigm shift, and engage my silk's brain.

Let us take a worst-case scenario. Let's say – for argument's sake – that J2 has been Jared all along. And let's say that he had some knowledge of what happened, or what was going to happen, to Bernard Hooper. Where would that leave us?

Well. Whatever knowledge Jared may or may not have had about the murder, he wasn't at the scene. That much we know. It throws parts of the peripheral evidence at trial into confusion, there's no denying that. But the core of the prosecution case would not actually be affected. There is nothing, when you stop and think about it logically, which would undermine the safety of either Craig or Jamal's convictions.

I breathe again, slightly more easily.

'I think it's OK,' I say to Rose. He looks at me, unconvinced.

'It is,' I say, hoping that my aggressive nodding is engendering confidence. 'It's OK.'

Isn't it?

CHAPTER 74

UNUSED MATERIAL (SENSITIVE SCHEDULE) ITEM 342: CCTV VIEWING LOG FROM CAMERA 54, TOP OF FIRE ESCAPE (PC SILVESTRE) – MARKED CLEARLY NOT DISCLOSABLE

Date	Time	Event
31/12/2023	23:00:00	Seized footage begins. A tree branch and foliage obscures half of the screen.
01/01/24	00:00:58	Blurred movement for four seconds near door at top of fire escape.
01/01/2024	00:05:03	Blurred movement for three seconds.
01/01/2024	00:05:06	No further recorded movement.

CHAPTER 75

Aliyah

Thoughts are compounding in my head quicker than I can register them, let alone organise them.

Let's say, for argument's sake, that Jared orchestrated the murder. For whatever reason. It is unlikely, for the very reason that there is no reason. But for argument's sake. Let us play this scenario through.

If Jared was involved in orchestrating, or organising, or encouraging the murder, then he could of course be charged and tried as an accessory, or a co-conspirator. That would depend on multiple factors, including, most importantly, whether he could even be identified or traced. There is, after all, no record for Jared Grimes on police systems. All we know is that that is the name attached to the new number in the J2 handset when Jamal added that number to his prison PIN. As a Cat A prisoner, there should have been checks to verify the identity of 'Jared' before the prison authorised the call, but they are likely to have been perfunctory, if they took place at all. Probably little more than a quick call to, and a verbal confirmation that, the recipient answered to the name of Jared Grimes.

'But,' I murmur to myself, 'if Jared *was* involved, then why would he take the risk of using the J2 number now?'

'Well, he hasn't,' Rose says. 'He's chucked the J2 SIM. He's just continued to use the handset. Like we told the jury, most people, even crims, don't understand IMEIs. They don't realise we can link two numbers used in the same burner.'

'Do the records show when the new number was first used in the J2 handset?' I already know the answer as Rose reads out the date, excusing himself from the table.

'The day before Jamal's confession,' I whisper. 'Jared put in a clean SIM just for this call, thinking that gave him enough distance.'

I continue playing the scenario out in my head. *If* Jared was involved in the murder from afar, and *if* he could be traced, then yes, he could be a co-defendant. But where would that leave us? What would be the impact – if any – on the trial? On the safety of the convictions? Perhaps very little. The forensic evidence showed at least two assailants. Given the acquittal of Arron Freeman, the jury must have rejected what Farid Suhail said about there being three assailants, and must have been sure that Craig Mervyn-Scott and Jamal Lowton were physically attacking Bernard Hooper. So a third party who was not present and who knew about the murder, or even assisted somehow – maybe supplying weapons? – does not actually affect the central issue.

Or does it? My mind flashes to the message sent by J2 to Arron Freeman on the night of the murder. '*MT O REGG*'. Meet *outside* Reggie's, is how all parties were happy to interpret it. But could it have been 'meet *at old* Reggie's'? And if so, and if – and again, we are piling conditionals upon conditionals here – but *if* it was Jared and *if* he was telling Arron to meet at old Reggie's, does that not tend to suggest that Jared was . . . there? Physically present at Garth Yard?

Would that, potentially, leave scope for a fourth assailant? Could Jared, somehow, have been waiting in Garth Yard for the others to arrive? Dancing in and out of the shadows? Surely he'd have been caught on CCTV entering Garth Yard? Unless . . .

Let us say yes. Just hypothetically. *If* Jared was actually present, and actually involved, would that undermine the safety of Craig and Jamal's convictions?

Certainly not Craig's. The evidence of his involvement was utterly overwhelming. The video recording of him with the zombie knife would be enough for the Court of Appeal to laugh in his counsel's face. And that is before you add in the lies, the bad character, the forensics – no. Even if someone else joined in with the attack, it would not have the slightest impact upon Craig Mervyn-Scott's guilt.

What about Jamal? Would the presence of a fourth person have any bearing on the safety of the conviction of a defendant who was recorded confessing to being involved? A defendant who did not give evidence to deny either his participation or his confession?

Absolutely not.

Although . . .

Would it not open the door to the possibility that Jamal *had* run off, missed by Paul Bell, before the violence began, and that the three people seen by Suhail and Bell attacking Bernard Hooper were Craig, Arron and Jared? The 'gap' that Jennifer Rennie stressed in her closing speech, between Bell leaving his window to collect his takeaway and Suhail hearing the violence starting – I dismissed it as a reach, but if there is in fact a possibility of another participant, does this . . . change things?

And would this opening not yawn even wider if the 'murder game' messages, which we all along attributed to Jamal, had in fact been sent by Jared? Would those possibilities not immediately render this new information about Jared not merely disclosable – not simply *capable reasonably of assisting the defence or undermining the prosecution* – but capable of exonerating Jamal?

And if the answer to that question is yes, then the inevitable inquest would interrogate why this information has only arisen post-conviction. And who was in the driving seat at trial. And who should, notwithstanding the ridiculous burdens placed upon her, have somehow spotted this the minute Jamal's prison call to J2/ Jared emerged. Who should carry the can, and what professional, career-defining, financially ruinous sanctions should follow.

I breathe hard, and close my eyes until the pressure bursting beneath them begins to dissipate. I am spinning out.

Yes. That is it. I am spinning out.

I am starting from an unreliable premise, and speculating in a way which is most unlawyerly.

All of this – all of this – is based on the supposition that Jared was controlling J2 on the night of the murder. And there is absolutely no evidence to support that contention. It has not even been hinted at by any of the three defendants, at any stage. Let alone by Jamal Lowton, who has been content throughout to allow the Crown to attribute J2 to him.

And is that not because the obvious, *obvious* explanation is that J2 *was* Jamal? That he tossed the handset on the night of the murder – or even passed it straight to his mate Jared, who for all we know may have lived near to where Jamal was arrested. And that Jared has just started using that handset. Is that not, in fact, the overwhelmingly likely scenario?

Against this backdrop, it seems to me – and I find that I am shaking my head and laughing at myself for my uncharacteristic catastrophising – that the information about Jared cannot possibly *reasonably* undermine the Crown's case, or assist *any* of the defendants. And that being so – unarguably, I now realise – then this information need not, and indeed positively should not, be disclosed to the defence.

It is a storm in a china teacup. An inconsequential, almost amusing, coda to a case in which the defendants have been fairly tried, and fairly convicted. As Chris Rose himself said when we first set off down this rabbit hole, just a funny thing he spotted after the event, to be tossed into small talk over a tepid G & T and a flat lager.

As Chris Rose emerges from the gents, tugging up his fly, I straighten my back and smile, ready to reassure him that our victory – justice's victory – remains intact.

CHAPTER 76

Arron

They're always listening. They tell us that on induction, and then every fucker reminds you once you're on the wing. Any call you make through your PIN, they can listen in. They don't listen to every single thing said by every dickhead in here, obviously, but they can. There's the risk. That's why if you've got any fucking sense, you get yourself a burner.

What Jared pointed out is that for me, Jamal and Craig, they was gonna be listening in to basically everything we said at all of our prisons, in case one of was thick enough to talk about the trial. Obviously, they'd be hoping that one of us grassed or coughed, but Jared said that they also had to look out in case any of us said something which could help one of the others. Because then the prosecution would have to give it to us in case we could use it.

The best example of that, Jared said, is if one of us, when we're just chatting to a mate like it's just the two of us and nobody's listening, says that another of us is innocent. That's the kind of shit which can cause a fucking earthquake.

The difficulty was getting the plan to Jamal. Obviously none of us can talk properly at court. Jamal is too fucking thick to get himself a burner. So Jamal's mam was the answer. Jared paid her a little visit that Friday night and told her what Jamal needed to do. He said to her what she needed to tell Jamal when she saw him for his Saturday morning visit.

Jamal's mam obviously doesn't know who Jared is, but she could tell he was someone she didn't want to say no to. He told her that the plan was dead simple, and it would get both me and Jamal out. Craig was done for, Jared said to her. He's fucked himself acting like a dickhead in his evidence. But Jared told her that he could still do something for me and Jamal. What he would do, he said, is talk to each of us over PIN, and get each of us to say that the other one did not do anything to Bernard Hooper. This would all be recorded, he told her, and when the prosecution listened to it, they would have to give it to the defence. When they did, it would create so much confusion, bang in the middle of the trial, that the jury would have no choice but to find us both not guilty.

Truth is, Jamal shits his pants every time he even hears Jared's name. Jared once showed us this TikTok of one of the youngers getting his kneecaps done for creaming a few grams from a delivery. That's why Jamal wouldn't breathe anything in court that might bring Jared into it. So the minute Jamal's mam told him the plan had come from Jared, he would have done it anyway. Jared didn't actually need to lie to him. He could have just said, Jamal is gonna do this because I say so. But Jared obviously thought that giving Jamal that little bit of incentive – making the daft cunt think he could save himself as well – would make sure.

The words were important. Jared made Jamal's mam repeat them back to him until she could remember them backwards, and told her to make sure she did the same with Jamal. 'Jamal's future,' he told her, 'depends on him getting this right.' Fucking hilarious, man.

To be fair to Jamal, he got the words dead on. When Mr Evans played the call to me in the cells, Jamal was proper convincing, like a fucking actor or some shit. Swear down, the first useful thing that kid's done in his whole fucking life. He was calm, he was natural. And obviously completely fucking clueless that, with every word he spoke, he was getting himself closer to a life sentence, and getting me closer to a walkout.

Thing is, once Jamal lost the box, the debt wasn't just his. Jamal was my runner, and Jared is my boss, so Jared is the one who has to answer. Making up half a key – 25k – was not gonna be easy.

When I mentioned to Jared about what Kayla had told me, Jared said it was 'fate opening a window'. We looked him up on Craigy's phone and found Kayla's old teacher was still alive, and had a company registered to his home address. It was one of them massive houses sitting in the hills above the town. 'A walking, noncing cash cow,' Jared had laughed.

Bernard Hooper had begged for a month to get the cash together. *That's fine*, Kayla had told him, with Jared listening as she made the call. *But that makes New Year's Eve your cut-off. If you don't make payment in full, I will be making a little visit to your wife. And then to the police.*

Old Reggie's was the handover spot. There's no cameras in the alley and some of Jared's boys had been using the old storage lockers for the previous six months with no issues, so he said we wouldn't be interrupted. When Jared sent me them messages, I knew we'd be doing more than just collecting the money. Getting blooded, he called it. And tying up loose ends.

I took Craigy with me, like Jared asked. The debt had nothing to do with him – I'd just told him he could earn some wages by bringing a rucksack to take the money, and that he'd get a chance to watch the man who'd nonced his sister get a bit of a slap. He didn't know about the game Jared had in mind. Jamal came with us coz, well. What else is that kid gonna do with his night?

That night, Jared texted Hooper the directions, and then messaged me around 11:30 telling us to meet him at the old Reggie's. When he messaged, it was dead confusing coz we already thought we'd seen Hooper and were following him, but then as I got Jared's message this rando went into some flat and Craig was like, 'That's not him,' and we realised. 'Jared's sent him to Reggie's,' I told them, and we headed.

On our way, we did then see Hooper near to Rowe Street. We legged it to catch up with him, and I sent Jamal over to make sure he knew where the meet was. Jared absolutely lost his shit when I told him this. It was the first call I made after I got my burner at Twyford, and he was asking what the evidence was and what the cops knew. 'You escorted the nonce through the streets of Ableford past hordes of CCTV cameras and eyewitnesses? If I'd known at the time that you'd been so fucking stupid, I obviously would have reconsidered what I took out of that locker, and what we went on to do, Arron. You're supposed to be the clever one, you dozy fucking cunt.'

When Jared unlocked the door and stepped out onto the fire escape, and walked down the clanging metal steps, us three and Hooper was already in the ginnel. Hooper had given us this shopping bag with the cash inside, but had also brought this tiny little knife with him that he was waving at Craigy. 'This is all I've got, you won't get a penny more out of me!' he was squealing. 'If I hear one more word from any of you, or that little whore . . .' Craigy gave him a slap for that, and Hooper proper whacked him on the hand with the knife.

'First blood to the nonce!' Jared announced as he appeared at the bottom of the fire escape, holding the zombie in the air like he was going into battle. Jamal skated straight away, absolutely pussied out. Craigy was just staring with his mouth open like a gormless fucking fish. But I understood. I'd been working for Jared for four months now.

He nodded at me. 'Let's play.'

Jared went first, swiping clean through Hooper's wrist, pretty much leaving his hand dangling from his arm and sending his little knife clattering to the floor. He handed me the blade, and I pulled it across the side of Hooper's face. He didn't make a sound, and at first I thought I'd not actually touched him, until I saw teeth spilling out of this gaping wound. The rush was incredible.

Craigy was still standing there shaking, so Jared took his turn, dragging the serrated edge across the back of Hooper's thigh. He fell to the ground, and it was around this point that Craigy sprung to life, like somebody had just changed his batteries. He charged over and started kicking Hooper's head like he was taking penalties. Me and Jared then carried on taking it in turns, with Jared shouting, 'Lovely bodywork!' and 'Avoid the arteries!' At some point, Craig had got hold of a metal pole – it looked like scaffolding or something, probably from that skip – and was smashing Hooper's knees as me and Jared did the cutting.

It must have been after about five minutes that I saw the lights on in some of the buildings across the road, and I thought I saw movement in one of the windows. I pointed this out to Jared, who brought the blade down across Hooper's neck to put an end to it. He twitched and gurgled for maybe ten seconds, and then it was over.

Craigy then asked for a go, which was pointless as the game was obviously over, but Jared passed him the blade. He told me to take a video of the nonce's body and to forward it to him. I picked up Jamal's phone that he'd dropped when he ran, but while I was recording, Craigy completely lost his shit, grabbing the blade and running out of the alley with it. I screamed at him to come back, and Craigy then runs back in and hammers the blade right into Hooper's chest, making even more blood bubble out of his mouth. Jared gave the zombie a quick wobble. 'It's fucking *Sword in the Stone* deep. That ain't coming out.'

When we heard the sirens, it was literally like an alarm going off. Literally. Like I'd woken up and found myself there, not knowing what had gone on. I completely panicked, to be fair. Jared has told me that when he grabbed Hooper's carrier bag and ran up the fire escape, he was shouting at me to follow him, but I was just in a daze. After what felt like for ever, I just ran out onto the street behind Craig, and, well. The jury heard the rest.

'Now it's up to me to find a way to dig you out of this shit, is it?' Jared said in that first call.

Fair play to him, he did.

Jared says that I'm worth it. That I'm the most reliable worker he's ever known. He says it was obvious from the first day we met that I was eager, smart and fearless. And, unlike most of the kids at Rosewoods who did jobs for Jared and his mates, I was clean. Obviously that's changed now, but even with what's happened, Jared still says I've got an amazing future ahead of me.

Other kids from Rosewoods liked Jared because he was flash, or because he gave them bottles of Jäger or the odd gram of white, but that wasn't what happened with me. He was just a decent guy, who listened and wanted the best for me. The day he told me he was gonna have to trade patches – coz one of the nosey old cunts at Rosewoods had seen me getting out of his BMW and threatened to call the cops on him – and I thought I wasn't going to see him again, I was proper wounded.

'This is goodbye,' he said to me, opening the car door. I wiped my nose and got out, but as I turned to shut the door, he was like, 'Unless . . .'

I was like, *What? What?*

And he said, 'Unless you wanna leave this shithole behind and come and work for me full-time?'

And that was that. I was in.

Only thing left to do was for him to remind me of the deal we'd made on the first day we met.

EPILOGUE

Rosewoods Family Centre is a shithole.

That assertion requires no inscription, nor any intemperate online review, nor indeed the submission of any formal evidence to substantiate it. One is not required to read the coruscating OFSTED reports, or inhale the rotting stench from the kitchens, or attempt to wash oneself in facilities where the bathwater runs a darker colour than the toilet water. One need only stand in the weeds of the car park, beneath the barbed-wire curls stalking the perimeter, and watch the lifeless, loveless faces at the windows staring enviously at an outside world which any other person would fight with their last breath to escape.

It is a conclusion which has evidently been swiftly reached by one fourteen-year-old, recently arrived and quickly apprised of his new surroundings. For even though it is dinner time – or teatime, as he would understand it – he is eschewing the promise of whatever the microwave threatens to eject tonight, in favour of the society of a fifteen-year-old from the local estate. Their venue – a bus stop. Their dinner – a small, badly rolled joint.

As Craig, the fifteen-year-old, sucks the last light out of their evening meal, they are approached by a man in his early twenties. He is dressed expensively, and as he catches the eye of the fourteen-year-old, he gestures ostentatiously to the BMW 4 Series parked across the street.

The smart man tells the fourteen-year-old that he does not recognise him, which is unusual, because the smart man makes it his business to know all of the young people bustling about this part of town. The fourteen-year-old replies, in duo-syllabic terms, that he has moved in to Rosewoods Family Centre as of two days ago. The smart man detects an accent, and asks the fourteen-year-old where he is from. The fourteen-year-old looks bored now, and is exchanging glances with his associate, the type of glance that teenage boys exchange when an adult in their company has not only overstayed his welcome, but is unwittingly contravening the unspoken social codes which teenagers know by instinct, and which adults can never hope to understand.

'Wythenshawe,' the fourteen-year-old offers, swinging his legs and kicking his torn trainers into the dust. 'Manchester.'

The smart man smiles. 'Just like Marcus Rashford, right?'

When the appeal to pop culture fails, the smart man opts for a more direct road to the boy's attention, taking three steps closer and holding out a small packet.

'Smoke?' he asks with a smile.

The fifteen-year-old reaches greedily, but the man's attention is on the younger of the two, who is still not engaging. With his arm still extended, the man endeavours to keep the conversation alive.

'What's your real name, Rashford?'

The boy rolls his eyes.

'OK. Well, tell me this – have you ever been in trouble before with the police?'

This elicits a snort, which the man supposes is a step towards a verbal response.

'No. But why the fuck do you care?'

The smart man is a fairy godfather of sorts, it emerges, with particular responsibility assumed for the young people at the boy's new home. The man looks out for them, he explains. Some of them even, from time to time, work for him. Just helping out. Doing odd jobs here and there. 'Maybe one day,' the man suggests, 'you will too.'

Whatever charms he may suppose himself to hold, the man's

patter does not look to have persuaded, but nor, yet, has he been outright rejected. So he stands his ground, cigarettes still extended, until the boy relents and helps himself. The man takes a lighter out of his jacket pocket and leans in.

'What's your name?' asks the boy.

'I go by Grimes,' comes the reply.

'Graham?'

'Fucking hell,' the smart man laughs. '*Grimes*. Jared Grimes.' He shakes his head affably. 'Do I look like a fucking Graham?'

'Well,' says the boy, staring him straight in the eye, 'I think you do look like a Graham. And maybe I'll just call you that.' They hold each other's gaze, the boy brimming with bravado in front of his new friend.

The man looks away first, concealing a smile so as not to burst the boy's bubble.

'Well, I tell you what, Rashford, I'll do you a deal. You can call me Graham, but the day you come and work for me, it stops. Do we have a deal?'

He holds out his hand and the fourteen-year-old flashes that look again at his friend, the raise of the eyebrows, a derisory *seriously*? passing silently between them.

'You really think,' the boy says to the man, waving his hand dismissively, 'that I'm going to come and work for *you*?'

'I do,' says the man, flashing a wink as he grabs the boy's hand mid-air, twists it down and forces it into a slow, firm shake. 'I think we'll make a killing.'

ACKNOWLEDGEMENTS

The coming-into-being of this book owes so much to so many people that it might be a shorter exercise to acknowledge those who have not contributed in any way. A list of grievances, as it were. If your name isn't on the list, you can take it as read that I am humbly grateful for all your love and support. If you do appear on the list, then do better.

That said, I am a lawyer. And the list of grievances that I would wish to include, while undoubtedly both justified and hilarious, would risk incurring the attention of Picador's legal department. So I should probably do this the conventional way. In doing so, I apologise in advance for inevitable, inadvertent omissions.

My parents, who force-fed me a diet of crime and legal thrillers growing up, are probably responsible in more ways than I can measure for what you have just read. My anonymity means that they are unlikely to ever be held accountable, but they know what they've done.

Chris Wellbelove, the world's greatest agent, remains ultimately liable for bringing me out of the blogosphere, into the bright lights of non-fiction publishing and across the bridge into fiction. Any good ideas I have stumbled across, at any point during the past nine years, are almost certainly his.

The team at Picador continue to astound me with their patience, professionalism and talent at navigating the restrictions and complexities created by an anonymous author while managing the ego of an anonymous barrister. Special thanks must go to Andrea

Henry, my wonderful editor, not only for her editing skill but for her boundless enthusiasm and belief in this project, without which I may well have ended the book after eleven chapters with a 'and then the trial finished and they all went home.' The cheerleading of Mary Mount can also not pass without gratitude; the hardest times during this process have only been surpassed because of the relentless positivity of the whole Picador family.

The wizardry of Katy Loftus in putting my flabby, lethargic first draft through an exhausting boot camp of structural editing and plot refinement is appreciated more than I was possibly able to express at the time, red-faced and wheezing heavily. Katy's Rumplestiltskinesque talent for spinning straw into gold has been a wonder to behold.

Outside the world of publishing, two hearty hails are owed to two friends I have never met: John, for pushing me to seriously pursue my crime fiction bug, and Nicky, for patience and support over many years, which I am yet to meaningfully repay. And a friend who does not know whether she has met me or not, but whose kindness and wisdom has been a constant throughout my avatar's existence: Mary. I'm sorry about all the swearing.

Veering away from gratitude, an apology. My purpose in turning to fiction writing was to try to offer something authentic. Something which married the reality of criminal justice with its complexity; the blurring of lines between absolutes of good and bad, of heroism and villainy. Of the moral codes of those in the dock, and those pontificating in wigs and gowns. Our courts and our laws are ultimately ordered by humans, with all of the messiness, irrationality and unpredictability that that entails. In these efforts, I have tried, wherever possible, to adhere to realism (an early, largely unreadable draft included copies of Defence Statements, skeleton arguments and an actual Sequence of Events). Almost all of what happens in this trial has happened either to me, or to somebody I know, although I concede not all within the same trial. However there will inevitably be parts where fellow pedants may spot creative licence winning the day over legal formalism, or simply my own shortcomings as a lawyer revealing themselves. For those who have read this book with as close and sceptical an eye as I would have, I am sorry if at times I have fallen short.

Thank you to the giants of the legal profession whose skill, endurance and humanity have filtered into some of the characters in this book. I would issue similar thanks in relation to other, less agreeable, characters, but those of course are entirely of my imagination and not inspired by anybody at all.

Finally, and most importantly, my family. By the time we reach a fourth set of book acknowledgements thanking you for your unstinting love and support, apologising for the burden that my second anonymous career imposes upon you all, and promising that I will be better next time, there is a chance that my words will start to ring hollow. Like a defence barrister assuring a sentencing judge that a career burglar has reached yet another 'turning point'.

So this time I make no such promise. I'm a helpless recidivist. I'm sorry, but that fate, it seems, is inescapable. All I can offer by way of mitigation is an assurance that I love you – truly, deeply do – a promise to share the buried spoils upon my eventual release, and an acknowledgement that none of this – not a single part of the ridiculous escapade of the past decade – would have been possible without you.